SECOND SHOT

SHANDI BOYES

Edited by
MOUNTAINS WANTED PUBLISHING
Illustrated by
SSB DESIGNS

COPYRIGHT

Written by
Shandi Boyes

© **Shandi Boyes 2017**

No part of this eBook may be reproduced or transmitted in any form or by any means, electronic or mechanical, including photocopying, recording or by any information storage and retrieval system, without written permission from the author.
30/12/2023
This is a work of fiction. Any names or characters, businesses or places, events or incidents, are fictitious. Any resemblance to actual persons, living or dead, or actual events is purely coincidental.

Editing: Mountains Wanted Publishing
Cover: SSB Designs!

Photograph: Shutter-stock account photographer
Some photo edits were made to the photographs.

ALSO BY SHANDI BOYES

Denotes Standalone Books

Perception Series

Saving Noah *
Fighting Jacob *
Taming Nick *
Redeeming Slater *
Saving Emily
Wrapped Up with Rise Up
Protecting Nicole *

Enigma

Enigma
Unraveling an Enigma
Enigma The Mystery Unmasked
Enigma: The Final Chapter
Beneath The Secrets
Beneath The Sheets
Spy Thy Neighbor *
The Opposite Effect *
I Married a Mob Boss *
Second Shot *
The Way We Are
The Way We Were
Sugar and Spice *
Lady In Waiting

Man in Queue

Couple on Hold

Enigma: The Wedding

Silent Vigilante

Hushed Guardian

Quiet Protector

Enigma: An Isaac Retelling

Twisted Lies *

Bound Series

Chains

Links

Bound

Restrain

The Misfits *

Nanny Dispute *

Russian Mob Chronicles

Nikolai: A Mafia Prince Romance

Nikolai: Taking Back What's Mine

Nikolai: What's Left of Me

Nikolai: Mine to Protect

Asher: My Russian Revenge *

Nikolai: Through the Devil's Eyes

Trey *

The Italian Cartel

Dimitri

Roxanne

Reign

Mafia Ties (Novella)

Maddox

Demi

Ox

Rocco *

Clover *

Smith *

RomCom Standalones

Just Playin' *

Ain't Happenin' *

The Drop Zone *

Very Unlikely *

False Start *

Short Stories - Newsletter Downloads

Christmas Trio *

Falling For A Stranger *

One Night Only Series

Hotshot Boss *

Hotshot Neighbor *

The Bobrov Bratva Series

Wicked Intentions *

Sinful Intentions *

Devious Intentions *

Deadly Intentions *

WANT TO STAY IN TOUCH?

Facebook: facebook.com/authorshandi

Instagram: instagram.com/authorshandi

Email: authorshandi@gmail.com

Reader's Group: bit.ly/ShandiBookBabes

Website: authorshandi.com

Newsletter: https://www.subscribepage.com/AuthorShandi

DEDICATION

To my readers who encourage me every day to follow my dreams.
You guys rock!
Shandi xx

PROLOGUE

HAWKE

"*H*it me." Chester, one of my field platoon brothers, bows his brow high into his thick, dark hairline as his light blue eyes glare into mine. "Are you sure, Hawke? You're sitting on sixteen. Any blackjack dealer will tell you that sixteen is solid."

He raises his voice to ensure I can hear him over the choppers landing in a dusty field a quarter mile from our base. Our squadron is bunkered down, waiting for the call on where we will go. We're on day five of a six-month deployment. A carefree sentiment prevailed since we've recently returned from a two-week break. My mood is extra relaxed as I only have six weeks before my four-year military stint ends.

My crew's two-week hiatus from Iraq passed in the blink of an eye, but it was fourteen days of amazing accomplishments for the entire platoon. Chester's prize-winning mare birthed a foal, Tallis got engaged, Miquel got divorced, London, well. . . he went back to London, and I married the love of my life.

Jorgie is the type of girl men can only dream of catching. Thick, luxurious dark hair, the fairest, unmarked skin I've ever seen, and eyes that look like Rembrandt himself painted them. I'm not lying when I say Jorgie is the prettiest girl I've ever seen. She didn't just knock me on my ass when I met her, she completely winded me—literally.

I've never been a man who believes in fate until I met Jorgie. I've known her brother, Hugo since he joined the Kappa Sigma Phi fraternity at our local university. Not once in those two years did he mention how hot his little sister was. Don't get me wrong, Hugo talked about Jorgie all the time, but from the stories he shared, Jorgie sounded like a female replica of him. Nothing against Hugo, but at six-foot-five and two hundred and fifty pounds of pure muscle, a female Hugo didn't sound like the type of girl I'd be interested in getting to know a little better.

Boy, was I wrong. So very wrong.

After taking an unexpected naked plunge in Lake George during summer break, I discovered that Jorgie may have had Hugo's dark hair, sky-blue eyes, and giant smile, but she was nothing like her big brother. She was all woman, a woman I would have given anything to become well acquainted with.

I won't lie. My endeavor to woo Jorgie over the following four months was an uphill battle. I wasn't just up against Jorgie's displeasure of me crashing into her canoe butt-naked after an impromptu skinny dip with a bunch of college girls. I was fighting a much harder challenge: Jorgie's older brothers.

The Marshall boys were raised by their father to protect their mother and sisters. Considering Jorgie is the baby of the family, Hugo and Jorgie's older brother, Chase, made it their mission to keep us apart.

But like every determined offensive lineman, their challenge only made the game more enticing to me. You can't achieve the greatest victory known to man without putting in a stellar effort. I did precisely that. I gave it my all. And, in the end, I won. Snagging Jorgie was the best game I've ever fielded. A triumph worthy of the record books.

I'm the luckiest bastard in the world because I not only caught Jorgie; I courted her, married her, and knocked her up with our son, who is due in a little under six weeks. It's been a great four years—some of the best I've had.

Now, don't take my admission the wrong way. I'm not saying things are always rosy in my relationship with Jorgie; we are like every other young couple out there. We fight, I get jealous, and we both have quirks we can't stand about each other. She hates that I bite my toenails. I loathe that she covers my house in hideous floral towels and knitted tea covers when I'm deployed, but just like every other couple, we take the good with the bad. It's what makes us stronger.

My reminiscing comes to a halt when a deck of cards is flung at my head, hitting me just above my left eyebrow.

Gritting my teeth, I snap my eyes to Chester.

"Hit or stay," he mutters.

He may have only said three little words, but his eyes relay much more. Peering into Chester's eyes is the equivalent of scanning an open encyclopedia. If you want to know anything about Chester's life he isn't willing to share, stare into his eyes. They disclose way more than his mouth ever could.

I rack my knuckles on the makeshift blackjack table. "Hit me. I'm feeling lucky."

A roar from the men seated around me sounds over the choppers in the distance. With four cartons of cigarettes on the table, my gamble is substantial, but I have a feeling something immense is about to happen, so I'm willing to take a risk on losing my bargaining chips for the next four weeks. My laidback mindset might also have something to do with the fact I don't smoke, so my gamble isn't as life-altering as Chester's. His brow is beaded with sweat, and the distinct scent of defeat is leaching from his pores.

As Chester flips over the black checkered card, the room falls into resolute silence. I divert my gaze to the late afternoon sky when a flock of doves fly over the dust-covered mesh tent we are camped under. The sky is void of a single cloud. It is beautifully serene but weirdly eerie at the same time—a patent imitation to the war-torn country I'm immersed in.

Shaking off the uneasy feeling growing in the pit of my stomach, I turn my eyes back to the table in just enough time to see a five of hearts flip onto my solid sixteen. The crowd surrounding me erupts into an ear-piercing holler. I stare at the cards, absorbing what should be a glorious victory, but for some reason unbeknownst to me, I can't celebrate.

When the hairs on the back of my neck stand to attention, I return my eyes to the sky. Something doesn't feel right. I have a terrible feeling deep in my gut that something is horribly wrong.

Jorgie.

I bolt out of my seat and rush to the improvised communications room the crew set up when we first landed. I hear Chester calling my name, but my frantic speed doesn't slow. Doctors have warned us numerous times over the past two months that Jorgie may go into labor early due to our son being a little on the large size. Unfortunately, that can't be helped. Jorgie is a stick of dynamite with a petite frame and mouth-watering curves, but she stands a little over six feet tall. Add that to my six foot three height and two hundred twenty pounds, and you have a recipe for a record-weight-breaking newborn. The guys in my platoon have been taking bets for the past six months. At last check, ten pounds is the clear favorite sitting at 2 to 1 odds.

When I enter the communications room, I scan the area, hoping to find a free station. Due to our secluded location, standard cell phone reception is spotty, so my regiment have stayed in contact with our loved ones via satellite internet for the past five days. The service is slow, but you make it work when it's all you have.

Failing to find an unoccupied computer, I prop my shoulder onto the thick canvas lining the room and patiently wait for a free station. You know that feeling you get when you know something isn't quite right, but you can't pinpoint the exact reason for your racing heart and clammy hands? That's how I'm feeling now. For every second that ticks by on the clock, the churning of my stomach grows.

When the wary feeling in my gut becomes impossible to ignore, I move toward the closest bank of computers, preparing to plead with a fellow squad member for a portion of their fifteen-minute allotment. If that fails, I'm not below yanking them out of their seats.

Just as I hit the first row of computers, Dangelo, a fellow platoon member, waves his hand in the air, signaling he's about to finalize his call. Breathing a sigh of relief that I won't be assigned mess duty for a week, I run my hand over my clipped hair as I quickly span the distance between us.

"Stay safe. I love you, D," I catch Dangelo's wife, Penny, saying when I stop to stand beside him.

"I will, baby; see you soon," Dangelo replies before pushing two fingers to his lips and pressing them onto the computer screen.

Once the screen goes blank, Dangelo stands from his seat and runs his eyes over my face, absorbing my stunned expression.

"Ah, shit, I better go and change my bet. I thought Jorgie still had a good three weeks to go, but from the look on your face, I have a feeling things may be happening a little sooner than predicted," he mumbles before sidestepping me and racing toward Hamilton, the money man behind Jorgie's bets.

Although Dangelo's comment is aiming for playful, it adds to the gnawing pit in my stomach. As much as I can't wait to meet my son, I'd prefer for it to happen when I'm on home turf and when Jorgie is closer to the safe zone the doctors have been aiming for the past two months: the magic thirty-seven weeks mark.

Ignoring the shake beginning to control my arms, I plop into the chair and lift my hand to the mouse. My heart is walloping against my chest so furiously that the cursor on the screen wobbles as I scan it across the monitor to click into my Skype account and connect to Jorgie's profile.

For every ring that goes unanswered, the weight on my chest grows.

By the time half an hour creeps past, I can barely breathe because the heaviness on my chest is so intense.

When another thirty minutes pass, my panic hits an all-time high.

Jorgie always carries her cell phone with her. From the day I was deployed two months after we started dating, she has ensured her cell is fully charged and accessible. Like every serviceman's wife, she knows the importance a five-minute chat with significant others have on the men and women on duty. When I return from a tiresome day in the field, sometimes those quick calls home are the only thing that keep me going. So, it isn't like Jorgie. She wouldn't not take my call unless something terrible has happened.

I sink deeper into the hard wooden chair, causing the rusted hinges to give out a creak. While running my hand over the scruff on my chin, I try to calm the mad beat of my heart. I've never felt more hopeless than I do right now. I try to convince myself that if Jorgie is in labor, our son will be okay. Although six weeks is early, with how advanced technology is, I'm certain he will be fine.

For all I know, the panic could be completely unnecessary; Jorgie may not even be in labor. She could be simply sleeping. She barely sleeps a wink when I'm deployed as it is, let alone with a heavily pregnant stomach to contend with. I just wish she would answer my calls so I can settle the unease swirling in my stomach.

Any chances of settling the gnawing pit in my gut are lost when Major General Carmichael enters the communication room with the chaplain following closely behind him. My breathing turns labored as I slouch deeper into my chair, praying to God the chaplain isn't here for me. I've only seen the chaplain once during my last deployment; it was when London's brother was killed in duty. Other than that, the members of my crew only seek the chaplain's assistance when they're either broken or on the verge of being broken.

The twisting of my stomach winds up my throat when Major General Carmichael turns his gaze in my direction. I crank my neck to peer behind my shoulder, certain his glistening eyes are peering at someone else. A stabbing pain hits my chest when I discover there's no one behind me. After swallowing away a bitter taste in the back of my throat, I return my eyes front and center, stand from my chair, and salute my senior officer as he spans the distance between us. Every step he takes tightens the stranglehold wrapped around my throat, silently asphyxiating me.

Carmichael stops in front of me, returns my salute, then gestures for me to sit.

"I'd rather stand," I reply, speaking through cotton mouth, the shakiness of my words unable to hide the hammering of my heart.

Snapping my eyes shut, I faintly mutter, "Thank fuck," into the late afternoon air when Carmichael hands me a satellite phone. In the military, bad news only ever comes in the form of a telegram, not a phone call.

My gratefulness is short-lived when I press the phone to my ear and am delivered the news no man ever wants to hear. "Hawke, it's Hugo. Jorgie's been in an accident. She's not good."

"Our baby?" I stutter, my words barely a whisper.

Hugo doesn't utter another syllable. He doesn't need to speak for me to know the words his mouth is failing to produce. I can hear every horrid comment through the heartbreaking sob sounding down the line.

As the room spins around me, I fall to my knees and howl.

Broken.

Shattered.

I'm completely and utterly destroyed.

CHAPTER 1

HAWKE

Nearly Five Years Later...

Two days after the call that ended my life, I met and held my son for the first time in the morgue he was resting in. The tuft of hair on top of his head was as dark as his mother's, his lips just as plump. Being six weeks early didn't take away from his chubby little cheeks and chunky thighs.

Parents can be biased, but I'm not lying when I say Malcolm was perfect in every way. Ten perfect little toes and ten perfect little fingers on a precious little boy who never had the chance to play catch with his dad, ride a bike, kiss a girl, or take his first breath.

Malcolm was everything I could have wished for and more. He was the perfect combination of both Jorgie and me.

As if the pain of losing my son wasn't tragic enough, I also lost my wife—my beautiful little firecracker. The injuries Jorgie sustained when she was hit by a drunk driver after having lunch with her best friend, Ava, were fatal, but, thankfully, against the doctor's advice, Jorgie's family kept her on life support so I'd have the opportunity to say goodbye to the love of my life in person.

It was a bitterly sweet day.

I'll be forever grateful that I was the man who got to place Malcolm into his mother's arms for the first time, but I'll never forget hearing Jorgie take her last breath only a short four hours later.

I thought the disturbing images of war I encountered during my years of service in the US Army would be the worst thing I'd ever see in my life.

It wasn't.

It was seeing my wife laid to rest two days after her death with our son, Malcolm, cradled in her arms. There has been no crueler image than that one. It still haunts me to this day.

Even more so since I'm standing at the foot of the church they were laid to rest in. A little less than five years have passed since that day, but I still recall it like it was yesterday. Jorgie was buried in the wedding dress she walked down the aisle in only three weeks earlier. Malcolm wore the outfit he was supposed to be christened in at this church. They were buried in a beautiful plot near an old oak tree only a few feet from here.

It's somewhere I haven't visited since the day they were laid in their final resting place—a place I'll never be strong enough to visit.

Jorgie and Malcolm aren't in that white coffin covered in dirt. They're in my heart. I carry them with me everywhere I go. It won't matter if another five years pass or fifty, they will forever be carried in my heart.

I gulp in a deep breath, trying to build the courage to push open the church doors that both haunt and appease my grief. When I married Jorgie in this church, I thought we were creating memories we would have forever to cherish. Little did I know I'd be saying my final goodbye to her at the same church only three short weeks later.

As I push down on the old brass handle on the whitewashed double doors, I remember a saying I've quoted numerous times in the past five years.

Memories last a lifetime, but not all of them are sweet.

CHAPTER 2

GEMMA

A late fall wind whips up my hair, adding to my already disheveled appearance as I slide out of a rusted old pickup.

"Thank you," I praise the lady who rescued me from being stranded at a B&B ten miles out.

The leanly built lady with dazzling brown eyes bows her head before pulling her truck away from the graveled-lined parking lot of a cute little church on the outskirts of Rochdale, NY.

When I requested my Uber driver to alter our initially agreed-upon route, I never considered that I'd end up stranded on the side of an isolated road. Thankfully, my bad timing corresponded with the knock-off time of the maid from the B&B, otherwise I'd be not only wrangling a tousled hairstyle but blistering feet as well.

Although I'm arriving at my friend's wedding a little ruffled around the edges, I'm glad I couldn't harness the desire to capture some sneaky snaps of Ava and her bridesmaids getting ready. Photography is my life. It nursed me through some of my darkest days.

When I have a camera in my hand, I truly don't feel fear. Which is incredible for me, as normally, anything that goes bump in the night frightens me, but magic happens when I'm behind the lens.

One click of a button can capture the smallest memory for eternity, but I treasure the beauty behind the image the most. A picture is a poem without words. So many things are said without a syllable needing to be spoken.

When Ava requested that I photograph her wedding, I graciously declined. Staged shoots aren't my style of photography. I like the raw emotions you rarely see when a camera is shoved in your face.

I love the pictures that capture the individual in their natural environment. When they're staring into space reminiscing about the past, or licking a stream of ice cream dribbling down their dirty palms.

When my clients look at their proofs, I want real-life memories to be triggered, not fake ones of an ideal life in a perfect world displayed every day on social media. Every red-blooded human knows there's no such thing as an ideal life. That isn't possible in the world we live in. Life can be both cruel and beautiful. My photos aim to capture both sides of the coin: the good and the bad.

That was what I did today. I photographed the real Ava. I caught the little tear in the corner of her eye when she ran her index finger along the picture frames containing photos of the loved ones who can only attend her wedding in cherished memories.

I captured the way her son Joel's nose screwed up when asked if he was excited to meet his brother or sister due in a few months, and I caught Ava's breathlessness when she slipped into her wedding gown for the very first time. I captured the real Ava today. It was a truly magical experience. One worth the risk of being stranded on an isolated country road.

Once my rescuer's truck is nothing but a speck on the horizon, I dig my hand into my oversized clutch and pull out my compact mirror.

I cringe when I spot my reflection. I wouldn't say I'm an overly girly type of woman, but I've been known to have sporadic moments of girliness.

Thankfully, today, I'm not having a moment. Although my sweat-slicked skin could benefit from a soak in a tub, my last-minute change of heart has stretched my time too thin to head to my hotel. My schedule is so tight I had no option but to touch up my makeup during the bumpy fifteen-mile trip from the B&B to the church.

Have you ever applied makeup in a moving vehicle? It's practically impossible. Well imagine doing it in a rusted old truck juddering down a road at forty miles an hour.

I nearly lost an eye while adding a coat of mascara to my lashes.

The driver swerved to miss a pothole, sending the mascara stick smearing across my face. I dabbed up the mess the best I could, but from the raccoon look I'm wearing, there's no doubt who won the mascara battle.

Mascara – 1.

Me – 0.

Lucky for me, smoky eyes are making a comeback.

After returning my compact to my clutch, I secure the handle on my bag and drag it across the gravel parking lot. Pretending I haven't noticed the little black stones ramming into the swivel wheels of my suitcase, I roam my eyes over the church Ava and Hugo are getting married in. It is charming, with large stained glass windows lining the entire east wing and a beautiful glass atrium housing the silver bell that will ring at the end of their ceremony. It is quaint and charming, a stark contradiction to the graveyard attached to it.

By the time I reach the wooden stairs at the front of the church, I'm sweating profusely, and my heart is hammering against my ribs.

My perspiring state isn't just from dragging my heavy suitcase up the small flight of stairs but from the prospect of walking into a church full of strangers. I've known Hugo for nearly seven years, but the only people I've met in his inner circle are his soon-to-be wife, Ava, and his mother, Mrs. Marshall.

In my industry, meeting strangers is a regular occurrence, but usually, it is only a handful of people at once. The last I heard, Hugo and Ava's wedding attendees were close to four hundred.

I don't even know four hundred people.

I shouldn't be surprised their guest list is so high, though. From the stories Hugo shared, his family have been upstanding citizens of the Rochdale community for longer than I've been born. And I'm sure when rumors circulated that Hugo's wealthy boss was funding an open bar, Hugo had relatives he didn't even know existed crawl out of the woodworks.

When I hit the top of the stairs, I run my fingers through my hair, not wanting to startle Hugo with my tousled appearance. The rake of my fingers stops halfway through my platinum blonde locks, closely followed by the beat of my heart. Hugo has seen me at my worst, so windblown hair and smeared mascara won't faze him.

After releasing a nerve-cleansing breath, I push on the church doors with all my might. Before I can grasp that the door is a pull design, not a push, the thick wooden door sails open and smacks me right in the nose.

If that isn't bad enough, the person fleeing the church like a groom with cold feet crashes into me, sending me sprawling onto my backside. My wrist jars on the hard wooden floor, and a breathless grunt parts my lips.

I inwardly squeal when my unladylike topple sends the free-flowing skirt of my dress flying over my head.

"Oh, shit. Are you okay?" says a profoundly deep voice from above.

Grimacing with embarrassment, I yank down my dress before mumbling, "Uh-huh. I'm fine. What were you doing racing out of there like a madman anyway? The groom is the only person allowed to flee a church like it's on fire. And considering Hugo has been waiting for this day for years, I highly doubt you're him."

After scampering off the floor, I lift my humiliated eyes to the man who just barreled me over.

Oh, for the love of god, Greek Gods do exist.

Strong, powerful jawline; dark, well-groomed hair; sculptured cheekbones; and rich, soul-absorbing eyes all assembled on a suit-covered body that looks like it eats gladiators for breakfast.

If I had to guess the mysterious man's age, I'd say he's a couple of years older than my twenty-eight years. It isn't that his chiseled face has signs of a man in his early thirties. He just has a mature approach about him. He has an edge of sophistication and seems well put-together—a stark controversy to the woman standing in front of him.

My gaped mouth gains leverage when the reality of the situation dawns on me. He just saw my panties—*my hideously ugly panties*. I'm not talking slightly frumpy with an edge of sexiness some men find appealing. I'm talking *about* contouring from the middle of my thigh to halfway up my stomach skin-tone panties.

Great!

Vainly pretending I can't feel my cheeks burning, I lock my gaze with the dark-haired stranger. "Don't panic. Despite mass hysteria, it was announced earlier this year that you can't catch the wedding bug." I tilt closer to his side and whisper, "Just don't tell my grandma. She's got everything crossed that I come home from this wedding with the full-blown nuptial virus."

I aim for my tone to be witty, but when the turmoil in his murky eyes escalates, I realize my attempts at humor are borderline. I've never been good at making jokes, but I gave it my best shot. I'll do anything to deflect the awkwardness of our meeting away from my contouring undergarments.

Before I can mutter another cringe-worthy syllable, gravel crunching under tires bellows through my ears. Cranking my head to the side, I spot two white Rolls Royces gliding down the church driveway.

"Shit, quick. It's the bridal party," I mumble, partly to myself and partly to the mysterious stranger eyeballing me like I'm a circus freak.

After snagging my suitcase off the ground, I loop my arm around the mute stranger's elbow and pace to the doors he just charged out. I won't need to lift weights for a week with how much effort it takes to drag him into the church foyer. Anyone would swear he's the one about to get married with how reluctant his steps are.

Once we enter the small white foyer, I release the dark-haired stranger from my grasp so I can dump my suitcase in a coat closet on my left. His eyes track me as I cross the room, but not a peep seeps from his hard-lined lips.

The hum of gleeful chatter beaming out of the church sanctuary causes the hairs on my arms to bristle and my heart to beat a little faster.

Well, I'm assuming it is the liveliness causing my body's odd reaction, but I can't one hundred percent testify to that, as my stomach did a weird flipping thing the instant I curled my arm around the mute stranger's elbow.

After closing the coatroom door, I run my eyes over the silent stranger as I pace back toward him. His well-fitting three-piece suit sends blood rushing to the lower regions of my body. Even with a heavy groove between his eyes and an unapproachable demeanor, he's insanely sexy—the type of man you'd expect to see on the cover of magazines.

Or do anything to see what he looks like under his clothing.

Swallowing down my surprise at my inappropriate inner monologue, I stop pacing when I'm within reaching distance of the stranger.

"Your tie is wonky," I mutter quietly, noticing the only fault in his entire package is his black bowtie dangling precariously to the left.

"May I?" I bounce my eyes between his stormy gaze and rumpled tie.

His Adam's apple bobs up and down in slow motion before he briefly nods. My hands shake when I lift them to straighten his bowtie.

My nervous response can't be helped. The idea of entering a room where a large group of people are already seated rattles me, but I'm just as cautious being in the presence of a single man, even if he both excites and intimidates me.

My anxious composure isn't solely based on the mysterious man's incredibly handsome features; it is because he's also ginormous. His substantial height towers over my five-foot-six stature by six to eight inches. His shoulders are double the width of mine, and the tormented look in his eyes sets me on edge, but if I'm honest, I'm drawn to him even with my insecurities on high alert.

Perhaps it's because he reminds me of Hugo? On the surface, Hugo also looks rough and brutish, but his heart is as big as his frame. I wonder if the same could be said for this mysterious stranger.

"There you go. Perfect," I mumble after ensuring his tie is straight and center.

I step back and run my hands down the front of my misty green Chi Chi knee-length lace dress.

"Do I look okay?" I ask, hoping my tumble didn't add to my already tousled appearance.

After slanting his head to the side, the stranger's eyes travel my body. As the arch of his brow grows, so does the swirling of my stomach.

I've gone through a lot of personal growth over the past three years. One of my biggest hurdles was learning not to care about the opinions of others, but for some reason, unbeknownst to me, I want his opinion, and I want it bad.

When he returns his eyes to mine, a tense stretch of silence crosses between us. My irritation swells. Not because he clearly doesn't find me as appealing as I find him, but because I haven't progressed as far as I thought I had in self-assuredness.

His rejection not only dents my ego but also makes me realize I still have a long road to travel before I fully recover from an incident that shook my core six years ago.

"Okay. Let's do this," I mumble when the thick tension in the air becomes too great for me to ignore.

The faint whizz of chatter trickling into the foyer turns rowdy when I swing open the double doors of the church sanctuary and walk two steps inside. Even with the burn of rejection hitting my chest, I can't help but crank my neck back to seek the attention of the stranger standing mute in the foyer.

"Are you coming?" I question when his haunted eyes connect with mine for a fleeting second.

His rich chocolate eyes peer past my shoulder to the wedding congregation before he locks them back with me. The edgy cloud in his gaze mimics mine to a T; we are both unnerved at the idea of entering the jam-packed church. I give him a small smile, pretending my heart isn't hammering against my ribs.

Although the man standing in front of me is technically a stranger, I'd rather walk into the church with him by my side than alone.

"Come on," I murmur with a nudge of my head, my words as shaky as my composure. "My dad has always said, 'even the most daunting tasks are less awkward with company.'"

His freaked-out mask slips away for the slightest moment and a spark of determination fires into his eyes. It feels like minutes pass in silence before he gingerly pushes off his feet and strides toward me.

As we walk down the aisle, side by side, he remains as quiet as a church mouse, whereas my eyes scan the packed room looking for two vacant seats while trying to ignore the outlandish current of electricity zapping through my body from his closeness.

For every step we take, the crease between my brows deepens. The energetic chatter filtering in the air vanishes as the room falls silent. Even a pin drop would be heard.

My hands dart up to smooth my air-blown hair when numerous pairs of eyes turn to gawk at us. I thought the stare my newfound friend gave me on the church stairs was daunting. It is nothing compared to the intensity of every pair of eyes in the room directed at us right now.

Although the mysterious stranger has heart-racing looks that would conjure inquisitive stares from lust-driven women of all ages, he hasn't just secured the devotion of every pair of female eyes in the room. He has acquired the zealous interest of nearly every attendee surrounding us.

When the tension in the room becomes throat-clutching, we gain the attention of the final pair of eyes: Hugo's mother, Mrs. Marshall. Her pupils widen when her neck cranks back to us, and she gasps in a staggered breath.

After clamping her hand over her O-formed mouth, only just suppressing a painful sob, she leaps out of her chair and races down the aisle.

The smell of floral perfume fills my senses when she throws her arms around the mysterious stranger's neck and hugs him tightly.

Feeling confused and awkwardly out of place, I excuse myself from the heart-strangling reunion and take an empty seat a few rows up. Only as I pace away from the dark-haired stranger do I realize the prying stares of hundreds of eyes weren't directed at me. They're solely devoted to the handsome man with the haunted eyes.

My curiosity about who the unnamed man is grows when Hugo emerges from the vestibule at the back of the church ten minutes later. His long strides come to a dead stop when his eyes lock in on the dark-haired man now standing at the end of the aisle.

Like Mrs. Marshall, Hugo's reaction causes tears to prick my eyes. He looks both shocked and relieved by the stranger's attendance.

With a smile I've only seen a handful of times, Hugo aids his mother back to her seat at the front of the church before eagerly striding to the unnamed man.

Their conversation not only attracts my full devotion but also demands the attention of every attendee in the room.

My gawking stare only stops when the whimsical voice of John Legend plays out of the speakers. Hugo spins on his heels to face the back of the church. My interest in the mysterious stranger's status in Hugo's life piques when Hugo gestures for him to stand next to him as the bridesmaids commence walking down the aisle.

If he's Hugo's best man, why was he fleeing from the church?

Any further debate on the stranger's identity is pushed to the background of my mind when the heat of a gaze secures my devotion.

Lifting my eyes from my intertwined hands, I lock my gaze with a pair of eyes that causes both tears of happiness and sadness to well in my eyes from one little glance.

Hugo: my ultimate savior.

The man who sacrificed his own happiness to ensure I kept mine.

CHAPTER 3

HAWKE

"*H*it me."

The bartender finishes polishing a crystal tumbler before placing it into an over-stacked steel rack on his left. Flinging a damp tea towel over his shoulder, he saunters to a wall of liquor at the back of the bar.

I've spent the last hour of Hugo and Ava's wedding reception guzzling down whiskey like my throat is on fire. Unlike the other wedding patrons, I'm not just taking advantage of Isaac's generosity of an all-expenses paid bar tab. I'm struggling to keep buried memories hidden.

Jorgie and Malcolm will always hold a special place in my heart, but in this town, I feel suffocated by the memories.

Memories are often my worst enemies. There are days when I think I'm doing okay. Then there are other days where everything I do reminds me of what I've lost.

Today is one of those days.

It isn't just the anniversary of Jorgie and Malcolm's death creeping closer. It is this place.

Every inch of this town has Jorgie attached to it in some way. This is the hotel Hugo and I crashed in the night of my bachelor party; the park three blocks over is where I took Jorgie after dragging her out of a college party kicking and screaming, and the radiology center two miles from here is where we discovered our unborn baby was going to be a little boy. Jorgie chose Malcolm's name while driving me to the airport for my next two-month stint in Iraq.

I can recall at least a dozen memories for every mile I travel in this town. That is why I haven't stepped foot in Rochdale since the day of Jorgie and Malcolm's funeral. I knew the instant I came home the truth would crash into me. And it is. No matter how much I wish it was all a nightmare and that I'll eventually wake up, that will never happen. Jorgie and Malcolm's memories will forever live on, but they're never coming back.

It is only now do I realize I've spent the last five years living in denial. Don't get me wrong, the truth has been staring me in the face the entire time. I just refused to accept it.

It was easier to believe I was doing an extended stint in Iraq than face reality, so that's what I did. The day following Jorgie and Malcolm's funeral, I reenlisted in the military. It wasn't that my grief was pushed aside too quickly—I'm still grieving to this day—I just had to do something to stop myself from absorbing the truth.

The morning of their funeral, I caught my reflection in the mirror. All I saw was a hollow, soulless man staring back at me. Since a heartless man fears nothing, reenlisting in the military felt like the obvious step. I had nothing to lose, so I had nothing to fear.

For the five weeks following their deaths, I was the ideal soldier. I was always first to volunteer to sweep the danger zones; I walked on point between command stations and crawled through more foxholes than I could count. It seemed even walking directly into the line of fire couldn't hurt me. I was invincible.

Well, so I thought.

Six weeks after Jorgie's passing, her brother and my best mate, Hugo, was reported missing. I only met Hugo during his first week of college, but I've classed him as family from the moment we shook hands. He's the brother I never had, and even the biggest boulder can't knock down two brothers standing shoulder to shoulder. Our unique bond saw me immediately heading to my superiors to request special leave. Since Hugo was not a blood relative, my request was denied. That was the first instance I regretted reenlisting in the military.

The second was two years later when Hugo was declared deceased in absentia of a body. Just like I knew something was wrong the day Jorgie was involved in an accident, fragments of Hugo's death didn't make sense. I knew in my gut that something wasn't right with his mysterious disappearance.

Although I refused to step foot in Rochdale, I kept my ears to the ground the years following Hugo's disappearance.

Four years later, with the ink on my discharge papers still wet, I set out to prove that my intuition was right. For months, I had nothing. Hugo was a ghost. I discovered my intuition was spot on when access to Jorgie's sealed court records was granted to an FBI agent. Hugo was alive and well, living in a town called Ravenshoe.

I wasn't surprised when the reasoning behind Hugo's disappearance was made apparent. Like he'd done his entire life, he protected his baby sister when the courts failed to. For that, I'll forever be in his debt. That is the sole reason I'm guzzling down overpriced whiskey in a town that equally haunts and appeases my grief.

When the bartender plunks an overflowing whiskey glass in front of me, excess liquor spills over the rim and soaks into the polished countertop. I jerk my chin up in thanks before lifting the glass to my mouth. Nothing comes close to easing the pain in my chest I've been living with for the past five years, but the burn of expensive liquor warms the area where my heart used to belong. And for the quickest second, my numbness is achieved by something more than grief.

After throwing back the generous serving in one fell swoop, I request a refill. As the bartender replenishes my glass, I scan my eyes over the congregation of people mingling in the opulent surroundings.

Just as they had done for mine and Jorgie's wedding, Mr. and Mrs. Marshall have gone all out for Hugo and Ava. I'm not surprised. Although Ava doesn't have a drop of Marshall blood running through her veins, from the stories Jorgie told me, she has been a Marshall longer than she was a Westcott.

You only need to attend one Sunday brunch in the Marshall residence, and you're classed as family. Chase's disdain may have taken me four months to get an invite to the Marshall brunch, but it's a morning I'll never forget. It was the day Jorgie and I officially became a couple.

A hiss parts my lips when I spot Hugo and Ava dancing in the middle of the crammed dance floor. I've felt every second of every day since Jorgie and Malcolm passed, but I still can't believe nearly five years has flown by since Ava and Hugo danced together at my wedding.

I recall in crystal clear detail Jorgie spending our entire bridal waltz orchestrating a way for Ava to catch her bouquet. She was so determined for Ava and Hugo to become a couple that she gave fate a stern push every chance she got.

What she didn't calculate was that I'd be dragging a red-faced Hugo off a Rochdale High alum only minutes later. Marvin got what was coming to him. If Hugo didn't deck him for the rumors he was circulating about Ava, another Rochdale local would have called him out.

Just like Jorgie, Ava grew up in Rochdale. She's loved by the community just as much as Jorgie was. Now, she holds the last name associated with the prestigious title. A rare smile cracks onto my lips. If Jorgie had it her way, I would also have the Marshall surname.

Grinning at the memory of Jorgie's sermon on how husbands taking their wives' surnames was all the rage, I stray my eyes back to the bar.

On the way, I spot a flurry of blonde in the corner of my eye. The unnamed lady who coerced me into the church hours ago has her face hidden by an outdated camera. Although she has spent the last hour taking snapshots of Hugo and Ava's guests, she hasn't spoken to a single attendee since she warily entered the ballroom.

When she peered up at me wide-eyed and slack-jawed after our collision, I would have never guessed she had a reserved personality.

Don't get me wrong, her fetching green eyes were clouded with mistrust and wariness, but their appeal was still strong enough to pull me out of the panicked state that was silently asphyxiating me.

The blonde is undoubtedly attractive: big worldly eyes, a little button nose, and soft, plump lips on an angelic face, but her entire composure demands solitude. If I hadn't seen the other side of her demeanor in the church foyer—the helpful, kind-hearted one—I would have assumed she had a prickly personality.

And from how numerous men eye her with zeal from across the room but fail to act on their impulses, her standoffish composure has the effect she's aiming for. Her attractive features gain their attention, but her unapproachable demeanor keeps them at arm's length.

When the blonde cranks her neck in my direction, I drop my gaze to my glass of whiskey. I've noticed her glancing my way numerous times in the past hour, but I've been avoiding her at all costs. It isn't because I'm ungrateful for her earlier assistance. If I hadn't run into her while fleeing haunted memories, I have no doubt I'd be halfway to Ravenshoe by now, but with my agitation already on edge from unavoidable memories, every sneaky glance she gives firms my annoyance.

Her interest doesn't bother me. It is the fact that every time she locks her eyes with me, she stirs something deep inside me I haven't felt in years. I'm not talking about the normal rush of lust any hot-blooded male gets when confronted by a woman with attractive features and a tempting body. I'm talking about the churning your stomach does when every assumption you've ever made is about to come undone.

I grit my teeth. Just having a thought like that pisses me off, even more so because of the location I'm sitting in, but even annoyed beyond comprehension, I know part of the reason why the unnamed blonde is causing such a fierce reaction out of me. It isn't just lust or yearning. It is because she's the only person in the room not staring at me with sympathy.

Ever since I walked into the church nearly three hours ago, I've had hundreds of eyes planted on me. Hers are the only pair that don't remind me of what I've lost. For the entire forty-minute church service she gazed at me with wonderment and intrigue, two looks I haven't seen in years.

Don't take my confession the wrong way. I'm not saying I've spent the last five years celibate. My needs are just as potent as any other man in this room tonight, but my sexual contact over the past four years has only been in the form of meaningless, sporadic one-night stands.

No connection.

No commitments.

Nothing but two consenting adults sharing an intimacy you can only achieve with a bed partner.

It would be nice if I could experience that type of satisfaction without needing a companion, but unfortunately, no matter how much you wish for something, not all your desires can be granted. I've begged and pleaded for years. The one wish I've requested on repeat has never been fulfilled.

While I'm being forthright, I'll admit, it isn't just my reaction to the blonde's inquisitive glances that has my agitation growing. Part of it resides from when she glanced up at me on the church stairs with a look of admiration.

While returning her stare, for a fleeting moment, my recurring plea of the past five years stopped. Not because my greatest wish was finally granted but because another wish passed through my mind, one I hadn't thought of before.

I wanted to be the man the blonde was staring at in awe.

I wanted to feel whole again, even for the quickest moment.

For the first time in over five years, I didn't want to be a broken man.

I just wanted to be me.

CHAPTER 4

GEMMA

"Excuse me. Did you drive here?"

The still unnamed man stops walking toward a dark blue car that's just pulled to the curb and turns to face me. His suit jacket has been removed and slung over his forearm, and he's grasping a valet card firmly in his hand. With his head slanted to the side, he cocks his brow high into his hairline and glares into my eyes. I return his ardent stare while racking my fried brain about why he seems so familiar but still remains a mystery.

Hours have passed since our embarrassing meeting on the church stairs, yet I'm still no closer to finding out the identity of the dark-haired man with pulse-racing good looks and unapproachable demeanor. If I'd put my alcohol-fueled courage to the test, I could have asked one of the many wedding attendees gawking at him the past six hours, but for some silly reason, I didn't want to find out his identity from anyone but him.

I want to say my reasoning is solely based on the great intrigue every good book has, but that would be a lie. Mystery is great, but not when it has you obsessing over a stranger. My interest in unearthing his identity has seen me going from an intrigued onlooker to a Class A stalker felon in just shy of eight hours.

With his demeanor screaming, "do not approach," I spent the last six hours of Ava and Hugo's wedding taking hundreds of pictures of the happy couple's guests, drinking half a bottle of wine, and stealing numerous sneaky glances at the broodingly handsome man from afar. He spent the first hour of the reception sitting at the bar drinking whiskey like the distillery went up in flames. Then, shockingly, his choice of liquor switched to bottled water.

He remained seated at the bar the entire time, not budging to eat, dance, or participate in the festivities, but he didn't touch another drop of alcohol. The self-control he exuded while surrounded by Hugo's rowdy alcohol-fueled ex-frat brothers intrigues me even more than discovering his identity. Even the most upstanding members of society can become cruel and heartless when influenced by those surrounding them. Not once tonight did the handsome stranger succumb to peer pressure.

My sweat-producing stare down with the dark-haired hottie ends when a valet throws a set of keys at him, momentarily breaking our bizarre connection. I wait for the valet to move on to his next client before mumbling, "Would it be too much if I asked for a lift to my hotel?"

When the stranger's brows scrunch together, I nudge my head to Hugo and Ava making out like teenagers next to the white Rolls Royce prepared to whisk them to their honeymoon suite for the night. The cheerful smiles they've worn the past eight hours are still going strong. Not even a two-hour-long grueling staged shoot with a photographer whose voice sounds like nails being dragged down a chalkboard could dampen their eagerness.

"Considering they're the only two people I know here, I could ask them, but that may be a little awkward." I return my breathing to a respectable level before shifting my eyes back to the dark-haired stranger. "I also didn't pack any sanitary wipes, so. . ." I screw my nose up, letting him choose the remainder of my sentence.

He tries to hold in his smile at my playful comment, but the corners of his lips tug high, exposing his deceit. He has a wonderful smile—even his dark eyes blaze with glee—but from the way the grooves on the edge of his plump lips face downwards, I'd say it is something he doesn't do very often, which is a real shame, as he has the kind of smile that makes me weak at the knees.

"Please," I shamefully beg when he maintains his quiet approach.

I'm not usually a begging type of girl, but with the rumors of an open bar ringing true, I soon discovered taxis are as rare as hen's teeth in Rochdale at this time of night. Realizing I'll never secure a paid service to take me to my hotel, I've spent the last hour building the courage to ask a stranger for a ride. Not a single request has been uttered from my lips until now. Don't ask me why, but the brooding stranger is the first person I've felt comfortable approaching.

"It's the least you can do after you nearly knocked me out," I jest, hoping a dash of guilt may lessen my chance of hitchhiking the nearly fourteen miles to my hotel.

Although Hugo would pitch a fit if he discovered I even contemplated hitchhiking, I'd rather cop the wrath of his fury than be the third wheel at the commencement of his honeymoon. Being the tag-along friend is never fun, let alone when it is a newlywed couple.

Not appreciating my attempts at candor, the smile is wiped off the stranger's face and replaced with the scowl he's worn most of the night. Before his faint grin at my attempt at humor, I've only seen him smile once in the past eight hours. It was an hour into the wedding reception. I'm not being devious when I say it was one of the most magnificent smiles I've ever seen.

"I hear the bar at the Grand Hotel has a great selection of liquor. If you can give me a ride, I'll buy you your last drink of the night. If you're lucky, I might even upgrade you from standard bottled water to sparkling." I bite on the inside of my cheek to hide my cringe. My jokes are getting cornier the more desperate I get.

While holding his stern gaze, my pleading eyes shamefully expose my desperation. With the late hour and the four hundred wedding guests dwindling to only a handful, I'm in full-blown desperado mode.

Just when I think he will deny my request, he briefly nods. His gesture is so quick, if I weren't stuck in the trance his captivating eyes put on me, I may have missed it.

Not speaking a word, he stalks to his flashy-looking car and curls into the driver's seat.

"I'll get my bag then, shall I?" I mumble to myself.

Blowing a wayward hair out of my face, I drag my suitcase toward the dark blue car with thick white stripes down the front. Although I've been known to have girly moments, that doesn't extend to my knowledge of cars. My dad has been a classic car lover for centuries. His admiration for beefy muscle cars was passed down to me before I enrolled in kindergarten. I have no trouble recognizing a fully restored 1969 Chevrolet Camaro Z-28 SS Coupe. She's a real beauty, nearly as enticing as the man sitting behind her steering wheel—*if he'd stop scowling at me.*

Grumbling under my breath at his sour demeanor, I swing open the passenger door, throw forward the seat, and jam my suitcase into the backseat of his car. Surprisingly, he doesn't cite a single objection to me manhandling his pride and joy. If I know anything about gearheads, it's that they hate when people manhandle their *babies.* Clearly, any presumptions I've made about this man over the past eight hours are completely off-base. I don't know this man at all. He truly is a stranger.

After taking a breath to soothe my jittering stomach, I slide into the front passenger seat and fasten my seatbelt. My hands are clammy with nerves, and my eyes are wide, but thankfully, my outward appearance doesn't give away the crazy thump of my heart.

"Nice ride—" I attempt to mumble. My words are rammed into the back of my throat when he slams his foot on the gas pedal, and we fishtail out of the hotel driveway.

Adrenaline surges through my veins when he weaves his car in and out of the small traffic surrounding us, like a race car driver striving for a podium finish. Taillights whizz past me in a stream of vibrant red lights as his speedometer goes well over the designated speed limit. Even with my gaze planted straight ahead, I can't help but notice how the cut muscles in his arms flex with every shift of the gears. He drives with controlled precision, like a man who intimately knows every dip and groove in the roads of Rochdale. His extensive knowledge makes me wonder if he's a born and bred Rochdale man like Hugo or an adopted Marshall family member like nearly half the town is.

His grip on the steering wheel tightens as his speed increases even more. If he's trying to scare me, he's miserably failing. There's nothing more intoxicating than the purr of a five-hundred horsepower engine showcasing its power. Classic cars like this were created to be driven, not gather dust in a collector's garage. Add the intoxicating smell of sweat-slicked skin to the hair-bristling energy bouncing between the mystery stranger and me, and you have a captivating combination that sets my pulse racing.

Like every time I flew around the track in the passenger seat of my daddy's car, the tension weighing down my shoulders lifts, and a rush of excitement blazes through my body. Even though the stranger's boorish demeanor hasn't lightened, the glimmer of life in his eyes brightens with every quarter of a mile we travel. Exhilaration roars through my body, and my heart rate reaches levels it hasn't achieved in years when the potent smell of burning gasoline streams into my nose.

Incapable of holding in my excitement for a minute longer, I flatten my palms on the roof of the Camaro and let out a glass-splintering squeal. My excited scream initially startles the stranger before it encourages him to push his car to the limit. As the compression on his accelerator boosts, so does the curve of his lips. His heart-clenching smile sends the pulse raging through my body to a needier region.

When he downshifts the gears and drifts around a corner with meticulous precision, I'm panting, wet, and on the verge of combusting. The control he exerts behind the wheel is nearly as stimulating as his panty-wetting good looks. It also makes me wonder if he exudes the same type of domination in the bedroom.

The width of my pupils grows when a set of blinking traffic lights enters my peripheral vision. A luminous orange glow from the out-of-order lights brightens the interior cabin of the stranger's car the closer we encroach the intersection. I sink deeper in my seat, my heart walloping, my mouth gaping.

"Come on!" I squeal when the stranger withdraws his pressure on the accelerator, dragging the needle on his gauge back to the designated speed limit marked on the nearly isolated roadside. "Bring it all or go home crying."

The stranger's gaze shifts sideways, his eyes flaring with alarm and excitement. I return his soul-intrusive stare while repeating one of my dad's famous quotes, "Bring it all or go home crying."

I lose the ability to secure a full breath when the stranger grins the most seductive smirk I've ever seen before planting his foot to the floor. I'm thrust deep into my seat when 3400 pounds of steel charges down the narrow street. We hit a dip in the intersection so fast the four tires of the Camaro lift from the ground. A smile cracks onto my lips when we sail through the air. I feel weightless and free even while being buckled into a flying deathtrap.

We land on the other side of the intersection with an almighty crunch. The metal underframe of the Camaro grinds against the asphalt, sending sparks shooting behind us, and the bumper of his pride and joy sustains numerous scratches, but we make it through the intersection relatively unscathed.

I suck in a deep breath, filling my lungs with much-needed oxygen before turning my massively dilated eyes to the unnamed man. "That was. . ." I stop talking when I fail to find a word to express how epic that was. I've always been a daredevil, but after some devastating events six years ago, I forgot what it feels like to let go. But even more astonishing than gaining back a piece of me I never thought I'd recover is the fact I entrusted my safety to a man I don't know. That is a massive step in the recovery I've been undertaking for the past three years. It's one of the biggest leaps I've taken thus far—literally.

After slowing his speed to the limit indicated on the signs whizzing by, the unnamed stranger drifts his eyes from the roadside to me. He stares at me, blinking and confused... and if I'm not mistaken, with a smidge of awe. I issue him a cocky wink, my mood still high and laced with adrenaline.

The wild thump of my heart kicks into overdrive when he asks, "Who are you?" The deep roughness of his voice adds to the excited shiver running down my spine.

Smiling, I slip my legs under my bottom and tilt my torso to face him. "So you can speak?" I jest, my tone crammed with wit. "I was beginning to wonder if the knock to my head was playing tricks on me."

Just like earlier, my attempts at humor are lost on him.

"Gemma Calderon-Lévesque. It's a pleasure to meet you..." I leave my greeting open, hoping he will fill in the gap.

His brows furrow together tightly. "Calderon-Lévesque? As in Matias Calderon-Lévesque?"

Ignoring the fact he didn't introduce himself, I nod. Years ago, my dad was well-known in the NASCAR circuit. With five championships under his belt and more podium finishes than any of his competitors, he was one of the best in the field. As the years moved on from his glory days, so did the glamour surrounding his name. Although no red-blooded creature is happy to let their limelight fade into the background, my father was a humble man who knew when to step aside for the new up-and-coming racers. Although his name is still associated with NASCAR to this day, it had a recent resurge in popularity from his induction into the NASCAR Hall of Fame two months ago.

"Matias is of Spanish heritage," the stranger mutters, shocked.

The smile I've been wearing the past ten minutes enlarges when his eyes roam over my lightly tanned skin, green eyes, and platinum blonde hair. His avid gaze enhances the uncontrollable throbbing between my legs. With the aftershock of adrenaline still pumping through his veins, the stranger's eyes are wild, and his lips still wear the effects of his devastating smile. He looks ravishingly beautiful and traumatized at the same time, two panty-wetting combinations.

After absorbing every inch of my American born body in dedicated detail, the stranger locks his eyes with me.

"I was adopted when I was four," I explain to his bemused expression.

His astonishment grows. "How old are you? Twenty-five? Twenty-six?"

"Twenty-eight," I correct.

His eyes bounce between the road and me for numerous heart-strangling seconds before he asks, "So Matias adopted you at the crest of his career?"

Warmth blooms across my chest at his extensive knowledge of my dad's illustrious profession. He must be a fan. That makes me like him even more.

Smiling, I nod. "He won his first championship the year he adopted me. He said I was his good luck charm."

A puff of air parts the stranger's lips; he looks equally shocked and intrigued. "Did he ever let you behind the wheel?" he asks, staring at me with blazing eyes.

I take my time replying, loving that I've finally secured a snip of his attention. Even though his excitement is attached to discovering who my father is, I'll take any leverage I can get on the man I've grown an impulsive obsession with. To be honest, part of my interest in him resonates from everyone's odd reaction when we entered the church hours ago, but the majority is trying to work out how I can keep his libido-bolstering smile on his face. Since he rarely smiles, they're like wishes from a genie. You treasure every one granted.

When the arch of his brow increases, it dawns on me that I failed to answer his question. Gritting my teeth, I shake my head. "Unfortunately, no. I've only ever been allowed in the passenger seat. My dad didn't want his lucky charm to get a single scratch." *That's why he was so devastated about my attack.*

My dad wrapped me up in cotton wool my entire childhood. I was even homeschooled to ensure I wouldn't have to endure the taunts children with famous parents usually suffer. He only unraveled me from his protective cocoon once I reached the safety of adulthood. Little did he know it would be grown men who would have the most significant impact on my quality of life.

"Now it makes sense why you weren't scared," the stranger mutters more to himself than me.

My grin fades. So, he was trying to scare me with his erratic driving? I can't fathom why. Other than shamefully begging for a ride to my hotel, I adhered to his do not approach demeanor. Even beyond riveted by him, I gave him the space he so desperately craved, so why did he set out to frighten me? Perhaps I'm not the only one who's grown a weird obsession in a short time?

Before considering the consequences of my actions, I grab his steering wheel and yank it to the left.

CHAPTER 5

HAWKE

"What the fuck are you doing?"

I shift down the gears as my car violently swerves toward the gutter. It's lucky I maintained the speed limit the last mile, or Gemma's abrupt yank on my steering wheel would have caused my Camaro to cartwheel down the asphalt.

Although my life over the past five years appears to have been protected by an invincible shield, I can't make the same guarantees for Gemma. And although she's practically a stranger, I was born with a naturally engrained protective instinct—especially when it comes to women.

My back molars smash together when the concrete curb scours across my expensive rims, matching the grinding of my teeth to a T. Although annoyed at sustaining more damage to a car that used to be my pride and joy, I'm not overly worried. Our dangerous midair sail already depleted my bank account of a few thousand dollars, so what are a few more scratches?

I haven't driven my Camaro in years. Before Jorgie, this car was my pride and joy. After Jorgie and Malcolm passed, just like every beautiful thing in my life, I couldn't stand the sight of it. It's been sitting in a storage shed for five years, doing what no classic car should: gathering dust.

It took more effort than I'd like to admit to slide into the driver's seat, but it was nowhere near as bad as walking into the church. Just like everything in this town, this car holds a lot of memories for me, but most were gained before I met Jorgie. I have fond memories of my life before Jorgie became a part of it, but like all couples, when you start making new memories, the old ones don't feel as compelling as they once did.

Once my car rolls to a stop at the side of Rochdale Village, Gemma drifts her massively dilated eyes to me. "You want to get your heart racing? I can get it racing. Move."

My brows tack when she kicks off her shoes, throws off her seatbelt, and climbs over the small parcel of space between us. "It's time for you to see how a real NASCAR driver does it."

With her ass thrust in the air and her blonde hair clinging to the leather lining of my roof, she slips her foot into the minute portion of space between my splayed thighs and the steering wheel. The adrenaline heating my veins turns to anger when her wild berry scent stirs my cock. It isn't just my cock's reaction to her closeness annoying me. It is the fact my attempts at scaring her were ineffective.

Although I was in control the entire time, I don't usually drive so erratically. I just had an irrepressible desire to scare Gemma away from me. To show her how dangerous and unhinged I am. Why? Because as the minutes on the clock slowly dragged by at Ava and Hugo's reception, Gemma's sneaky glances my way increased. This may make me sound conceited, but her reaction isn't abnormal.

When entering a room, I conjure the curious stares of women of all ages. Usually, my large frame and height initially attract their attention. Then, for some insane reason, the more brooding my temperament is, the more attention I gain.

Women these days seem to like a challenge. They flock to men with aloof personalities with the hope they will be the one to change them—to make them better and feel whole again. What they don't grasp is that it will never happen. Men with personalities like mine don't want to be saved. We want solitude. That is the reason we are so standoffish.

Well, that's usually the logic I work with. Tonight, my approach did a complete one-eighty. The more my brutish behavior secured the inquisitive stares of Gemma, the more my fucked-up mind strived for her attention. That pissed me off even more than my pointless wish on the church stairs.

I was sitting in the hometown my wife was born, raised, and buried in, guzzling down bottles of water to force myself back into sober territory, and all my fucked-up mind was worried about was attracting the attention of a pretty blonde across the room. That alone proves I should have never stepped foot in this town.

My grief for the past five years has been a sickening mix of remorse and guilt, but when I add the idea of moving on to the volatile concoction, the guilt becomes crippling.

Every breath I take without Jorgie feels like I'm betraying her. So, shouldn't spending even a second without her on my mind make it hard for me to breathe?

To me, it should, and it's been that way the past five years, but every time Gemma glanced at me tonight, for the quickest moment, I wished I could return to the man I was before I lost everything. To know what it feels like to breathe without heaviness sitting on my chest. To smile without guilt. To enjoy the company of a beautiful woman without feeling like I'm betraying my wife.

I'd give anything to become the man I used to be, the man I was before I was broken.

Gritting my teeth, I swallow down the guilt bubbling up my throat before gripping Gemma's hips and hoisting her toward the driver's side door. Once I've clambered into the passenger seat—which is no easy feat for a guy my size—Gemma cranks the driver's seat mechanism, dragging it closer to the steering wheel. Her pupils are dilated, and a fine layer of sweat is beading her forehead, but she takes control of my car with a confident approach not many women exude when sitting at the helm of a vehicle with a five hundred horsepower motor.

After checking her mirrors, she flicks on the blinker and pulls my

Camaro onto the isolated street. My car shudders when she gingerly shifts the gearstick from first to second. Her brows join when her heavy compression on the accelerator sends the speedometer into the red zone.

Guilt creeps up my esophagus when Gemma shifts her eyes to me and mutters, "I don't know how to drive a shift." It isn't her confession causing my odd reaction. It is the little chuckle toppling from my lips after seeing the panicked expression on her face. I didn't mean to laugh, but it spilled from my mouth before I could push it into the small crevice in my chest not suffocated by guilt.

"Keep going. You're doing fine," I force out through the tightness of my throat when Gemma removes her foot from the pedal and veers my car toward the edge of the road.

Gemma's brows meet her hairline. "Really? As I'm fairly certain your gears won't have any teeth on them by the time we make it to my hotel," she replies while grinding the gears from second to third.

I shrug my shoulders. "After tonight, this old girl is being returned to storage."

Gemma scoffs. "My dad would have a coronary if he knew you kept this beauty locked up. Collectors are not car enthusiasts. They're sadists only determined to make the less privileged envious," she quotes her father, a saying he used numerous times during his long NASCAR career.

Excitement thickened my blood when I learned Gemma's dad is Matias Calderon-Lévesque. I've been a fan of NASCAR racing for as long as I've been breathing. If I had the skills, I would have loved to become a professional racer, but like all young boys, my dreams were not within my reach. They did get close enough that I could smell them, but not quite close enough to grasp them with both hands. Perhaps if I'd spent more time at college concentrating on my career aspirations instead of chasing skirts, I would have gotten closer to achieving my dreams.

It is another thing I can add to my unachievable wish list.

The further we travel out of Rochdale, the lighter the heaviness on my chest becomes. Recognizable locations streaming by my window still conjure up memories, but most are pre-Jorgie ones. Although I wasn't born and raised in Rochdale like Jorgie, I spent most of my teen years here. To be honest, before I met Jorgie, I couldn't wait to see this town disappear in my rearview mirror. That all changed the instant I attended my first Marshall brunch. It wasn't Rochdale's location that had me calling it home; it was the people in it.

"Take a left," I instruct Gemma when a familiar street enters my vision.

Nodding, Gemma follows my demand. Her pupils are still massive, but she stopped chewing on the corner of her lip half a mile ago. Although I'm still hesitant at the odd reaction her presence incites, I need to do something to ease my guilt from trying to scare her. This is a small step, but it's better than nothing.

"This road has a steep descent perfect for learning how to shift gears. As you roll down the hill, take your foot off the accelerator, push in the clutch, and glide through the gears. Get a feel for the stick and how it moves."

A faint smile creeps across my lips when I remember saying something similar to Jorgie. Like Gemma, Jorgie had never driven a stick shift before we met. I gave her lessons on the side streets of her university most weekends I drove up to visit her. The only difference this time around is that Gemma is driving the car I refused to let Jorgie behind the wheel of. I never let Jorgie drive my pride and joy as I didn't want to risk her getting even a hairline scratch on my expensive paintwork. How ludicrous is that? I wouldn't let my partner of four years drive my car, but I hand her care over to a lady I only formally met minutes ago.

My lips quirk. I thought my confession would have guilt boiling in my veins, but surprisingly, it doesn't. I'm sure if Jorgie is looking down at me now, she would be laughing. She'd say the damage to my car was Karma's way of kicking my ass for trying to scare Gemma. I do agree with her. What I did wasn't nice. If Gemma wasn't raised by a NASCAR icon, I could have scared the living hell out of her.

When metal grinding comes through my ears, I turn my attention to Gemma. Her first run through the gears grinds at the teeth of my gearbox, but her second attempt is more convincing that she was indeed raised by Matias. Gemma's teeth graze over her bottom lip as her apologetic eyes relay her sympathies to my car without a word seeping from her mouth. Just like Jorgie, Gemma has attractive features that cause men's heads to turn when she enters the room, but the hesitancy in her eyes weakens her appeal.

Don't get me wrong; I'm not saying the timid look makes her less attractive. I'm saying it is why the dozen men gawking at her from across the room tonight never built up the courage to talk to her. Some made it close. For others, it was a dismal failure. The two who got within handshaking distance soon regretted their decision when Gemma blinded them with the flash of her camera before she used their hindered sight to escape.

One good thing that came from watching the cringe-worthy attempts of the men striving for Gemma's attention was that it took my focus off the fact I couldn't wash away my haunted memories with a bottle of liquor. It was only after guzzling down four shots of whiskey did the burn of my car keys in my pocket become too great to ignore. With my head ordered into lockdown mode, I completely forgot that I drove to the hotel where the reception was held. After calling the local taxi company and discovering my limited transportation options, I switched my beverage selection from whiskey to water. Jorgie and Malcolm were killed when a man driving three times over the legal limit struck Jorgie. That alone ensures I'll never drive drunk.

The juddering of my car vibrating through my body drags my mind away from the thoughts souring my already hostile mood. Gemma's panicked gaze flicks between the road and me numerous times before she faintly mutters, "I didn't do anything. I swear."

When a familiar clomping noise sounds through my eardrums, the reason for my car's violent shudders make sense. "Pull in the alleyway. We've got a flat."

Gemma's grip on the steering wheel tightens so much the lightly tanned skin covering her knuckles turns ghostly white. "The alley?" she stutters, her voice rickety.

When I nod, her throat works hard to swallow while her skittish eyes check her surroundings. After ensuring the coast is clear, she slowly glides my car toward the alley. Although she pulls in far enough that we are out of the danger zone of oncoming traffic, not even half the hood of my car is sitting in the alleyway.

Once she finishes scanning the area for a second time, Gemma shifts her massively dilated eyes to me. She looks more frightened now than when I was trying to scare her with my erratic driving, but even with her eyes shrouded in uncertainty, her panicked glance still stirs something deep within me. I don't fucking get it. Honestly, I don't. Gemma is attractive. One hundred percent, but that isn't what is causing my astonishment. The fact that a stranger can spark a reaction out of me at all makes it so bizarre.

When you're a man living with grief, inexplicable instances of happiness that occur with family and friends can be written off without too much thought. A smile at a playful antic or the way my heart rate quickened when I found out Hugo had a son – rare occurrences like that I can explain, but when the glance of a stranger gives me a pinch of hope that not every word in my story has been written is an absurd notion I cannot explain. A look can't give me back my heart I buried five years ago. It can't erase every bad thing in my life, so how can it encourage hope? It can't. That is why it is such a ridiculous notion. It is nothing but a fantasy – the misguided hope that I'm not a wholly heartless and broken man.

A humid July wind smacks me in the face when I throw open the passenger door of my car and peel out of it. I need to get this tire changed and Gemma to her hotel before any other idiotic ideas formulate in my dysfunctional head. Maybe I should just come out and tell Gemma who I am. Then she will look at me with the same amount of sympathy everyone else does, and the little spell she has me under will break. I considered doing that earlier tonight when she introduced herself, but no matter how often my name sat on the tip of my tongue, my mouth refused to relinquish it.

Any chances of keeping my head out of idiotic territory evaporate when Gemma curls out of my car and stands next to me at the trunk. "If you break it, it's your responsibility to fix it," she mumbles, quoting another of her dad's famous sayings.

My brow cocks into my hairline. "You're going to change the flat tire?"

The startled expression on her face fades as she spreads her hands across her tiny hips. "You don't think I can change a tire?" she asks, a whip of edginess to her voice.

Not waiting for me to reply, Gemma snatches the jack out of my grasp and saunters toward the front passenger tire of my car. Inwardly grinning at her fire-cracking self-assuredness, I unscrew the lock clamps on my spare tire, drag it out of the trunk, and roll it to her. My lips twitch as I struggle to conceal my smile.

Gemma kneels on my suit jacket with her expensive-looking dress tucked in the hem of her *panties*. I hesitate when I say panties as I have no clue what the hell she's wearing underneath her dress. From what I saw earlier today, her panties are a cross between gym clothes and the spandex pants bicyclists shouldn't wear. With her hair tied off her face, held by the piece of thread holding my jack together, she looks like a NASCAR pit model who decided to glam it up for the night.

"I know how to change a tire, but I never said I intended on getting dirty while doing it," she informs my mocking expression.

She surprises me when she rolls the jack under my car and hoists the front passenger side of my Camaro off the ground without requesting assistance. My attempt to conceal my smile grows when her hearty endeavors to unfasten the lug nuts on the tire don't budge them the slightest. After blowing a rogue strand of hair out of her face, she increases her pressure on the wrench. If I had anyone to share them with, I'd be tempted to snap a sneaky picture of her kneeling on the filthy ground wrangling with the tires on my Camaro. The little veins in her forehead have darkened from her almighty pushes, and a beading of sweat has made her damp hair stick to her temples. She looks flustered and desirable at the same time. It's an enticing visual for any red-blooded car guy, let alone a NASCAR fanatic who knows of her connection to the industry.

Spotting the corners of my mouth tugging higher, Gemma turns her eyes to me. "You think you can do better? Be my guest." She waves her hand across the front of the tire like the models on *The Price is Right* do when displaying the latest prize up for grabs.

My feeble smirk turns into a smile when my first crank of the wrench undoes the nut Gemma's been working on the last ten minutes. Unable to hide my naturally deep-rooted cockiness, I drift my eyes to Gemma and arch my brow.

"Lucky shot," she mumbles under her breath. "That one was easy as I loosened it for you."

She crosses her arms over her chest when the second lug nut closely follows the first one. The cute little pout she's wearing increases with every nut I remove. By the time I have the flat tire replaced with the spare, her entire forehead is lined with a heavy set of wrinkles, and she wears her sexy scowl with pride. I can't remember the last time anyone scowled at me like that. Jenni, the mark I've been protecting for the past six months, is the only female I've been around lately. Even after surviving a traumatic six months, Jenni wouldn't know what a scowl is. Inflamed cheeks. . . that's an entirely different story.

"Whatever," Gemma hisses, taking my smile as a dig at her epic failure. Her voice is aiming for stern but it comes out with more spiritedness than she hoped for. "Who needs to know how to change a tire when you have an entire pit crew at your disposal to do it for you?"

She tries to keep her gaze narrowed. She miserably fails. After wiping the grease from my hands with a rag tied around my jack and lowering my car back to the asphalt, I return my eyes to Gemma. Once she finishes scanning the alley for the tenth time in the past three minutes, she locks her wide eyes with mine. A flush of color creeps across her cheeks when she notices she has secured my prying stare. Although I can see a snick of embarrassment forming in her eyes, she maintains my gaze.

This is probably more my grief talking than logic, but being looked at through the eyes of a stranger is a nice change. Even with Gemma's horribly fake annoyance, not being seen as a damaged man for even the shortest period makes the weight I've been carrying on my shoulders for the past five years a little lighter. Although I said earlier my wish not to be a broken man for just a second frustrates me, it doesn't stop it from being true. I know the insane feeling I get when Gemma looks at me won't last, but when you're grasping at straws, even a nanosecond of being treated normal is a huge deal to a man who has nothing to look forward to.

I know why people stare at me in sympathy. Everything I wanted in my life was working out how I had envisioned. Then faster than I could snap my fingers, my entire world changed, but their silent sympathies can't undo what happened. It just adds to the grief I'm already drowning in.

While standing from my crouched position, I remember the quote Mrs. Marshall said to me on the day of Jorgie and Malcolm's funeral. "Grief is not a straight line that disappears into the horizon with time. It's just like the beat of your heart. It goes up and down, slows for a while, then speeds up when you least expect it. Your soul knows what to do to heal itself, Hawke. The challenge will be to silence your mind."

Deciding to test her theory, I shut down my mind before thrusting my hand out, offering to help Gemma off the ground. A trace of a smile curls on her lips before she accepts my friendly gesture. When her smile causes an even bigger impact to me than her inquisitive glances, I calm the guilt trickling into my veins by repeating Mrs. Marshall's quote over and over again.

After running her hands down the front of her dress, Gemma locks her curious eyes with me. "Considering you don't have the Marshall heirloom blue eyes, I'm fairly certain you're not Hugo's brother, Chase. So, who are you?" she asks, unable to leash her nosiness. She peers into my eyes, her curiosity growing by the second.

"Carey," I reply, my voice as uncertain as my facial expression. "My name is Carey."

I know I'm being somewhat deceitful with my introduction, but for every second Gemma glances at me, it feels like an hour is taken off the lifetime sentence I was handed five years ago. If one second in her presence is that potent, imagine the impact an entire minute or hour could have on a broken man.

Would you lie for a chance to feel normal again?

CHAPTER 6

GEMMA

Carey's mood bounced between dour and passive the first twenty minutes of our trip, but the ten minutes following our impromptu battle of the sexes tire-changing game exposed a new side to him.

It is an approachable side that welcomes the occasional question and awards my attempts at wittiness with sporadic smiles. Although his true personality is still a little hard for me to gauge, I've thoroughly enjoyed our time together—even with the flare of victory brightening his dark eyes.

I'm not going to lie; my efforts at changing his tire were woeful, but in my defense, I've never changed a tire in my life. And despite that, just leaving the safety of Carey's car was a remarkable performance for me. I only grew the courage to face my fears when I recalled the steps Dr. McKay taught me during the first six months of my intense recovery.

Wanting to bolster my belief that I didn't lose any power in a dark alleyway years ago, I became a woman on a mission. I was more determined than ever. I just never fathomed how much muscle it would take to remove the lug nuts on the tire. I don't care how often Carey denies it. I swear on my grandfather's grave that those lugs were seized in place from years of corrosion while sitting in a storage shed.

While I'm being forthright, I'll also admit I don't feel guarded around Carey. I don't know why. Maybe because he has such a reserved demeanor, I need to bring a more outlandish personality to the party to even us out. It's funny. Six years ago, a word like "outlandish" wouldn't have made a dent in my former personality. Now the only outlandish thing I do is switch my coffee order from artificial sweetener to sugar. I wouldn't say I was an extrovert before the event that changed my life course, but I honestly didn't believe anything could ever bring me down. *How naive was I?*

Any further thoughts on my naïveté are left for dust when familiar scenes zoom by my window. With my heart beating at a double speed, I shift my eyes to the driver's seat. I blink, slightly confused, when my excited gleam is met with a pair of inquisitive dark eyes I don't immediately recognize. With cherished memories engulfing me, it takes me a few moments to remember where I am in time.

Once I grasp that I'm no longer a ten-year-old girl sitting in her father's truck, my excitement swells. "Do you have anywhere you need to be right now?" I ask Carey, my voice high.

Carey's eyes flick from the radio clock, showing that it is nearly midnight to me. He takes a few moments to absorb the excited expression on my face before he briefly shakes his head.

Barely holding in my squeal, I request, "Take a right on Lewis."

Carey eyes me with silent reserve before doing as instructed.

For the next twenty minutes, I direct him to our destination using nothing but happy memories. The further Carey's Camaro glides down a narrow black road, the more my backside lifts off the seat. The crackling of energy in the air is electrifying, sparking every fine hair on my body to bristle with excitement. I'm not the only one excited; enthusiasm also beams out of Carey in invisible waves.

I squint my eyes as I scan the familiar location. Although several years have passed since I've been here this late at night, cherished memories are real-life snapshots. You never truly forget them, no matter how much they fade.

"Stop," I demand when a white wooden mailbox enters my peripheral vision.

The sound of gravel crunching under tires booms into my ears when Carey pulls his Camaro into the driveway of my dad's first country estate. Before he sold this property four years ago, we lived here six months out of the year. From the outside, there's no clue of the beauty hiding behind the overgrown hedges and unkempt lawn.

When Carey's car stops at a large twelve-foot-high electric gate, he looks at me. He seems baffled and unsure. From the scared look in his eyes, anyone would swear I just guided him to a scary country rendition of Blood Manor.

Our necks crank to the side in sync when a luscious female voice asks, "*Hola, puedo aydarte?*"

An excited squeal ripples from my lips when I recognize the sultry voice. The muscles in Carey's thick thighs flex when I lean across his chest to roll down his driver's side window. "*Hola, Valentina, es Gemma,*" I greet into the intercom hidden in the stonewall of the entrance gate.

Valentina squeals nearly as loud as I did when I identified her voice. I haven't seen Valentina in over two years, but I'd never forget her hot-enough-to-melt-chocolate voice. It's as seductive as her curvaceous body. Ignoring Carey screwing up his nose from Valentina's ear-piercing squeal, I apologize in Spanish for arriving at such a late hour but plead with her to grant us access to the back half of the property.

"We'll be so quiet, you won't even know we're here," I add in English to strengthen my plea.

Seconds feel like hours before Valentina agrees to my terms but with one stipulation. The next time I'm in her neck of the woods, I have to visit at a more appropriate hour and introduce her to the dark-haired hottie I'm rubbing my boobies against. My cheeks initially flame from her witty request, but considering Carey didn't flinch the slightest, my embarrassment quickly subsides. I'm confident he doesn't understand a word of Spanish.

"*Gracias, Valentina*, and I will, I promise," I reply.

The sound of a loud buzzer drowns out Valentina's farewell. I blow an air kiss to the camera recording my every movement before sliding back into the passenger seat. After the electric gate slowly chugs open, Carey pulls his car down the asphalt driveway. My eyes shoot in all directions, eager to absorb the space that hasn't changed in nearly three years. Although this residence looks rundown and scary on the outside, magic happens once you enter the rusted old gates. With rolled turf, established manicured gardens, and a residence that puts Graceland to shame, this property is not only superb; it is one of a kind.

"Follow the path on your right," I request.

The further Carey's Camaro rolls down the isolated side track, the more recognition dawns on Carey's face. New NASCAR billboards are scattered between the original ones my dad had installed nearly twenty years ago.

"Valentina. . ." Carey leaves his sentence open like I had earlier, hoping I'll fill in the blanks.

"Valentina Cratis. Wife of—"

"Andre Cratis," Carey fills in before he cranks his neck back.

Although the former Calderon-Lévesque mansion is shrouded in darkness from the cloud-filled sky, the light illuminating the main stairs of the residence makes it easily distinguishable to any NASCAR fan. My dad was photographed on those stairs ten years ago with his vast collection of championship trophies surrounding him, and Andre and Valentina wed on those stairs three years ago. That was the day my love for photography flourished. I still have the picture I snapped of them with an old retro Polaroid camera their wedding photographer lent me. It is sitting on the duchess in the bedroom of my apartment in New York. It is one of my most treasured possessions. That picture saved my life in more ways than words could ever express.

"We're at Matias's private ranch?" Carey asks, his voice the highest I've heard.

Smiling, I nod. "This isn't my dad's private ranch anymore, though. This is Andre and Valentina's home. They have lived here the past four years."

The shock on Carey's face grows when his car stops at the edge of the race track my dad had built in the late 90s. When it became apparent my dad's grueling training program and my school schedule weren't melding, my dad built a replica NASCAR training track in the back paddock of our winter residence. When it was finished, he never practiced on another track. Critics slammed him, saying he was reckless and that he'd lost his passion for the sport. He proved them wrong. He won his final three championships the years following his decision to upend his training program to an unknown town fifty miles outside of New York.

Carey sits in muted silence when I crank open the passenger side door and curl out of his car. After flicking on the overhead flood lights, I pace toward the large steel gate of the track. My heart swells in pride when I notice Valentia and Andre have kept the track in its original condition. Even the track's name remains the same: Calderon Mile.

After swinging the gate open, I turn my eyes back to Carey. "Come on."

A childish giggle rumbles up my chest when Carey throws open his driver's side door and starts climbing out of his car.

"Not you. Your car," I shout, laughter in my voice.

Even with the brightness of Carey's Camaro hindering my vision, I don't miss the confused arch of his brow.

"Do you want to drive your Camaro on the same track champion NASCAR drivers Matias Calderon-Lévesque and Andre Cartis have driven on?" I overemphasize my voice with dramatic flair, hoping to conceal the nervous butterflies jittering in my stomach. I've seen this track more times than the back of my hand, so I'm not here to recall old memories. I'm here because every second I spend with Carey creates hairline splinters in the protective barrier I built around my heart six years ago. Just the excited gleam in his eyes as he runs them over the track has a jackhammer working through a wall I assumed was impenetrable.

When Carey briefly nods at my question, I say, "Then let's do this!"

The smile that cracks on his face is brighter than the headlights on his car, and it drowns out the warning bells ringing in my head that I'll never come out of this night unscathed.

Once Carey guides his car through the narrow opening, I close the gate and switch on the automatic timer. Pretending Carey hasn't already seen my hideous contouring undergarments, I strut toward the start line while gesturing seductively with my hands for him to follow me. If my dad could see me now, he'd be mortified. No matter how often I wished to be a NASCAR pit girl for just one day, it was a dream my dad would never allow to come true. If my dad had it his way, still to this day, I would wear nothing but overly baggy race suits with a grease-covered face.

Once Carey's fat-rimmed tires are pressed against the edge of the thick white start line, I snag a rag out of the makeshift starters box on my left and wave it in the air.

"Are you ready?" I shout, ensuring Carey can hear me over the loud rumble of his engine.

My cheeks burn from their sudden incline when Carey revs his engine, advising he's good to go.

"One point five miles of track is waiting to be dominated. Bring it all or go home crying!" I scream into the muggy night air.

Swiveling my flag, I add to the suspense firing the dark night sky with stifling heat. "Go!" I scream while throwing down my rag.

The intoxicating scent of burning rubber and gasoline stream through my nose when Carey's Camaro shoots over the starting line like a rocket. I knew from his earlier performance tonight that his driving skills were impressive, but my astonishment grows when he charges past the first half-mile sign with just over twelve seconds on the clock. My eyes follow the blue blur of his car as he moves through the track at lightning speed. His incredible performance pushes me back to ten years ago, back to an age where I thought I was invincible.

My eyes snap to the timer when he flies over the finish line. My breathing halts when I notice only 32.84 seconds on the clock.

"Holy shit," I mumble to myself. Champion NASCAR drivers struggle to get over the 1.5-mile line in under thirty seconds, and they're driving cars designed for these conditions. So for a novice to achieve that in a standard car... that's phenomenal.

"How the hell did you do that?" I query when Carey pulls his Camaro to the side of me.

The crazy thump of my heart merges into dangerous territory when the most alluring smile I've ever seen crosses Carey's face. I'm not talking about a half-smirk or even a full-toothed smile. I'm talking a genuine smile that extends all the way from his chest. His true smile is... *wow*. If I thought this man was breathtaking before, I had no clue. He's truly outstanding.

"It's not the first time I've driven on a NASCAR track," Carey confesses while curling out of his car.

My eyes bulge. "It isn't?"

Like it could get any larger, Carey's smile increases before he briefly shakes his head. "I participated in two of the future NASCAR driver programs your dad organized in my late teens."

"You did!?" I catch my eye roll halfway from the daftness of my questions. "Then how come I've never met you before? I attended all my dad's events." This time, my voice sounds like it usually does: friendly but inquisitive.

Before Carey can answer, I wave my hand through the air. "Never mind. I already know the answer to my question. Associating with handsome young drivers was also on my dad's no-go list."

Carey cops my compliment on the chin without the slightest switch in his composure. Rumors circulated throughout the NASCAR industry that my dad threatened any drivers chosen to participate in his advanced training program to stay away from his daughter.

"If you so much as share the same air as my daughter, the closest you'll get to a NASCAR will be when you're polishing my hubcaps with your toothbrush," I quote. A smirk curls on my lips when my impersonation of my dad's thick Spanish accent comes out to perfection.

Carey chuckles. "That was one of Matias's regular sayings, but my favorite one was, 'You even glance in my daughter's direction, the only rubber you'll be smelling will be the scent of my boot up your ass,'" he replies with a smile.

My mortification grows. I love my dad—truly I do—but he gives overbearing protective parenting a new name.

Acting like my dad's tactics were perfectly normal for a caring father, I ask, "So what happened to your NASCAR dreams? Why aren't you out there breaking records in the sprint circuits? You have the skills, as only the best up-and-coming drivers were invited to join my dad's program."

"Life happened," Carey replies a short time later with a shrug. His voice is low and crammed with sentiment.

I prop my backside onto the hood of his car and scoot backward until my back is resting against the windscreen. "Sounds like the excuse of a young man without aspirations," I quote, still mimicking my dad's accent.

The heat of the Camaro's engine adds to the sweat slicking my skin, but it is nothing compared to the fiery range of emotions brewing in Carey's eyes. The happy sparkle they wore mere seconds ago has vanished, and his unapproachable demeanor is back full force, but even with him holding a gaze that would terrify any woman, I'm remarkably unafraid.

I strive to capture the devotion of Carey's absconding gaze before saying, "Life is 10% what happens to us. The other 90% is how we react to it."

"Another quote from Matias?" Carey's voice is as reserved as his personality.

I shake my head. "No. It was a statement my therapist said to me when I was fleeing our first court-appointed session four years ago," I admit, hoping my honesty will ease his agitation.

I wait with bated breath, fully anticipating that he'll react as shocked as every man does when I admit to court-appointed therapy. I'm the one who ends up shocked when the expression on his face doesn't change the slightest. He maintains his normal impassive yet intrigued expression.

Fiddling with one of the many gold bracelets wrapped around my wrist, I say, "I have numerous contacts in this industry if you're interested in pursuing racing. I'm not offering my support because I find you intriguing. I truly believe you have talent that should be exploited—"

"Exploited or explored?" Carey interrupts, his tone changing from antagonized to astonished.

A grin curls on my lips. "People whose talents are not exploited become disenchanted and disruptive."

Feeling the heat of Carey's curious glance, I lift my gaze to his. "That one was Terence Conran," I advise his questioning eyes. When the confusion on his face grows, I ask my question in a way that only requires a simple yes or no reply. "Is a career in racing something you want to exploit?"

Carey takes his time configuring a response before he mutters, "You don't think I'm a little too old to be an aspiring NASCAR driver?"

"God no," I reply dramatically with a roll of my eyes. "Age shouldn't be a deterrent when you're destined for greatness."

I pat my hand on the hood of his car, offering for him to join me. When he surprisingly does as requested, I continue with my endeavor to reignite the glimmer of content his eyes bore earlier. "Casey Mears, Jamie McMurray, David Gilliland, and Jimmie Johnson are all drivers in the Sprint Cup Series, and they're all over forty."

"And they've all been driving for the past twenty-plus years," Carey adds.

I knock my knee against his thigh. "You're acting like you already have one foot in the grave." My high voice exposes my excitement at his closeness. Just the warmth radiating off his body has every nerve ending in mine sparked, and paying careful attention to his every move. "How old are you, anyway? And pre-warning, if you say anything over the age of thirty-five, I won't be held accountable for my actions."

He locks his gaze with me, his eyes confused, his lips twisted.

I smile at his confusion. "If you're over thirty-five, I'm going to hold you down until you cough up the location of the fountain of youth you've been drinking out of. A million dollars will be nothing but chump change for me once I've distributed that age-defying concoction to all the old, wrinkly ladies of America."

The vibrant spark flaring in Carey's eyes from my compliment bolsters the euphoria pumping through my veins from sitting so close to him.

"I'm thirty-one. Old enough to know my racing aspirations belong in the grave I already have my foot in," he replies. From the roughness of his tone, I can't tell if he's trying to be witty or forthright.

I scoff, feigning repulsion before shifting my eyes to the sky. Stargazing is a mandatory requirement whenever I'm outside after dark. There's a magical beauty in a dark sky full of stars.

A pout slips onto my lips. With a heavy set of clouds in the sky, the usually sparkling visual isn't as enticing as normal. Or perhaps it is because nothing comes close to the allure of the man sitting next to me? Who needs to look at a beautiful sky when you have the very definition of a man sitting next to you? If just the meekest touch of Carey's thigh against mine is sending a thrill of excitement down my spine, imagine what a purposeful contact would do.

A few minutes of silence pass between us. I turn my eyes away from the sky twenty minutes later when Carey murmurs, "It's been a long time since I've just sat and did nothing."

I'm not surprised by his revelation. He seems like a guy who would constantly be on the go. For some people, keeping their minds occupied is the only way they can keep their thoughts in neutral territory.

I lick my dry lips before asking, "Don't you know doing nothing is one of the hardest things to do?"

My pulse quickens when Carey drifts his eyes to me. "Doing nothing is hard work?"

I nod. "Because you never know when you're finished."

My lungs stop working when Carey throws his head back and laughs. No dream I've ever had can compete with the accomplishment I feel by making Carey laugh. In the cruel and twisted world we live in, making another person happy is one of the kindest things you can do. That is what this feels like. No matter what happens from this point out, nothing can ruin this night. I achieved the seemingly impossible. I made the man with dark, haunted eyes laugh, and it was everything I could have wished for and more.

Carey's laughter stops as quickly as it begins. Although the stormy cloud dimming his dark gaze has cleared away, a new, unreadable filter occurs.

Another stretch of silence passes between us as we watch the clouds in the sky slowly reveal a beautiful star-filled night. Just like in life, sometimes walking through the darkness is the only way to truly appreciate the brighter things in life. If the sky wasn't so dark, you'd never see the beauty of the stars.

I suck in a nerve-clearing breath before turning my eyes to Carey. "Just because someone plays poker for twenty years doesn't mean they have world-class skills. The same can be said for driving. You either have it or you don't. You have it."

My greedy gasp of air entombs halfway between my lungs and my throat when more than inquisitiveness brightens his gaze. If I'm not mistaken, his eyes are enhanced with the unique mix of confusion and hankering.

Unable to determine if it is my declaration causing the new shimmer in Carey's eyes or the fact our thighs have been touching the past forty minutes, I mutter, "Dreams are like memories. No matter how old you get, you never stop creating them. You just have to decide if you're strong enough to pursue them."

The small section of skin between Carey's eyes becomes heavily creased—adding to his confused expression. He appears just as baffled as I am about our bizarre interactions tonight. It is so peculiar that a man I only met hours ago has such a sense of familiarity about him. If I didn't know any different, I'd swear I've met him before. It's probably his worldly eyes adding to the confusion clustering my mind. He has eyes that look damaged and broken, but they also plead not to misread his outward appearance. Although his standoffish demeanor gives the impression he wants solitude, the aura beaming out of his eyes tells an entirely different story. He's just like every other human being out there. He's waiting for someone to throw him a lifejacket, to show him that there are rays of sunshine even in a storm-filled sky.

My voice comes out with a quiver when I begin to speak. It isn't shaking with nerves; it is hindered by anticipation. "There's only one rule in life. If you don't go after what you want, you'll never have it."

"And how does fate play into this?" Carey asks, his voice gritty and deep.

"It doesn't," I reply with a headshake. "Fate only takes you to a certain point, then it is up to you to make it the rest of the way. I'm not saying life is a sunset walk on a Caribbean beach. Sometimes it can feel like everything is falling apart, where, in reality, everything may be falling into place."

I slide across the hood of Carey's car as I battle to keep buried memories hidden. It took an intense amount of therapy and the love and guidance of those surrounding me before I could even consider the prospect that my life didn't end six years ago. Only now do I realize my life plan may have veered slightly off-track, but it never came close to crossing the finish line.

The hot metal hood of the Camaro sticks to my sweat-slicked skin, dragging the hem of my dress up high on my thigh when I slide off the side. The oddness of our exchange this evening grows when Carey maintains my eye contact even with a scandalous amount of my skin exposed. I don't know if that makes him an admirable man or me a foolish woman for chasing someone clearly not interested in me.

I stop wallowing in self-pity when Carey mumbles, "Fate brings people together, but it takes more than that to keep them together."

Smiling, I nod. "Fate decides who comes into your life. Your heart chooses who gets to stay." As I pace to the driver's door of his Camaro, an idea formulates in my head.

"So what do you say, Carey? Can you spare a couple of minutes of your time to help a girl achieve a lifelong dream? Or will you wait for the sun and moon to align and let them choose your path?"

CHAPTER 7

HAWKE

For every second that passes in silence, the width of Gemma's pupils increase. Although she only asked for a few minutes of my time, the look in her eyes tells me she wants so much more. I can't say I don't understand the bizarre mix of intrigue and confusion in her heavy-hooded gaze.

I'm battling the same range of emotions. The past hour has been unlike anything I've experienced in the past five years. When I raced around the track, it felt like I was speeding past every horrid thing that has happened in my life and that I was finally making headway in my grief.

In the twenty minutes that followed, I secured a full breath for the first time in years. To others, that may not seem like much of an accomplishment, but when you're a man drowning in grief, inhaling a lung-filling gulp of air is a treasured moment.

But do you want to know what is even more astonishing than that? My race around the track didn't just make a small crack in the grief that's been crippling me the past five years; it also cleared away some of the mistrust Gemma's eyes have been carrying since I barreled into her nine hours ago.

It makes me wonder what is going on in that head of hers if

crossing a dream off a broken man's bucket list eases the pain in her eyes.

Peering into Gemma's eyes is like glancing into a kaleidoscope, so many different colors and emotions reflect back at me. Although her eyes have never been filled with sympathy the past hour, there have been an array of emotions I can't recognize.

Don't play me for a fool. I can read the ga-ga glint brightening her eyes the past hour as clear as the sun in the sky, but there's something much deeper than lust there. And for some reason, unbeknownst to me, identifying that glint is just as important to me as my next full breath.

After a few moments of silent contemplation, only one thought crosses my mind. When you're a man living your life as if you're on death row, anything that gains your attention should be explored, shouldn't it?

"Come on, Carey. What man accepts a favor without giving one in return?" Gemma whines, her voice quivering with both nerves and excitement.

My eyes roll skywards. There she goes again with the guilt trip. That is how I am certain she has no clue who I am. Guilt is swallowing my life whole, so her little nicks don't cause the slightest ripple in the ocean of grief I'm treading in.

Gemma takes a step closer to me. Her wild berry smell adds a feminine touch to the virile surroundings we're immersed in. "Unless you're afraid I'll show you up," she murmurs, her tone as cocky as the competitiveness in her eyes. "A little bit of competition never hurt anyone." She spreads her hands across her hips and stares straight into my eyes. "Will being beaten by a girl bruise your massive ego?"

I arch my brow. Maybe she does know me? Even with my usual personality watered down with remorse, I've always been cocky – although I usually only unleash my bloodthirsty desire to win on a male opponent. Out bench-pressing my trainer at my local gym or forcing Hugo to tap out on the boxing mat are competitive games that keep blood pumping to the region my heart used to be, not competing against a woman who both confuses and intrigues me.

When the glint in her eyes I can't recognize weakens, my intentions to turn down her request do a complete one-eighty. Ignoring the uneasy feeling in my stomach that she has instigated more times than I can count tonight, I mutter, "The only way you'll drive around that track is while wearing the full get-up."

Gemma's eyes flare in excitement as she curtly nods. Her excitement fades when I add, "Fire suit, helmet, and all."

The smile her disgruntled moan caused widens when she moves into a pit station at the side of the track and drags a pair of coveralls up and over her dress. The sides of the legs are black and white-checkered in color and they have a red band around the midsection.

After pulling the zipper to her chin, she kicks off her heels and pulls on a pair of black boots. For how quickly she transforms from runway model to NASCAR driver, I'd say this is something she has done regularly, but from her flamed cheeks and wide-eyed expression, I'd say it is something she would prefer to do in private.

Snagging a helmet from a shelf at the back of the pit station, Gemma paces to me. If the moon wasn't bouncing off her platinum blonde locks, and she didn't have a face that can make a heartless man's pulse beat a little faster, she looks like every other NASCAR driver out there, even more so because of the determination in her eyes.

Clearly, this is something she has wanted to do for a long time. I don't know why, but the fact I get to help her achieve one of her dreams makes my chest puff high. Perhaps it is the desire to even the ground between us? Or maybe it is because I've always believed a good deed brightens a dark world.

I crank open my driver's side door and gesture with my head for Gemma to enter. Her breathing turns excited when I lean over her shoulder to pull the five-point safety harness over the seat.

Although she is practically a stranger, I still don't want her getting hurt. The idea of her getting in a wreck causes my hands to shake, making it hard for me to latch the harness together.

Peering into my eyes, Gemma stops my jittery movements with her hands while mumbling, "I've got this." After clipping the harness together, she exhales a ragged breath. "All right, tighten me in firmly," she requests. Her words are strong, but her eyes relay her uncertainty. From how she watches me, I know not all her insecurities come from nerves; some of it resonates because she's unsure of my odd response to strapping her in.

Acting like I can't feel the air shifting between us, I grip the tethers on the harness and yank down hard. The panic thickening my blood thins when Gemma grimaces, faking asphyxiation from the harness' death-tight grip. Wanting to ensure there isn't a space of air between the harness and her body, I give it another rough yank.

"Okay. Now I'm not joking. I can't breathe," she wheezes, her whitening face adding strength to her admission.

"Good. Because that's how it's supposed to feel," I inform her.

Her brows stitch. "It feels like I've gone back to my pre-teen days." When she notices my confused expression, she adds, "My boobs have gone back to 2010. I'm once again flat-chested."

I swear, I give it my best shot, but the instant the word "boobs" leaves her mouth, my eyes dart to her chest. Even knowing I shouldn't be looking, it takes me several seconds to tear my eyes away from her wildly thrusting chest. It is nearly as tortuous as when I had to maintain her eye contact when the hood of my car exposed inches of her smooth thighs. Even with Gemma's inquisitive glances agitating me, it doesn't take away from the fact she's an attractive female with an enticing body.

After giving myself a few moments to get over the fact I fell for one of the oldest tricks in the book, I lift my eyes to Gemma. When I see the mortified look on her face, I realize she didn't purposely set out to goad me. She appears as mortified as I am over my lack of self-control when I'm around her.

Spending the past hour with her is like being stabbed with a double-sided sword. Her inquisitive glances give me a moment of reprieve from the grief I've been wading through the past five years, but the fact a stranger can exonerate me at all adds to my agitation.

When you're sentenced to a life of misery, shouldn't even a second of your time be suffocated by misery? Normally, I'd say yes, but for those thirty seconds, I flew around the track, and for the forty minutes that followed it, miserable was not a word I could use to describe that time.

Free. Encouraged.

Me.

If I could push them past the guilt curled around my throat, those are words I'd use to describe the range of emotions pumping through my veins right now. Words I never thought I'd utter again in my lifetime.

Ignoring the crosswire of emotions overwhelming me, I close the driver's side door of my car and amble to the other side. When I slide into the passenger seat, Gemma bows her brow and glares at me. The longer she stares, the foggier the screen on her helmet becomes.

"What?" I eventually ask when I fail to comprehend what caused her lightning-fast personality switch. She's gone from her eyes beaming with apologies to looking like a woman who crushes balls for a living.

Gemma nudges her head to the side. "Are you going to put on your seatbelt?" Her words come out strained through the mouth guard of her helmet.

My right shoulder lifts into a shrug before I briefly shake my head. "I have nothing left to lose," I mumble.

Her grip on the steering wheel tightens as she revs my car's engine, sending a deep rumble through the seats. "Having nothing to lose means you have a lot to gain. Put on your seatbelt," she demands, her voice bossy and straight to the point.

Deciding an argument isn't worth the effort, I pull my seat belt across my body. The instant the belt mechanism latches, I'm thrust into my seat from Gemma's heavy compression on the gas pedal.

For a woman who struggled to change gears not even an hour ago, she does remarkably well this time around. She shifts from first gear to second with only the smallest grind of the gearbox, and second to third is even smoother than that.

When she reaches the first bend in the track, my foot slams onto the floor of my Camaro as I search for the invisible brake. My heart rate reaches levels I haven't achieved in years when she glides my car around the bend without touching the brakes. The back end of my Camaro drifts out, but with a relaxed and calm approach, she admirably maintains control of my car.

My head flies back to check the timer on the side of the track. A ghost of a smile cracks onto my lips when I notice only twenty-two seconds on the clock have passed. That's a stellar effort any novice driver should be proud of.

When Gemma's endeavors of switching from third to fourth crunches at the gears, I curl my hand over her tight fist and guide the gearstick into place without pause for consideration. Even though I can't see her face through the reflective mask of her helmet, I know she's smiling. I can feel it deep in my bones.

Adrenaline scorches my veins when she hits the one-mile marker with only forty-two seconds on the clock. "Come on," I silently chant. "Bring it all or go home crying."

Like she can hear my private thoughts, she increases her pressure on the gas pedal, and my gauge stops recording her speed. Even with guilt trickling into my veins at the excitement roaring through my body, I can't stop the smile etching onto my mouth when Gemma releases a squeal, similar to the one she made earlier tonight when she zooms over the finish line with an impressive time of 59.53 seconds recorded on the timer.

"I did it!" she squeals through the face shield of her helmet. "One and a half miles in under sixty seconds!"

After pulling my car into the pit lane at the side of the track, she unlatches the five-point harness and curls out of the driver's seat. She throws off her helmet and places it on the hood of my car before undoing the zipper on her race suit. I mimic her movements minus the removal of safety equipment.

"I swear on my grandpa's grave that was better than sex," Gemma confesses, her words breathy and laced with excitement.

A chuckle topples from my mouth before I can stifle it when she does a little jig on the spot. Her dance moves look like a bronco-riding line dancer who had a baby with the person who invented the chicken dance. Her feet are kicking up dust as her arms flap out wildly at her sides. It is a hideous and oddly enticing boogie.

Hearing my laughter, she snaps her eyes to me. Even with her cheeks flaming in embarrassment, she smiles a grin that makes me feel like I stepped back in time ten years. Back to when my only concern was not being the frat brother who drew the short straw as designated driver. It's the type of smile that impacts me way more than I'd like to admit. A smile that forces stupid thoughts to trickle through my mind. Like, what if I pretend not to be me for just one night? Or can widowers take a night off from their grief just to feel normal for a few measly hours? But the stupidest ones, the ones that turn my blood black with anger, are these: what if my life didn't end with Jorgie and Malcolm? What if there are still chapters of my story yet to be written?

The heaviness that cleared off my chest mere minutes ago comes steamrolling back in as a wave of guilt swamps me. The tightness around my throat firms as anger steals my ability to breathe. While Gemma yanks her race suit down her thighs, I charge for the driver's side door of my car, more than eager to end this night before any more foolish thoughts enter my mind.

"Wait," Gemma requests when I open my driver's side door.

Even with my brain screaming at me to get in the car and leave now, my eyes unwillingly lift to Gemma.

"Good memories never fade, but there's no harm in suspending a moment in time for eternity."

In haste, she dumps her race suit into a bin on her left before placing her helmet back onto its rack. When she pivots around to face me, the urge to dive into my car and leave her here overwhelms me. Like the past nine hours, her briefest glance stirs something deep within me. Something I want to dig out of my chest and bury in a pit where it will never be found.

Not noticing the switch in my composure, Gemma issues me another heart-strangling smile before pacing to my car. My brows scrunch when she leans into my car and removes a retro-looking camera from the front pocket of her suitcase.

"Have you ever just wanted to fully let go? To pretend that nothing matters more than making memories that will steal your breath away every time you think of them?" she asks after fiddling with the ancient camera.

I nod before my brain has the chance to protest.

"That's what tonight is about: a chance to forget the things that will still be there tomorrow. The hardest part of waking up every morning is remembering what you spent all day yesterday trying to forget. Tonight has ensured I'll not wake up tomorrow with the same amount of regret I woke up with today. The bad memories will still be there, but I've added a few good ones as well."

I remain quiet, unsure exactly how to reply. The weary haze in Gemma's eyes shows she has her own set of issues she's dealing with, but there's a difference between us. Gemma is guarded and weary. Two faults that can be fixed with time. I'm broken. Nothing can fix broken.

My eyes squint, and I step backward when a bright flash of a camera light blinds me. Gemma lets out a little giggle at my reaction before the sound of heels clicking on asphalt overtakes her laughter. It takes me several blinks to clear away half of the white spots dancing in front of my eyes, but even with my vision hindered and a stranglehold of emotions pumping into me, I can detect Gemma's closeness when she leans into my side. It isn't just the warmth of her body pressed up against mine that gives it away; it is the way her closeness calms the unease swirling in my stomach.

Before I can cite an objection, Gemma lifts the Polaroid to snap a selfie of us together. A grin unwillingly tugs my lips higher. I've spent the last six months as a bodyguard to a chart-topping pop group, so I know all too well how selfies are all the rage right now, but seeing Gemma take one of us with a chunky retro Polaroid camera brings a whole new meaning to the fad.

After snapping our photo, Gemma pivots to face me while shaking the Polaroid image. Over time, our picture sneaks out of the blackness. Even with the odd angle because of our difference in height and the fact we're both wearing the effects of a long day, the photo is surprisingly decent. Gemma is wearing her devastating smile, and her eyes are bright and alive. My dark gaze exposes the range of emotion pumping into me, but against my wishes, the lines in the corner of my mouth are facing the sky.

"We aren't friends nor enemies, just two strangers who'll share the same memory for eternity." Gemma's voice is filled with sentiment.

I lift my eyes from the photo to her. As the glint of happiness in her eyes dampens, I say, "Every person in your life was a stranger at one point."

My statement has the effect I'm aiming for when Gemma's eyes flare in excitement as her lips curve into a smile I'll never forget. "Strangers can become friends just as quickly as friends can become strangers." She tilts into my side like she did on the church stairs hours ago. "You just have to stop treating me like I'm the enemy."

With that, she slips into the passenger seat of my car and fastens her seatbelt, shifting the air between us even more quickly than our selfie developed. After rolling down my car window, she drifts her lively eyes to me. "So what's next, Mister? Am I going to show you up on the go-kart track? Or take you down during a round of glow-in-the-dark bowling?"

"You don't want to go back to your hotel?" I ask with shock evident in my tone.

Gemma stares into my eyes for several moments before faintly muttering, "I don't want to go back to reality."

CHAPTER 8

GEMMA

"For future reference, if you had disclosed that carrying a gun was a requirement of your job, I wouldn't have put Mr. Bunny on the negotiating table," I inform as I crank my neck back to the giant stuffed rabbit strapped into the back seat of Carey's Camaro.

My love affair with Mr. Bunny was brief but long enough to last me a lifetime. Although his hairy face is as cute as fluffy clouds in a blue sky, he's nothing but icing on a big cake from spending the last two hours with Carey in a twenty-four-seven amusement parlor.

I won't lie; my endeavor to strong-arm Carey into the arcade was nearly as difficult as coercing him into the church hours ago. His unease only lasted as long as it took for me to challenge him to a NASCAR stimulator showdown. If he won, I agreed to leave the parlor without a single protest. If he lost, he couldn't leave until we played one round of each game in the entire arcade. Carey thought he was a sure-fire winner. Considering Mr. Bunny is sitting in the backseat tells how the story went. I won. I'm not bragging when I say I won by at least half a bonnet. If you asked Carey, he'd probably tell you it was a dead heat. Either way, it doesn't matter. A win is a win.

Letting my cockiness get the better of me, I threw in one final showdown on our way out of the arcade. The best out of three in the duck hunting game would become Mr. Bunny's owner. Let me just say defeat has never been something I've handled well. Tonight is no different.

Pouting at being slaughtered and losing my beloved stuffed bunny, I return my eyes front and center. My brows furrow when Carey pulls his car into the driveway of my hotel, and the odd expression of relief filters through his eyes. Although the ten minutes following our showdown at the training track was plagued with mood-strangling awkwardness, the last two hours have been void of any confrontation. Carey still has a mysterious edginess attached to his composure, but he willingly participated in the activities we undertook the past two hours. He even instigated a conversation on how our twenty-minute drive to my hotel ended up being a four-hour-long adventure fifty miles in the wrong direction.

When Carey parks into a space in the dimly lit parking lot, disappointment consumes me. Even tired after an exhausting day, I'd give anything for our night not to be over. Carey truly intrigues me more than any man before him. Every second we spend together has me craving another. This is only the third time in my life that I've met a stranger whom I feel the need to get to know better. The first time I had this feeling, I was so young, the only thing I can remember is my dad's dark eyes and gentle smile. The second time was when I caught the quickest glance of a stranger sitting across the room. That inquisitive stare not only saved my life, but it also saved his as well. So, if I have the same feelings about Carey, should they be explored and not ignored? *Shouldn't it?*

Masking my confusion with a neutral expression, I scan my eyes over my hotel. The Grand Hotel is not as elaborate as the hotel Ava and Hugo's wedding reception took place in, but it has a nice vibe to it with a chandeliered driveway and sparkling glass facade. I had initially planned to stay at the hotel where the reception was held, but with my tenancy to leave things until the last minute, this was the only hotel I could find in a thirty-mile radius of Rochdale that had a vacancy and advanced security features. Wesley, my roommate/best friend, said it served me right to leave my booking until this morning.

Grasping the Camaro's door handle, I shift my eyes to Carey. He's watching me with the same unusual mix of interest and uncertainty he has bestowed on me most of the night. His brows are stitched with confusion, but evidence of the smile that snuck onto his face during our playful antics tonight remains in place. Although not being able to read his true intentions is off-putting, the unique vibe radiating out of him is intriguing and pulse-quickening.

Snubbing the tremors making my body shudder, I ask, "Did you want to come in?" I smash my back molars together when my words come out with a hint of shakiness. The weakness of my words expose that the calm outward appearance I'm striving to display isn't as authentic as I'd like Carey to believe.

Even with an invigorating blast of adrenaline and excitement heating my veins, I'm still a ball of skittish nerves. If I'm being upfront, I'll admit that not all the butterflies fluttering in my stomach are nerves. Most are excitement from spending the last four hours in the presence of a man with strikingly handsome features. I thought the swelling of desire his pulse-racing good looks incite would fade the more time I spent with him. It hasn't in the slightest. He's just... *wow*. Not just his looks but the entire package.

When Carey remains quiet, I stop absorbing the fine details of his face and return my eyes to his. I really shouldn't look directly at him. Just the defined cut of his jawline freezes my heart, and don't get me started on his murky irises.

When he stares at me with confused eyes, I add, "I did offer to buy you a drink in exchange for a ride to my hotel. I can't do that if you don't come inside." I try to keep my tone as impassive as his facial expression. My efforts are borderline. Not even shock at my recently rediscovered boldness can conceal the eagerness in my voice.

Carey's brooding mask that vanished hours ago slides back into place before my very eyes. The brightness in his eyes dulls, and his jaw muscle tightens. Taking his lightning-fast switch from alluring stranger to grouchy recluse as an answer to my *invitation*, I issue my gratitude for a fun night with a smile before swinging open my door and peeling out of his car.

This time, I remove my suitcase from his back seat with more respect to his pride and joy. Although my hackles are bristling from his abrupt and cold demeanor, his car doesn't deserve to cop the wrath of my fury. Don't get me wrong. I'm not mad because he rejected me—rejection has never been something that overly worries me—it's the fact every notion I thought I knew about myself has been unraveled tonight. To be honest, I don't know if that is a good or bad thing. I guess only time will tell. For all I know, it may not even be Carey pushing me out of my comfort zone. It could just be the next phase in my long-winded recovery process.

Standing my luggage to my side, I dip my torso into the cabin of Carey's car and attempt to secure the attention of his absconding eyes. "Thanks for the ride... and everything in between. It was a lot of fun," I praise when I capture the devotion of his dark gaze. "I'll practice my tire-changing technique and driving skills over the summer. If ever given a second shot, I'll live up to the Calderon-Lévesque name."

The corners of Carey's lips tug high before he briefly nods. After issuing my final thanks with another smile, I close the passenger door, secure a grip on my suitcase, and make a beeline for the entrance of my hotel. My steps are fast and frantic as the creepiness of being in a poorly lit parking lot rattles my free-spirited composure my night with Carey instigated.

It takes several yanks on the hotel's front door before I realize I need to push a buzzer to be granted access to the foyer. The advanced security features of this hotel were the sole reason I chose it over the other numerous hotels in this area.

After pushing the intercom buzzer, I peer over my shoulder to ensure no one is sneaking up on me. It is a bad habit I've had since my attack six years ago. Although I've reined in a lot of my obsessive-compulsive disorders over the past three years, my need to constantly check my surroundings remains intact.

My regular breathing pattern returns. Other than Carey eyeing me with a strange gleam, the area is vacant of another living thing.

Noticing he has captured my attention, Carey smirks before dropping his gaze to his hands. Pretending I can't feel the enthralling tension that's been buzzing between us all night still hanging thick in the air, I return my eyes front and center and impatiently wait for the hotel clerk to buzz me in.

The dampness slicking my skin spreads to another region of my body when not even ten seconds later, Carey's baritone voice booms out into the night, "The sign on the door says the bar in this hotel closed at 1 AM. You can't really invite me in for a drink if the bar is closed." The rough grittiness of his voice causes the hairs on my nape to prickle.

Lifting my downcast eyes, I spot Carey's reflection in the glass door beside the sign he's referring to. He's standing in the nook of his car door, like he's anticipating his confession will force me to give him his marching orders. His apprehension bolsters my campaign to spend more time with him.

After exhaling a sharp breath to settle the butterflies fluttering in my stomach, I reply, "The online brochure said there's a mini bar in my room."

My body goes on high alert, waiting for Carey to respond. I don't know if it is months of yearning restlessness instigating my boldness or adrenaline from our heart-starting activities tonight, but whatever it is, it has ignited a cluster of hope in the pit of my stomach. Even if Carey turns down my offer, the fact that I made it at all is a massive achievement for me, one I will no doubt spend hours deciphering tomorrow.

The nerves making my skin a sticky mess increase when the loud shriek of a buzzer pummels into my eardrums. After clutching my chest to ensure my heart remains in its rightful place, I secure a firm grip on the brass door handle and carefully pry the door open. Any chance of calming the crazy beat of my heart comes undone when a large, manly hand curls around the door handle above mine and assists me in opening the door. I don't need to look up to know who is standing beside me, but I do.

Lust rockets through my body when my eyes connect with Carey's dark gaze. From this vantage point, his well-built frame and height are even more beguiling, but they're nowhere near as ravishing as his rigid jawline. Just like the blistering heat bouncing between us during our two hours in the arcade, the energy flanking us now causes an out-of-control inferno to rage in my womb.

I stand mute in desire as I fantasize about kissing every sharp edge of his jaw until it softens against my mouth. Shock gnaws at my stomach. I haven't been driven by the desires of my body in well over three years. I'm not saying I'm pure by any means. After the incident that shook my core six years ago, "promiscuous" was a word I'd use to describe my sexual endeavors. It was only after a tense bout of therapy and finding Wesley did I discover my self-worth wasn't lost during my attack. It was simply misplaced for a few dark and very lonely months.

Shaking my head to snap myself out of the mood-dampening disposition of past memories, I slip by Carey and enter the hotel's foyer. My breathing labors when my budded nipples graze past Carey's rigid chest. They tighten even more when, after a short moment of quiet reflection, he follows me into the foyer. His long, agile steps have him reaching me in less than a heartbeat.

The hotel clerk with dazzling sapphire eyes and a friendly smile greets me when I saunter to the highly polished check-in desk. "Good evening, welcome to the Grand Hotel. What name is your reservation in?"

"Quincy Mac Jones. I made an online booking early this morning," I reply, placing my clutch on the counter.

I don't need to look at Carey to know he's smirking at my immature alias. I can feel it deep in my bones. Ignoring the desire to witness another one of his all-inspiring smiles, I pull my credit card out of my clutch and hand it to the hotel clerk. Her eyes scan the company card associated with my photography business before she lifts them to peer past my shoulder. "And your guest? Will he be included in your booking?"

While following the direction of the clerk's gaze, I stammer out, "He's not a guest. He's just coming up to my room for a drink."

My words come out brittle, strangled by the large rock her silent accusation rammed down my throat. The stronghold wrapped around my neck tightens when I catch Carey's cajoling gaze. Although technically I only invited him to my room for a drink, the sexual current firing between us indicates he understood the hidden innuendo in my suggestion.

Squeezing my thighs together to lessen the ache between my legs, I return my eyes to the desk clerk. Her eyes drift between mine for several seconds before she faintly murmurs, "Okay." Placing a hotel keycard on the counter, she points to a bank of elevators on her left. "Your room is on floor twenty-three. You need to swipe your key on the security panel at the front of the elevator for the doors to open. Upon exiting, take a sharp right; your room is halfway down the hall. Once you've unlocked your door, slide the room key into the holder next to the light switch. It will keep the lights and air-conditioner running."

After gathering my receipt from the printer at her side, she places it in a white embossed envelope and hands it to me. "Normally, we would have an usher take you to your room, but with the late hour—"

"That's fine. I'm sure we can find our way," I interrupt, my voice high in anxiety.

It isn't that I care about the hotel clerk's opinion; I'm unsure exactly what I'm doing inviting a male guest to my room at 4 a.m. I'd like to plead innocence and pretend my motive is solely to thank Carey for the ride, but the excitement blazing in my tingling womb indicates otherwise.

After breathing out my nerves, I accept my room key from the hotel clerk and head to the elevator bank. My stomach churns for a moment when Carey shadows me, and then it heats with excitement. Although he doesn't utter a syllable, the energy crackling off him adds to the teeming mugginess consuming the elevator car. Carey has his brooding nature down pat, but something greater between us makes me want to jump into the air with excitement before begging him to leave.

I thought our extended drive to the hotel would be our most

spine-tingling event tonight. It wasn't. Our short ride in the elevator is even more electrifying than our earlier antics.

When the elevator dings, announcing it has arrived at my floor, my nerves get the better of me. "I think we should—" The remainder of my sentence entombs in my throat when I lift my eyes from the plaid carpet lining the elevator to Carey. His pupils are massive, inundating his haunted eyes, and a beading of sweat lines his forehead. He appears just as petrified as me. His edginess soothes the nerves twisting my stomach.

"—Limit our drinks to two since I have an early start tomorrow," I add on, pretending I wasn't about to demand that he accept my thanks for a ride with a handshake.

With his brows furrowed together, Carey nods before shadowing me down the elegant corridor. Paintings of the New York skyline line the hall, but I'm too immersed in maintaining my breathing to pay them any attention.

Even rattled, for every step I take, the throbbing between my legs grows. I'm not ashamed to admit *many* months have gone by since I've had sex. For the most part, I'm perfectly happy with the lack of sexual contact, but there are times when I miss the feelings you can only achieve with a bed companion. Don't get me wrong, sex toy technology has improved drastically in the past six years, but nothing compares to being wrapped in a pair of solid arms or the smell of sweat-slicked sheets. Although manufacturers have tried to bottle up that scent, they failed. Nothing comes close to the real thing.

As per the hotel clerk's instruction, after pushing open my door, I place the swipe card into the electricity mechanism and then flick on the lights. I wait for the room to be fully illuminated by artificial light before entering. Dimly lit rooms are another weakness I haven't conquered yet. The only room I'll happily enter while dark is the dark room in my home office. If there was a way I could develop my photos in a lighted room, believe me, I'd do exactly that.

While placing my suitcase on the luggage stand in the middle of the room, I ask, "What's your drink of choice?" A smile etches onto my mouth when my question comes out with only the slightest quiver.

When Carey continues his quiet stance, I spin on my heels to face him. He's standing in the hallway with his fists balled at his side, and his handsome face contorted with confusion.

My uneasy steps toward him falter when he mutters, "I'm going to go," while nudging his head to the elevator. His words are stiff and crammed with shame.

"Okay." I gently nod. I only smothered my own doubts seconds ago, so I can't argue bias at him harboring the same qualms.

Although the cloud of concern in his eyes adds strength to his admission he wants to leave, his feet remain planted on the ground as I stroll toward him. My already slow pace slackens even more when I spot his zealous gaze running over my body. I nearly miss his perusal as it is concealed by his thick, luscious lashes. Even with my astuteness clouded by a dense haze of lust, I can't miss the interest flourishing in his stormy eyes the closer I get to him, but not wanting to push him into doing anything against his wishes, I say, "Thanks for the lift."

I attempt to thrust out my hand in offering, only to have one of the gold bracelets lining my wrist snag the lace on my dress. The thread caught in my bracelet is as fine as a strand of hair but stronger than titanium. The more I struggle to free my wrist, the firmer my arm becomes pinned to my body. Usually, this type of thing would have me rolling on the floor in a fit of laughter, but since it is happening in front of one of the most fascinating specimens I've ever encountered, the hilarity of the situation is lost on me.

When my efforts to untangle myself become tiresome, Carey silently offers his assistance. Although I'm tempted to take a pair of scissors to my $400 dress, just like Carey's Camaro, my dress doesn't deserve to cop the fury of my idiocy. So, with a nod, I accept Carey's offer.

When Carey clasps my wrist in his, I mumble, "The prettiness of my dress made me forget the no lace rules my bangles demand." My words come out shaky, my voice incapable of hiding the thrashing of my heart from his simplest touch. The instant he touched me, the butterflies in my stomach cleared, and potent yearning took their place.

The corners of Carey's lips crimp at my attempt at candor before he drops his eyes to my snagged wrist. In silence, he weaves the tiny thread around the twisted design of my charm bracelet. I watch him eagerly, categorizing the way his lips twist and the top of his nose crinkles when he concentrates. He truly is a beautiful man: straight, defined nose, dark, trimmed hair, and alluringly beautiful eyes.

By the time my wrist is released from the death clutch of my dress, I've absorbed every fine feature of his face in meticulous detail. Now I'm even more disappointed he wants to flee. I've never been so captivated by a man before. Don't misconstrue my statement. Like all women my age, many intriguing men have graced my crush list in the past fourteen-plus years, but none have been worthy enough to be placed on the top of the list. *None until now.*

After tucking the felonious string of lace into my dress, Carey lifts his eyes to me. My breath catches halfway to my lungs when I come face to face with his fascinating gaze. The sparks of lust firing between us in the elevator car were nothing compared to the frenzy of emotions brewing between us now. It is so uncontrollable I have no chance of extinguishing it.

Acting purely on the desires of my body, I lunge forward and press my lips onto Carey's hard-lined mouth. I gasp a throaty moan when the softness of his mouth graces my lips. His mouth is soft and scrumptious for a man whose lips spend most of their time frowning.

Doubt dampens my eagerness when Carey remains entirely still, neither accepting or neglecting my daring advance. Deciding to either bring it all or go home crying, I run my tongue along the seam of his stern, shut lips. My pussy throbs as the flavor of his mouth engulfs my senses. He has a manly, virile taste that adds to his brutishly handsome appearance.

The fire raging in my womb combusts when Carey's lips weakly crack open at the request of my tongue. Fighting the urge to do a jig of victory, I sweep my tongue into his mouth in a slow and devoted stroke. My pussy becomes wetter. The inside of his mouth tastes even more intoxicating than his lips.

Dizzy with desire, I band my arms around his neck and draw him closer. My boldness ramps up the pace of our kiss, pushing it from a one-sided affair to a lust-driven production. Carey's fingers weave through my hair as his tongue delves into my mouth in a confident and controlled lick. I mimic the strokes of his tongue as he kisses me with the same measured discipline that rules his personality. His kiss is mind-spiraling and knee-weakening, and it douses any panic roaring through my veins as we stumble clumsily into my room.

The ache between my legs cultivates as my fingers fumble with the buttons of his shirt. My movements are frantic, wanting to ensure there's no opportunity for either of us to back out for a second time. Growing impatient at the tiny pearl buttons on his crisp white shirt, I fist the material in my hands and yank it open. My brutal force sends small buttons shooting in all directions. Carey smiles against my mouth when they clatter on the floor around his feet. Not wanting to miss seeing one of his rare heart-stopping grins, I detach my lips from his and pull back. He seizes the moment to drop his mouth to the curve of my neck. Goosebumps rush to the surface of my skin when the roughness of his five o'clock shadow scratches the delicate skin on my neck.

After giving myself a few moments to drink in his intoxicating scent, I continue with my mission to remove his clothes. Seconds later, his shirt becomes reacquainted with his buttons scattered on the floor. I gasp in greedy breaths when my eyes roam over his body. It is. . . *oh my god.* Seeing him in the flesh is mind-boggling. If I wasn't so immersed in capturing every dip and plane carved in his magnificent torso and rippling six-pack, I wouldn't hesitate to pull out my camera to capture the magnificence of his body in time forever. That's how awe-inspiring his body is.

I stiffen when Carey slips his hand under my dress to grasp the waistband of my panties. It isn't haunted memories holding me captive. It is wondering what his reaction will be to my hideous undergarments. He doesn't bat an eyelid as he yanks them down my stomach.

Feeding off his eagerness, my hands shoot to the waistband of his trousers. I pop open the button of his pants and slide down the zipper as my panties slip down my quivering thighs. Passion scorches every inch of my skin when the coolness of the air-conditioning blows on the exposed heated region of my body.

The softness of bedding caresses my taut muscles when we fumble carelessly onto the bed. Usually, the weight of a man pinning me down would send my panic skyrocketing, but just like every moment I've spent with Carey thus far, it feels natural and relaxed.

Keeping his head buried in the crook of my neck, Carey drags his trousers down his thighs. I writhe beneath him, incredibly turned on when seductive portions of his V muscle come into view. My eyes go wild, absorbing every inch of him. I swear there isn't an ounce of fat on his entire body... *well, except there.*

The wetness of my pussy grows when his impressive cock springs free from his trunks.

He's hard, thick, and ready to go.

His hot breaths hit my neckline when he says, "One night."

Although I could construe his statement as a question, the roughness of his tone doesn't indicate that.

He waits for me to nod before he guides his impressive cock toward my quivering entrance. When he sheathes me in one fluid thrust, I snap my eyes shut and throw my head back. With no guarantees of a re-run, I'm going to yield to the brilliance of my first sexual contact in over a year without a single moment being ruined by hesitation.

CHAPTER 9

GEMMA

Groaning, I kick sweat-slicked sheets off my body and roll onto my side. The pleasurable tightness of my muscles reminds my blurry mind of the events that occurred in this bed last night.

Although Carey continued with his reserved composure, last night was unlike anything I'd ever felt.

Hours of touching, stroking... *fucking.*

Usually, the mystery and intrigue a man holds ends up being nothing but a lie the instant we step into the bedroom. Carey defies that logic. If I thought the man was magnificent before, it is nothing compared to my awe for him now.

The thrilling ache of my muscles is worth waking up alone. I don't need to open my eyes to know Carey is gone. Even with the intoxicating mix of pheromones confusing my perception, a man with an aura as compelling as Carey's can't be concealed. Let alone the fact a man of his size isn't something I'd ever miss. I can still feel the heaviness of him inside me.

You'd expect me to be annoyed at Carey's vanishing act. I am not. I'm somewhat pleased he snuck out in the darkness of the night. Usually, when my dates discover who my father is, they become what

Wesley calls Stage One I Want To Meet Your Daddy Clingers. They're the guys who follow me around like a shadow, send inappropriate gifts to my work, and pretend I'm the girl they've been waiting for their entire life. Where, in reality, they only like who I'm associated with.

Fifty percent get the hint within days that I won't introduce them to my dad until I've been dating them exclusively for six months. Since only a small minority of men in New York City are seeking a long-term relationship, they run for the hills the instant the dreaded C word leaves my mouth.

The next forty percent take a little longer to grasp that their penis won't be a magic wand that will have them miraculously meeting my dad after two so-called "dates." The chances of them jumping my firm six-month rule for a parental meet-and-greet are as unlikely as them being invited into my bed before my prerequisite 90-day date rule.

The other ten percent of the men I've dated are the worst of the worst. They're the guys who have no interest in NASCAR racing whatsoever. Who in their right mind hates NASCAR racing? Bile forms in the back of my throat just entertaining the idea that NASCAR racing isn't the sport of Gods. In no particular order, NASCAR, photography, my dad, and Wesley are my entire world.

And perhaps a dark-eyed stranger with pulse-racing good looks and worldly eyes.

My eyes bulge, shell-shocked by my silent admission. Even reveling in the high only a night of earth-shattering orgasms can produce, I never thought I'd have those types of reckless thoughts again. Beyond Wesley, Ava is the only person I've allowed in my inner circle since my attack six years ago.

When you go through a crisis like I did, you're incredibly wary of anyone new entering your life. You wonder what is behind their sudden interest in you, so you lose the joy you get from meeting and befriending a stranger.

Maybe that is why last night was so intriguing. For the first time in a long time, I allowed a stranger in. Not just into my bedroom but inside my heart as well.

There's another reason I'm so astonished by my behavior last night. For the past three years, I haven't participated in a one-night stand, and for the past two and a half years, I've never come close to breaking my 90-day rule. Not once. Not even when a hot he-who-will-never-be-named movie star had me seriously reconsidering my determined morals. However, one glance into Carey's tormented eyes blew my entire plan, and I don't even know his last name. Wesley will have a field day when I update him on my adventurous night.

Grumbling at the thought of that conversation, I throw back the covers and swing my legs off the bed. The thumping of my skull from a measly two hours of sleep overtakes the pounding of my pussy as I slowly shuffle toward the bathroom door.

My sloth-like speed quickens to a snail's pace when I hear the shower beckoning me to its heavenliness. I'm not eager to wash away the intoxicating scent of sex slicking my skin, but I'm keen to remove the heaviness of a long, tiring day—both mentally and physically.

My brows stitch when I flick on the bathroom light, and it fails to illuminate the windowless room with artificial color. Acting like I don't know the inner workings of a light switch, I continue flicking it on and off over and over again. My annoyance festers when my incessant switch-flicking does nothing but chip the polish on my index finger.

While cursing the unresponsive lightbulbs under my breath, I pace to the entranceway table so I can call the hotel desk and advise them of the blown bulb. When I catch sight of the time on my cell phone, I cross my fingers that they will send someone straight to my room as my late night has stretched my time extremely thin.

Upon picking up the phone receiver, I notice the room keycard I placed in the electric mechanism by the door has been removed. I remain still, blinking and confused. Only after racking my tired brain for numerous minutes does the reason behind my missing keycard trickle into my fried mind. Carey couldn't gain access to the elevators without taking my card.

"Well, shit," I curse under my breath.

I take another few moments I don't have to consider a solution to my situation. When a brilliant idea formulates in my tired brain, I pace to the large double windows of my room and draw open the curtains. Bright late morning sun causes me to squint, but it isn't bright enough to illuminate the bathroom to allow me to feel comfortable showering in there. Even giving myself a mental pep talk about how I'm a grown woman who should be able to shower in a dim room doesn't help matters.

Throwing my hands in the air at my skittishness, I pad to my suitcase and get dressed. A pair of fresh panties and a dash of perfume won't clear away the scent of sex on my skin, but when you're running on empty, you take any leverage you can get.

When the Uber app on my phone dings, advising my driver is waiting at the front of the hotel, I snag my dress and panties I wore last night off the bedroom floor, stuff them into my suitcase, and then make a beeline for the door.

Like I could feel anymore daft this morning, it takes me numerous pushes on the elevator button for recognition to dawn that I can't access the elevators without my room key. Gritting my teeth to hold in an annoyed squeal dying to break free, I throw open the emergency fire exit stairs and step into the stairwell. My heart falls from my chest when a loud siren shrills through my ears.

"I'm so sorry," I strangle out through a lump in my throat when a maid comes frantically rushing out of the room next to the emergency exit like Armageddon was just announced. "I accidentally tripped the alarm."

The middle-aged maid with rosy cheeks and ample breasts curses at me in Spanish.

"I'm sorry for frightening you," I apologize again, except this time in Spanish. "I left my swipe card in my room."

The embarrassment heating my cheeks doubles when the maid offers to open my door so I can retrieve my card.

"My keycard isn't in my room," I admit, my tone low and laced with embarrassment.

She eyes me curiously, her brows pulled together tightly, her lips pursed.

"A *friend* took it with him when he left my room this morning," I disclose.

I hold my breath, fully anticipating her to *tsk* or jeer at me.

She does nothing but look at me with sympathy.

"Gracias," I thank her when she swipes her employee card over the elevator security panel to summon the elevator car to my floor. I strive to keep my tone neutral, but the embarrassment dangling off my vocal cords impedes my efforts.

The maid runs her hand down my arm. "Rejection doesn't mean you aren't good enough. It means the other person failed to notice what you have to offer."

I try to put on a brave front, but her words have more impact on me than I care to admit. The year following my attack, I truly believed I'd never be good enough for anyone. That is why I was so promiscuous. Sexual contact meant nothing but a meaningless night with another consenting adult.

Last night was the first time I felt a connection during a sexual act since that horrid night in the alleyway six years ago. I felt worthwhile and treasured, and for the first time in years, I honestly thought I was enough, but the fact I woke up alone makes me wonder if I misread the entire evening. Perhaps it was nothing more than a meaningless night of fun?

The unease twisting in my stomach morphs into unchartered waters when the elevator doors ding open. Because the car is empty, it takes me under a second to spot my keycard squeezed between the two glass panels lining the back wall. Although my room key has no distinguishable marks associating it with my room number, just having my card left in such an unsecured environment swirls my stomach. What ifs run rife through my brain.

What if my room number was scanned on the back of the card?

What if the maid hadn't been in the room beside the elevator banks to save me from being trapped on the twenty-third floor?

What if my card ended up in the hands of a person like the sick and twisted man who haunts my dreams every night?

While swallowing the bitter-tasting bile creeping up my windpipe,

I enter the elevator and snatch my room key from its conspicuous hiding place. I ignore the curious glance of the hotel clerk who served me last night as I stroll across the tiled lobby floor to dump my keycard into the advanced checkout box. I pretend I can't feel the inquisitive glances of men drinking their hangover concoctions in the bar I offered to buy Carey a drink at last night, and I act like the numbness that cleared off my chest last night hasn't returned stronger than ever when I curl into the back of my female Uber driver's SUV and smile a greeting.

For the twenty-mile drive to my destination, I try to rationalize every irrational thought running through my blurry mind. All I achieve is thirty minutes of a flipping stomach and the loss of polish from two of my nails.

When the SUV pulls into the driveway of a modest but well-kept house, I sit in silence for several minutes, striving to build the courage to enter a residence I've heard about numerous times but never visited.

Any thoughts lingering in the back of my mind about fleeing become impossible when a cherry-red Chevelle pulls in beside the SUV. The smile Hugo was wearing the entire eight hours of his wedding yesterday tugs higher when he spots me sitting in the back seat of the SUV.

Smiling, I return his wave while every cuss word I've ever heard silently seeps from my lips.

Once I've extinguished any possibility of going to heaven, I secure a grip on my suitcase and slide out of the SUV, thanking the driver for her service on my way out.

A refreshing woodsy smell soothes the agitation swirling in my stomach when Hugo curls out of his car and stands next to me.

"Sorry I'm late, I had... traffic issues," I mumble, my tone as weak as my excuse.

Any anger boiling my blood simmers when Hugo's hearty laugh sounds through my ears. "A New Yorker having traffic issues? Anyone would swear you just left Ravenshoe."

My heart warms when Hugo hugs me. Like Carey last night,

Hugo's caress doesn't cause me to flinch. He's one of only a handful of men who can touch me without making me inwardly cringe. He is undoubtedly gorgeous with dark hair, ocean blue eyes, and a body that makes grown women say ga-ga out loud, but it wasn't his panty-melting good looks that initially attracted me to him. It was his laugh.

Don't get me wrong, I'm in *no* way attracted to Hugo now. I'm talking way before I knew of his Ava fascination, and way before I realized he would be the big brother my father wished he'd given me years ago.

Although we haven't seen much of each other in the past six years, it doesn't matter how much time passes, he will always be family to me.

"I'm glad you finally made it to one of the Marshall family brunches, Gem. My mom will shit a brick." Hugo removes my suitcase from my grasp before leading us down the side of the house.

I smile at the glee in his tone before running my eyes over the Marshall residence. It is a modest house in a leafy, safe neighborhood of Rochdale.

From the stories I've been told, Mr. and Mrs. Marshall purchased their home when they were pregnant with their first child, Chase. They raised their four children in this house.

Just the vibe lingering in the air reveals that many fond memories were made here... and perhaps even some not-so-fond ones.

After storing my suitcase in a coat room at the side of a large eat-in kitchen, Hugo places his hand on the curve of my back and guides me through the residence. The warmth of his hand pacifies the nervous butterflies taking flight in my stomach.

"Where is Ava?" I query as we walk through an expansive but empty dining room. "Where are we eating brunch?" Confusion is evident in my tone.

Hugo smirks at my inquisitiveness. "Ava ran out of blueberries, so I went and got some more," he replies, jingling a plastic bag into the air I didn't even know he was holding until now. "And we always eat under the patio outside."

My lips quirk. "Very retro."

Hugo laughs. "More like convenient. Joel and my nieces leave so much food on the floor that my mom would be chasing raccoons out of the house for weeks if we ate inside."

A giggle bubbles up my chest, fully pushing out my desire to chase my Uber driver's SUV rolling down the street.

When we stop outside a pair of double screen doors, an energetic hum of chatter streams through my ears, overtaking the shrill of my pulse ringing in my eardrums.

"Are you ready?" Hugo asks, his tone kind.

He knows I find meeting strangers a challenging task.

After licking my lips, I nod. The beat of my heart kicks up a notch when the delicious taste of Carey's lips fills my senses. Even with my annoyance sitting on the edge of a cliff at him putting my safety at risk, I can't stop the smile that sneaks onto my mouth. Last night was so magical, even frightened anger can't take away from it.

Spotting my odd expression, Hugo angles his head to the side as one of his heavy brows cocks high into his hairline. "I might need to push you out of your comfort zone more often, Gem. You look remarkably calm considering the storm you're about to be thrown into."

I swallow, harshly.

He laughs before curling his arm around my shoulders. "I'm just playing with you."

My chance to reply is lost when a small gathering of Hugo's frat brothers, whom I had steered clear from last night, smack their hands onto the tabletop and holler when Hugo and I merge onto the patio.

"No camera to hide behind today, sweet cakes," one of the blond men jests.

"It looks like my bland morning is about to become a raging all-nighter," heckles another.

The playful jeering stops when Hugo glares at them with a tight smile.

After issuing his warning solely using his eyes, Hugo guides us to the less rowdy section of the table. "Don't let them scare you. They're as harmless as puppy dogs, even with their brains living in their cocks."

A smile creeps across my face. If Hugo says I can trust them, I will trust them because that's how much faith I have in Hugo's opinion.

As we pace down the long patio, my eyes scan the three dozen or more guests spread across the sizeable makeshift table. My curiosity piques when I notice a man a few spots down talking to Ava. With his ocean-blue eyes and strikingly handsome facial features, it isn't hard for me to decipher that he must be Hugo's big brother, Chase. They're a spitting image of each other.

My assumptions are proven spot on when Hugo introduces me to Chase.

After accepting Chase's handshake, I greet Ava with a kiss on the cheek and a little rub on her belly.

Names are thrown at me hard and fast when Hugo points to each member at the table to introduce them. I hope I don't have to take a test after this, as I lost track of my own name once I'd been introduced to guest number eleven.

Halfway through Hugo's introductions, my breathing pattern quickens as the hairs on my arms prickle. A warm summer breeze blows onto the patio, but my intuition tells me it isn't early summer temperatures causing my body's prompts.

Not wanting to be rude, I nod at Hugo's introductions as I sneakily swing my eyes to my right. My breath catches in the back of my throat when my inquisitive scan locks in on a pair of dark and confused eyes gawking at me.

Carey is standing at the end of the table with a glass of water in his hand and a nasty scowl on his face. His throat works hard to swallow as his eyes rake over my frozen form.

When his narrowed gaze returns to my face, I leave my dignity at the door and hesitantly wave at him. He doesn't wave back.

Acting like his coldness didn't punch me in the stomach, I drop my hand to the side and hold his gaze.

If anyone has the right to dish out death stares, it's me.

He not only compromised my safety this morning, but he also

stupidly threatened to unravel the personal growth our exchange last night instigated.

Even if it was just a night of fun for him, our time together smothered some of my haunted memories by replacing them with much happier ones. That admission alone eases the agitation slicking my skin with sweat.

My attention diverts from returning Carey's belligerent glare when Hugo barges me with his shoulder. I try not to jump at his playful touch, but with my nerves rattled by Carey's irate composure, I flinch before my body can shut it down.

"Shit, Gem, I'm sorry. Are you okay?" Hugo asks, worry in his tone. Although Hugo kept his voice as low as a hushed whisper, his question still garners the attention of several nosy glances.

"I'm fine," I mumble before taking the empty seat next to Ava. "I'm just starving, that's all. Can we save the rest of the introductions until after we've eaten?" Guilt clutches at my throat when my words come out with a hint of bitchiness.

Thankfully, my snarky tone is put on the backburner when Mrs. Marshall says, "Of course we can. She slings her arm around Hugo's shoulders. "We wouldn't want any of the food getting cold. Especially not your pancakes."

Hugo's eyes light up like a kid on Christmas morning.

"Snap frozen is the only way anyone should tackle Helen's scrambled eggs," jests Chase, his timber brimming with wit. "Because you can only hope the freezer burn will kill your taste buds."

A broad grin stretches across my face when a bread roll flies across the table and smacks Chase in the nose. I swing my eyes in the direction the bread roll came from. Considering the dark-haired beauty with pretty green eyes is the only one not laughing at Chase's antics, she must be Helen, Chase and Hugo's sister.

Like all the Marshall family members I've met, Helen has jealousy-boosting good looks. If her eyes didn't hold the same amount of integrity and friendliness as Hugo's, she has the type of beauty that makes me want to dislike her on sight.

I know that sounds callous, but unfortunately, it's true. Sometimes we women are our own worst enemy. We hate when men judge us on our appearance, but then we do the same thing to each other, but instead of appreciating someone's God-given graces, we get green with envy and act immature.

Helen handles my inquisitive gawk with a friendly smile. After returning her greeting, I shift my eyes to my rapidly growing plate Hugo is over-stacking with food. On the way, I catch a glare that sets my heart racing with both fear and excitement. Just like last night, Carey is eyeing me through thick lashes, but this time, zeal isn't beaming from his heavy-hooded gaze. It is downright fury. His irate glare adds to the repulsion I'm feeling from sitting at a breakfast table reeking of sex while everyone surrounding me looks like they've just been featured in a six-page spread on life, love, and prosperity in the Hamptons.

Swallowing away a lump in my throat, I keep my gaze fixed on my plate of food as I rack my brain about what has caused Carey's sudden shift in demeanor. Although his composure ran hot and cold most of last night, it never had this edge of rawness to it. I acted purely on the desires of my body last night. I have no doubt Carey did as well. So if he's worried I'm expecting a lifelong commitment from one night between the sheets, he doesn't need to be. Although he intrigues me, that doesn't mean I saw last night as anything more than it was. I'm an adult. I understand the rules of engagement associated with a one-night stand as well as anyone else in this room. There are no rules or expectations, nothing but awkwardness and hours of queasiness. That is the reason I had such a strict 90-day date rule. To avoid horrific confrontations like today.

If only Carey's eyes weren't the key to unlocking my heart from years of misery.

CHAPTER 10

GEMMA

After watching Hugo devour enough pancakes to make anyone sick and copping enough stink eyes from Carey to last me a lifetime, I ask Ava for directions to the bathroom before excusing myself from the table. The scent of Ava's blueberry pancakes makes my mouth salivate, but Carey's glare makes my usually robust appetite wane.

Sitting at a table with dozens of strangers is already challenging, let alone being glared at by a man who was eyeing me with desire only hours earlier.

"Do you want me to come with you?" Hugo asks, peering up at me with a set of eyes that soothe the annoyance Carey's glare initiated.

I smile. "Thanks for the offer, but I've got this covered."

He understands that there are times in my recovery when I think nothing will rattle me, but occasionally, a slip-up has my recovery backpedaling.

Thankfully, today is not one of those days.

Ignoring Hugo's pleading eyes, I place my napkin onto my half-empty plate and head to the bathroom. My bladder relishes being relieved of the three Long Island ice teas Mrs. Marshall served me throughout brunch.

Just as she has been the two times we've previously met, Mrs. Marshall is a little ball of sunshine wrapped up in a lady any child would be privileged to call their mother. It is events like these that make me wish I had a mother. Don't get me wrong, my dad is the greatest parent in the world, but there are some things a girl can't discuss with her father.

As I wash my hands in the vanity sink, I scan my disheveled appearance. I look remarkably put together for someone still wearing the makeup she applied in a rusty old truck as it sped down the highway sixteen hours ago. Good genes from a lady I only know from hazy memories deserve a gracious pat on the back. My dad adopted me when he discovered me scrounging for food after an event at San Antonio Raceway nearly twenty-four years ago. Just like the inexplicable connection I developed with Carey in a matter of seconds, the unique bond between me and my dad was instantaneous. He had the eyes of a warrior and a heart even stronger than that. Although adding me to his family was one of the toughest competitions he had ever raced, he often quotes it was his greatest win.

After ensuring no immature sentimental tears have welled into my eyes, I exit the bathroom. My heart plummets from my chest when my wrist is seized, and I'm dragged toward a set of French doors. I only manage to hold in my frightened scream when I realize the energy buzzing around my body isn't associated with fear. It is excitement.

Lifting my gaze, I spot Carey's stern profile. His jaw muscle is ticking so furiously that the heavy stubble on his chin cannot hide it. His eyes are narrowed into tiny slits, and his plump lips from our hours of kissing are set in a hard, rigid line.

I gasp in a shocked breath when he angrily asks, "What the hell are you doing here?" He drifts his gaze behind my shoulder to ensure we haven't gained the attention of unwanted eyes before returning them to me. "You need to leave right now."

After yanking my hand out of his grasp, I take two steps back and crank my neck so I can peer into his eyes.

It takes me a few moments to realize it isn't just anger clouding his eyes—it's remorse.

Sickened at the thought he regrets spending the night with me, I stutter out, "Are you angry because I'm here or because of what we did this morning?"

He doesn't need to answer my question. The truth is relayed in his murky gaze. He's angry about both choices on my limited list.

For the quickest moment, the shame beaming from his eyes pushes my recovery back to the days following my attack, but it only lasts as long as it takes for me to recall that our actions last night were a two-sided affair. I may have initiated our *gathering* by kissing him, but he's a grown man who could have stopped things the instant they became uncomfortable for him.

The sick gloom spreading through me morphs into anger when I connect my eyes with Carey's irate glare. When he first dragged me in here, I was willing to let my anger slide just to avoid having an awkward confrontation like this, but since he isn't grown up enough to throw down the towel without first whipping me with it, I'm not inclined to leash my anger anymore.

"Just a word of advice, when you're out trolling bars tonight for another naive fool to warm your sheets, go back to the feel-sorry-for-me recluse personality you were working like a pro last night because it's shitloads more appealing than the chauvinist asshole you're portraying today," I grind out before I can stop my callous words.

Carey's face lines with anger. "That's sweet coming from a lady who can't grasp that a man sneaking out of her bed isn't an open invitation to brunch."

"I was invited here." I cross my arms under my chest and firm my stance. "And you need to get over yourself if you think I'm that desperate for round two I followed you here. Last night was good, but I wouldn't go cashing in all your tickets."

My words are strong, giving no indication of the deceit in my statement. Last night was above and beyond anything I've experienced, but when a woman must resort to defending her integrity, you bring out the big guns. Every woman knows even the most self-assured man has a hard time accepting a knock to his ego.

As I predicted, Carey reacts to my taunt like every egomaniac man I know. The invisible feathers of a peacock fan out behind him as the arrogance in his eyes strengthens. "I didn't hear you complaining last night."

"It's hard to complain with a tongue rammed down your throat," I fire back, my voice doused with sarcasm. I swivel my finger in the air to mimic the movements of a slithering tongue. "I visit the dentist every six months, so cavity checks during sex aren't necessary."

I force a cocky smirk onto my mouth to mask the grimace attempting to cross my face. Every word I'm saying is a vicious lie, but I refuse to let a man make me feel unworthy, even if every word spilling from my lips causes little papercuts to my heart.

"Ha!" Carey's loud voice bounces off the walls and jingles in my ears. "You didn't get a chance to complain?" He steps closer, engulfing me with his manly smell. "That wasn't because my tongue was rammed down your throat. It was because you were too busy pleading to cite an objection."

Ignoring how his coffee-scented breath fans my lips, I roll my eyes skywards. "Pleading? *Please*. The only pleading I was doing was for you to stop jackhammering my uterus into the next century."

My pulse quickens when the most seductive smirk I've ever seen sneaks onto his mouth. "'Oh god, don't stop. More. I need more.'" He lowers his voice to a deep, manly tone as he takes another step closer to me. He stands so close our chests compete as we struggle to fill our lungs with air. "'Harder. Faster. Oh, god, right there.'"

Not thinking, I slap him across the chest. "You're an asshole. Jerk. Asshat. Dickwank," I immaturely taunt, each insult a strike to his chest.

Electricity jolts through my body and clusters low in my pussy when he seizes my wrist with his big, manly hand. My breathing switches from rapid pants to greedy gulps when I lift my eyes from his expanded chest to his face. He stares down at me, eyes blazing, lips twitching. He looks a cross between angry and turned on.

Not willing to reel in my embarrassment, I snarl. "You're an ass—"

My vicious words are forced down my throat when my mouth is assaulted by a set of lips no amount of anger will ever make me forget. Teeth clash, tongues mingle, and callous words switch to moans as Carey kisses me like a man starved of oxygen.

My fingers weave through his hair when he bands his arms around my waist and draws me in. He hoists me up his big body before he strengthens the intensity of our kiss. The hem of my skirt bunches around my waist when I curl my legs around his hips. I need to tether myself to him to ensure I don't go floating to heaven from his soul-stealing kiss.

Just as quickly as our kiss began, it ends. Carey violently yanks away from me. His abrupt movements nearly send me tumbling onto my backside as I stumble back onto my feet.

After his wide eyes scan the room, he locks them back on me. The guilt in his eyes grows tenfold when he drinks in my kiss-swollen lips and disheveled clothing.

"Fuck!" He rakes his fingers over his scalp. "*Here*. Of all the fucking places in the world, *you* make me lose my mind *here!*"

I stare at him, muted and confused.

He scrubs his hands over his eyes before balling them into fists at his side. "Jesus Christ, Gemma! Fix yourself up," he demands before stepping closer to me so he can yank the hem of my skirt to a respectable level. "*Here*. I can't believe you made me fucking do that *here*."

"It was just a kiss—" My attempts at calming the tornado of anger brewing in his narrowed gaze halts when he locks his eyes with me. If I thought he harbored ill feelings towards me earlier, it is nothing compared to the downright fury his eyes carry now.

When he lifts his hands to my hair to settle the wispy pieces his fingers created to my dead straight locks, I step back, unnerved by his anger. "I've got this."

Hearing the rattle of my words, Carey drops his hands and peers into my eyes. The hurt in his dark gaze escalates when he spots the tears in my eyes. He runs his thumb across my cheek as if he'll catch my tears before they fall.

He doesn't need to worry. A tear hasn't spilled from my eyes in years.

After ensuring his thumbs are dry, he barely mutters, "I'm sorry," before making a beeline for the door.

Even confused, my heart yearns to ease his pain. "Carey, wait."

Once I've ensured my clothing is sitting right, I follow him to the door. His steps are so long and fast he disappears down the hallway before I exit the room.

I stand in the doorway for a moment, trying to work out what just happened.

Time only gives me more confusion. Since I'm so immersed in working out Carey's bizarre switch in moods, I fail to notice Ava standing at my side.

I jump out of my skin when she says, "I wasn't aware you knew Hawke."

I turn my bleary eyes to her. "What?" I ask, confusion in my tone.

I've heard of the man Ava is referring to, but I don't understand why she's bringing him up now. Hugo mentioned Hawke numerous times during our deployment to Afghanistan before my attack, but I've never had the chance to meet him. After his wife and son were killed by a drunk driver five years ago, Hawke became a ghost.

Most people say he died right alongside his family that day.

My brows stitch when Ava points in the direction Carey just left. "Hawke. The person who just left this room like it was on fire," she whispers, like she's afraid of my reaction. "I didn't know you knew each other."

I swallow to relieve my dry throat before asking, "You mean Carey, right? I've never met Hawke."

The unease in my stomach grows when Ava locks her dark eyes with mine. They're beautiful but full of silent apologies. "Carey is Hawke, Gemma. His real name is Carey Hawke, but everyone calls him Hawke."

The room spins around me as every second I spent with Carey last night runs through my mind.

That's why everyone stared at him with sympathy all night.

That's why his emotions were so hot and cold.

Oh my god.

That's why he reacted so fiercely.

We just kissed in the house his wife was born and raised in.

I clamp my hand over my mouth to ensure the contents of my swishing stomach don't see daylight as I stumble to a bench seat halfway down the hall. I don't feel sick because I regret a single moment I've spent with Carey. I'm devastated at the thought our kiss is causing him pain. If I'd known this was the home his wife was raised in, I would have never kissed him here.

Pain strikes my chest. That's a lie. It wouldn't have mattered if I'd known. I would have never denied his kiss. All thoughts vanish when I peer into his eyes. Pain. Fear. None of it matters during our exchanges. Not last night, and not during our kiss this morning. I don't feel anything but a bizarre sensation of kinship.

The sweet smell of candy filters through my nose when Ava crouches in front of me. "Is Hawke the reason you look more rumpled now than you did while wrestling in the bushes around my cabin yesterday?"

An unexpected giggle spills from my lips. I'm so fanatical about angles and lighting that I spent two hours yesterday wrangling prickly bushes in a meadow field to capture perfect pictures of Ava. Although I won't know the outcome of my country adventure until I spend a few hours hiding in my dark room, I'm sure the sacrifice to my appearance will be worth the effort. Just like my adventures with Carey this morning are worth the sacrifice of feeling betrayed.

Pushing aside the desire to pretend last night was nothing but a fantasy, I lock my eyes with Ava. "He told me his name was Carey."

She scoots closer to me so her extended seven-month pregnant belly braces against my knee. "Don't take that as a negative, Gem. He didn't lie to you. His name is Carey."

I run the back of my hand under my nose. "Yeah, but anyone who knows him calls him Hawke. It kind of makes me feel a little dirty. Like I'm not privileged enough to know the real him."

"Hawke introducing himself as Carey makes you privileged." Ava peers at me with a set of stern but understanding eyes. "If you're the reason he walked into this house this morning still wearing the suit he wore at our wedding yesterday, you shouldn't feel dirty. You should feel honored."

Wrinkles line my forehead as confusion engulfs me. "That doesn't make any sense."

"You gave Hawke back something he hasn't had in years," she explains to my confused expression. She squeezes my hand before standing from her crouched position. "You returned the spark of life in his eyes. It might be hidden by remorse and guilt he shouldn't be feeling, but it's still there. You gave him that. You gave him something no one's given him for years. You gave him peace. That makes you privileged. Not dirty."

For the first time in over four years, a single tear wets my cheek.

CHAPTER 11

HAWKE

I take the stairs two at a time, my mind as scrambled as my stomach.

I can't believe I just did that. I kissed a woman I've known twenty-four hours in the sunroom of my deceased wife's family home.

I knew I should have never come back to this town. All I keep doing is making one stupid mistake after another. I just wanted one lousy night of pretending to be someone else. To act impulsively instead of cautiously. To be a man with nothing but his libido to take care of.

This may make me sound like an ass, but Gemma gave me that. She freed me from the torment weighing down my chest and returned me to the man I was before I lost everything.

For hours, I truly forgot. Nothing was on my mind.

Nothing but fulfilling the pleas of a beautiful blonde with tormented green eyes.

Last night was a stark contradiction to the way my normally unmoving trysts go. Usually, I'd do anything I could to keep the physical connection to a bare minimum, which is ridiculous considering the event I'm undertaking.

This *will* make me sound like an asshole, but it's the truth. The only attention I typically give my bed companions is trying to find their similarities to Jorgie.

Before Gemma, I hadn't slept with a woman whose hair wasn't the shade of a storm-filled sky or whose eyes weren't the color of the ocean.

It is easier to pretend I'm reliving memories when the person I'm using to recreate them looks like Jorgie. It might make me sound sick and twisted, but when you're a man living in the shadow of what your life used to be, sick and twisted is the least of your worries.

Although guilt lingered in the back of my mind the entire time, last night was the first time I didn't shut down all emotions and solely concentrate on myself. I wanted Gemma's attention. No matter how much I try to deny it, the more attention she gave me, the more I wanted.

I fucking craved it.

Part of the reason I so desperately wanted her devotion was because she doesn't look at me like everyone else, but only today do I realize that's not the only reason.

Gemma sees past the mask I wear warning others to stay away. She sees the man I've tried to bury with my family five years ago. Every glance she gave me last night filled me with hope that I haven't been sentenced to a life of misery. That I have more life left to live than just striving to recapture memories that will never fully fade.

Don't get me wrong, last night, guilt meddled with my composure, but unbridled lust kept it to a bare minimum.

It wasn't until this morning, when the midmorning sun snuck into Gemma's hotel room, did guilt make itself comfy in the area where my heart used to belong. I laid in the bed next to Gemma for what felt like hours, but was actually minutes, trying to rationalize with myself that I had no reason to feel guilty.

It wasn't my choice to be a widower, and it wasn't my choice to live my life without Jorgie. Any rationalization I made only angered me more. I may not have chosen to live without Jorgie, but she didn't choose to die either.

When the remorse became too much for me to handle, I quietly snuck around Gemma's room, gathering my clothes left strewn on the floor before ambling to the door.

On the way, my eyes locked in on the keycard slipped into the electricity mechanism on the entryway wall. I hesitated for only a moment before slipping it out of its spot and sliding it into my pocket.

Like I could feel any worse, the instant I stepped into the elevator, more guilt crashed into me hard and fast. The only difference that time around was it wasn't solely from using Gemma for a night of forgetting.

I knew she would feel ashamed when calling the concierge desk for assistance. Gemma wore a brave front, but I saw the torment in her eyes during her exchange with the hotel clerk. Clearly, I wasn't the only one treading into foreign waters last night.

I paced the corridor of Gemma's hotel for nearly an hour, waiting for a sign of life to stream through the tiny crack underneath her door.

The entire time, I racked my brain trying to think of a way we could both get out of this predicament unscathed. Only when I saw a maid enter the room next to the elevator did an idea formulate in my weary mind.

For the next five minutes, I ignored the inquisitive stare of the hotel maid as I repetitively called the elevator car to the twenty-third floor. The instant I heard Gemma wrangling with the heavily weighted hotel room door, I slipped into the elevator and rode it down to the lobby. I knew the panel glass on the elevator wall wasn't an ideal place to leave Gemma's room key, but I figured it was better than her explaining to the checkout clerk how she lost her key.

After pushing the twenty-third floor on the elevator dashboard, I slipped out of the elevator and headed to my Camaro in the hotel parking lot. Gemma emerged onto the sidewalk not even five minutes later. She appeared in a hurry as she raced toward an SUV idling at the curb. Call me a sucker for punishment, but even with guilt bubbling in my veins, I wanted one final chance to be seen as a normal man.

I glided my Camaro up the side of the SUV when it stopped at a red light. I stared at Gemma. She didn't glance my way once. I thought the little knock my ego took from my intrusive glare going unnoticed would be the biggest hit I'd take this morning; it wasn't. It was seeing shame wash over Gemma's face as she sat in the back of the SUV looking dazed and confused. I don't know why, but knowing she felt ashamed of what we had done cut me deeper than I'd like to admit.

The look on her face started a tidal wave of emotions to slam into me. With a vast array of feelings pummeling me senseless, I drove to the Marshall family home in autopilot mode.

At the start, I didn't even second guess why I was attracting numerous glances when I entered the back patio. Since the day I buried Jorgie and Malcolm, that is all I seem to achieve. Only when Ava offered to lend me some of Hugo's clothes did I realize not all the glances were sympathy-filled. Some were inquisitive stares.

I turned up to brunch wearing the same suit I'd worn last night. If that wasn't bad enough, my dress shirt was missing numerous buttons from where Gemma yanked it open.

Guilt unlike anything I've experienced the past five years crashed into me hard and fast when I used the joined bathroom between Jorgie and Hugo's childhood bedroom to get changed. Jorgie's childhood room is like a shrine to her life.

Every detail of her short twenty-four years is displayed in her family bedroom. The pom-poms from when she was the head cheerleader in senior high. The map pinned to her wall where she circled the destinations around the world she wanted us to visit; and the veil she wore at our wedding added to my guilt. For every second I didn't have her on my mind last night, an ounce was added to the weight I've been carrying on my chest for the past five years.

Imagine how much that weight increased when I left Jorgie's room and was confronted with the image of the lady who caused me to forget her. Technically, it isn't Gemma's fault I forgot Jorgie for even a second, but it was easier to blame her than to face the truth. So that's exactly what I did.

While fighting the urge not to storm over and drag Gemma out of the chair Jorgie used to occupy, I issued her every belligerent, malicious, life-threatening stare I could. I was horrible, a man Jorgie would have been ashamed to know if you could even call me a man.

When I confronted Gemma, it went nothing like I'd predicted. Just like last night, the instant she stared up at me, my past vanished. I knew every word spilling from her lips was a lie. Even with her eyes dampened with mistrust, they're truthful and honest. I didn't mean to kiss her. I truly got caught up in the moment.

The way she put me in my place without a single qualm made her one of the most intriguing women I've ever met. It thickened my blood with excitement and had me dying to prove her wrong. If I'm being honest, I also wanted to wash away the shame her eyes were still carrying, to show her that what we did was not something to be ashamed of. Not me and definitely not her.

Like every other idiotic thought I've had the past twenty-four hours, I acted on them instead of evaluating them first. I should have known better. Acting on impulse is for fools. Although I'm certain I won't need to worry about my impulsive desires outweighing my shrewdness anymore.

Ava may have acted unaffected when I stormed by her, but from the look of shock on her face, I know she either witnessed the exchange between Gemma or me or read the guilt my eyes relayed.

It will only be a matter of time before Gemma discovers my real identity. I know it shouldn't bother me because technically, I didn't lie, but I hope she realizes that I didn't tell her my name was Carey to deceive her; I just wanted to hold on to feeling like an unbroken man for a few more moments.

When I reach the top of the stairs, my eyes swing to the right before drifting to the left. With my attitude already teetering on the edge of a cliff, I head to the detached washroom at the end of the hall to throw some cold water on my face.

After drying my face with a towel, I grip the vanity and peer into the soulless eyes in the mirror. Just being in this house spears the truth into my chest. Jorgie isn't coming back. Even in a house full of strangers, she had so much spirit you couldn't help but notice its absence.

Jorgie and I may have only had four years together, but I knew her better than anyone. So, as much as it kills me to admit, I know she isn't looking down on me consumed with jealousy. Jorgie didn't have a jealous bone in her body. That neurosis solely belonged to me in our relationship.

We'd discussed the possibility of moving on if one of us passed many times in the weeks prior to my first stint in Iraq. Back then, I never put much thought into my replies, as I genuinely thought it would be Jorgie moving on, not me. I was in a war-torn country where soldiers lost their lives every day, so the idea of losing Jorgie and Malcolm was never something I fathomed.

Deep down in my soul, I know that what Hugo said to me months ago is true. Jorgie would hate the way I've been living the past five years. She's probably begging me not to give up every day, but that is easier to say than do.

No one can tell you how to handle grief. I've been living it for five years, and I wouldn't have any advice to give a man who was about to enter the hell I live in every day. My ideas are simple. The fact that blood is still pumping through my veins is considered living to me. Anything above that is an achievement in itself.

After taking a few moments to ease the heaviness on my chest enough so I can secure half a breath, I exit the bathroom and trudge down the stairs. If there was a way I could leave this brunch without looking like a coward, I'd take it, but since I'd rather die like a man than live like a coward, I head back out onto the patio.

I don't need to lift my gaze to know Gemma is aware of who I really am. Instead of the three dozen pairs of eyes glancing at me in remorse like they did the first half of brunch, I now have thirty-seven sets of sorrow-crammed eyes burning a hole in the side of my head.

Keeping my head low, I slip into my chair at the end of the table and push food around my plate with a fork.

Five minutes later, when I can't leash my curiosity for a second longer, I lift my eyes from my plate of untouched food. People appear to be holding conversations around the table, but even with their sneaky glances concealed by thick lashes or wine glasses filled with mimosas, I can feel the heat of their gazes on me.

My brain screams for me not to, but I slowly drag my eyes along the table until I stop at a pair of pretty green eyes usually filled with mistrust. As I'd predicted, Gemma's eyes are no longer brimming with mistrust. They're crammed with sympathy.

And just like that, her spell on me is broken.

CHAPTER 12

GEMMA

The smell of exhaust fumes and the hustle and bustle of city life grow with every mile my Uber driver travels. The closer I get to my apartment building, the more the pain in my chest subsides. There were times after my attack six years ago when I never felt content. I've never once had that feeling since I moved to New York. This city is my home. More so because of the man I live here with.

When the sedan idles at the curb of my apartment building, I step out and admire the tree-lined street that obscures the liveliness of an overly populated city mere blocks from here. The beauty of this building's architectural design first drew me to this area of New York. Then, the convenience of having all my necessities within walking distance made me fall in love. A Starbucks is half a block down, and a little cupcake store is next to it. If the winds blow in the right direction, I can stand out on my balcony and sniff in the calories I'll spend my day running off.

George, the doorman of my building, taps his top hat in greeting before opening the gold-embossed door. "Welcome home, Ms. C— "

His greeting stops when my brow bows high into my hairline.

"Gemma," he adds on.

"Thank you, George," I reply before gliding into the foyer.

Like every building in New York, chatter filters into the air as I span across the pristine marbled floors to the elevator banks at the back of the energy-filled space. An elevator attendant I haven't met before requests the car to the foyer when he notices me approaching. I smile a greeting before dropping my eyes to the gold name badge pinned to his chest indicating his name is Jeremy.

"Do you mind if I ride this one alone?" I request to Jeremy.

I have nothing against him, but considering he's under the age of thirty and he has his eyes hidden by the brim of his hat, I don't feel comfortable getting in a small four-by-four box with him alone.

Guilt clutches my heart when Jeremy cranks his neck to the desk in the foyer before turning his gaze back to me. "I really can't afford to lose my job Ms..."

"Gemma," I fill in, inwardly cringing when my voice comes out with a quiver.

I can tell by his worn shoes and the way his hair is greasy at the ends that Jeremy needs this job, but with a broad range of emotions hammering into me from my heart-strangling confrontation with Carey at brunch, I can't stomach the idea of entering a small space with him alone.

Before Jeremy has the chance to reply, the elevator doors swing open, and a deep, profound voice says, "Get your ass into the elevator, Lil Lady."

Jeremy jumps when an excited squeal ripples through my lips. "You're home early," I shriek before launching into the elevator car and throwing my arms around Wesley's neck. "You have no idea how much I was praying you were home."

"I might go to San Fran more often if this is how I'll be greeted upon return," Wesley mutters into my ear while returning my embrace.

As Wesley, Jeremy, and I ride the elevator to the 33rd floor, I scan my eyes over my very best friend in the world. Wesley is leanly built with a smattering of muscles in all the right locations. He stands a little shy of six feet tall, has blue eyes, and dark, delicious skin. The sprouts of hair on the top of his head are a little fuzzy from the oppressive humidity swamping us, but the Boston Red Sox cap he's wearing backward as he vainly clutches onto his dwindling youth conceals his indecision about growing out his afro. Wesley is gorgeous. If he weren't my best friend, I'd have a hard time keeping my hands to myself.

Don't get me wrong, Wesley and I came very close to crossing the friendship line on New Year's Eve three years ago. It was only after we started mauling each other did we realize what our joint therapist told us was true. We had an addiction to sex. Wesley's self-medicating habits switched from drug abuse to sex. His addiction was strongly based on confusion surrounding his sexual orientation. Mine was solely focused on convincing myself that I didn't lose any control from my attack. During sexual activities, I felt more empowered, but it was extremely short-lived. More times than not, I was left feeling more powerless after sex than before.

When the elevator car arrives at our floor, I loop my arm around the nook of Wesley's elbow and amble to our apartment.

"How did you know I was home?" I ask Wesley when he swings open our apartment door and gestures for me to enter.

After dumping my suitcase next to the entryway table, I pivot to face Wesley. "George buzzed to say you had arrived. Jeremy only started his shift an hour ago and figured you'd be a little freaked if you had to ride alone with him," he reveals.

My heart swells. This type of attentiveness is nothing new for Wesley. He's my crutch in life. As I am his.

Wesley throws a set of keys into a crystal bowl by the door. "If I could get a peek at him out of that ghastly elevator get-up, I think Jeremy could become a good *friend* of mine," he jests with a waggle of his brows.

I roll my eyes before pacing into our living room. "What happened to the girl who works at that Italian restaurant we get our 'Oh Wesley' discounts from?" I query. I overemphasize my sentence's "Oh Wesley" part in a long, breathy moan.

Wesley has been driving his headboard into his bedroom wall for the past four weeks with a pretty redhead from a restaurant a few blocks over. I've never seen Wesley in a relationship in the past three years, but things seemed to be getting serious between them. Especially considering she spends more time in my apartment than I do.

My nose screws up when I fail to recall her name. Because of our revolving door meet and greets, I never received a proper introduction. And although this is selfish of me to say, when I'm with Wesley, I want his sole devotion, so I never thought to ask the name of his latest bed companion. Although Wesley admits he's a sex addict, he hasn't fully come to terms with the repercussions associated with the title. He has reined in his sexual conquests compared to the number it was three years ago, but he still has a lot of steps to work through.

A grin curls on my lips when Wesley flops into one of the suede couches in our sunken living room. "I hope your fascination with creamy pasta laced in garlic up and left town like your fashion sense today. That discount is done and dusted."

Ignoring his snide comment at my disheveled appearance, I take the empty seat next to him and sling my arm around his shoulders. "You all right?" My tone is sincerer than the one I was using earlier.

Wesley connects his blue eyes with mine. "Perfectly A-Okay. She was just another female who couldn't comprehend she didn't have all the necessary equipment a guy like me requires."

Quicker than a flash of lightning brightening a pitch-black night, the glint in Wesley's eyes changes. I roll my shoulders and straighten my spine when I notice the suspicion his usually candid eyes are carrying.

When Wesley doesn't buy my attempts at acting unaffected by his inquisitive stare, I leap from the lounge chair while blubbering, "I'm going to grab a quick shower."

My brisk pace slows when Wesley demands, "Wait right there, Ms. Gemma-I-never-sleep-with-a-guy-unless-we-have-been-dating-a-minimum-of-90-days."

He graciously rises from the sofa and teeters toward me. I hold his gaze as he spans the distance between us with blazing eyes and a smug grin. He runs his heavy-lidded gaze down my body before locking it back with mine, making me squirm.

With one brow arched, he declares, "You had sex."

Before I can respond, he slings his head to the doorway. "I spent the entire trip in the elevator trying to work out where Jeremy did the naughty as he didn't smell like sex when I arrived home an hour ago." He returns his eyes to me. "But that intoxicating scent wasn't coming off Jeremy. It's coming from you."

My mouth moves as a range of lies filter through my brain, but not a syllable escapes my lips. It would be pointless for me to lie anyway. It would be like the time I told my dad I didn't eat an entire jar of Nutella in one hit while it was smeared all over my face. Wesley would see straight through any ruse I dangled in front of him.

Wesley's spurred-with-excitement eyes stare into mine as he asks, "Who was it? And please, for the love of god, don't say it was the stockbroker with the gap tooth you went on a date with last month. I know the economy is bad, but taking a pay cut doesn't mean you date a man who isn't even close to a six." He stares me straight in the eyes, his composure stern, his nostrils flaring. "Tens never date below a seven. Say it with me, Gem."

"Tens never date below a seven," we recite.

Rolling my eyes at the ridiculous drunken pledge we made three years ago, I spin on my heels and pace to my bedroom. Although Wesley remains quiet, I know he's shadowing me. It isn't just the shuffling of his bare feet on the thick, plush carpet that gives it away; it is because I can hear his brain ticking over as he tries to work out whom I broke my stern 90-day rule on.

Wesley flops onto my bed. "At least give me a number."

I brace myself on the dresser in my room and remove my shoes. "Do you remember that up-and-coming actor I was seeing in the middle of last year?"

"The one I'd happily give up pussy for?" Wesley asks, his tone unwavering and calm, a complete contradiction to his admission.

I throw off my second stiletto and kick it to the side of my drawers while nodding. "This guy was even hotter than him."

"Bullshit," Wesley retorts, shaking his head. "It's not possible. He'd need to be a god."

I cock my brow and stare him straight in the eyes. "*Gladiator.*"

"No fucking way," Wesley yells when he reads the truth in my eyes. He runs his hand across the five o'clock shadow on his cut jawline before muttering, "What about down…" He gestures his head to his crotch. "The rules of not dating below a seven don't just apply to looks. They also refer to inches."

My teeth catch my bottom lip as images of Carey's fat cock rush to the forefront of my mind. I can use only one word to describe Carey's impressive package: anaconda.

Spotting my flushed expression, Wesley throws one of the scatter pillows from my bed across the room. I grunt when it hits me in the chest. "That good?" he asks, surprise in his tone.

Wesley knows I'm not the type of girl to overly gush about my dates. Don't get me wrong, they get credit where credit is due, but if they fail to reach the high standards I set for myself three years ago, I don't hesitate to call it how I see it.

"Better than good," I reply with a precise nod.

Wesley curls off my bed and follows me into my large bathroom. "So when's round two?"

I cringe as a whiny moan involuntary parts my mouth. "I'm pretty sure it was a one-time-only deal."

Wesley props his backside on the granite countertop as I move into the shower and switch on the faucet. "If it was better than good, why no round two? He's either an idiot or no nookie for nearly a year has played tricks with your head, and he wasn't really an eleven."

As I undo the buttons on my shirt, I choose between giving Wesley the short version of events or the long-winded one. Deciding I need any help I can get in this awkward predicament I've managed to get into, I give Wesley the entire rundown of everything that happened the last twenty-four hours.

"So what did you say when you discovered who he really was?" Wesley asks once every sordid detail has been revealed.

I sweep my hand across my forehead, removing a beading of sweat

I'd like to blame on the steam pumping out of the shower, but unfortunately, it isn't the muggy environment making me a sweaty mess. It's my stupidity the hour following finding out Carey's real identity.

After swallowing away a lump in my throat, I mumble, "I said it was a pleasure meeting him and that I was sorry for his loss."

Wesley flops his head to the side as his mouth gapes open. "Gem! What the fuck? Why would you say that?"

"Because it was the truth," I reply, throwing my hands into the air. "What was I supposed to say? 'I'm not sorry for kissing you in the house your wife grew up in?' Or perhaps, 'Hey, last night was a lot of fun; if you ever get over your grief, look me up.'"

"Now you're just being a bitch."

You'd expect my feathers to be ruffled by Wesley's bluntness, but they're not. After seeing the flare of disappointment in Carey's eyes grow from my statement, I feel like a complete and utter bitch.

"I didn't mean to treat him like everyone else at brunch, but the words slipped out of my mouth before I could stop them. It's like a double-edged sword. If I didn't express my sympathies for his loss, wouldn't that make me callous and heartless?"

"No, Poppet, it wouldn't have." Wesley slips off the counter and strides to me. "You know what it was like for you after your attack, and only a handful of people knew what happened to you. Carey can't escape the pity stares as he couldn't keep something like that a secret."

The guilt weighing down my shoulders increases. I understand what Wesley is saying. Wholeheartedly. I kept news of my attack to a bare minimum so only those involved in the case knew the entirety of what happened that night. I couldn't stand the thought of people looking at me differently, so I did everything in my power to keep myself and my assault out of the spotlight. I still can't stand the sympathy my dad's eyes hold every time he looks at me, and I love him more than anything, so I can imagine what Carey is going through.

I prop my backside onto the bathtub and drop my head into my hands. "Oh god. I'm a terrible person."

"No you're not. You're human," Wesley replies. The warmth of his hand on my back soothes my shaking. "Everything happens for a reason, Gem."

"You know I don't believe stuff like that. Everything doesn't happen for a reason. I wasn't attacked for a reason," I snap, my voice getting louder with each word I speak. "Carey didn't lose his family for a reason. That's just a cop-out people use when they can't find a reason for a fucked-up situation."

"Whether you believe it or not doesn't make it untrue." Wesley drops down so he can meet me eye to eye. "You know I'd give anything to go back six years ago and warn you about what was going to happen just to stop your pain, but I can't, but do you know what? If that horrible thing didn't happen to you, this beautiful, creative, kind-hearted woman sitting in front of me would still be afraid of her shadow, and I'd probably be singing show tunes with Frank Sinatra in heaven."

The concept of not having Wesley in my life causes tears to prick in my eyes.

"You saved me, Poppet because you understood what I was going through. If you ever get a second shot with Carey..."

I attempt to interrupt him, but he keeps talking like he hasn't noticed my endeavor, "*If* you get a second shot, remember that he doesn't need your sympathy. He has it in bucket loads - he's probably drowning in it. Treat him how you'd want him to treat you if he ever discovered your secret."

My throat tightens at the thought of Carey looking at me differently. Last night was so magical, as for the first time in years, I was the Gemma I was before my attack. I wasn't guarded or weary. I was open and adventurous. I will forever cherish every minute that Carey made me feel whole again.

I stop staring into space when Wesley says, "Now get your sexy ass into the shower before my ego can no longer hold back its desire to wipe that puppy love look out of your eyes. How dare you let another man steal the glint only I can place in your eyes!"

A smile spreads across my face. "Jealousy is a good look for you. You should wear it more often."

My last statement comes out in a hurry when Wesley snags the hand towel off the bathroom vanity and whips it against my thigh. A loud crack splinters through the air, closely followed by my girly scream as I race out of the bathroom with a grinning Wesley snapping at my heels.

CHAPTER 13

HAWKE

I step back in time when I enter the main bedroom of Hugo and Ava's home in Rochdale. Even though nearly five years have passed since Jorgie and Malcolm were laid to rest, the bedroom I shared with Jorgie remains in its original condition.

Her favorite perfume bottle sits on her chest of drawers; her clothes hang in the closet, and a hideous lace-edged towel is draped over her dressing chair. If there was a speck of dust to be seen, I'd assume no one has entered this room in five years, but since every surface is clean and well-presented, I know that isn't the case.

Placing the keys to my Camaro in the silver tray on the dresser, I pace to our bed. My blood thickens when the faintest scent of Jorgie's perfume lingers into my nose.

My visual memories of Jorgie are as clear today as the day she passed, but little things like her scent, the smoothness of her skin, and the softness of her hair aren't as vibrant as they used to be.

It isn't from lack of trying to keep her memory alive; it is the fact I've been grieving Jorgie longer than she was mine. We only had four short years. She's been gone for five.

Ignoring the shake encroaching my hands, I snag one of the

moving boxes from the bed and set to work on packing away Jorgie's belongings.

The first half of her clothing is done before my brain can register what I'm doing. The second half is a little more challenging. The more items I pack away, the more reality dawns on me.

I guess that is why Ava and Jorgie's mom have kept both of her rooms in their original condition. Neither of them have been strong enough to face the reality of the situation either.

Don't get me wrong, I'm not saying I've been suddenly engulfed with a mass surge of courage. I'm only here because I don't have a choice. With Hugo and Ava moving to Ravenshoe at the end of the month, this property will once again become vacant. Although I haven't decided what to do with this house I once called home, I know I will never live here again, so why should Jorgie?

Packing away Jorgie's belongings is a hard task, but it is also freeing. It is easing the pain in my chest from my betrayal this morning by replacing it with memories we created in this room. It is in that bed our son Malcolm was conceived. That's also the same bed I asked Jorgie to marry me in.

It was the most unromantic proposal in the history of proposals. I didn't even get down on one knee, but I didn't need to show Jorgie that I loved her by using flowers and gimmicks. It was how I expressed it. She knew I loved her because I still wanted to marry her even when she had messy bedhead and horrid morning breath.

Being yourself is one of the biggest indications that you're on the right track to finding your better half. When you can take someone at face value and accept that you will never change them, that's true love. I knew the instant I saw Jorgie that I would fall in love with her. Just like I knew the instant I saw Gemma, my life would change. If you asked me right now if it will be a good or bad change, I wouldn't be able to answer.

For the quickest moment on the front stairs of the Marshall residence this morning, I both hated and appreciated Gemma. I hated that she could make me forget Jorgie, especially considering she's a stranger, but I also appreciated that she could make me forget because if she hadn't, I would have never been strong enough to endure this weekend on my own.

I tried to rationalize with myself the last two hours of brunch that the spell Gemma had on me cleared away the instant she discovered I was a widower, but that isn't true. She looked at me with the same amount of empathy everyone does when they express their sympathies for my loss, but there was something much deeper in her eyes that said way more than her words did. They told me she didn't just wonder what I was feeling, she understood. Part of me wonders if that's why she causes bizarre feelings to stir deep within me.

This kills me to admit, even more so because of the location I'm standing in, but I'm drawn to Gemma. I don't just mean in the physical sense. I mean mentally as well. Something about her brings out a side of me I swore I'd lost years ago. A side I never thought I'd see again in my lifetime and one I'm more than tempted to explore. *A side I wish I could bury right alongside my heart.*

My thoughts stray from dangerous territory when I detect another presence in the room. Hugo has his arms crossed in front of his chest and his shoulder propped against the doorframe. The small section of skin between his eyes is creased, and his lips are quirked. His baffled expression makes me wonder if I have said my private thoughts out loud.

I release the breath I'm holding when he mutters, "I didn't realize you were planning on packing up Jorgie's things today."

"Someone has to do it," I mumble more to myself than Hugo. He must hear my statement as a puff of air parts his nose, and he nods.

"I've been trying to pack up this room for months, but Ava wouldn't let me," he confesses. He rubs his hands together as his eyes, identical to his sister's in every way, scan the room. "I know you probably feel like decades have passed since that day, but to me, it only feels like yesterday when Jorgie had us shifting furniture around this room over a dozen times. No matter how often we told her the bed wouldn't fit under the window, she was adamant it belonged there."

"A dozen? More like thirty," I banter as my lips curl into a grin. "I didn't think either of us would make it out of that den alive when she found us hiding down there hours later with half a bottle of whiskey in our stomachs."

Hugo's boisterous chuckle quickly fills the room. "I got off easy by buying pizza for dinner. I'd hate to think of what you had to do to get into her good graces again."

Hugo makes a gagging noise when I waggle my brows. The bitter coldness sitting in my chest warms from our playful conversation. Hugo is my best mate, but I still struggle to talk to him about Jorgie. It isn't because he doesn't understand my grief; I can tell just by looking into his eyes that he still hasn't come to terms with losing his baby sister. I just don't talk about Jorgie to anyone. It isn't because I don't have stories to share—we made plenty of memories—I just find it hard to talk about her without letting my emotions get the better of me. Then, when Malcolm is added to the mix, I can barely function, let alone articulate a conversation.

After a few moments of silence, I say, "What are you doing here? I thought you and Ava were heading off on your honeymoon today?" My words come out shaky since they were forced through the tightness of grief wrapped around my throat.

"We were supposed to, but when Ava said you were packing up Jorgie's room, we set it back a day as I want to help. When you married a Marshall, you didn't just get Jorgie; you got all of us," Hugo replies, his deep tone low and crammed with sentiment.

Even though Hugo's statement is one hundred percent accurate, I can tell he's holding something back. Hearing an "and" hanging in the air, I verbalize it.

Hugo pushes off his feet and secures a flattened box from the bed to assemble it. "And I thought it would be a good chance for us to talk. We've got years of catching up to do."

I barely stifle a groan. Hugo has always been a communicator. Before he vanished, you could only shut him up by placing a stack of pancakes in front of him. That guaranteed you a minimum of fifteen minutes of peace. It was fifteen minutes filled with him drooling while shoveling pancakes into his mouth like he'd never eaten a thing in his life, but it was still fifteen minutes of peace.

Although we've been back in contact for the past nine months, we've never had the chance to talk like we did before Jorgie passed. That isn't Hugo's fault. He has tried numerous times, but with the rawness of my loss thrust in my face, I immediately shut down any attempts he made. Unfortunately, most of the time, my way of expressing that I didn't want to talk wasn't in an overly friendly manner.

Although I'm technically employed as a bodyguard for a chart-topping music group, my prime asset is a little boy named Jasper. When Hugo first called requesting me to keep an eye on a family member of his boss while he was out of town, he failed to mention it was a young lady who was heavily pregnant. Jenni is nothing like Jorgie, but the fact she was pregnant awakened haunted memories, but when Hugo said she was in danger, I pushed my grief to the side to fulfill Hugo's request.

When I was offered to become the full-time bodyguard to Jenni and Jasper, my initial response was a resounding no. The last thing I wanted was to be responsible for the safety of a newborn baby when I hadn't come to terms with my own loss.

Everything changed when I was leaving a meeting with Hugo's boss, Isaac. Jenni, Nick, and Jasper arrived at his office earlier than expected. Like the odd feeling that twisted my stomach when I peered down at Gemma sprawled on the church floor yesterday, something deep inside me shifted when I spotted Jasper in Jenni's arms. He was tiny, like breakable tiny. Just the thought of someone trying to hurt him brought out a side of me I was certain vanished the day I laid Malcolm in his mother's arms. I know Jasper isn't Malcolm, but that didn't stop me from wanting to ensure he was protected and safe.

I figured if I accepted Isaac's offer, I'd just turn up and do my job. I didn't have to interact with Jenni or Jasper. That wasn't in my job description. Boy, was I wrong. Jenni's personality would be best described as exceedingly friendly. My first evening on the job, she walked straight up to me and handed me Jasper. I didn't even get the chance to shake my head at her request before he was placed in my arms. If I didn't keep ahold of him, he would have ended up on the floor.

I'm not going to lie. That was one of my hardest nights in the past five years. The night Hugo called me in Iraq has been the only time I've failed to hold in my grief. The night I held Jasper was nearly the second time. Jasper represents everything I lost. He's the first baby I've held since Malcolm. He's also the reason I'll never fail at my job. I don't want Jenni or Nick to ever experience what I went through losing Malcolm. I wouldn't wish what happened to me on my worst enemy, let alone a young couple in the prime of their lives like Jorgie and I were before it was cruelly torn apart.

With my mood sitting on the edge of a cliff, I ignore Hugo's inquisitive glance and set back to work on packing Jorgie's belongings.

By the time we've stored years of memories into twelve small boxes, hours have flown by on the clock. Miraculously, Hugo didn't utter a syllable the entire time. I don't know if I should see that as a miracle or a curse. Only when I swing my eyes to him do I realize why he has been so quiet. I'm not the only one still grieving Jorgie and Malcolm. He's hurting just as much as me.

"Beer or whiskey?" My low tone is unable to hide the sentiment in my voice.

Hugo locks his eyes with me. "I'll take anything you're offering, as long as it isn't being served here."

CHAPTER 14

HAWKE

My head lifts from a drawing Joel, my four-year-old nephew, is creating, to the entrance of the kitchen when I hear the shuffling of feet. Ava slowly trudges into the room with her curly hair sprouting in all directions and the crease of a pillow indented in her cheek.

"Rough night?" I query, my voice groggy with dryness from downing too many nips of whiskey in one sitting.

Ava moves to the fridge to grab a bottle of milk before waddling to the island to prepare a large cup of coffee. "Have you ever tried to wrestle a thousand-pound colorful gorilla who is a loved-up drunk?" she asks, her brow inching higher with every word she speaks.

Joel's head lifts from his drawing when my hearty chuckle fills the space. "Is that what people are calling it these days? Wrestling?" After covering Joel's ears with my hands, I add on, "I didn't know they classed spanking as a sport."

Ava has gorgeous African American skin, and usually only Hugo's attention can cause her cheeks to flame, so I'm somewhat pleased when my little snide remark has the effect I'm aiming for.

"I'm just playing with you, Ava. I was out before my head hit the pillow," I confess.

My confession doesn't clear Ava's blemished cheeks. If anything, it inflames them more.

A few minutes pass with nothing but the noise of Joel's pencil scratching on paper sounding through my ears. Ava sips on a mug of coffee as she struggles to settle down her heated cheeks, and I sit in muted silence, shocked I managed to laugh without a snippet of remorse. Only two days have passed since I entered Rochdale with the full intention of leaving as soon as possible, but in regards to my grief, it feels like years have flown by.

Once Joel has finished his drawing, he looks up at me with his big blue eyes. "Here you go, Unky Hawke."

The corners of my mouth tug high. "Is this for me?"

"Uh huh," he replies with a nod before he slides off his seat. "Now you'll never forget the night you won Mr. Bunny."

He wraps his little arm around Mr. Bunny's neck and pulls him down from the kitchen counter. The stuffed bunny is so large, even with Joel clutching him around the neck, his feet drag along the tiled floors.

Once Joel exits the kitchen, I drop my eyes to his drawing. My lips twist. Considering Joel is only four and a half, his picture is remarkably good. It even has the detail of the black and white checked ribbon Gemma tied around Mr. Bunny's neck as an added token of our night together.

Even with Joel capturing part of my adventurous night with Gemma in his drawing, I'll never forget the night I shared with her. What Gemma said that night was true. We weren't enemies nor friends, just two strangers creating a memory we will share for a lifetime. That is why I gave Mr. Bunny to Joel. I don't need an artifact to remind me of the night we shared. I have it stored in my memory bank.

I raise my eyes from the picture when Ava says, "Joel must really like you, Hawke. The chance of him giving up his drawings is as low as Hugo sharing pancakes. Your odds of winning the lotto are better."

I chuckle. "He's a great kid, Ava. I see so much of you in him.

Except his eyes. They're an exact replica of Hugo's." *And Jorgie's, but* I keep that snippet of information to myself.

"Thanks. I think he's pretty awesome." A gloss of sheen forms in her eyes when she locks them with me. "Maybe you two can spend a little more time together when we move to Ravenshoe next month?" she asks hesitantly.

Pain strikes the area my heart used to belong. Joel is my nephew—not just because I married Jorgie, but because no matter what happens, Hugo will always be my brother—but I barely know him. Although Joel is a cruel reminder of what I lost, he's also a reminder of the joy I could still have in my life if I could just open up to the prospect of letting others back in.

It was only while spending the last hour with Joel did I truly realize how much I've missed the past five years. I miss Jorgie and Malcolm for every minute of every day, but coming back to Rochdale and seeing family I haven't seen in years and spending an unforgettable night with Gemma made me realize I also miss living. It is a harsh notion to admit, but it doesn't make it untrue.

"I'd really like that," I reply, not even attempting to hide the emotional undertone of my voice.

Ava smiles a grin that displays why Hugo lost his heart to her before they were even adults. She's a beautiful lady, no doubt, but it isn't just her attractive outer shell that makes her beautiful – it is the gigantic heart sitting in the middle of her chest.

The smell of honey infuses the air when Ava takes the empty seat next to me. "So where did Mr. Bunny come from? I didn't see a single *hare* of him when I collected you and Hugo from the bar last night." She barges me with her shoulder. "Hare, get it?"

Lucky for Ava, her sex appeal has Hugo overlooking her dorkiness.

"With that poor effort, it is clear you're not the one teaching Joel jokes," I jest, playfully barging her back.

Ava takes a sip out of her mug of coffee before turning her dark eyes to me. "Which one?"

"What did Peter Rabbit say to his girlfriend when they broke up?"

"Now you're just some bunny that I used to know," Ava replies, laughing. "Hugo can't even take credit for that one. That was Ms. Mable."

I rub my hands together before crossing them over my chest. "I can't believe Ms. Mable is still going. How old is she now?"

Ms. Mable lives in the house next door. She made herself known within five minutes of Jorgie and me moving into this house. Over the following year, I saw her more than my own mother. Jorgie loved her as if she were her grandmother. I know why. Ms. Mable is an exact replica of what Jorgie would have been if she ever had the chance to make it to that age.

"She turned ninety-two last month," Ava replies, her voice high with respect. "I tried to convince her to move to Ravenshoe with us, but she can't leave Rochdale. She said it's her home."

"Home is where your family is," I reply before I can stop my words.

Ava smiles. "Clearly you've been spending too much time with Hugo. That is exactly what he said to me while convincing me to move to Ravenshoe."

"Ravenshoe is a nice place, Ava. You and Joel will really like it there," I assure her.

She bumps her shoulder against mine again before sliding off the breakfast stool and pacing into the kitchen. After placing her mug in the sink, she spins around to face me. The suds in the sink from me washing up Joel's breakfast dishes cause her nightie to cling to her rounded belly. Ava's stomach is the first pregnant belly I've seen that doesn't make my gut knot in grief. Pregnancy looks good on her; just like it did on Jorgie. I'm glad this time around I got to see her pregnant.

As much as I hate admitting this, what Hugo said yesterday was true. When I married Jorgie, I didn't just get Jorgie. I got her entire family. And although I'll never stop wishing that I'll wake up and discover this was all a prolonged nightmare, I need to start living again. Not just for me, but for those surrounding me. Particularly, the little ones in my life who don't understand I'm grieving, like Joel and Chase's twin daughters. All they have witnessed this weekend is a grumpy old stranger. I want to change that.

My eyes lift from Ava's belly when she quietly murmurs, "I'm glad to see some of the remorse has cleared from your eyes this morning, Hawke."

I attempt to respond, but my words stay entombed in my throat. So instead, I briefly nod. Although Hugo and I did more drinking than talking last night, our time together still helped remove some of the guilt I felt for kissing Gemma in the Marshall's home. It's not all gone, but I haven't struggled to breathe as much this morning as I normally do.

"Why didn't you tell Hugo what you saw at brunch?" I struggle out through the guilt clutching my throat.

Ava holds my gaze as she answers, "It's not my place to tell him. If it's something you want him to know, I'm sure you can tell him yourself."

She pushes off the kitchen counter and paces to me. "I know nothing I could say would ever make your life easier, Hawke, but I'm going to say it anyway."

I brace myself, preparing for impact. When Hugo has quoted similar things the past six months, I didn't handle the situation in a brotherly manner, but this time is different. This isn't coming from a man who can read my emotions without a word seeping from my lips. This is coming from Ava, my wife's heavily pregnant best friend, and a woman I've respected for years. I not only want her advice, I need it. She knew Jorgie better than anyone, so if I'm going to accept advice from someone on handling my grief, Ava will be that person.

My stomach launches into my throat when Ava simply says, "You can't fight fate."

That was Jorgie's favorite saying. It wouldn't matter if it was when I was getting hot under the collar during an incident of road rage or when I wanted to deck her brother, Chase, for keeping us apart. She always believed fate would eventually play its hand. Don't get me wrong; she knew fate only took you so far, but she didn't believe people just met by pure coincidence. She was determined it was fate.

I suck in large gulps of air to calm the furious beat of my pulse as

Ava pulls a business card out of the top drawer in the kitchen and slides it halfway across the counter.

"I know even the prospect of moving on is hard for you." She shifts her eyes to the main bedroom of her house. "I don't even want to do it. I keep praying one day Jorgie will just magically walk out those doors." She returns her eyes to me. They're brimming with tears. "But that will never happen." She curls her spare hand over my clenched fist as a tear slides down her cheek. "The day we had lunch. . . the day of the accident. . . Jorgie made me promise that if anything happened to her, I'd make sure you were okay." She pushes the business card across the remaining half of the counter. "I'm going to keep my promise."

Her tears soak into the collar of my shirt when she wraps her arms around my shoulders and gives me a brief hug. "You weren't the only one who took a huge leap that night, Hawke. Gemma did too," she faintly whispers.

When she pulls back and I spot the pain in her eyes even a heavy set of tears can't hide, the vital part of my body I thought I lost years ago stops beating.

"What happened to Gemma? Why are her eyes full of mistrust?" I question, my voice softer than a whisper as the questions that have been running through my head the past twenty-four hours finally see daylight.

The tears in Ava's eyes grow exponentially. "That isn't my story to tell. When the time is right, Gemma will tell you what she wants you to know."

"There's no Gemma and me, Ava. If was just a night of fun." I try to keep the deceit out of my voice. My attempts are borderline.

Ava's brow crinkles. "It's funny you say that, as that's the exact thing Jorgie said to me after you crashed into her canoe. Obviously, even the most intelligent people in the world are wrong sometimes. I've loved and admired you from the moment Jorgie introduced you to me, Hawke, but you're a fool if you try to deny these signs. You didn't meet Gemma in this town, at that church, this month, for no reason. It was fate."

After issuing me a tight grin, she spins on her heels and walks out of the room.

A strange thumping noise comes out of the large cavity in my chest when I drop my eyes to the business card Ava handed me. "Capturing memories one picture at a time," I read off the card that has Gemma's name and cell phone number scrawled across the back.

A riot of emotions holds me captive for several moments. For the first time in years, it isn't just anger and grief swirling my stomach. It is... *hope*. Before I have the chance to decipher why Gemma's business card would give me an upwelling of hope, Hugo staggers into the room. From his disheveled appearance and bloodshot eyes, it doesn't take a genius to realize he's hungover. For the past five years, Hugo used alcohol to support his grief, but that type of grief counseling was placed on the backburner when he moved back to Rochdale six months ago. He looks as wretched as the torment swirling my stomach.

"Hair of the dog?" I query when Hugo chugs down the half a bottle of flat beer he left on the kitchen sink yesterday. Mercifully, the laughter tainting my voice ensures he can't hear the sentiment my heavy tone is unable to shield.

"I'm not hungover, but I'd drink out of a dog's bowl just to get rid of the horrid taste in my mouth. What the hell did we drink last night?" he replies, his voice raspy and low.

"Pretty much anything under five dollars a nip," I answer, still chuckling.

Hugo screws up his nose. "Darn Isaac and his expensive taste."

"Spoiled taste buds? That's the excuse you're running with?" I glare into his eyes, silently calling him out.

Hugo grins while nodding.

A smile tugs my lips high. "Then what's your piss-poor excuse for your bloodshot eyes?"

A flare of excitement blazes through Hugo's eyes. "Keeping up with the demands of a pregnant lady is hard work. The more I give Ava, the more—"

Hugo chokes on the remainder of his sentence when Joel enters the kitchen. After drifting his inquisitive eyes between Hugo and me, his little hands shoot up to cover his ears.

"You can continue. I'm not listening anymore," he yells, projecting his voice over the laughter spilling from Hugo's mouth. "Mommy said it's not polite to listen when adults are talking."

Keeping his ears covered, he paces deeper into the kitchen and attempts to climb onto the stool next to me. Seeing him struggle, I place my hands under his arms and hoist him into his seat.

"Thank you," he stutters politely. Clearly, he has Ava's manners.

With his ears still covered, he lifts his big blue eyes to his dad. "You owe me ten dollars." His voice is nothing like you'd expect a four-year-old to sound. . . until he adds on, "I not only stayed in my bed *all* night when I heard Mommy calling for help, I also get the pancake boganus."

I spit my coffee halfway across the kitchen floor. Hugo doesn't even flinch when coffee stains sprinkle his white shirt. My brow shoots up into my hairline when the excitement flaring in Hugo's eyes doubles.

"Mommy's making pancakes?" Hugo asks, eagerness in his voice. "On a Monday?"

Even with his ears covered, Joel nods. "Yep! And I get to help." The happiness in his voice matches Hugo's grin to a T.

THREE HOURS after witnessing Joel and Hugo demolish more pancakes than I've eaten in my life, Hugo walks me to my Camaro.

"You got lucky, Man. Ava has always been great, and Joel adds that little extra sweetness to the package."

Hugo cranks his neck back to peer into the window of his family home. "It isn't luck. It's—"

"Fate," I interrupt before I can stop my words.

Hugo returns his gaze front and center.

"Don't," I request when I see the same pleading look his eyes hold every time he suggests it is time for me to move on. "I'm glad things with you and Ava have worked out how they should have years ago, but that doesn't mean you need to shift your focus to me. I'm trying, Hugo. It might not be at a pace acceptable for others, but I'm putting one foot in front of the other. Let me get used to walking again before you line me up for a marathon."

"I wasn't going to say anything," Hugo mumbles, his deep voice laced with deceit. "I wasn't," he adds on more forcefully when he spots my cocked brow. "I was just going to say you seem to be walking around a little lighter than you were last month."

A flare of cheekiness brightens his eyes when he playfully backhands my chest. "Clearly, it wasn't just the cobwebs on the Camaro's engine that cleared away this weekend. Your balls got a little lighter as well."

Before I can respond to his accurate but highly inappropriate comment, Hugo hotfoots it into his house. I can hear laughter in his voice when he yells out, "I know Ms. Mable and Betty White are around the same age, but damn boy, I didn't realize you were so desperate."

Pretending I can't feel Ms. Mable's indiscreet stare through the lace curtain of her home, I grit my teeth, slide into the driver's seat of my car, crank the engine, and reverse out of the driveway. Overcome by another bout of stupidity I seem to be having a record run with this weekend, I roll down my driver's side window and shout. "Betty White is a fox! Always has been and always will be!" at the top of my lungs.

I swear I can hear Hugo's boisterous chuckle ringing in my ears for the next three blocks.

CHAPTER 15

HAWKE

When I pull my Camaro into the driveway of the storage unit she's been housed in the past five years, I curse under my breath. With the advancement in technology, you're no longer greeted by an employee when you visit this establishment. The man with the greasy comb-over and half lit cigarette dangling out of his mouth that served me years ago has been replaced with a computer program. Even just to enter the main gate you need a four-digit PIN code—a code I recall scribbling on a piece of paper Saturday morning while grumbling about how I would take my business elsewhere. I didn't realize at the time this was the only storage building within twenty miles of Rochdale.

After throwing my gearstick into neutral and pulling on the park brake, I open the glove compartment and rummage through the slips of paper stored inside. Since the storage shed owners placed my monthly receipts in the glove compartment, it is bursting at the seams with papers. Halfway through my search, the midday sun beaming in the passenger side windows casts a flicker of light onto my black gearstick.

"There you are," I mutter under my breath when I spot a recognizable scrunched-up piece of paper lying on the passenger floor.

As I'm dragging my hand back to the steering wheel, a scratching sensation hits the edge of my palm. With my head angled to the side and my brow arched, I dig my hand under the passenger seat to find what caused the scratch. Unwillingly, a smirk etches on my mouth when the polaroid photo Gemma took of us two nights ago comes into vision. It must have slipped off her lap and got stuck down the side of the seat.

I'm glad I'm only discovering this photo now. If Ava or Hugo had seen it, they would have said it wasn't an accident and that it was fate coming into play. If I'm being totally honest, half of me is wondering the same thing. Gemma intrigues me. So much so, she managed to sneak her way into my dreams last night. It wasn't long. Only the quickest flash of her beautifully tormented eyes. It was short enough I didn't feel guilty about it, but long enough it had me wondering why even half a bottle of liquor couldn't shake the hold she has over me.

For several moments, I sit in the driveway of the storage building staring at the photo of Gemma and me, trying to work out why I'm so drawn to her. I don't know what it is about Gemma, but even looking into her eyes through a photo causes something inside me to shift. Maybe it is the desire to find out what caused the mistrust in her eyes? Or the fact she gives me a break from reality? Whatever it is, it is strong enough to have me yanking my cell phone out of my pocket and dialing a familiar number before I can stop myself.

Hunter answers three rings later. "Hey, Paige and I will be ready to roll out in a few hours. Did you want us to pick you up? Or will you meet us at the airstrip?"

"Is Isaac not travelling back with us?"

Isaac, Isabelle, Paige, Hunter and I flew to Hugo's wedding in Isaac's private jet. When I first began working with Isaac, I thought a lot of his wealth was a reflection of his billionaire friends' generosity. It isn't. From what I've witnessed, Isaac is a lot wealthier than he lets on. I don't even think his fiancée is aware of his true wealth.

I can hear Hunter running his hand along his scruffy beard. "Nah, Isaac has some matters to handle in New York before he can return to Ravenshoe."

"Getting Izzy to Town Hall?" I mutter, laughter in my tone. There are two things every red-blooded man in Ravenshoe knows: Izzy is 110% off limits, and the only woman in Ravenshoe not trying to drag Isaac down the aisle.

"If given the chance, I have no doubt, but no. Just some business stuff he needs to take care of," Hunter replies, chuckling. "So. . ."

Hunter leaves his question open, no doubt confused by my call. Hunter is my supervisor, and although I've been working under him for the past seven months, I've never called him out of the blue before.

"There's been a change of plans. I'm going to drive my Camaro back to Ravenshoe." I strive to keep my tone neutral, my efforts are marginally acceptable. "This old girl has been locked up long enough; it's time to end her sentence."

"Your Camaro or you?" Hunter asks, his tone no longer having a whip of edginess attached to it.

"To be honest, I don't have a fucking clue," I mumble, my voice reflecting the insanity of my decision.

I've reversed out of the storage building driveway and clocked my first quarter of a mile on the odometer before Hunter's shocked gasp finishes sounding down the line. Deciding to use his shock to my advantage, I ask, "If I have someone's name and cell phone number, can you give me their address?"

I hear Hunter's cheeks inclining over the line. "Is the Pope Christian?"

My brows furrow. "I don't know. Wasn't there something in the news about the new Pope being an a—"

"It was a rhetorical question," Hunter interrupts, with humor in his deep tone. "Give me the digits and watch me work my magic."

The sounds of fingers stroking a keyboard at a lightning fast pace filter down the line seconds after I recite Gemma's cell phone number to Hunter.

My ears prick when Hunter releases a heavy sigh. "Usually, I'd have no trouble giving you someone's address, but. . ."

I stop breathing as I wait for him to continue. "But?" I mutter when he fails to hear the inquisitiveness in my silence.

"If I want to keep the integrity of my clients, I can't give you her address," Hunter slowly breathes out.

"Gemma is a client of yours?" I ask with surprise in my tone.

Hunter's silence answers my question. I don't want it to, but disappointment clouds me.

"But. . ." Hunter slowly drawls out again, his one word overly dramatic. "I can tell you there's a little cupcake store in Greenwich Village, New York you should totally check out while you're in the area."

My grip on the steering wheel tightens as confusion swamps me. "Thanks, but sweets are Hugo's weakness. I'm more a savory type of man."

A breathy chuckle resonates down the line. "Fuck, Hawke. Those years you spent in the military messed with your head. I was talking in code," Hunter laughs.

"Why?" I interject. "Why not just say what the fuck you're trying to say? Why does everything always have to be secret squirrel shit with you?"

"Because it's more fun this way," Hunter replies, still chuckling.

Hunter's laughter strengthens after a winded grunt escapes his lips. "Hey, Hawke, it's Paige," greets Hunter's girlfriend I've met a handful of times the past three months. "Hunter might have to keep his integrity for his clients, but I don't. Gemma lives in a fancy apartment building on University Place, Greenwich Village." Her words come out in a hurry as the sound of feet stomping thumps down the line. "Hunter traced her cell; she's at the cupcake store he told you to visit."

Girlish laughter shrills through my ears before the faintest, "Don't you dare, Hunter," sounds over the line. A grin curls onto my lips when Paige's contagious laughter barrels through my phone before my call is disconnected. Smiling, I shut down my phone and place it onto the passenger seat next to the photo of Gemma and me.

When I come to a stop sign on the outskirts of Rochdale, I take my time deciding which direction I want to go. If I head left, I'm going back to the life I've been living the past five years. If I turn right, I'm driving straight into what could be the equivalent of a tornado for me.

When I flick my signal left, one of Gemma's sayings from our night together plays through my mind. "Dreams are like memories. No matter how old you get, you never stop creating them. You just have to decide if you're strong enough to pursue them."

A motorist sitting behind me beeps his horn when my blinker signals that I'm turning left, but my hands yank my steering wheel to the right. I blink several times in a row as I try to shake off the unease stiffening my back. I'm not going to Gemma with the hope of reigniting the obvious attraction firing between us two nights ago. I'm going to prove a point. To demonstrate beyond reasonable doubt what I said to Ava was fact, not fiction. There's no Gemma and me. We were just two strangers having a night off from our tormented lives.

"If you believe that, Hawke, you're even more sick and twisted than I thought," I mumble to myself, confirming my suspicion that returning to this town has made me lose my mind.

FORTY MINUTES LATER, and three failed attempts at turning around, I pull into a spare parking space on University Place, Greenwich Village. The liveliness of the late Monday afternoon pummels into my ears when I crank open my car door and step onto the sidewalk before I lose my nerve. The frenetic flow of foot traffic on the sidewalk replicates the streets of Ravenshoe, but the smell of exhaust and food vendors are an element Ravenshoe has not yet gained.

Even only knowing Gemma for a short period of time, I can imagine she loves living here. The dynamic atmosphere suits her personality to a T. It is lively and upbeat, just like her. Although Gemma's eyes are shrouded in mistrust, they also show that behind her weariness is a woman dying to break away from the stigma her eyes portray. Just like me, she's praying that one day someone will see through the safety shield she wears to protect herself. That they will finally see the real Gemma hiding behind the mask. The Gemma I was privileged to spend time with two nights ago.

The guilt churning my stomach eases when a frisson of awareness jolts through my body. I stand muted on the sidewalk when I spot an unforgettable smile in a sea of a hundred faces. Gemma is striding down the sidewalk across the street with a white bakery box in one hand and a cell phone in the other. Even with wearing a simple pair of white fitted knee-length pants and a pasty pink short sleeve shirt hanging off one shoulder, heads turn to watch her as she saunters by. She has effortless beauty that doesn't need to be accentuated with priceless jewels and designer threads. As much as I wish it weren't true, just like Saturday night, she stirs something deep inside me. It is an odd and peculiar feeling, but also unmissable.

Feeding off the hope Ava's conversation ignited, I follow Gemma as she continues strolling down the street. When I notice an opening in traffic, I step onto the edge of the sidewalk and prepare to cross the road. Aggravation hits me with brutal force when my scan of the street has me stumbling upon the image of Gemma being greeted by an African American man. I step away from the road when Gemma smiles before throwing her arms around the man's neck.

I take another retreating step when the unknown man swings Gemma around the sidewalk. They look like they know each other very well. Like they're an intimate couple. Guilt twists all the way up my throat. Is that why Gemma wanted the night off? It wasn't a night to be free of the event that caused the mistrust in her eyes; it was a night off from her life. *From her partner.* How the fuck did I misread her so badly? I may only be a shadow of the man I used to be, but I had no clue my perception was so clouded. I could have sworn the doubt in her eyes was mistrust. If I hadn't seen her interaction with the unnamed man, I would have never known it was guilt.

"Sorry," I apologize when my unsteady steps back to my car have me tripping into a lady walking her poodle on the sidewalk.

The corners of her lips crimp into a snarl as she yanks on her dog's lead and sidesteps me. I don't register a single disdained hiss from

New Yorkers pushing past me standing muted in the middle of the sidewalk. I'm too shocked to register anything. I shouldn't be surprised, though This is what I get for believing I have suffered long enough.

This is fate's way of showing me that when you've been sentenced to a life sentence, it is exactly that: LIFE.

CHAPTER 16

GEMMA

One month later...

"Did you find him today?"

I stop scanning the faces of the people hustling past the window of my apartment building and clutch my chest. "You scared the poop out of me," I declare before spinning on my heels.

The cheeky gleam in Wesley's eyes pauses for a moment when he notices the disappointed sheen in my eyes. Although it is utterly ridiculous of me to do, every time I'm waiting for my Uber driver in the lobby of my building, I search the crowd for a familiar face. Wesley thinks I'm insane, but I swear to god, the Monday following Hugo and Ava's wedding, I spotted Carey standing on the sidewalk across the street from my building.

Wesley assures me he can sniff out an eleven in a crowd of millions, but I'm certain his hottie radar was on the blink since he was riding a career adrenaline high. Wesley has looks that could have him gracing the covers of magazines for years to come, but his passion isn't modeling. It is singing. And he's darn good at it.

The afternoon the hairs on my arms bristled in awareness was the same afternoon Wesley discovered an up and coming record label requested a copy of the demo CD he produced three years earlier. Considering Wesley has been shipping his CDs across the country the past two years, to have the record label request it was a surefire indication that he was onto a winner.

But even with glee beaming out of Wesley in invisible waves, I couldn't shake the peculiar feeling prickling every nerve-ending in my body. The dizziness clustering in my brain wasn't from Wesley spinning me around the sidewalk like a man much younger than his twenty-eight years; it was my heart pleading for me to listen to the prompts of my body.

By the time Wesley placed me back onto my feet, a pang of guilt overwhelmed me. I didn't know why I felt guilty, but it increased tenfold when I caught the quickest glimpse of a dark blue 1969 Camaro before it vanished over the horizon. I was so sure the Camaro was Carey's, I pushed off my feet and chased it half a block down. Uneased by my erratic behavior, Wesley shadowed my every movement.

Now, I can laugh about my absurd behavior that afternoon, but at the time, when I lost sight of the Camaro as it merged into the heavy clog of rush hour traffic, I was devastated. That afternoon was the first time in years I didn't stop to evaluate the prompts my body was giving. I acted purely on instinct, and all it gave me was blisters on my feet, and a heart even heavier than it was the morning I left Carey dumbfounded on the stairs of the Marshall residence.

This shames me to admit, but after inconspicuously asking for Carey's number from Ava, I texted him that very evening and for the seven days following. He never texted me back. That blow was nearly as brutal as me being winded from chasing pipe dreams down a crammed New York sidewalk.

My attention reverts from childish wallowing when a black stretch limousine pulls onto the curb of my apartment. When George, the doorman of my building, nudges his head to the limousine, my brows meet my hairline.

"They sent a limousine?" I practically squeal, staring at Wesley with wonderment. My loud scream startles an elderly lady entering the revolving doors of our building.

Wesley flashes his mega-watt smile, causing a few cheeks in the foyer to become inflamed with desire. Any pity left lingering in my mind clears away when a professional looking lady dressed in a thousand-dollar pantsuit and wearing more jewels than I own crashes into a round table in the middle of the decadent space. She was so immersed in categorizing every inch of Wesley that she failed to notice the six-foot-wide table decorated with a large arrangement of chrysanthemums.

After issuing me a nasty-stink eye, she runs her hands down her crisp black jacket and turns her eyes to Wesley. Only just holding in my immature retort, I drift my eyes to Wesley. "She wants you to go and kiss her boo-boo."

Wesley laughs. "I don't think that's what she wants me to kiss," he jests, his tone low and abundant with self-assuredness.

After immaturely sticking out my tongue at the snarling middle-aged lady, I loop my arm around Wesley's elbow and exit our apartment building.

"Finally. She's back," hollers Wesley as we merge onto the sidewalk. "I was starting to think your one night stand with the gladiator stole your sense of humor."

My hackles stiffen from Wesley's snide comment, but I fail to refute his claims. You can't deny the truth. I've been a bit of a wet blanket the past month. To such a degree, this is the first time I've gone out with Wesley since he returned home from a week-long visit to his hometown of Tiburon. Don't get me wrong, Wesley has begged and pleaded a minimum three nights a week for the past month, but I didn't feel like going out. He was so concerned about my lack of social life, he scheduled a crisis appointment with Dr. McKay. Unfortunately for Wesley and his hectic social calendar, Dr. McKay was on my side. As long as I was occupying my desires for solidarity with healthy mind expanding tasks like reading or working in my darkroom, much to Wesley's dismay, Dr. McKay wasn't concerned with my pleas to spend a few nights indoors.

SECOND SHOT

The driver of the limousine, a fit-looking man in a crisp black suit and dazzling smile, taps his hat in greeting before opening the back passenger door of the stretch Phantom Rolls Royce. Although this area of New York is known for its wealth, there's still a bristling of excitement hanging thick in the air. Just like the day the church door smacked me in the face, it feels like something magical is about to happen. And I'm as pleased as punch I get to experience it with Wesley.

Oddly, when the record company called to request a meeting with Wesley, they also requested my attendance. Although shocked, I was also pleased. Like in any industry, most of my contacts are made through word of mouth. This was the sole reason Wesley asked me to design and shoot his demo album cover two years ago. Over the past two years, Wesley's album cover has bestowed me with the privilege of photographing a handful of rising stars in both the music and movie industries. It makes me both humble and thrilled that industry professionals could see past Wesley's heart-cranking good looks and recognize that the entire picture is just as beautiful as the man standing in the middle of it. Anyone can take a photo, but a person with passion sees the picture before it is taken.

I grip Wesley's hand before turning my eyes to the vibrancy of New York City streaming past my window. I've lived in this city the past three years and I still feel like a fraud. It probably has something to do with my inability to hide my love for the city that gives away my deceit. The unique smell, the vibrancy, the way you never feel alone. They're only a small handful of reasons why I love this city so much, but the biggest one, the one that ensures I will never leave is the fact I feel safe here.

After wrangling through the tightly packed cars with the precision of a native New Yorker, the limousine driver pulls onto the curb of a glass building in the middle of Manhattan. I tip my head back and follow the smooth lines that soar into the billowing clouds promising to cool the ghastly muggy temperatures with a few drops of rain. Although a few hours of reprieve from the stifling New York summer heat would be a godsend, the humid conditions that follow an afternoon storm aren't something I welcome with open arms.

I squeeze Wesley's hand one final time in silent support before scooting across the cool leather seats. Although we are both here with the hope of advancing further in our careers, he needs this more than I do. The smell of exhaust fumes and food vendors rush memories of days at the track with my dad to the forefront of my mind when I step onto the sidewalk. It is also a reminder of his stern demand that we are to call him with an update the instant we leave our meeting.

After rolling my shoulders to shake off my nerves, I accept Wesley's hand and saunter into the architecturally marvelous space. I struggle to keep a neutral expression on my face when the full wonderment of the building engulfs me. With dark gray veined marble floors and artist-designed glass and chrome chandeliers, it is a seriously impressive building that would only look better captured in black and white film.

"We need to come back here," I whisper, tilting into Wesley's side. "I'd give up cupcakes for a month for the chance of photographing this lobby."

Wesley nods in greeting to the two large security officers manning the turnstiles before replying, "That's the plan, Poppet. If I have it my way, we will be having many visits to this building over the next century."

The jitters in my tummy ramp up a notch when I hear the unease in his voice. Nerves have never bothered Wesley. He typically oozes confidence, so his shaky composure has my anxieties sitting on edge.

After having our IDs scanned by one of the security officers eyeing us with interest, a lady in a one shoulder stark white dress gestures for us to follow her. Nerves tingle the hairs on my arms, and just like it did every time my dad rolled his car onto the track during a race, my bladder decides now is the perfect time to announce its desire to be emptied. Now is not the time to let my nerves get the better of me, so I push them to the side and force a professional front onto my blood drained face.

Any chance to portray a professional facade is left for dust when

Wesley mumbles, "Holy shit," under his breath when the pretty brunette walks us into a boardroom bristling with energy.

It doesn't take me long to realize what caused Wesley's abrupt response. We are standing in a room with one of Wesley's newest idols. Noah Taylor, lead singer of the number one band in the country, Rise Up, smiles a dimpled blemished grin at Wesley's star-struck response. After picking Wesley's jaw up from the floor, I pace to Noah and accept the hand he's holding out in offering. I'm not going to lie, even with Noah being several years younger than me, my mouth is salivating so badly, I'm tempted to run my hand across it just to ensure I'm not drooling. He's gorgeous. A ten out of ten. No doubt about it.

"Hi, I'm Gemma," I greet him, loathing that my voice comes out shaky. "And this is my...business associate, Wesley."

I yank a still slack-jawed Wesley to my side.

"It's a pleasure to meet you both," Noah replies, his voice rough and gritty, and 100% sexy. "This is my wife, Emily," he introduces, gesturing to an equally gorgeous specimen seated at the end of the table. "And these are my bandmates, Nick, Slater, and Marcus."

I'm mentally snapshotting each band member of Rise Up as Noah greets them. Nick has charming good looks and the aura that screams of a player. Slater has a more manly and brutish appearance than Nick, but just peering into his dark eyes tells me there's more to his story than the headlines the tabloids have been running on him the past two months. And Marcus . . . *my, oh my*, he has gorgeous dark unblemished skin and a pair of soul-stealing green eyes that hit a few of my hot buttons. If you stared into his eyes too long, you'd combust into ecstasy without him even needing to touch you.

If I wasn't a fan of Rise Up's music, I would have assumed their record label signed them purely on their looks. They have a set of faces that would sell CDs by the truckloads even if their music sounded like nails being dragged down a chalkboard. They're all attractive but in a unique and completely individual way.

After giving me a few moments to fully absorb the beauty

surrounding me, Noah turns his dark eyes to me. "I believe you've been in contact with Cormack?"

I nod. "Yes. That is who we're meeting with today?" The hesitancy of my words make my statement come out sounding more like a question.

My knees wobble when Noah smiles. "Cormack is running a little bit behind, so he asked us to start the formalities." He gestures for us to take a seat at one of the many vacant chairs housed around the long rectangular table.

Pulling out the chair closest to me, I thrust a still-muted Wesley into his seat before taking the empty one next to him. Noah surprises me when he sits into a vacant chair two spaces up from us. Normally, any meetings I've attended in this industry, the help and talent sit on opposite sides of the table.

Heat spreads across my chest when Noah connects his dark eyes with Wesley. "We've listened to your demo CD numerous times the past month. You have real talent. A smooth edginess to your voice not many singers can produce."

"Thank you," Wesley graciously replies. "Coming from you. . . that's a real compliment."

I squeeze Wesley's hand, grateful he has finally worked past his shock.

My grip on Wesley's hand firms when Noah swings his eyes to me. "We've also been perusing your photography portfolio online. The pictures you took of the O'Reilly Brothers tour earlier this year were phenomenal. My wife Emily is a huge fan of theirs, and she said your photos captured not just the band, but the men standing behind the instruments."

I lift my eyes to Emily. "You have good taste. Pictures can't lie. The O'Reilly Brothers aren't just talented musicians; they're also wonderful human beings."

Wesley sighs loudly when Emily smiles. I can understand his response. She has natural grace and beauty any young woman would love to have, but when she smiles, my god, it makes me green with envy.

"I told you she'd be perfect," Emily says, glancing at Noah.

Noah nods as he sinks deeper into his chair. His laidback approach shows how comfortable he is leaving decisions about his career in his wife's hands. I guess I shouldn't be surprised. They only married two months ago. They're still in the newlywed love haze I hope one day to experience.

Masking my shock at my inner monologue with a smile, I return my eyes to Emily.

"As Rise Up's publicist, it's my job to ensure the band is seen by the public in the best light. That won't happen by slapping a half-naked photo of them with oily chests onto an album and mass producing it. Don't get me wrong; I'm not saying sex doesn't sell, but there's so much more to this band than just their sex appeal."

"I understand. I don't photograph people to capture their smiles. I photograph them to capture their souls," I reply, my words coming out heavy with pride. I shift my eyes to Noah. "I'm sure you and Wesley don't turn up to a recording booth and sing in the same tone as every other singer out there. Every artist brings their own unique flair to their industry. Capturing that unique quality is my specialty."

All my nerves clear when Emily, Noah, Marcus, Slater and Nick nod their heads in agreeance.

Noah claps his hands together. "Our very first unanimous vote?" he mutters, his voice sounding shocked. "Hell must have frozen over."

When the band members break into laughter, I drift my eyes to Wesley. He appears just as confused as I am. His confusion intensifies when the boardroom door flings open and a blond-haired man in a dark blue suit enters the room. When Wesley straightens his spine, the spicy scent of the cologne I bought him for his birthday lingers into the air.

"You're the talent scout I spoke to two months ago." Wesley drifts his eyes to me. "You remember that talent scout we saw that night at Karaoke City."

My heart rate kicks into overdrive when recognition dawns. Although he's more professionally dressed now than he was when we saw him two months ago, there's no doubt the blond-haired man is the same man who had all the females entranced at Karaoke City.

I jump in fright when a deep, manly chuckle booms through my ears. "You still pretending to be the help?" Slater chuckles.

"If that's what it takes to find the best talent in the country, that's what it takes." The blond flings off his suit jacket and hangs it across the chair before extending his hand in offering to Wesley. "Cormack McGregor, owner of Destiny Records."

My eyes snap to Wesley. He looks just as shocked as I am at discovering the man we've been corresponding with the last month is the owner of the record company interested in signing him. My chest swells when, before my very eyes, Wesley seizes the life-altering opportunity standing in front of him with both hands. With a smile that would stop traffic, he rises from his chair and accepts Cormack's offer of a handshake.

"Wesley Heart, next year's Grammy award winner for Best New Talent."

CHAPTER 17

GEMMA

I wait for our limousine to chug into the bumper-to-bumper traffic before turning my massively dilated eyes to Wesley. "What the hell just happened?" I ask, shocked.

Muted into silence, Wesley's mouth gapes open and closed like a fish out of water, but not a syllable escapes his parched lips.

"You got a record deal," I answer for him. "A real-life record deal."

I'm so thrilled for him and so very proud. He has worked hard the past five years, and he deserves this recognition more than anyone I know. He is proof that hard work eventually pays dividends.

Wesley hesitantly nods. "I did, didn't I?" His heavy brows stitch together. "Did I?"

I arch my brow high into my hairline before nodding. "You did! I'm so proud of you, Wesley."

He throws his arm around my shoulders. "Just as I am of you, Poppet. You killed it in there," he praises. "You practically had Cormack eating out of your hand to sign you on as the band's photographer. I'll have to take a page from your book and occasionally play the not interested card. It might have forced the decimal point on my contract down a few places."

"That wasn't a ploy," I reply, leaning into the plush leather seats.

"New York is my home, Wesley. I don't know if I could cope not seeing it for weeks or months at a time." Even with New York having so much energy it could crush a weak person, I love it here.

Wesley angles closer to me. "Home is where your heart is, Gem, not your zip code." He runs the back of his hand down my cheeks, drawing my attention to him. "So I guess it is lucky we're going to Ravenshoe together, or you would have been left heartless for two months."

Even with my heart warming from Wesley's playfulness, confusion swamps me. "Ravenshoe?" I query, uncertainty in my tone.

Wesley nods. "Yeah, that's where we're going."

The bile in my stomach climbs up my windpipe. "Cormack said we were going to Hopeton. Didn't he?"

Wesley shakes his head. "No, he said the headquarters of Destiny Records were in Hopeton, but wanting to keep the number one band in the country happy, he's bringing us to them."

"The band lives in Ravenshoe?" My pulse quickening as my heart freezes.

Overlooking the daftness of my question, Wesley nods.

My mind spirals with endless possibilities. I'm both excited and petrified.

"What's going on, Gem?" Wesley asks when he's unable to read the bizarre mix of emotions pumping out of me.

I lick my dry lips before replying, "Carey lives in Ravenshoe." I can't hide the excited nervousness of my tone.

Wesley smiles a grin that does nothing to ease the turmoil plaguing my stomach. "What clearer sign do you need than that?" he asks, his voice as high as his brows. "That's fate, Poppet."

I roll my eyes. "Are you sure you and Ava aren't long lost siblings? You both love pulling out the fate card as often as possible."

Wesley barges me with his shoulder. "That would be totally gross if we were, as I've thought many times about banging her."

I pop my elbow into his ribs. "Don't ever let Hugo hear you admit that."

"He doesn't need to be jealous. There's plenty of Wesley to go around."

I laugh before switching my eyes to the bustling flow of activity out my window. Only the brave dare to drive in New York City. The traffic is bumper-to-bumper. Bike couriers meld with a sea of yellow cabs; wealthy stock brokers share the same footpath as the less fortunate, and native New Yorkers cruise past wide-eyed tourist snapping photos of the well-renowned landmarks without a pause in their stride. It is a confronting and magnificent sight.

After a few moments of silence, Wesley tilts into my side. "Sometimes the road of life takes an unexpected turn, and you have no choice but to follow it until you end up in the place you're supposed to be. This may be a forced fork in the road, Poppet, but nothing worthwhile comes easy."

A solid lump of sentiment forms in my throat. "Dr. McKay would be so proud," I push out past the bulge.

Mortified at being busted quoting our therapist, Wesley deflates into his seat and shifts his eyes to the stream of traffic moving at a snail's pace. Even with the sound of sirens wailing and the hum of the heavy clog of traffic surrounding us, I can hear his brain ticking over. I know this record deal is everything he has ever wanted, so I'm somewhat surprised by his lack of excitement.

"You are stronger than you were back then, Wesley," I mumble when reality finally dawns.

Looking at Wesley as he is now, you'd never guess the lifestyle he was raised in. My upbringing would have mirrored his to a T if I hadn't been adopted by my dad.

"If you're worried this lifestyle is too tempting, don't. Look at Slater for example. At the first sign of trouble, the record label got him the help he needed."

"Drugs aren't my only addiction, Poppet."

I nod. Wesley has been a sex addict nearly as long as he has been a drug addict. I scoot across the leather and grasp his hand in mine. "You have no reason to be worried. Back then, you didn't have me as your kickass side kick. Anything starting with a P won't get close to you. I'll make sure of it."

The pain in my chest soothes when a grin curls on Wesley's lips. "P?"

"Powder, pills, pussy, and penis." I impress myself when I hold in the childish giggle dying to break free from my snickering lips.

Smiling, Wesley shakes his head. His expression is both mortified and disgusted. That's all it takes for my girly laughter to spill from my lips.

Once my laughter settles down, Wesley locks his hopeful eyes with me. "Does that mean you'll do it? You'll come to Ravenshoe with me?"

My cheeks incline as I nod. "I'll do the special edition cover, but I can't sign up for more than that right now. Besides, who in their right mind would pass up the opportunity of photographing a group of men who look like that? They're so hot, I'm considering changing my business slogan from upstanding memory capturer to pin-up photographer."

Wesley throws his head back and laughs. "You need to do one of those artistic shoots that require no clothing," he strangles out between vigorous bouts of laughter.

"I'd be the most famous photographer in the state," I laugh.

"State? Try the world. Especially if you get a sneaky dick pic of Noah."

When our chauffeured limousine glides down our street, Wesley rests his cheek on my shoulder. "Thanks for doing this for me, Poppet. Although this is something I've wanted for years, it doesn't make it any less daunting."

"It's the least I can do after everything you've done for me," I reply, truthfully. Wesley thinks he's the only one benefitting from our friendship. He isn't. He has saved me more times than I can count.

"I'll always be there to keep you sane," Wesley taunts as the limo pulls into the curb of our building.

George opens the rear door for us and we climb out. Just like they have every time I'm standing outside of my building, my eyes scan the street. The sidewalks are packed with people dodging the refreshing sprinkle of rain that will blanket the city with steamy heat the instant it is over.

When I nudge Wesley with my shoulder, he locks his beautiful eyes with mine. "Ravenshoe is a huge town, so the chances of running into Carey would have to be..."

"Slim, minuscule, no fucking chance in hell," Wesley fills in, believing he's articulating the response I want to hear. He isn't.

I not only want to see Carey again; I want to feel him as well.

CHAPTER 18

GEMMA

The chances of my wish being granted grow when the first face I spot while exiting a private jet on an abandoned runway on the outskirts of Hopeton is Carey. He's standing to the side of a white stretch limousine. My pulse quickens when I absorb the crisp black suit and white dress shirt he's wearing. The fitted design of the suit showcases his tall, powerful frame fittingly and adds to the stifling heat consuming me from the midday sun. From his protective stance, it doesn't take a rocket scientist to reach the conclusion that he's on duty. He has the dark and brooding composure all security details seem to have, but his eyes are void of the shock mine are carrying. *Did he know I was coming?*

The commanding appeal his protective stance demands isn't as effective on me. I've seen him naked. Nothing strips away a man's guard more effectively than removing his clothes. After giving my eyes a few more minutes to scandalously drink in every inch of Carey, I crank my neck back to Wesley. I don't need to ask if his hottie radar is working. His slackened jaw and bulging eyes are a clear indication he's also spotted Carey.

"You owe me twenty dollars," I declare before walking down the private jet's small flight of stairs.

Wesley was adamant my lack of sexual contact the past year screwed my hotness radar, so he happily pledged to cook dinner for a week if he was proven wrong. Considering cooking isn't Wesley's strong point, I negotiated the provisions of our bet to a monetary value.

"I don't owe you shit. You said he was an eleven. He's *clearly* not an eleven," Wesley argues.

After waving a greeting to Emily and a pretty blonde lady pacing toward us, I shift my eyes to Wesley. "Are you jealous?" I ask, laughter in my tone.

Wesley has no reason to be jealous. Although Carey is insanely gorgeous, so is Wesley. If they were put side by side in a room, you'd have more than a few ladies—and maybe even a handful of men—passing out from high blood pressure.

"Ah, no," Wesley retorts, his voice surprisingly stern. "Carey isn't an eleven because, just like me, there isn't a number high enough to rate that hotness." He flings off his reading glasses and inappropriately rakes his eyes over Carey. "If you don't go round two with him, Poppet, I'll be tempted to break our no fraternization policy."

Before I get the chance to reprimand Wesley for even considering breaking our no dating the same guy rule, Emily appears at our side.

"Hi! We're so glad you're both here," she greets before wrapping me up in a tight hug.

Not being an overly huggy type of person, I return her embrace before taking a step backward. "Thanks for believing in us enough to offer your support."

Emily waves her hand across her body. "All I did was place your work into the hands of the right people. Your talents are what deserves the credit."

A normal person could construe Emily's statement as butt-kissing, but she expresses herself with a sense of confidence that displays the genuine truth in her statement. She may be gushing, but she believes in what she's saying.

After greeting Wesley with the same amount of enthusiasm she instilled on me, Emily introduces us to her friend, Jenni, who looks young. If I had to guess her age, I'd say late teens, early twenties. She has strawberry blonde hair and petite facial features. Her eyes are a similar color as Hugo's but a shade lighter, and she stands a good six inches shorter than Wesley's six-foot height. She's beautiful, but has an aura like Emily, one that encourages positive thoughts instead of jealousy.

While pacing to the limousine, Emily updates us on the plan for today. On route to the studio Destiny Records has created for me in Ravenshoe, Wesley will be dropped at Destiny Records headquarters in Hopeton for a one on one meeting with their song writer, Mickey. If all goes to plan, I'll be photographing the members of Rise Up tomorrow afternoon, while Wesley will have his first recording session with Noah tomorrow morning.

"I know it is all a little frantic, but the record label wants to ride the high the band is having as long as possible," Emily explains halfway to the limousine.

I suck in deep breaths, trying to ignore my body's acute consciousness of Carey's encroaching closeness. It's a pointless endeavor.

Failing to notice my inflamed cheeks, Emily continues, "If we keep the schedule we are aiming for, Wesley's collaboration with Noah will be included on the one year anniversary CD, and your photos will capture a side of the band the public has not yet seen."

"Sounds ideal," I reply, excitement in my tone.

"Brilliant," Wesley adds after giving my hand a squeeze.

The more I strive to ignore my body's perception of Carey, the more alert it becomes. He's impossible for me to ignore. Especially since his unique virile smell gets stronger with every step we take. He smells divine, and looks even yummier.

"Don't let Hawke frighten you," whispers Jenni, leaning into my side. "His hard shell is just a cover for the big squishy heart he has inside."

The flushed hue of pink on my cheeks escalates. Although Carey acts like he didn't hear Jenni, I know he heard every word she said. His straight-lined lips hardened with every syllable she spoke.

Pretending I can't feel Carey's muscle-quivering stare, I mumble,

"From the way he looks in that suit, I'd say that's the only squishy thing on his entire body."

Jenni's cheeks flame with heat as her wide-eyed gaze rockets to Carey. The more she takes him in, the more her pupils dilate. "Yeah, I'd have to agree with you," she admits, her words muffled with girlish laughter.

I feel like I've stepped back into my college days when Jenni loops her arms around Emily and they giggle like schoolyard children. I'm not going to lie, their laughter is contagious, and it takes all of my effort not to snicker alongside them. The only reason I don't is because my witty banter didn't lessen Carey's furious scowl the slightest. If anything, it made him more irate. Even scowling, he's ridiculously striking.

When we reach the edge of the limousine, I gesture with my hand for Emily and Jenni to enter before us. They slip into the back seat without a snick of hesitation. Not a word escapes Wesley's lips when I nudge my head for him to follow—unless you include the throaty moan he indiscreetly emits after raking his eyes over Carey standing guard by the limo door.

After playfully kicking Wesley's ankle, I raise my heavy-hooded eyes to Carey. Even with his murky gaze clouded with anger, I can't stop my lips from curving into a smile. I truly didn't believe I'd ever gain back the raw hunger you feel when standing next to a man as appealing as Carey. His scent alone is a serious aphrodisiac for me. The rush of desire. The vortex of emotions. The unquenchable thirst. Those are stimuli I regained during my night with Carey. If one night was so rewarding, imagine what could be achieved with another. The possibilities are endless.

When my blatant gawk is awarded with silence, I squeak out, "Hello."

I bite on the inside of my cheek when my one word expresses way more than it should have. *Why didn't you return my texts and calls? Why have I spent more time missing you than I've known you? And why do I want to kiss the sadness from your eyes even when you're evilly glaring at me?*

"Hello," Carey replies, his tone as clipped as his reply.

I wait for a deluge of questions to bombard me. All I get is silence. When he gestures his head to the limousine, soundlessly advising for me to enter, I swallow down the sick gloom spreading through me and do as requested. I'm clueless as to what has caused Carey's cold demeanor. I know our last meeting didn't exactly follow the protocol of a typical one-night stand, but I didn't realize our situation was so dire. We're both adults, so cold shoulders are not required. If his interest in me isn't as gripping as my interests in him, I'm woman enough to gracefully bow out of my endeavor to spend more time with him. He just needs to say the word.

Since Emily and Jenni are seated on one side of the dual leather benches, I take the empty seat next to Wesley, who is sitting across from them. Late August temperatures make the interior stuffy, but the climate turns calamitous when Carey slides into the empty seat next to Jenni. After he speaks into a device tucked in the sleeve of his suit, the limousine lunges forward.

"Very James Bond," Wesley murmurs.

Ignoring how the confined space compromises my efforts to act unaffected by Carey, I lean in to Wesley's side. "You don't think it's a bit overkill?"

He scoffs before shaking his head. "No. You know as well as anyone, Poppet, there are some fucked-up people in this world. If I could afford to hire a fleet of bodyguards to shadow your every movement, you'd never pee alone again."

Even knowing what he says is true, I pop my elbow into his ribs. "You sound like my father."

"Who do you think planted the seed in my head?" Wesley replies, chuckling.

For every mile we travel, the bristling energy bouncing between Carey and me grows. Unlike our night together five weeks ago, this time, the energy isn't fired with lust. It is an uncomfortable, stomach-churning vibrancy that makes me wish the limousine had barf bags dangling from the headrests like the private jet did.

My attention diverts from trying to work out Carey's shift in demeanor when Jenni questions, "How long have you two been together?"

My pupils widen to the size of dinner plates. "Oh…umm… Ca—" I attempt to refute, believing Jenni has detected the irrefutable connection between Carey and me.

"Nearly a month," Wesley interjects, sliding his hand into my sweaty, clenched fist.

I balk before snapping my eyes to Wesley. I stare at him, blinking and muted when he adds on, "It was lucky I jumped in early and snapped her up before anyone else got the chance."

Emily and Jenni sigh in sync. I sigh too, but mine isn't as pleasant as theirs. Wesley keeps his head hanging low, refusing to look at me. He's lucky, as I'm glaring at him with more anger than my eyes have ever possessed. He may not survive this death stare.

The anger heating my veins gets a moment of reprieve when a shiver runs down my spine. Pushing my anger aside, I swing my eyes to Carey. He isn't peering out the window, pretending to act unmoved by Wesley's false declaration. He's staring straight at me—cold-eyed and emotionless. It hurts me to see the vulnerability in his eyes. So much so, I nearly blurt out the truth. The only reason I don't is because the limousine comes to a stop at the front of a glass-front building marked Destiny Records.

Feeling the thick tension suffocating the air, Emily says, "We'll give you two a few minutes to say goodbye."

"Yeah… umm… I need to pee anyway," Jenni declares, strengthening Emily's suggestion. From the pink coloring adorning her cheeks, I can tell she's lying.

At Jenni's request, Carey clambers out of the stationary vehicle. Disappointed, I turn my eyes to Wesley. "What the hell, Wesley?" I grumble under my breath. "Why did you say we're a couple?"

Wesley waits for Carey, Jenni, and Emily to fully exit the limousine before drifting his eyes to me. "I like him, Poppet; he's gorgeous, and I could imagine how good he looks under that suit, but he isn't the man for you."

"What? What are you talking about? You haven't even formally met him yet."

"The ten-minute trip was all I needed," Wesley retorts, glancing into my eyes. "You were practically humping his leg outside the limo, and all you got in response for your eagerness was a brief hello he'd give a stranger on the street. Then he spent the last ten minutes glaring at you like you're the person who dwindled his grandmother's retirement fund. If I treated any of the girls I shared a bed with like that, you would have me lynched."

"You don't understand him. He has a lot going on." I defend Carey the only way I know how, by using his grief as an excuse for his erratic moods.

The anger in Wesley's eyes dampens. "I understand that, Poppet, but being a widower doesn't give him the right to be an asshole."

"He isn't. You just need to give him a chance."

"A chance to destroy you. I can't do that. You can't ask me to do that."

Tears burn my eyes because it hurts my heart just thinking that Wesley can't see the qualities I've already witnessed in Carey. To outsiders, his brutish demeanor and standoffish approach may make him appear dark and dangerous, but that isn't who he is. He's a man struggling to emerge from the suffering he's endured. That doesn't make him heartless and mean. It makes him real.

"Wesley," I breathe out when he slides across the leather seat in preparation to exit the limo.

The pain in my chest triples when he cranks his neck back and peers at me. "Have I ever steered you wrong?"

It kills me, but I shake my head.

"Then trust me, Gem. He will *never* give you what you deserve."

After pressing a kiss to my sweat-drenched forehead, he exits the vehicle without a backward glance.

CHAPTER 19

HAWKE

When Wesley exits the limousine, it takes all my strength not to reward his cocky smirk with a knock to his chin. Although I should take comfort in the fact he and Gemma didn't become a couple until after the night we spent together, reining in my desire to unleash my anger on him is proving to be a difficult task.

The past month has been both a challenging and rewarding one. My night with Gemma five weeks ago created the first solid crack in my grief in nearly five years; then, with each day that has followed, smaller—nearly invisible—cracks are slowly chipping away at the heaviness sitting on my chest. Don't get me wrong, I'm not even close to being a tenth of the man I was when I married Jorgie, but I'm trying to bring back some of the qualities she loved about me the most. Particularly, my sense of family.

That's been a whole heap easier to do since Hugo, Ava, and Joel moved to Ravenshoe two weeks ago. As per Ava's request, Joel and I have been spending some time with each other the past week. It is amazing how you can take the best of two people and cram it into one little four-year-old with big, inquisitive eyes and a brain like a sponge. Joel is the perfect combination of both Hugo and Ava. He has Hugo's cheeky personality and fondness for sweets, but he's kind-hearted and smart just like Ava.

Although every minute I spend with Joel has me wondering what things Malcolm would have accomplished if his life wasn't cruelly cut short, surprisingly, I don't feel any guilt when I'm with him. The innocence in a child's eyes is remarkably comforting to an adult wading through grief. There are times where I'd give anything to see the world through Joel's eyes. To see a world without the filter of cruelty.

My eyes swing to the side when a deep voice says, "So there's a soul hidden in there somewhere. I was starting to wonder why anyone would hire a heartless man to protect them. When you love someone, you protect them from the pain; you don't cause it."

Wesley straightens his spine, extending to his full height. Even if I weren't wearing my black commando boots, I'd still be a good two to three inches taller than him. Although his eyes are screaming of arrogance, and his demeanor is giving off the potent smell of cockiness, I can tell he cares for Gemma. He has the same protective gleam in his eyes mine always held when I defended Jorgie. It's the same gleam that fired in my eyes when I saw the panic wash onto Gemma's face upon hearing Jenni's intrusive question. Jenni is a great girl, wonderful mother, and an even better friend, but she has no filter whatsoever when it comes to privacy. Both she and Emily have the unfortunate knack of wanting to know every single detail of your life. I've been caught unaware by them many times the past two months. No matter how much I silently plead with Nick and Noah to save me, they don't throw me a lifejacket.

When Jenni asked Gemma how long she and Wesley had been together, I initially thought she was referring to Gemma and me. Even angry at seeing Gemma and Wesley together again, I couldn't shut down my body's perception of Gemma's closeness. My attraction to her is like a thirst no amount of water can quench. It is unquenchable, which is ludicrous considering she's the equivalent of a stranger. . . *and she's taken.*

Gritting my teeth, I lock my eyes with Wesley. "I don't need a soul or a heart to do my job. Just a gun."

Wesley's brows become concealed by the band of the cap he's wearing backwards. The shock in his eyes proves without a doubt that he read the hidden threat in my statement. I don't know where the threat initiated from, or why I felt the need to use it, but Wesley's stunned reaction makes me glad I couldn't leash a side of me I haven't seen in years. Jealousy has always been a curse of mine. Clearly, grief hasn't altered my idiotic neurosis.

Ignoring Jenni's gaped mouth, I gesture for her to enter the limousine after Emily. Once she does as requested, I slide in after her and slam the door shut. Gemma jumps in fright from the loud bang before her massively dilated eyes lift from the ground. The urge to guard her from the torrent of pain raging through her eyes grows exceptionally when she locks her downcast gaze with me. Just like the morning we kissed in the sunroom of the Marshall residence, her eyes are brimming with tears, and her face is awash with panic.

Even knowing I shouldn't care she's upset, I silently mouth, "Are you okay?"

A raw and intense feeling hits my chest when the faintest smile creeps across her lips as she nods. The impact of my three small words to her is so great, fragments of the protective wall she has built around herself crumble before my eyes. I don't know what it is about Gemma that provokes such a response out of me, but I do know one thing. She didn't build the walls surrounding her heart to keep people out. She built them to protect whatever is left within. That may seem conceited of me to say, but it's not because I'm bragging about the response my concern created; I'm saying it because I understand, as I do the same thing. Maybe that's why our connection is so bizarre? There's no greater connection two people can have than understanding. Words, sexual attraction, and desire mean nothing if you don't understand how the person came to be who she is.

Although Gemma's name was never mentioned during Emily and Jenni's discussion on the way to Cormack's private airstrip, I knew the person Emily described was Gemma. Not because Emily described her looks and personality with accurate precision, but because something deep inside me awoke with every mile we traveled.

When Gemma first stepped out of the plane, I was left breathless. I knew she was going to exit the jet before the hostess even opened the door, so that wasn't what caused my breathless state. It was the range of emotions pummeling into me from seeing her for the first time in weeks. You know that tingling feeling your hands and feet get when, after an extended period of absence, you see the welcome home sign of your home town coming over the horizon? That's the feeling I got when I saw Gemma. A feeling like I was going home.

That feeling was squashed the instant my eyes zoomed in on the man exiting the plane behind her. Even though I didn't get a clear visual of the man Gemma was greeted by five weeks ago, I knew Wesley was the same man. They have a unique bond even a man who spent months of solitary in trenches couldn't miss. *A bond a soulless man would give anything to feel again.*

"Huh?" I ask when Jenni nudges me with her elbow.

She looks up at me with her light blue eyes. Just like they do every time she senses Nick's closeness, a pink hue graces her cheeks. "We're here."

Shaking my head at her eagerness to see a man she only left an hour ago, I slide out of the limousine. Jenni and Emily practically dive out of the limo and sprint into the converted warehouse the band is hiding out in. With their album being one of the biggest selling albums of all time, things have become extremely hectic for the band the past three months. You know you've reached the pinnacle of stardom when you can't trust a pizza delivery man anymore. Yes, we had an incident last month. A member of the paparazzi paid off a local pizza store so he could deliver pizza to Noah and Emily's cabin at Bronte's Peak. After barging his way past Emily, he took numerous shots of Noah holding their newborn daughter, Maddie. Although the paparazzi was technically trespassing, it is lucky Noah is friendly with the local law enforcement agency, or he may have ended up with battery charges. Security for all members of the band has been ramped up since that day.

My head slants to the side when Gemma says, "There's nothing sweeter than young love." A film of mistrust dampens the brightness of her pretty green eyes. "I'd give anything to go back to an age where something as simple as being held could make you feel safe and protected. Like nothing could ever hurt you."

"Don't you have that with Wesley?" I ask before I can stop my words.

Gemma peers past my shoulder for several moments before briefly nodding. "Wesley will always make sure I'm safe and protected," she murmurs ever so quietly. "But he doesn't understand that one day I'll need more than he can give me."

She runs her hand down my forearm, sparking every nerve in my body before pacing toward the converted warehouse.

HOURS LATER, I lower the speed on my treadmill, adjusting it from a sprint to a leisured walk. While running a white towel over my head, I drift my eyes to Hugo working out on a leg press machine a few spots over. A grin curls on my lips when I notice every piece of equipment beside him has been swarmed by scantily clad women, looking more like they should grace the cover of *Vanity Fair* than undertake a sweaty workout. I've also noticed a few women flocking to my side of the gym the past hour, but with my mood still on edge from my exchange with Gemma this afternoon, their eagerness to socialize with me isn't as robust as usual.

When Hugo notices me walking to the weights station, he finishes his rep on the leg machine and comes over to spot me. A chuckle parts my lips when half the female population scrambles to secure the machines next to Hugo and me. I'm not laughing at their desperateness; I'm laughing at Hugo's ignorance. I swear, even if the pretty blonde working on the barbell bench press two spots up from us were stark naked, Hugo wouldn't notice her. That's how ignorant he is when it comes to any female not named Ava.

After doing enough reps that the pain in my chest is replaced with exhausted muscles, I mutter, "How well do you know Gemma?"

The quickest flare of emotion passes through Hugo's eyes before he shuts it down just as swiftly as it sparked. "She's a good friend of mine. We lost contact a few years ago, but just like me and you, it's like no time passed at all," he answers, his voice lower than his normal tone.

He assists me in raising the weight bar back onto its holder while asking, "Why? What's your interest in Gemma?"

I incline to a seated position. "Cormack hired her to shoot a special edition album cover for the boys. She arrived in Ravenshoe today."

Hugo smiles a grin that shows his genuine affection for Gemma. "She called Ava a few nights ago to say she was coming, but I didn't put two and two together when she said she was doing a shoot here," he informs me as his lips curl even more. "It's amazing how small the world seems sometimes." He hands me a towel embossed with M.S. Gym on it. "Have you seen her work? She's very talented. Ava is dying to see the photos she took at our wedding."

My eyes dart around the gym, preferring not to look directly at Hugo while I slide a white lie under his nose. "I haven't really had the chance to talk to her. She seems a little skittish and unapproachable."

Hugo closes his mouth before briefly nodding.

"Is she normally like that?" I struggle to keep interest out of my voice. "Or just cautious around people she hasn't met before?"

Hugo's brows join, enhancing the frown marring his face. "You've met Gemma," he says, his voice high in uncertainty. "Mom said you gave her a lift home from our reception."

My heart rate kicks into overdrive as the first ravel in my net of deceit comes undone.

Hugo peers at me in confusion. "Gemma was also at brunch the following morning. . ." His words trail off as the suspicion in his eyes doubles. "She said it was a pleasure to meet you on the front porch when she was leaving."

Quicker than a lightbulb switching on, recognition dawns on Hugo's face. "You never forget anyone you've met. Let alone a woman who looks like Gemma." He runs a towel down the side of his sweat-drenched face, dumps it into a linen basket at the side, then crosses his arms in front of his bare chest. "Gemma is Betty White, isn't she?"

I shake my head. My efforts of deception are utterly pointless when I mutter, "Yes," at the same time.

My response can't be helped. I'm fucking desperate to talk to someone about what the hell is going on with me. It's been a month since I've seen Gemma, and all it took was one glance into her eyes to stir up the conflicting array of emotions I've been spending the last month wading through. Even knowing she's in a relationship doesn't dampen my interest in her the slightest.

The entire drive back to Ravenshoe last month, I assured myself it was just haunted memories messing with my composure at Hugo's wedding. It wasn't. It was the pretty blonde with the tormented eyes, the only person in years who gave me back the ability to breathe without feeling guilt. The only person who filled me with hope that my life was still worth living. *The only person I want to protect and push away at the same time.*

Analyzing the storm of emotions pumping through me, Hugo says, "I knew there was something different about you that morning." His loud voice gains us even more attention than our half-naked frames. "It was the night of my wedding, wasn't it? Gemma's the reason you turned up to brunch wearing the same suit you wore the night before. You old dawg, playing Austin's overly used skit from *Wedding Crashers*."

Before I can utter a word, the cheeky gleam in Hugo's eyes switches. "Oh, fuck. Did you. . ." He swallows harshly before continuing, "Treat her right? You didn't hurt her or anything. Did you?"

"I'm not a complete fucking ass," I snarl through clenched teeth.

Hugo's brow cocks, no doubt shocked by my abrupt reply. "I'm not saying you are, but Gemma isn't the type of woman you shag then dump the following morning."

Guilt roars through my body – not just because Hugo pretty much described what I did to Gemma the morning following our one-off romp, but because Hugo isn't just my best mate. He's my wife's brother for fuck's sake. I can't talk about this kind of stuff with him. I can't taint Jorgie's memory by discussing my sexual conquests with the man who has eyes identical to hers.

Gritting my teeth, I peel off the weight bench and head to the locker rooms. "Forget I said anything," I strangle out through the tightness curled around my throat.

Hugo tails me. "No, fuck that, Hawke. You started this conversation; you don't get to end it too."

When I fling open my steel locker door, Hugo slams it shut, blasting my face with cool air from the air conditioning vents above our head. A middle-aged man with a towel wrapped around his expanded hips darts his eyes between Hugo and me. Feeling the thick tension hanging in the air, he drops his gaze to the floor and shuffles across the tiles to collect his clothing hanging on the wooden bench lining the corridor of lockers. He doesn't speak a word as he leaves the room with his hairy backside on display for the world to see.

After ensuring the coast is clear of any other spectators, I turn my eyes to Hugo. "Now is not the time to discuss this."

"Not the time, or the wrong person?" Hugo calls me out, knowing me well enough to guess what I really wanted to say. *I can't talk to you about this.*

"I'm your best mate, Hawke. I was years before Jorgie, and I'll be years after you throw me against the locker, as you aren't going to like what I say next."

Reading the determination his eyes always get when lecturing me about moving on, I brace myself for impact. Hugo would never resort to violence, so I'm not preparing for a physical blow; I'm preparing for a mental one.

Just like Ava, Hugo shocks me by keeping his reply short and simple. "It's been five fucking years."

"I know that," I sneer viciously, my voice cracking with emotional anger. "I don't need you to tell me how long it has been. I've felt every goddamn minute of every goddamn day in this fucking nightmare I've been living the past five years."

I fully expect Hugo to argue that I've grieved long enough, and that it is time to move on. What I'm not expecting him to say is, "Then imagine what it's like for Gemma, because she's been living in her nightmare even longer than you."

I balk like I've been physically hit. A frantic wave of feelings overwhelms me. Confusion. Anger. An uncontrollable urge to protect Gemma. I'm also shocked. Our conversation began with Gemma, but the instant it switched to Jorgie, I never fathomed it would return to Gemma.

Just hearing Gemma's name hammers me with more emotions than the clusterfuck of feelings I've been dealing with the past month. Although the guilt I feel for how I treated Gemma last month will never compare to my guilt for continuing to live without my family, it's still enough to add pain to my hollow chest. To know some of the hurt her eyes carried today could have been put there by me utterly destroys me.

"What happened to Gemma?" I surprise both Hugo and myself that my concern for her has me looking past my grief. "Why are her eyes full of mistrust?"

Hugo scrubs his hand over the shadowing of hair on his chin before locking his despairing gaze with mine. "Just like you, she discovered the world isn't full of people determined to make it a better place."

He swings open his locker door to gather his keys and wallet. I can tell he wants to say more—hell, I want him to say more—but even under the influence of a bottle of whiskey, he doesn't loosen his lips. He guards people's secrets as well as he protected his sister.

"I won't hurt her." I don't know why I felt the need to say that. It just came out of my mouth before I had the chance to stifle it.

Hugo places his hand on my shoulder. The rattle of his hand exposes way more than his words ever could. "I never had a doubt, Hawke. You're a good man. One Gemma could use in her life, but you need to tread carefully with her. Gemma is like the world's finest crystal, beautiful to look at and worth every penny it costs, but one crack may completely shatter her."

After squeezing my shoulder, he spins on his heels and ambles out of the locker room.

While changing out of my sweaty gym clothes, I run my conversation with Hugo through my mind on repeat. Hugo has always been overly protective, but there's something more than protectiveness in his eyes when he talks about Gemma. If I'm not mistaken, it's regret... *and perhaps even disappointment.*

My conversation with Hugo was one of the shortest ones I've had since Jorgie and Malcolm passed, but it shook my core hard enough that the impenetrable wall surrounding me has permanently shifted. *Similar to my evening with Gemma last month.*

I wait for the guilt my private confession should create. It doesn't come.

Ignoring the suggestive smile of the brunette manning the counter at the gym, I exit the single glass door. My night with her four months ago was good for reliving memories I'll never truly forget, but not great enough I'm tempted for round two. There has only been one woman who has given me that desire. Her hair is the color of the full moon hanging in the sky, and her eyes as glistening as the stars.

Humid, hot winds pummel my chest when I stride down the sidewalk to my Camaro parked a few doors down. The muggy temperatures add to the sweat coating my skin from a vigorous gym session. I've always been a bit of a gym junkie, but my obsession grew the past five years. The burn of a hard workout lasts for hours, and I figured it was better to feel pain than nothing at all.

After throwing open my car door, I slide into the driver's seat and roll down the window. Wanting to keep my Camaro in its original condition, I've never bothered having air-conditioning installed. I'm now regretting my decision. Ravenshoe is a great city, a mecca of a town that Isaac is growing into a thriving community, but its ghastly mugginess takes some adjusting to.

When a large truck roars past my stationary vehicle, gushes of hot air blow into my car. The force of the gust is so brutal, it rattles my visor and knocks down a picture I tucked in there five weeks ago. Snubbing the peculiar feeling swirling in my stomach, I pick up the photo Gemma took of us together last month to appraise it.

Gemma's eyes are holding the same amount of excitement in this photo they held when she peered up at me earlier today. I thought she'd look at me differently once she found out who I really am. This photo proves my assumptions were wrong. She glanced at me today with the same amount of wonderment and intrigue she did before she knew I was a broken man. Perhaps that is because she understands what I'm going through? The hurt in her eyes mirrors my own. She may do a better job of masking her pain, but it is still there all the same.

After placing the photo back into the strap of my visor, I crank my engine and pull my Camaro onto the street clogged with traffic. A shocked chuckle escapes my lips when the first song played over the radio is Rise Up's hit song "Hollow." This song resonates a lot with the barrage of emotions I've been dealing with the past five years. And more particularly, the past month. I wouldn't say I was suicidal after I lost my family. It wasn't ever something that crossed my mind, but during times of silent reflection, I realize I may not have consciously considered suicide, but it was obviously playing in the background of my mind. I didn't hold a gun to my head, but I walked directly into the line of fire without any concern for the repercussions of my actions. *The most dangerous people are those who believe they have nothing left to live for.*

"You've got to be fucking kidding me," I murmur into the muggy night air when the song on the radio switches to another Rise Up record-breaking hit. I shouldn't be shocked. The disc jockeys in this town—along with half the state—have been giving Rise Up an endless amount of radio time. They either have a genius sitting behind the helm of their album launch, or a sadistic bastard set out to torture the miserable fucks who drive classic cars with no CD or Bluetooth capabilities.

As the lyrics of Rise Up's song "Surrender Me" plays through my ears, I'm struck by the way Gemma's glances from earlier today are still making an impression on me. This song isn't about despair and anguish like "Hollow;" it is about surrendering your heart to the person who finally broke through your walls and fought through your resistance. It is about promising to protect and love them with as much tenderness as they bestowed upon you. It is a song that proves you can find love again after loss.

Snubbing the shake encroaching my hands, I shift my eyes to the sky, which is as open and as beautiful as my wife's heart used to be. "I hear you," I whisper to the glistening night sky. "I hear you loud and clear."

CHAPTER 20

GEMMA

"Can you feel it?"

Reluctantly, I tear my eyes from the spectacular view of Bronte's Peak gracing every window of the two-bedroom cabin Destiny Records rented for Wesley and me. His eyes are bright and full of life, no doubt also overwhelmed by the beauty of a town that has managed to capture my soul in less than three heartbeats. This town is picturesque, but it is the people inside that take your breath away.

"The magical feeling?" My words are laced with sentiment.

Wesley nods. "Like something marvelous is about to happen."

"Is happening," I correct, my brows inching as high as the excitement in my voice.

I pull my lightweight cardigan in close to my body before burrowing my nose in Wesley's neck. I barely hear the sound of waves crashing over the furious beat of his heart. I can understand his excitement. I'm still reveling in the high of an awe-inspiring day. Wesley had a meeting with a man who had no hesitation in recognizing his god-gifted talent, and I spent my afternoon with my mouth gaped open, drinking in the world-class studio Destiny Records set up for me. Clearly, money is no object for a man like Cormack McGregor. In the five days following me accepting his offer to shoot Rise Up's commemorative cover, he turned a run-down warehouse into a studio any photographer would be proud to call their own. A place I'll struggle to give up when my assignment is complete.

The only dampener on my entire day was my encounter with Carey this afternoon. During our brief conversation in the parking lot of the warehouse, I wanted to tell Carey the truth—that Wesley and I are nothing but friends—but my loyalty to Wesley saw me continuing with his lie. Normally, nothing affects me when I'm backing up Wesley and any decision he makes, but guilt made itself comfy in the middle of my chest today. It is so strong, every time I caught the quickest glimpse of Carey from across the room, the desire to tell him the truth nearly crippled me.

You'd figure a month of silence would have lessened the spell of intrigue Carey cast on me from the moment we met. It didn't. Those three little words he mouthed when he sat across from me in the limo were the final nails in my coffin, pushing my fascination with him from awkwardly uncomfortable to creepy and skin-crawling. I'm now not only intrigued by him; I'm in complete awe.

Every beautiful thing in Carey's life was cruelly snatched away from him. He has suffered more loss than any man should ever have to go through. That alone would warrant him the excuse of being a heartless and callous man, but seeing him have enough compassion that he was concerned for my welfare shows he's far from being callous. There's a man inside that shell dying to break free. I want to help him do that.

"We need to tell Carey the truth," I mumble into Wesley's chest. My hot breath bounces off his cologne-scented neck and fans my heated face.

Wesley inhales a large breath of air that expands his chest. "I already have," he slowly breathes out, shocking me.

I pop my head up and peer into his eyes. The truth in his wholesome gaze instantly clears the guilt off my chest.

A new type of unease churns my stomach when Wesley asks, "Did Jenni tell you he threatened me today?"

"He did?"

A smug grin curls onto Wesley's lips. "Not in so many words, but the premise was there."

"Why would he do that?" I ask, shock evident in my tone.

"Because I provoked him." Wesley's voice is crammed with shame. "I pretty much said he was heartless."

"Wesley! Why would you say that?"

"Because it's my job to protect you, Poppet. If he reacted badly, I wouldn't let him within sniffing distance of you."

"*Again*. Within sniffing distance of me *again*." My lips twitch as I struggle to hold in my smile. Although mortified that Wesley feels so obliged to protect me, I also love it. It is nice having someone other than my dad in my corner.

Wesley's growl vibrates through my chest. "*Again*. Although I'm glad your sexual rut was *finally* taken care of—as you get a little bitchy when you're horny—I still can't believe you let a stranger into your hotel room. What's wrong with a little nookie in the backseat in the middle of suburbia?"

I slap his chest. "Umm... cops for one?"

A girly giggle parts my lips when Wesley's eyes roll skywards. "The only reason they would interrupt you and the gladiator getting hot and heavy is because they want a better angle."

"And popcorn," I add on. "Even the best movie in the world is crap without popcorn."

I gag. I need to limit the amount of time I'm spending with Jenni and Emily. They're wonderful girls, but one afternoon with them has already dragged my maturity back to an unacceptable level for a woman approaching thirty.

Ignoring the cringe crossing my face at the recognition I'm inching closer to the flirty thirties era of my life, I rest my head back onto Wesley's chest. "Why did you come clean with Carey if he threatened you? Wouldn't that set off your alarm bells, not appease them?"

Three lengthened heartbeats pass before Wesley confesses, "He came and saw me at the studio tonight."

Even beyond curious as to what occurred at their meeting, I can't get my mouth to cooperate with my brain to fire a range of questions at Wesley. Thankfully, I don't need to speak for him to hear my pleas.

"He has an odd way of showing it, but even hidden by the remorse in his eyes, I can tell he cares for you," Wesley eventually fills in. "It's clear he isn't a fan of mine, but he was man enough to push that to the side to ensure your safety was our utmost priority."

My heart stops beating. "Does that mean he knows what happened to me?"

"No," Wesley replies with a curt shake of his head. "I wondered the same thing when he was so pedantic about everything, but his desire isn't to take away your hurt, it is to ensure you don't get hurt. That's something only a man who assumes you haven't already been hurt would do."

Sweet relief engulfs me. It is short-lived when Wesley warns, "I still don't think he's the right man for you, Poppet. You have dreams you're striving to achieve. He's waiting for the day he can return to his family."

I tug my cardigan in tighter, pretending the chill running down my spine's from the pleasant summer breeze blowing off the ocean and not from Wesley's unease. "I don't believe that, Wesley. Yes, he's a man living with an immense amount of grief, but there's something in his eyes that begs for me to look deeper." I lift and lock my eyes with him. "If you had met him the night we shared, you wouldn't think the way you do. Carey's life is far from over. He just needs someone to show him that. He needs someone to believe in him like you believed in me."

"Like we believed in each other," Wesley corrects.

A stretch of silence passes between us. Although uncomfortable, words aren't needed to express what we are feeling. I understand Wesley's hesitation—wholeheartedly—but that doesn't lessen the overwhelming urge deep inside me to stand in Carey's corner as strongly as Wesley stands in mine. Wesley also understands this isn't something I'd undertake lightheartedly. I used to believe the only way I could protect my heart was by keeping it locked up and guarded. Carey has proven that isn't true. The only way I can keep my heart safe is by opening it, because sometimes the greatest lessons in life begin by taking a chance.

Reading the determination beaming out of me, Wesley says, "If you can look me in the eyes and tell me you're strong enough to take on a man with as much baggage as Carey has, I will support you, one hundred percent."

"You're assuming Carey wants me, which means you're forgetting he didn't return any of my calls or messages the past month." I loathe that my words come out needy. If I want any chance of forming a relationship with Carey, I need to be at my strongest. Not just for me, but for him as well.

Wesley smirks. "There's no cure for idiocy, but that isn't what we're discussing here. Carey wants you, but like half the male population, he let his ego steer him in the wrong direction."

Even with my brows stitching in confusion, I manage to jest, "Half?"

Wesley rolls his eyes. "All right, *most* of the male population." He adjusts his position so he can see my face without needing to remove me from being glued to his chest. "This kills me to admit, but my hottie radar was on the blink last month," he confesses, sending my heart rate skyrocketing. "Carey was outside your apartment that afternoon."

"Then why didn't he come in?" My voice is laced with confusion and a smidge of excitement.

Before Wesley can reply, my own idea formulates. "He saw us together..." I feel the blood draining from my face. "And he assumed we were a couple."

"Bingo," Wesley confirms.

I grit my teeth before slapping his chest.

"Hey!" Wesley wails. "He's the one who fucked up, so why am I getting slapped?"

I slant my head to the side and cock my brow. "He saw us together and thought we were a couple."

Wesley nods like I'm asking a question. I wasn't.

"Then you went and added salt to his wounds by saying we *were* a couple."

Wesley chuckles. "Salt to his wounds? It was one night, Poppet. That's not long enough for wounds to be inflicted. From the cute little moans I've heard coming out of your room the past three years, I have no doubt I'd put a big tick next to your name in my little black book, but open wounds? *Please.*"

I slap him again. He laughs even louder.

After laughing so hard, little tears form in the corner of his eyes, he gathers me back into his arms. His heart is racing even faster now than it was earlier. "Are you strong enough to handle this, Gem?" he asks, his voice the sincerest I've ever heard.

"If he'd give me a chance, yes," I respond, speaking directly from my heart.

Wesley pinches my chin and forces my eyes to his. "The rejection when his memories become too great for him to ignore? The wondering if he's only with you because you were his second choice? Sharing his heart with another woman? Are you sure you're strong enough to handle that?"

"Yes," I reply again without pause for hesitation. "A broken heart never mends, but it can swell to accommodate more people in it," I quote, referencing a book I read during our plane trip to Hopeton. "Carey will never stop loving his wife and son, but that is one of the reasons I'm so drawn to him. Imagine being loved by someone so fiercely they'll never forget you. I want that."

"You deserve that." He draws me into his chest. My heart squeezes when he adds on, "If this is what you want, I'll support you, Gem, but, if he destroys you, I'll take him down. He may be big, but that don't mean shit when it comes to protecting my Lil Lady."

I tighten my grip around his waist. "Oh, Wesley. If I didn't want the neighbors to get the wrong idea, I could kiss you right now."

"When have the opinions of others ever bothered you?" Wesley questions before smacking his hands on the side of my face and planting a big sloppy kiss directly on my lips.

Pulling back from my gapped mouth, Wesley snickers, "Good luck explaining that," with a waggle of his brows.

Before I can request an explanation for his odd behavior, the noise of tires crunching under gravel sounds through my ears. My pulse quickens when I swing my gaze sideways and spot Carey's Camaro rolling down the driveway. From the heavy groove between his eyes and his hard-lined lips, I'm certain he witnessed my exchange with Wesley.

Snarling, I return my eyes to Wesley. "You're a butthole."

Wesley grins. "Hey, I said I'd support you; that doesn't mean I'll make it easy for him," he advises, not the slightest bit intimidated by my furious scowl.

After winking cockily at Carey exiting his car, Wesley walks into our rental cabin, disgracefully leaving me to clean up his dirty work.

The wooden stairs of the cabin creak, protesting about Carey's well-built frame when he climbs them. "Hey," I greet him. Just like earlier today, my one word expresses way more than it should.

"Hey," Carey replies, his word as ruffled as my nerves.

Leaving my dignity somewhere between New York and Ravenshoe, I observe, "We can pretend we're strangers, but that's pretty pointless. I've seen you naked."

Goddammit! That came out sounding way more like a creepy peeping tom than the witty sophisticated lady I was aiming for.

I loosen the invisible noose around my neck when Carey's beautiful laughter fills the awkward silence between us. Now instead of my cheeks being flamed with stupidity, I'm flustered with desire. Carey can fill a suit like no man I've seen, and his face is the type sculptors dream of carving, but his laugh, my god, it hits every one of my hot buttons. Everything is better when it is surrounded by laughter, even a gladiator-sized man with a locked-up heart.

When Carey's laughter simmers, I question, "Can I get you a drink? I have beer, wine. . ." My words trail off when I spot him shaking his head.

"I'm not here on a personal level," he admits, his tone low and unsure.

I try to mask my disappointment. I miserably fail.

"Oh," I mumble, "umm… then what can I do you for?" My words come out shaky and hindered with unwarranted bitchiness.

I should have known Wesley's admission wouldn't change anything between Carey and me. He made it very clear last month that our night together was a one night only affair, so I have no reason to be annoyed, but I can't help it. How can he not feel the connection between us? The earth moves under my feet every time he's near me. Is it not the same for him?

Carey coughs to clear his throat. "Cormack mentioned that you want to photograph the band in a more natural setting than your studio."

I nod. "Staged shoots aren't my style. I work with natural light and textures. Props hide a person's soul. By placing someone in their natural habitat, I expose not only their shell, but their insides as well. You can't hide who you truly are when you're naked and exposed."

Most of my statement refers to my photography career. The last sentence was for Carey.

"With the band's success, organizing an event like that takes time. It's not something their security team could organize on short notice," Carey replies. Although his tone is the same deep timbre it always is, there's more roughness to his words that reveals he knows part of my declaration was for him.

I pat the seat next to me, offering for him to sit. Even beyond riveted by him, photography is one of my greatest loves. It is so strong, I can set aside the feeling of rejection maiming my heart to ensure the vision I've conjured for Rise Up doesn't suffer.

Once Carey takes the seat next to me, I explain, "I don't need to have the band in public; I just need them in their natural environment. A place they feel comfortable in. Where they can be the men they were before they were famous." I tuck my feet under my bottom and swivel so I'm facing Carey front on. "I want to see their world through your eyes."

Carey's brows bunch together.

"That bad?" I quip.

Carey smirks. "It's been a rough few months."

I'm tempted to ask if his statement is referring to himself or the band, but I don't need to. I know whom it refers to. His honest eyes expose the truth. He was referring to himself.

"I'm sorry for what I said to you at brunch," I blubber out before I have the chance to stop my words.

The color in Carey's face drains as he briefly nods.

"But I'm not sorry for kissing you. Or for the night we spent together. I'll never be sorry about either of those things." My words come out in a frantic rush, like I've suddenly been engulfed with a bad case of verbal diarrhea. "That night gave me back portions of myself I never thought I'd see again. I'll never regret any time we've spent together."

A small cluster of hope forms in my heart when Carey faintly murmurs, "Me neither."

Acting like he didn't just spark a flame in my aching womb, he stands from his seat and peers down at me. Even with a vast range of emotions taking away the effervescence of his eyes, they're still breathtakingly beautiful.

"I'll have to discuss it with Cormack, but I think I have a solution for your predicament," he advises.

I issue him my thanks with a smile.

"I'll call you later if everything works out?" The unease in his voice makes it come out sounding like a question.

I leap up from my chair. "That will be great. Let me grab you my number."

My brisk pace to the door stops when Carey sheepishly admits, "I already have it from when you texted me last month."

Although I can appreciate his honesty, it doesn't ease the brutal sting of rejection. The twisting of my stomach calms when he leans into my side and presses a kiss to the edge of my mouth. "It is not the environment that makes a picture, Gemma. It is the person standing behind the camera. You forcing me out of my natural environment exposed the real me, and you didn't have a camera wrapped around your neck."

Not waiting for me to reply, he spins on his heels and ambles to his car. Just before he enters, he lifts his fired-with-hope eyes to me. "I'll see you around?"

Biting on the inside of my cheek to hide my smile, I nod. "But only if I don't see you first."

I wait for the taillights of his Camaro to disappear from view before walking into the cabin. My steps are sluggish, weighed down by the conflicting array of emotions swirling in my stomach. Although Carey said he wasn't here on a personal level, it felt like a personal visit. Everything he discussed could have been handled over the phone. A fourteen-mile trip wasn't necessary... *unless he wanted to see me?*

My confusion switches to hope when Wesley says, "First thing tomorrow, I'm going to the store to buy popcorn. That was one of the best firework shows I've seen in a long time."

"Do you think?"

Wesley smiles a grin that should be gracing the fashion magazines of the world while nodding. "He wasn't here to discuss business. He was here to ensure this cabin has more than one bedroom. He wants you nearly as badly as I want to keep him away from you."

"Give him a chance before you woo him with your martial art skills," I plead, my words tainted with laughter.

After being approached on the street by the gorgeous instructor from our local martial arts class, Wesley signed up for three months' worth of lessons. He lasted five minutes. The time it took for him to see the wedding band wrapped around the handsome man's hand. Flirting seems to be the latest marketing craze in New York this year.

"If I were to give him a real chance, it wouldn't be my martial arts impressing him." Wesley waggles his brows before adding on, "It'd be my—"

I throw one of the scatter cushions from the couch into his face before he can finish his sentence. "The only person in this room who gets to wrestle Carey's anaconda is me," I warn, my tone half-serious, half-playful.

"If I weren't worried about your dad having your phone tapped, I could offer up some suggestions on how we could both wrangle Carey's beast, but not wanting to find myself buried in a shallow ditch, I'll keep my dirty thoughts to myself."

Concerns that Wesley's taunt may be factually based race to the forefront of my mind when my cell phone shrills with my dad's private ringtone not even two seconds later.

Wesley hooks his thumb to his room. "I'm going to say my final goodbyes."

Laughing, I answer my phone. "Hey, Dad, I was just about to call you."

CHAPTER 21

HAWKE

I know my grief is a sickening mix of remorse and guilt—I just had no clue it also made me a coward.

CHAPTER 22

GEMMA

"Will this work?"

I crank my neck to Carey as a grin tugs my lips high. "It's perfect," I breathe out in a long, breathless pant that mimics the moans I make in the bedroom. "And a little freaky," I add on, struggling to ignore the way his lazy smile at my wide-eyed response causes an ache between my legs.

I twist my lips and turn to face the cabin Cormack rented for Wesley and me to use during our two-month long stay in Ravenshoe. "If I'd known Noah and Emily lived in the cabin next door, I would have taken sneaky shots of them. With the going rate sitting at a few thousand per picture, I'd never have to work again," I jest.

Carey laughs, enhancing the lively throb surging through my body. It is well known that my dad is a wealthy man, but his wealth doesn't just stem from racing; it is also based on his very shrewd business mind. Considering I'm his only child, everyone assumes my personal wealth is attached to his. That isn't true. I don't spend a single penny I haven't earned myself. And although my bank account show I could retire at any time I see fit, I choose to work. Not just because photography is my life, but because I refuse to live off money tainted with deception and malice. Truth doesn't cost you a thing, but a lie can cost you everything. I learned that the hard way.

After granting my eyes request for one last gawk at Carey standing at the edge of an infinity pool that seamlessly merges into the brilliant blue ocean of Bronte's Peak, I bend down to fiddle with my camera bag. My heart rate picks up when I feel the heat of Carey's gaze on the bare skin high on my thighs. The late afternoon summer sun has made the temperature so stifling, I'm tempted to jump into the pool fully clothed. I've opted for a pair of frilly-edged denim shorts and a white and blue checkered shirt, and although I'm not representing my company to the best of my ability, I'll let it slide since I've gained Carey's attention. *I'd sell part of my soul for another night with him.*

Swallowing my absurd inner monologue, I gather four rolls of film out of my bag and slip them into my pocket. In the reflection of Carey's sunglasses, I notice the sun is bouncing off my blonde locks, shrouding me in a golden halo, and my shoulders are already sun-kissed. I'm not the only one taking advantage of the sun. Carey's black suit jacket has been removed, the sleeves of his shirt have been rolled up to his elbows, and the top two buttons of his shirt are undone, erotically showcasing a chest that should be as illegal as my shameful ogling.

"What do you need?" Carey asks, assuming I'm staring at him because I require his attention. I do need his assistance, but not with anything appropriate to demand while we are both working.

When Carey's brow arches higher than the rim of his glasses, shamefully calling me out, I mumble, "You." *If he can already read my private thoughts, why not just say them out loud?*

Carey smirks a wicked grin that sends a rush of desire to my throbbing core. "I meant what did you need from the guys?" he clarifies, his deep voice adding to my excitement.

"Five minutes alone with you," I wish, letting my unbridled hankering speak on my behalf.

When the heat radiating from Carey's eyes scorches my body more than the searing sun, it dawns on me that I said my naughty thoughts out loud so he could hear them. His gaze spears me in place, sending my libido into haywire. I rub my thighs together, hoping to ease the insane throb his sunglasses-concealed glare incites.

My awkward squirming halts when a rowdy chuckle comes from behind my shoulder. After masking my excitement with a neutral expression, I spin around to face the ruckus. The four band members of Rise Up are standing behind Carey and me, watching what I assumed was a private exchange. Their eyes are eager, their mouths quirked into mischievous grins. They look a cross between flabbergasted and fascinated.

Pretending my flaming cheeks are from the sweltering sun, I say, "Act exactly how you would any other day you're here. We're not shooting the cover today; I'm just capturing your everyday life."

The temperature rises even more when Slater shrugs his shoulders before whipping off his shirt and dive bombing into the pool.

"Dear Mother of Joseph," I mumble when Noah, Marcus and Nick soon follow Slater's lead. If I knew that was all I needed to say to be inundated with rippled abs and banging guns, I would have said it hours ago.

As the bandmates frolic in the pool, I snap several candid shots of them while striving to ignore Carey's watchful eye. Because his eyes are covered with reflective sunglasses, I can't tell if he's watching me with zeal or disinterest. I'm hoping it is interest, but with pendulum-swinging moods and a demeanor I can't read, I can only hope that is the case.

By the time I've gone through half a dozen rolls of film, the band soon forgets I'm here. Now the real magic happens. Gone is the pop group whose bank balances are rocketing into the next galaxy even faster than their songs are shooting up the charts; it's been replaced with a group of friends spending their Friday afternoon lazing by the pool.

By the time the sun has become a forgotten memory, I've run out of film, and my feet are aching. Although some of the photos I've taken will never be released, I'm sure the band will treasure them for years to come. I caught how Nick runs his hand down the side of Jenni's inflamed cheeks after he playfully teases her. I seized the moment Noah fell asleep on a lounge chair with his two-month-old daughter, Maddie, lying on his chest. I netted for eternity Slater peering out into the ocean deep in thought, and how Marcus seems like a solitary man, but his eyes expose he's so much more.

I even managed to capture a sneaky picture of Carey holding Jenni and Nick's eight-month-old son, Jasper. When Jasper crawled over to play with the shoelaces on his military boots, Carey peered around to ensure no one was watching before he cradled Jasper in his arms. Their embrace only lasted long enough for Jasper to cover Carey's cheek with a sloppy kiss, but it was an event no time will ever erase from my memory.

"How come you use film?"

Holding back my gasp of shock that someone snuck up on me, I lift my eyes from my camera bag. A pair of intense green eyes meets my curious gaze. They're brimming with silent apologies for scaring me.

"Film is light; digital is electricity," I answer, my shaky words divulging the hammering of my heart. "I'll most likely use a digital camera for the album cover, but for the commemorative photos, I prefer to use film. Nothing compares to holding an image in your hand. You can't touch and smell a photo through a monitor."

Marcus nods. "Kind of like people. Internet dating sucks."

I laugh. "Yes. I'm glad I'm past the era of internet dating."

"You're a good match for Hawke," he mutters after running his hand over the scruff of his chin. Spotting my shocked expression, he adds on, "He also acts years older than he is."

"Events in life age you," I mumble before I can stop my words.

"That they do," he responds. From his tone, I know he isn't just referring to Carey and me. He has experienced his own demons. "I'm sorry for whatever happened to you that caused the pain in your eyes, but you shouldn't see it as the end of your life; you should see it as the beginning. Every tragedy has a lesson equal in significance to its heartbreak."

I peer at him in silence, shocked the words of a stranger can spark such a response from me. Although I'd never wish what I went through on anyone, what Wesley said last month was true. I wouldn't be the woman I am now without leaping over the obstacles my life has thrown at me. I just wish I handled the aftermath of my attack with the attitude I have now. If I had done that, those closest to me wouldn't still be hurting years later.

Marcus rubs his hands together. "That's enough of this buzzkiller discussion. What's your drink of choice?"

My first thoughts are to decline his offer. My brain has other ideas, blurting out, "Wine," before I have the chance to cite an objection.

When I finish zipping up my camera bag, Marcus removes it from my grasp and slings it over his shoulder. "Go find a vacant seat around the fire pit; I'll return with a bottle of wine and some dessert," he suggests, nudging his head to the fire pit the rest of his bandmates and partners are gathered around. "I promise, none of them bite. Except perhaps Slater, but he'll do it as gently as possible."

I don't know why, but the first image that rushed into my mind from Marcus's playful taunt was his deliciously plump lips biting smooth, milky skin. My intuition tells me there's something more to that man than his humble personality and pulse-racing good looks.

Just like it did around the picnic table earlier today, the conversation between the band members and their friends flows as easy as water out of a tap. They all appear so comfortable around each other, which is a rare treat when you have so many strong personalities. Even Wesley has settled into the group dynamic without the awkwardness that plagued him last month.

Five minutes after I take an empty seat between Wesley and Jenni, Marcus exits the cabin. A grin curls on my lips when I notice what he's holding in his hands. It isn't the bottle of wine causing my girly response, it is the fact he's dragged a reluctant Carey away from his post on the front porch. From the mischievous gleam brightening Marcus's already glistening eyes, I can tell the reasoning behind his sudden interest in Carey. *He's bringing me my dessert.*

"Jasper fell asleep hours ago." Jenni stands from her seat so Marcus can shove Carey into her spot next to me.

Marcus's abrupt movements cause the back of Carey's fingers to brush the skin high on my bare thigh. When a flash of a memory from our night together rockets to the forefront of my mind, I writhe in my seat, doing anything to lessen the jolt of ecstasy sparking my core. My lips part as I gasp in greedy breaths. That night. . . my god! Those fingers are magic. Long enough to reach the sweet spot inside me only a handful of men have found, and thick enough to ensure I'll never forget feeling them. *Magic.*

My juvenile response to Carey's simplistic touch fades when he notices my awkward squirming. The smug look on his face when he runs the same set of fingers I was daydreaming about down my flushed cheek—god! If I weren't worried about rejection dousing the fire raging in my womb, I'd give my best shot to extend that cockiness to his guilt-riddled eyes. I hate that he feels guilt when he's with me, but I'm also grateful I can make him feel anything. *Something is better than nothing.*

My eyes shift sideways when Slater brutally gags. His reaction isn't from eating Noah's beef patties that were charcoal on the outside and undercooked on the inside. It is from the throaty moan Nick released when Jenni slipped into his lap. With Carey taking up the last seat around the fire pit, Jenni presumably had no other option, but after photographing the band for the past six hours, I know that isn't the case. Jenni and Nick are an extremely affectionate couple who have no qualms about displaying their fondness for each other in front of an audience.

"I'd sign up for another six weeks of rehab just to erase that noise from my mind," Slater pushes out through a gag.

Jenni's cheeks turn the color of the embers in the fire when Carey backs up Slater's pledge. "I'd work for free for a year if Cormack would approve my request of placing *at least* three floors between our hotel rooms when we go on tour."

Everyone circling the fire pit breaks into laughter, including Jenni and Nick. I'm not shocked by their response. The band and their partners appear to have a relationship similar to Wesley and me. They can be serious when they need to be, but for the most part, they're each other's biggest supporters.

Bristling with happiness, I tilt toward Carey's side. My palms grow sweaty when Carey inhales a sharp breath from my closeness. Clearly, I'm not the only one affected by brief, feather-like touches.

"That wasn't very nice," I mutter softly.

He leans in closer, filling the minuscule speck of air between us with his unique virile scent. My heart kicks into overdrive when he mutters, "That's what she gets for trying to set us up."

I connect my heavy-hooded gaze with a pair of eyes that are even more dazzling than the flames dancing in the fire. "Is that a bad thing?"

I hold my breath, preparing my lungs for a hard knock to my ego. Air whooshes out my gaped mouth when Carey surprises me by timidly shaking his head.

"Then I'll be sure to send Jenni a box of chocolates tomorrow to show my appreciation." I'm shocked my mouth cooperates with the instructions my lust-driven heart is issuing.

Carey doesn't respond to my remark, but the corners of his lips curl into one of his wish-granting smiles. I need to be careful. Not only is every second I spend with him making me cash in my genie wishes at a record pace, it's also encouraging my unhealthy obsession with him. Usually, I'm not attracted to men I date until I feel a strong physical connection with them. Those rules don't apply to Carey. My rules are nonexistent when it comes to him.

While sipping on the glass of wine Marcus handed me thirty minutes ago, I struggle to ignore my body's awareness of Carey's closeness as I participate in a range of conversations being held around the fire pit. I'm glad I didn't let my silly phobia of not leaving New York stop me from journeying to this area of the country. Bronte's Peak is gorgeous, but it can't compete with the people living here.

Two glasses of wine and several belly-crunching laughs later, Jenni locks her glistening light blue eyes with me. "Truth or dare?" she asks, her eyes flaring with mischievousness.

"Oh, no, I'm happy sitting this one out," I reply. Although I would have enjoyed games like this back in my teen years, that desire packed up and left town a long time ago.

My strong stance falters when Wesley discreetly nudges me with his elbow. I grit my teeth, loathing that my inability to keep my tipsy mouth shut revealed my latent desire to experience the teen parties my homeschooled persona missed out on.

"Truth," I mumble, wiping the disappointment off Jenni's face.

Jenni and Emily clap their hands together, making me feel like I've stepped back ten years in time. "Best and worst lay," Jenni questions, waggling her perfectly manicured brows.

My eyes bulge. Not just because of her personal question, but because Carey stiffened enough his knee brushed the bare skin on my thigh for the third time in the past five minutes, sending my body's awareness of him into meltdown.

Ignoring the hairs on my arms prickling in excitement, I answer Jenni's question. The first half of her question is easy for me to answer—it fires off my tongue without pause for consideration. It was the night I spent with Carey. Although I keep my answer to a bare minimum, I have no doubt he knows it was the night we shared. If the whole mysterious stranger element of my story isn't enough of a clue, the mention of the race track is a sure-fire indication.

I stop trying to secure a sneaky glance at Carey's reaction at being my best lay when Jenni questions, "And your worst?"

My hands become clammy as my knees rattle. I attempt to shake off the horrible bile crawling up my esophagus by swallowing several times in a row, but nothing I do rids me of the despair that's haunted me every day the past six years.

For the first time in years, I flinch when Wesley curls his arm around my shoulders. I can feel Carey's concerned eyes boring into me, but I don't dare look at him. I can't. If his eyes hold even the smallest smidge of pity, all the ground I regained from our night together could vanish. That's not a risk I'm willing to take.

"Come on, Gem, don't be shy," Wesley mutters, his tone hinting at a joke. I know he isn't goading me. That is something Wesley would never do. He would never turn my nightmare into a joke. "You remember that guy you told me about years ago? The one who thought body parts were on a menu, because once he finished, he always said—"

"Compliments to the chef," we recite at the same time. Wesley's voice is firm and clear, mine is nowhere near as strong.

The laughter that roars around the fire curtails the shakes impeding my body. I swallow down the bile sitting at the back of my throat before lifting my eyes to Jenni when she says, "You'd swear he thought your . . ." she stops talking and waves her hand over the lower half of my body, "was a buffet table."

"He did," I retort, my words half-shaky, half-playful. "He only said it after burping. Like he literally just sat down for a meal. . ." My words trail off when I realize my panicked state has me revealing more than I intended.

I keep my massively dilated gaze front and center, not the slightest bit tempted to gauge Carey's reaction to the second half of my confession. My attempts at acting ignorant only last as long as it takes for Carey to excuse himself from the gathering and pace toward the edge of the property that showcases the coastline of Bronte's Peak in all its glory.

Over the next twenty minutes, the heaviness on my chest lightens as the Rise Up crew continue with their game of truth or dare. I try to participate to the best of my ability, but my constant sneaky glances at Carey dampen my efforts.

I tilt toward Wesley. "Are you ready to head out soon? My feet are killing me."

My feet are screaming in pain, but that's just an excuse I'm using to talk to Carey. My dad's family is proof that there's no better way to spark a conversation than to say goodbye. I swear every time they visited when I was younger, hours of the day were wasted chatting in the driveway.

"Yeah," Wesley replies with a concise nod. "I'm dying to call home and tell them about my week."

I snuggle into his neck, taking a moment to bask in the excitement beaming out of him. I'm so glad his career is progressing forward in leaps and bounds. He deserves the recognition for his years of dedication to the music industry more than anyone.

"Give me a few minutes to say goodbye to Carey, then I'll meet you at the gate," I suggest, nudging my head to the dividing fence between Noah's property and the cabin Cormack rented for us.

I laugh when Wesley says, "From what I've been told, you only need five."

After ramming my elbow into his ribs, I rise from my seat. Just before I pace away, Wesley seizes my wrist. "Chin up, Poppet. He wasn't looking at you with anything but concern."

My heart swells, beyond pleased he knows me well enough to know where my thoughts drifted without me saying a word. "I love the way you love me."

Wesley smiles so broadly, the moon no longer exists. "I love the way you let me love you."

Grinning, I stride toward Carey with a newfound spring in my step. I've learned a lot the past three years, but my biggest lessons were discovering that my past can only affect my present if I let it, and only I have the power to influence my future.

The crackling of energy overtakes the sound of waves breaking on the shore when Carey lifts and locks his eyes with me. I can tell just by looking at him that he's still hurting from losing his family, but that isn't the only flare of emotion I see. I know he's interested in me. I just don't know if he wants to forget his past or create a future that yields his interest.

"Hey," I greet him, my one word breathy.

"Hey," he replies.

An awkward grin tugs my lips high. "One day we'll get past these lame greetings."

My smile turns genuine when Carey replies, "God, I hope so – this is fucking awkward."

"Not as awkward as being eyeballed from afar," I quip, gesturing my head to the fire pit. I don't need to crank my neck to know we have gathered numerous pairs of eyes. I can feel their intrusive stares.

Carey laughs a scoffing chuckle. "True."

A zing of pleasure jolts up my arm when he encloses his hand over mine and guides us into the unlit pool area. Even surrounded by darkness, I'm not afraid. Astonishingly, I don't remember what fear feels like when I'm in Carey's presence, which is both a terrifying and heartening notion.

Once we're shadowed by the pool patio, our eyes meet. Something so great passes between us, it forces words out of my mouth I never wanted to say to him. "Ask me anything you want to know. I'll answer any of your questions."

I stare at him with my stomach twisted in knots, my hands shaking. Every therapist will tell you that admission is the first step to recovery. Even if it is true, it doesn't make it easy to do.

Carey scrubs his hand across his chin and asks, "You described our night together?" The unease of his words make his statement sound like a question.

Shocked by the simplicity of his question, I nod. I truly expected him to start with the big hitters and work his way down. I never suspected he'd begin our conversation at a point that instantly eased my hesitation.

"Why?" he asks, shock evident in his tone.

I shrug my shoulders, aiming to lessen the impact of my reply. "Because it was the truth."

When my confession gains me nothing but silence, I add on, "That night was wonderful, Carey. A night I'll treasure for years to come." I throw all my dignity out the window when I say, "A night I'd give anything to experience again."

I take a step closer to him, fortifying the undeniable connection between us. It is so strong, even a man trapped in the hell of grief would be able to feel it. I stand so close to him, my wine-scented breath bounces off his lips and fans my mouth. When he lifts his hand and places it on the edge of my jaw, the muscles in my cheek twitch. He sweeps his thumb across my cheek, removing the invisible tearstains my watering eyes are begging to release. The gentleness of his touch and the concern in his eyes tell me he didn't miss my earlier panic, he just chose to leave the decision up to me on how much I'm willing to share. This makes me like him even more.

I nuzzle into his hand, ecstatic to once again feel his skin on mine.

Reading the relief in my eyes, Carey mutters, "I'm broken, Gem. You can't fix broken," ever so quietly. The pain in his words adds to his confession. He truly believes he's beyond fixing.

"Nothing is unfixable. You just haven't found the person holding the right type of glue." I balance on my tippy toes so we share the same breath. "Give me the chance to prove that to you," I shamefully beg.

My every wish, desire and want is granted when several seconds later, the most delicious pair of lips I've ever tasted push against mine. Carey strokes his tongue along the ridge of my lips before sliding it inside my mouth in a slow and controlled lick. I fall into his kiss, carried away by the sensuality of it. Carey knows how to kiss. Contrary to the lie I told last month, he adds the perfect amount of tongue and pace to have my toes curling and my libido skyrocketing. I could garner a lifetime of treasured memories from just one of his kisses and erase a mountainload of nightmarish ones.

When a rowdy cheer pummels our eardrums, Carey pulls away. I try to hold in my whiny moan about the loss of his contact, but my mouth relinquishes it before I have the chance to fully shut it down.

A grin curls on my kiss-swollen lips when Slater yells out, "She only requested five minutes alone with you, GI Joe, not an in-depth frisk."

My small smile turns into an idiotic grin when Carey's threatening charge towards Slater has him diving out of his seat and hotfooting in to the cabin. "Abort mission!" Slater chuckles.

Happy he has subdued the cheeky banter firing from the men of Rise Up, Carey returns his eyes to me. After rubbing his thumb over my kiss-swollen lips, he says, "I'll see you around."

Silly giddiness clusters in my womb as I reply, "Not if I see you first."

As much as it kills me to do, I pace toward the gate Wesley has his hip propped against. The cheeky grin on his face indicates he not only witnessed the exchange between Carey and me, but his concerns about Carey are weakening.

"I either need a few minutes alone or a cold shower," Wesley jests before curling his arm around my shoulders. "That kiss was nearly hotter than my wicked thoughts of seeing Emily and Jenni make out." He moans in a way only appropriate for the bedroom.

I slap him on the chest. "You've seen how protective Noah is of Emily. He'd have a coronary."

"Yeah because all the blood in his body would be rushing to his cock," Wesley fires back, laughing.

When we merge onto the patio of our cabin, I swing my eyes back to Noah and Emily's pool house. My heart beats triple time when I spot Carey still standing in the same spot I left him. Childishly, I wave at him. My pulse surges into dangerous territory when he waves back. *Yes!*

CHAPTER 23

HAWKE

I should feel bad for kissing Gemma. Guilt should be making it hard for me to breathe, but all I'm feeling is hope—hope that I get to do it again.

> *Love and heartache do not define you.*
> *They are a part of your story.*
>
> *-Author unknown.*

CHAPTER 24

GEMMA

Music blasts my eardrums as I move through a crowded living room jam-packed with Ravenshoe's finest. The scent of sweat-slicked skin on overheated bodies lingers into my nostrils, adding to the horrific thump of my head. When news of the band's upcoming tour circulated through the town, Ravenshoe locals got together to send the boys off with a mighty bang, bang being the prime word for my pounding head. Throw together Ravenshoe's stifling temperatures, dozens of horny young adults, and a DJ whose idea of party music is soundtracks with nothing but bass, and you have the perfect recipe for a migraine.

In my attempt to dull the ache, I push through the throng of people grinding against each other to reach a quieter region of the party. My lungs are replenished with fresh air when I enter the back patio of Nick and Jenni's modest four-bedroom house. Although there are still a decent number of people mingling on the manicured lawn, it is nothing compared to the numerous bodies lining every inch of the floor space inside.

I loosen the strap of my camera so I can rub a kink in the nape of my neck. While relieving the tension of a long day, a flicker of light in the back corner of the property obtains my attention. Okay,

I'll be honest. It wasn't just the flicker of light, it was the quickest glance of a profile standing behind the light that secured my devotion. *Carey.*

The blaring music roaring out of the speakers dulls with every step I take down the paved path. When I stop on the stoop of the pool house I saw Carey in, I run my hands over my hair and ensure my clothing is sitting right before raising my hand to tap on the glass sliding door. My knock stops midair when the door suddenly slides open, startling me.

"Hey," Carey greets me before propping his shoulder onto the doorjamb.

His efforts to ease our awkward greetings have improved dramatically compared to mine. I don't even bother issuing him a greeting. My eyes are too fixated on categorizing every dip and crevice of his bare torso to articulate a response.

After absorbing his unbuttoned business shirt and bare feet, I drift my eyes past his shoulder. "Are you busy?" I cringe, loathing that my voice comes out tainted with suspicion.

My eyes rocket back to Carey when a rare smile etches onto his mouth. "No," he replies with a curt shake of his head. "Did you want to come in?"

"Do you want me to come in?"

Carey responds to my pathetically woeful question by waving his hand across the front of his body. Ignoring the way my arm brushing past his nearly naked torso sends my libido into overdrive, I pace into the small but homey space.

"Is this your place?" I question after taking in the well-designed in-law's suite with muscular features and smooth artistic lines. The space isn't overly large, but it is well furnished.

Nodding, Carey walks to a small bar set up between two antique bookshelves. "Isaac wants me to stay on site when Nick and Jenni are home." A grin tugs my lips high when he grimaces. "There was no way in hell I'm sleeping inside—their walls are paper thin—this was Isaac's compromise."

"It's nice," I reply, my voice conveying my honesty. "Private too," I continue when I notice he has his own entrance attached to a back alley.

Acting like I can't feel the chill my brief glance in the alleyway caused, I turn my eyes to Carey. I smile and shake my head when he soundlessly offers me a drink by shaking the whiskey decanter in his hand.

"I wouldn't say no to a bottle of water if you have it, though? My head is thumping."

Not speaking, Carey sets down the whiskey decanter and walks into a sleek, manly kitchen on his right. He returns not even two seconds later with a bottle of water in one hand and headache tablets in another.

Smiling at his thoughtfulness, I accept the items. After swallowing down three tablets and half a bottle of water, I connect my eyes with Carey. "Why are you half-naked?" I stumble out before I can stop myself. My response can't be helped. My brain has turned to mush just from spending the last thirty seconds ogling his rock-hard six pack.

I suspect my question will have Carey tugging at the edges of his shirt. What I didn't fathom was that he would thrust his hands into his pockets—exposing even more of his deliciously taut skin—before answering, "I was about to take a shower."

Wickedly dirty images of us in the shower rush to the forefront of my mind. They all involve Carey and me in a vast range of Kama Sutra positions, and it reminds that I should look at doing some Yoga classes in the near future. There's no use conjuring up advanced sex positions if you can't even handle the Downward Dog.

Mortified at my lack of self-control, I stray my eyes to the floor. "Well, I better get going so you can have your shower." The throatiness of my words gives away my excitement. "Thanks for the water."

With my gaze planted on the ground, I make a beeline for the door. Well, I assume I'm heading towards the door as I have no clue which direction the exit is. My frenetic speed slows when Carey asks, "Do you like pizza, Gemma? I just placed an order if you want to stay for a slice?"

Fighting the urge to do a little jig, I reply, "Obviously, I love pizza. That's why I had to wear those hideous panties you shredded off my body last month. They help keep the cheese on my backside instead of on my thighs. Don't you know big booties are all the rage right now?" My mouth gapes, shell-shocked at the bluntness of my reply. The only wish I'm making when I blow out my birthday candles next year is the wish for a filter.

My panic recedes when Carey's beautiful laugh sounds through my ears. Not wanting to miss witnessing the core-crunching event, I snap my eyes to him. Just as I suspected, his beautiful smile clears away my insecurities.

"If you think that's funny, you should see me trying to get into them. Achieving world peace would be easier."

I feel like I've hit a home run in the playoffs when Carey laughs again. *God he has a beautiful laugh.* Manly with an edge of huskiness that hits every one of my hot buttons.

Once his laughter settles down, he locks his glistening eyes with me. "Make yourself comfortable. I'll grab a quick shower and be out in a few."

It's a painstaking fight, but I manage to hold in my inappropriate reply that I'd prefer to join him in the shower than sit on his fancy couch alone.

Awkwardly pretending I can't feel his heated gaze, I pick up one of the car magazines off his coffee table and sit down. I stop aimlessly flicking through the magazine when Carey calls my name. "If the pizza man comes, my wallet is on the coffee table," he advises, nudging his head to his wallet.

"Okay," I reply, smiling.

Twenty minutes later, I've flicked through every magazine on Carey's coffee table, and adjusted the bracelets lining my wrist numerous times.

"How long does it take to shower?" I mumble to myself, my words snarky.

I'm not annoyed at Carey; I'm peeved at myself. The past twenty minutes have been pure torture. Imagine knowing a gladiator-sized man with an anaconda cock you know intimately—and would do anything to experience that level of intimacy again—is naked only mere feet from you, yet you can't do anything about it because you have morals and principles to abide by. It is days like today I wish I was even ten percent of the woman I used to be. That Gemma wouldn't have doubted the chemistry bristling between us. She would have seen an opening and ran for it.

Tortured—there's no other word to describe how I'm feeling right now.

Doing anything to quell my desire to interrupt Carey in the shower, I snag his wallet off the coffee table and crank it open. A chuckle parts my mouth when I see his horrible license photo. Carey is a beautiful man, but this photo is atrocious. My gaped mouth snaps shut when I notice his date of birth. It is the same day as mine: June sixth.

Feeling guilty for prying, I close his wallet. Before it fully snaps shut, the overhead lighting in Carey's house reflects on a shimmering of color peeking out behind a stash of crumpled bills. Curious to discover if he has replenished his condom stash we depleted our first night together, I pry his wallet open further.

"Oh my god," I stammer out, my words choked by remorse.

A wave of emotion slams into me when I carefully open his wallet more, fully revealing the black and white image hidden between notes. My breathing pans out as I cautiously remove the picture. Even faded, it doesn't take a genius to realize what this photo is. It is an ultrasound picture of Carey's son, Malcolm. From the small portion of white writing still visible on the edge of the black surface, it appears it was taken mere weeks before his death. It is a cruel, yet beautiful reminder of what Carey had and lost.

As I stare at the image of a little boy whose life ended way too prematurely, an idea formulates in my head. I dump Carey's wallet on the coffee table and race out of his suite. The heavy stomps of my steps as I run toward the main residence threatens to spill the tears welling in my eyes, but thankfully, even with my heart hammering against my ribs, they stay at bay.

When I reach the spare room on the second floor of Nick and Jenni's residence, I'm wheezing and out of breath. My hand shakes when I place the ultrasound picture on a white dresser before yanking my camera bag off the floor. No care is taken with my beloved equipment as I search for an item generally stashed in the bottom of the bag. It is not an item I use very often, but I swear it should still be here.

For the first time in nearly ten minutes, I inhale a full breath when the item I'm searching for leaps into my hand. I frantically gather my disregarded equipment back into my bag before hoisting the strap over my shoulder. Being extra cautious, I carefully lift the ultrasound picture off the dresser and trudge down the stairs. The paper is so fragile, I can't be guaranteed it won't break just from touching it.

My steps back to Carey's suite are slow as I struggle with my heavy camera bag. Numerous partygoers acknowledge my struggle with a peculiar glance, but not one offers assistance.

My sloth-like pace completely stops when I reach the back door of Carey's place. He's frantically tearing apart his living room. He showcases his strength when he yanks the fixed cushions off his expensive-looking couch without a strain crossing his face. Feathers from his scatter cushions and filling from his couches disperse over the rug, covering his floor when he shreds them open as if they are nothing but tissue paper. After destroying his two couches beyond repair, he opens the drawer of his coffee table. Discovering the drawer is empty, he upends the table and moves to the antique bookshelves.

I slant my head to the side and rake my eyes down his body. I'm not shocked he's destroying his living room in the blink of an eye. It is the fact he's stark naked. Not slightly naked—fully *naked*.

My eyes sweep to a towel dumped at the edge of the living room as my heart rate skyrockets. I stop staring at the drenched towel when a faint voice says, "Ma'am."

A teenage boy stands at the door with a pizza box in his hand and a wide-eyed expression. The panic in his eyes snaps me out of the frozen trance Carey's violent rage caused. After putting my camera bag onto the kitchen counter and carefully setting down Malcolm's ultrasound picture, I snag Carey's wallet dumped halfway down the hall and yank out all the notes inside.

"Thank you," the delivery driver praises when I thrust a wad of bills into his hand. His words come out laced with concern.

Smiling to ease the worry marring his handsome face, I accept the pizza box from his grasp and gesture for him to leave. I'm in so much of a trance, I don't stop to acknowledge his concern for my safety. I'm too dazed trying to work out what has caused Carey's erratic behavior to add another item to my exhaustive list. I've never seen him so unhinged. With how much pain and guilt his eyes show, I never thought they would have the time to emit anger.

I shake my head when the driver asks, "Would you like me to call the police?"

"No, I can handle this." The shakiness of my words detracts from my honesty.

After closing the front door, I drop the pizza onto the floor and release a nerve-cleansing breath. Deep down in my soul, I know Carey would never hurt me, but it doesn't stop panic scorching my veins.

I stand at the side of Carey's living room for several minutes watching him move around the space, pulling open drawers and rummaging through every nook and cranny in his house.

"What are you looking for?" I eventually ask when it dawns on me that he seems to be searching for something. Surprisingly, my voice comes out strong, corroborating what I already know. I may be frightened by Carey's demeanor, but I'm not frightened of him.

I take a retreating step when he swings his barren eyes to me. He looks lost and haunted. Just the pain radiating from his eyes breaks my heart.

"A picture. M-Malcolm's picture," he stutters, his voice as broken as his eyes.

My hand darts up to rub the pain in my chest. "Oh—Carey. I'm sorry."

The pain in his eyes doubles. "Have you seen it? Do you know where it is?"

My brisk nod nearly sends a rogue tear rolling down my cheek. "I took it," I admit.

Carey's face lines with shock, and he seems stumped by my reply. "Why? Why would you take it?"

"I was going to fix it for you," I mumble before pushing off my feet to gather it from the kitchen.

Moisture forms in the corner of Carey's eyes when he spots Malcolm's scan in my hand. He charges for me, his movement so quick, a blast of air hits my face when he comes to a dead stop directly in front of me.

"Careful." My words are strangled by a sob sitting at the back of my throat.

My eyes burn when he gingerly removes the picture from my hand. After roaming his eyes over every inch of the photo, he releases a deep breath, which physically loosens the tightness of his shoulders.

"I thought I lost it," he mutters more to himself than me. "When I went to pay the delivery driver, and it wasn't in my wallet, I thought I lost it. I thought I lost him."

The pain in my chest turns deadly. "I'm sorry, so very sorry," I mumble while struggling to keep my tears at bay from the dejected tone of his voice.

Keeping his eyes planted on his son's picture, Carey paces into the living room and sits on the edge of his ruined couch. I want to comfort him. I want to express my remorse for causing him so much pain, but no matter how much my mouth moves, nothing comes out.

With my mouth refusing to cooperate, I force my legs to walk across the trashed living room and place a comforting hand on Carey's shoulder. I wouldn't have blamed him if he did, but relief engulfs me when he doesn't pull away from my touch.

The odds of holding in my tears diminish when Carey discloses, "I don't even know what color Malcolm's eyes were. Were they blue like Jorgie's? Or brown like mine? Some days I'm certain they would have been as dark as mine. Then other days, I'm not so sure."

Since he appears to be speaking to himself, I don't compile a response.

I'm too stricken with remorse to say a thing. I honestly wanted to help him and didn't stop to think of the repercussions of my action first. With my mouth still in lockdown mode, I run my thumb across Carey's sweat-slicked collarbone as I issue silent apology after silent apology.

After a few moments of quiet reflection, Carey jerks his head up and peers into my eyes. "Why did you take it?" Thankfully, all I hear in his voice is inquisitiveness.

My lips are dry, so I lick them before replying, "I was going to restore it for you."

His pained eyes bounce between mine before he asks, "You can do that?" The hope in his voice can't be missed.

Biting on my bottom lip, I nod. "It won't be like it was the day you got it, but it will be close."

Fighting against my shaking knees, I take the empty seat next to him. "If you don't want me to touch it, I won't, but it won't last much longer in that condition. The paper is very brittle and the image is badly faded."

When Carey runs his thumb along the edge of the thermal paper, it crumbles under his touch, reinforcing my warning.

His throat works hard to swallow before he mutters, "What if it gets wrecked?"

"It won't. I promise you. I'll be very careful," I vow, my voice barely a whisper.

I'm filled with bitter relief when, after a few moments of silent consideration, Carey hands Malcolm's photo to me. It is bitter because I hate we even need to have this conversation, but I'm relieved Carey believes in me enough to trust me with something so precious to him.

After running my index finger under my eyes to ensure no sneaky tears spilled, I stand from the couch and pace towards my camera bag. Carey tugs a pair of black trousers up his thighs before joining me in the kitchen.

"Because Malcolm's image was scanned on thermal paper, you can't use the same techniques you'd normally use for photo restoration." I yank a photo scanner out of my bag and lift my eyes to Carey. "Do you have a computer?"

Remaining quiet, he nods before spinning on his heels. I follow him into the main bedroom of his residence. I'm not surprised by its manly appeal.

I sit down in the chair in front of his desk and connect my scanner to his laptop. "I'll scan a digital copy of the image to your laptop for safe keeping." I drift my eyes to Carey standing at my side, watching me with caution. "Just in case it gets lost."

The quickest flare of emotion passing through his eyes relays that he heard the hidden apology in my statement. With a super fine brush and a pair of cotton gloves, I remove the excess dirt and grease distorting the image from years of being carried in Carey's wallet. Once I'm satisfied all the residue has been removed, I scan the image onto his laptop and email a copy to my private email address.

A deep line grooves in the middle of Carey's brows when I place Malcolm's picture onto a clean, flat surface before unwinding the cord of my hairdryer. "Images are printed onto thermal paper by using heat. By gently applying heat to the back of Malcolm's picture, it will encourage the natural coloring to resurface," I explain.

Although I'm planning on digitally restoring Malcolm's ultrasound picture, the sentimental value this photo holds for Carey is more important than the quality of the restoration.

Carey watches me in silence as I carefully heat the back of Malcolm's picture.

"Why are you wearing gloves?" he questions a short time later, his words raspy.

I lift my eyes from the photo to him. "Natural oils found on your skin contribute to fading."

His eyes drift between the photo and me. "So I should put it in a protective cover to stop it from fading?"

I briskly shake my head. "No. Don't do that. That will speed up the fading process. The best thing you can do is take care of this photo as well as you would have taken care of your son. Be gentle and handle it with care."

My chin quivers when Carey mutters, "Just like your heart?"

Not wanting him to see the tears welling in my eyes, I return my moisture-flooded gaze to Malcolm's picture.

It takes several minutes of careful dedication for the faded sections on his photo to return to the surface. It isn't the same quality it would have been when Carey placed it in his wallet years ago, but it is in a lot better condition than it was earlier.

After scanning the improved image onto Carey's laptop, I print out several copies on cheap printer paper. The little inkjet printer doesn't produce the best quality pictures, but it will do until I can professionally restore the image and print copies for Carey in my dark room.

With my heart not as heavy as it was earlier, I hand the original photo of Malcolm back to Carey. Numerous heart-thrashing seconds pass as he absorbs the restored image in resolute silence.

A surge of blood rushes to my heart when Carey locks his eyes with me and simply mutters, "Thank you."

CHAPTER 25

GEMMA

"How are you finding Ravenshoe?" Ava finishes draining the lettuce leaves in her kitchen sink and turns to face me. "It's good. Surprisingly busy."

I laugh. "Wesley and I thought the same thing, which is ludicrous considering the location of our apartment."

I finish cutting up the roma tomatoes and place them in the salad bowl at my side before washing my hands in the sink. "Did you find a suitable location for your practice?"

Even not being a fan of dentists, I will admit, Ava is a good one. She has been the only one I've felt comfortable seeing since. . . well, forever!

"Isaac has some great locations on the table, but I want to wait until I get a feel for the area." She places the lettuce in the bowl of salad and tosses it with her hands. "This side of Ravenshoe is gorgeous, but the other side still has a long way to go. As much as Hugo doesn't want me working on that side of town, they need my help more than this area."

I nod. "Ravenshoe is a beautiful place, but it does appear to have two completely unique facades."

Ravenshoe could be a metaphor for my recovery. There are days where I feel like I've fully recovered from my attack, then there are days like today that I struggle. Part of me knows my uneven composure is from the cold-sweat nightmare Wesley woke me from this morning, but the other half wonders if it is more to do with the fact I haven't seen Carey today.

Don't construe my statement the wrong way; nothing has happened between Carey and me the past week, but that is more because we barely get a moment alone. *Well, I hope that is the case?* With the band's tight schedule and their desire to release their one year commemorative album before they go on tour next month, everyone's free time is stretched to the absolute limit.

If I'm not photographing the band, I'm hiding out in the dark room of my studio editing and processing their photos. Because Carey is the band's head bodyguard, he goes where they go. With their rocketing fame, even something as simple as buying a loaf of bread requires a dedicated security team.

Although I've barely had a minute to mumble a hello to Carey since our heart-strangling time together in his suite, that doesn't mean we haven't shared numerous sneaky glances and heart-clutching smiles throughout the week. Carey's silence doesn't bother me. Sometimes it is best to stay quiet when you want to know someone's true self. Silence can speak volumes without a word needing to be said, and people who don't understand your silence will not understand your words anyway. Besides, words can lie; actions can't. Carey's actions show he's a man struggling to be freed from his past so he can enjoy the present. It's lucky for him I'm a patient woman.

I prop my hip onto the beautiful granite countertop of Ava's kitchen. "So what *exactly* does Hugo do for Isaac?" I ask with curiosity in my tone.

I met Hugo's boss, Isaac, at the Marshall brunch last month. Although he has panty-melting good looks and a bank account to rival my dad's, he has an aura to him that makes me a little more scared than impressed.

Ava's well-manicured brows stitch together before she shrugs her shoulders. "To be honest, I don't have a friggin' clue." A smile graces her plump lips. "But it pays well, and according to Wesley, money won't make you happy, but it's shitloads better than being broke."

I wrap my arm around her expanded waist and giggle. God, I love Ava. She's the female equivalent of Wesley: kindhearted, beautiful, and intelligent. All those years ago when I stirred Hugo about his Ava obsession, I had no clue he was onto a real winner. I should have known. Hugo's intuition has never steered him wrong. That's why I wish I'd taken up his offer that night six years ago. Then both of us would have been saved from a life of heartache.

"Gem," Ava murmurs softly, intuiting where my thoughts have strayed. "Hugo doesn't blame you for anything that happened."

"If I hadn't been so stupid—"

"No," Ava interrupts sternly. "You are not to blame for what happened to you, just as you're not to be blamed for Hugo's decision."

I want to tell Ava the truth. I want to explain that Hugo's decision to plead guilty to my assault was solely my fault, but no matter how hard I fight, my mouth refuses to relinquish my confession.

My guilty conscience eases when Hugo enters the back entrance of the kitchen with a broad grin stretched across his face. Whether you're a stranger or have known him half your life, Hugo has the type of personality that can calm any storm brewing on the horizon.

The smile I issue him in greeting grows when Carey enters the kitchen shortly after him. Unlike every day I've seen him the past week, he's void of his standard work attire. His black suit with crisp white shirt has been replaced with a pair of well-fitting cargo shorts and a round neck t-shirt. Seeing him dressed so casually adds to his appeal. Not many men can pull off cargo shorts, but Carey can, and he does it very well.

My slack-jawed response to Carey's presence awards me with a heart-fluttering smirk. The crackling of energy between us is so dense, the ribs sitting on the counter beside me won't need to be grilled. It's that roasting.

After Hugo presses a kiss on the side of my cheek and plants a sloppy smooch onto Ava's mouth, he snags the ribs and steak from the kitchen counter and exits the kitchen from the other end. Unfortunately, Carey closely follows him... but not before he gives my hand a sneaky squeeze on the way by. I swear, his briefest touch caused the next sixty years of our life to flash before my eyes. If my premonition is anything to go off, it will be a rollercoaster ride that gets better with every dip and weave we take.

Shaking off my reckless thoughts about achieving a happily ever after, I set back to work on finishing the salad we're having with dinner.

OUR IMPROMPTU double date goes better than I'd hoped. Although it was odd sitting across from Carey and pretending every word he spoke didn't cause of rush of desire to scorch my veins, it has been a pleasant evening full of laughter and conversation. You know it is a good time when you can spend hours with people and you're not once interested in looking at your phone. It is moments like these that fill me with hope that the best years of my life are still waiting to happen.

"We will get this cleaned up and be right out," Hugo advises, gesturing his head to Joel and Ava to help him with the dishes.

When I stand from my seat to assist, Hugo says, "No, leave it, Gem. We've got this."

"Yeah," Joel adds on. "We Marshalls know how to treat the ladies." I smirk when he stumbles over the last half of his sentence with a devilish wink.

Ignoring Ava's livid glare at his suaveness rubbing off on their son, Hugo gathers our dirty dishes before he, Ava, and Joel bolt for the house like their backsides are on fire.

I wait for Ava to close the glass sliding door before shifting my gaze to Carey. "Hugo knows, doesn't he?"

I don't know why my words are laced in panic, but they are. I guess I could use the excuse that Hugo is like my big brother, so it's a little odd for him to know about my sexual activities.

A cringe crosses my face when Carey nods. "I accidentally let it slip," he confesses.

I sink deeper into my chair, my heart walloping, my mouth ajar. This feels worse than the time my dad found a condom in my purse the night of prom. Even more so as Hugo has not only seen me at my worst, he has also seen me naked. It was a complete accident. When I snuck into the male latrine when his squadron was out on a training drill, I thought I would be in and out before anyone returned. I was wrong. *So very, very wrong.*

I snap back to the present when Carey's heated gaze gathers my attention.

"Did you know I was going to be here?" I strive to keep the panic out of my voice. My efforts are reasonable.

My heart beats even faster when the concern in Carey's eyes escalates. "No. And I'm taking it by your surprised response you didn't know I was going to be here either?"

"No," I reply with a concise shake of my head. "Not that I'm disappointed. I like spending time with you. Even if you have to do it with your clothes on." I keep my tone playful, wanting to ensure my pendulum-swinging moods don't cause any more alarm to form in Carey's eyes.

The coolness of the chilled wine I'm sipping does nothing to ease the panic roaring through my veins when Carey says, "If Wesley hadn't told me about your ninety-day rule, I would have assumed you were a sex addict. Nearly every conversation we've held has you mentioning my nakedness."

Overlooking the fact Wesley and Carey had that type of conversation about me, I chug down the remaining fruity liquid inside my glass, praying it will stop unwilling words spilling from my lips. As much as I'd love to deny Carey's cheeky taunt, I can't. Sex addiction is just like every other addiction. You never fully recover from it.

Choosing avoidance as the best option for this awkward situation, I gather Carey's empty schooner glass off the table and attempt to charge for the door. "Refill. You look like you need a refill," I mumble on my way.

My brisk pace halts when Carey seizes my wrist. His grip is soft enough he doesn't hurt me, but firm enough to demand my attention. It also sends a zap of lust rocketing to my core.

I suck in a nerve-clearing breath before locking my eyes with his. Just like every time he glances at me, the understanding in his eyes forces words out of my mouth I never thought I'd speak. "I did some *stuff* when I was younger I'm not proud of. Stuff I'd prefer you didn't know," I disclose, deciding honesty is the best policy I can work with right now.

The empathy in Carey's eyes switches to a gleam I can't recognize. "Does Hugo know about this *stuff*?" he asks, his voice low and risky.

I take a moment to consider my reply. "Some of it, yes, but not all of it," I admit. Although Hugo knows of my attack and the events that directly followed, his disappearance nearly five years ago means he doesn't know about every shameful thing I've done.

Carey works his jaw side to side before questioning, "Wesley?"

I nod without pause. "Wesley knows everything about me, Carey. The good and the bad."

The scruff on Carey's chin can't hide the tick in his jaw. His annoyed response fuels my anger. If I didn't have men like Wesley, my dad, and Hugo in my life, I wouldn't have a life. It is that simple.

"Wesley isn't your enemy, Carey," I caution, my voice shaky and brimming with emotions. "You are. There's no greater enemy to a man than his own self-consciousness."

CHAPTER 26

GEMMA

My confrontation with Carey quickly sees the mood shift from energetic and playful to stifling and uncomfortable. Although Hugo and Ava do their best to pretend they can't feel the negativity plaguing the air when they return from doing the dishes and putting Joel to bed, it is too uncomfortable for me to ignore. Carey hasn't said or done anything to irk me, but as I said earlier, words aren't required to express a person's sentiment.

Unable to handle the inquisitive glances of Hugo and Ava for a second longer, I place my empty wine glass on the patio table and stand from my seat. "I have a lot of editing to do tomorrow so I better head off."

Hugo pushes back from the table. "Let me grab my keys; I'll give you a lift home," he offers.

Before I have the chance to cite an objection, Carey perks up, "I'll take Gemma home."

Quicker than the strike of a cobra, Hugo dives back into his chair. "Great," he and Ava shout at the same time, their faces lined with glee.

Ignoring their glaringly obvious matchmaking, I shift my eyes to Carey. "It's fine. I can call a taxi."

Even with his eyes doused in agitation, Carey holds my gaze. "I'm heading off anyway. It's no trouble."

"You live in Ravenshoe; my cabin is at Bronte's Peak – fourteen miles in the wrong direction," I retort, my voice coming out with a hint of bitchiness.

I'm not angry at Carey; I'm fuming at myself for allowing an event six years ago to still hinder my quality of life today. Last week I said I'm the only one who can allow my past to affect my present, but today is different. Normally, on this day every year, I chase away haunted memories with decadent cupcakes and an expensive bottle of wine. I don't sit across from the man who sacrificed his own happiness to ensure I kept mine, and I don't spend it with a man who sends my mind into a tailspin from his briefest touch. There are so many emotions pumping through me right now, I don't even know which way is up.

A length of silence stretches between us when we undertake a sweat-producing stare down. If it were any other day than today, I'd succumb to the pleading look in Carey's eyes and accept his offer, but the events six years ago have my agitation on edge and my composure ruffled.

Hugo and Ava's heads bounce between Carey and me like they're watching a tennis match. Their mouths are gaped, and their eyes wide. They stop bouncing when Carey snarls, "I either drive you to your cabin or you stay at my place. The choice is yours."

Ava's mouth gapes open as far as mine. I know Carey's eyes could reach my soul with one sideways glance, but I never fathomed he could read my emotions so easily. Although my standoffish demeanor is pleading for seclusion, my eyes are begging for me not to be left alone. Silence is great when you're watching someone from afar, but when you're alone, sometimes silence can be your worst enemy.

When several seconds pass by without me responding to Carey's statement, Ava kicks me in the ankle under the table. "Ouch," I wince before rubbing the sting to my ankle with my other foot.

After issuing Ava a stink-eye that only makes her smile grow, I shift my eyes to Carey. "Do you have a spare toothbrush?"

Hugo spits out the beer he was gulping, sending speckles of malted liquid all over the tabletop.

When a flare of panic ignites in Carey's eyes, I snarl, "Don't *ever* put anything on the table you aren't willing to lose, because you can't guarantee who will sneak up behind you and steal everything you've ever wanted."

Part of my remark is from the disappointment of seeing panic in Carey's eyes, but most of it resides from my attack. I tried to shake off the horrid feeling I get on this day every year a majority of the night, but no matter what I do, I can't pretend like nothing happened. All it took was accepting a drink from a man I'd been fascinated with for weeks, and my entire world came undone.

I instantly regret my outburst when Carey replies, "You don't think you're preaching to the choir? I *did* have everything I've ever wanted stolen from me."

Guilt curls around my throat, silently asphyxiating me. I can't believe during a low moment in my recovery I completely forgot that, more than anyone in this room, Carey knows what it feels like to have your life upended in an instant. He knows how cruel the world can be just as much as I do. *I'm a terrible and horrible person.*

Before I have the chance to stumble out an apology, Carey yanks his car keys out of his pocket and nudges his head to the driveway. If it wouldn't hurt him more than I already have, I'd beg Hugo to take me back to my cabin, but unable to add pressure to the knife I just stabbed in Carey's chest, I gather my purse hanging off my chair and follow him to his Camaro.

"I'm so sorry," I whisper into Ava's ear when I hug her goodbye.

She tightens her grip around my shoulders. "A reaction is a reaction, good or bad, because only a lifeless person can't respond."

Blood surges to my heart when I connect my eyes to Hugo and he silently offers to drive me home. That proves what I've always known; Hugo will stop at nothing to ensure everyone surrounding him is safe and protected. Even giving up his freedom, and perhaps even his life.

"I trust him. I know he won't hurt me." I don't know why I

murmured my statement. I'm fairly sure Carey didn't hear anything since he's already sitting in the driver's seat of his Camaro.

"He'd never hurt you, Gem," Hugo confirms before wrapping me up in a tight hug.

I sigh heavily, fanning his neck with my hot breath. "If only you could say the same thing to him about me."

"I know today is hard for you, but remember the only way you can erase bad memories is by replacing them with good ones," Hugo whispers into my hair.

God—I should have known he would have never forgotten the significance of today.

"I wouldn't have bad memories if I listened to you six years ago." Not giving Hugo the chance to reply, I slip into the passenger seat of Carey's Camaro.

Unlike last month, Carey drives the entire fourteen miles at the designated speed limit. The further we travel, the tighter the hold around my throat becomes. I feel sick. Not just from the cold sweat of my nightmare this morning still clinging to my skin, but from guilt for the callous words I said to Carey.

Maybe Wesley was right? Maybe I'm not strong enough to pursue a relationship with Carey. My heart refuses to listen to the pleas of my brain, but my intuition is telling me to evaluate all the options. Carey and I are the equivalent of lightning and thunder. Alone, we already have people on edge, but put together, we could be catastrophic.

When Carey's Camaro rolls down the gravel driveway of my cabin, I swing my eyes to him. The air is forcefully removed from my lungs. My god he's beautiful. In pain, choked with remorse, but beautiful still the same. I gasp in a shocked breath when the unidentifiable glint in his eyes finally dawns on me. His eyes carry the same amount of concern my dad's did the day he peered down at me rummaging through a dumpster twenty-four years ago. He isn't angry at me or my closeness to Wesley. He's concerned for me.

His worry makes it easier for me to say, "Something bad happened in my life six years ago. Something I still have trouble processing how to explain." My words are shaky and full of emotion.

My assumptions about his concern are proven on point when it grows from my confession. "Is that what caused your frightened response two weeks ago?" he asks, his voice dripping with worry.

"Yes," I force out.

My one word hits Carey like a physical blow. A predatory glimmer sparks in his eyes, and his fists snap into tight balls. I can tell he wants to say something, but unlike my inability to hold in my comments, he seems to have control over his mouth.

As a stretch of silence passes between us, I pluck at the hem of my shirt.

"I want to tell you what happened, but that's not something I can do right now," I mumble when the silence becomes too great for me to ignore.

I'm barely holding it together as it is, let alone running the risk of having a man who intrigues me more than any man before him look at me differently. That is not something I could handle. That may very well be the final straw that makes me crack.

Disappointment floods Carey's eyes. "You have to go through pain to understand it." He locks his beautiful dark eyes with mine. "You don't look at me the same as everyone else, as you understand what I'm going through."

"Partly," I reply, my voice low.

Although I don't fully comprehend what Carey is going through, I do understand it is something that will never go away. No matter how much we both wish it would.

"Give me the same chance," he pleads. The worried tone of his voice swells my heart.

"I want to," I mutter, my voice croaking with emotion. "And one day I will, but not today." My emotions are too raw for me to hold this type of conversation right now.

When I feel stupid tears welling in my eyes, I lean over and press a kiss to the edge of Carey's jaw. I need to ensure I'm as far away from him as possible in case my silly tears decide to fall. I refuse to let another man see me cry about what happened to me six years ago. Tears are a sign of weakness. I'm not weak. My attackers are.

"Thanks for the ride," I mumble before throwing open the car door.

Before I can get one foot onto the driveway, my wrist is seized. I inhale greedy breaths as I strive to wipe the panic off my face. When I'm happy I've returned my cheeks to their normal coloring, I twist my neck to Carey. He stares at me with concern, worry, and another glint I can't recognize.

I surface from the sea of pain I'm drowning in when he leans over and seals his lips over mine. When I gasp to fill my lungs with life-replenishing air, he slips his tongue inside my mouth. The heat of his passionate kiss dries my tears and fills my heart with hope, while also freeing me from the tornado of emotions that has been hammering me all day. He kisses me until every doubt niggling in the back of my mind that my life ended six years ago vanishes, and nothing but begging for more overtakes my thoughts.

Toeing off my shoes, I climb over the small space between us and straddle Carey's lap, all while keeping my lips attached to his. A burning of lust rises to the surface of my skin when I feel the heat of his cock through his shorts. He's thick, hard and long, undoubtedly surging my confidence to a summit it hasn't reached since my attack. My hands are all over him. Under his shirt, raking my nails over the hard bumps on his stomach, and weaving them through his hair that is overdue for a trim.

I'm so immersed in heating every inch of Carey's skin with my touch I don't notice Wesley sneaking up on us until it's too late. When he taps on the driver's side window of Carey's Camaro, I jump so high, I smash my head on the lining of the roof.

My furious stink-eye does nothing to lessen the shit-eating grin on Wesley's face when Carey rolls down his foggy window. Not speaking a word, Carey interrogates Wesley's motives with a snip of annoyance in his eyes that sets my pulse racing—in a good way.

Perking his lips, Wesley drops his eyes to his watch. "Would you look at that... it's still August."

My brows join in confusion.

While drifting his eyes between a disheveled Carey and me, Wesley questions, "You guys met in June, right?"

I smash my back molars together when Wesley's sudden interest in our gathering dawns on me. Not catching the reasoning behind Wesley's unwanted meddling, Carey nods.

"July, August, September," he recites, flicking out his fingers as he counts down the months my usual ninety-day rule would force to pass before I undertook in any sexual activities.

The line between Carey's heavy brows smooths when he figures out Wesley's intrusive tactics. The fire in my belly simmers to a dull flame when Carey's thick penis braced against my aching core softens.

Sensing my disappointment, Wesley cockily winks. "I'll see you inside, Poppet." My vicious snarl increases when Wesley smiles a traffic-stopping grin.

Once Wesley climbs the stairs of our cabin, the fire of need in my belly switches to hope when Carey mutters, "I want to know you as well as Wesley does."

There's no chance I can hold in my smile, so I set it free. "If you play your cards right, you'll know me better than Wesley."

A heavy line of confusion marks the space between his dark eyes.

"Wesley hasn't seen me naked," I announce with a cheeky wink.

The heaviness weighing down my chest clears when a spark of lust explodes in Carey's eyes at the same time a soul-shattering grin graces his kiss-swollen lips. It takes all my strength not to react to the thickness growing beneath me, but I give it my best shot. Although I'd love to spend a few hours with him hoping he could turn my haunted memories into good ones, I'm still balancing on the crest of an emotional wave, and I can't guarantee how I'd react if this were to go any further than an innocent grind-up.

Snubbing the protests of my tingling womb that it can handle anything Carey is willing to give it, I ask, "Do you have any plans two weeks from Saturday?"

My stomach knots when I spot a blemish of unease in Carey's eyes. His wary response reminds me that I'm not the only one silently requesting to be handled with care. He needs to be taken care of with just as much caution as I do. He might have a much bigger and harder exterior than me, but our insides are exactly the same.

"Your schedule is so busy you have to plan dates two weeks in advance?"

The worry in his eyes fades when I explain, "It's not a date. The Bristol half mile is on. Wesley may be many things, but he doesn't know a clutch from a gas pedal. I like talking shop during races."

Carey cocks his brow. "You're not one of those girls who talks nonstop during races, are you?"

A conceited grin curls on my lips when his voice comes out super husky and laced with arousal. "God no," I push out, pretending to gag in disgust. "Although I can't make any guarantees I won't scream at the TV numerous times throughout the night."

Giddiness clusters in my muddled brain when a smile I haven't seen before etches onto Carey's plump lips. It's a smile of a man who isn't broken, a smile that fills me with hope that I'm not the only one baffled by our bizarre connection. You'd swear days have passed since our heart-clutching disagreement at Hugo's, where it's only been a matter of an hour. I shouldn't be surprised. Time doesn't matter when you're truly getting to know someone. Relationships are not measured by time. They're measured by undeniable connection. Two broken people will either fit together perfectly, or break each other beyond repair. If given the chance to fully explore a relationship with Carey, I believe we could have something truly beautiful.

The tingling between my legs I've only just controlled revamps when Carey says, "You screaming for hours? Hmm. . . what type of man would I be if I turned down an offer like that?"

I bite on the inside of my cheek—hard. Even with our combined emotions being potent enough to launch a rocket, only a naïve idiot would have missed the innuendo in his reply.

I'm not the only one astonished. Carey appears just as stunned as me. Shocked is a good look for him. It makes his eyes brighter and adds a vibrant coloring to his cheeks.

Struggling not to curve my knees together, I work on persuading him to spend more time with me. "We could eat greasy burgers and drink tasteless beer. Have the real NASCAR experience! What do you say? Can you squeeze another memory-creating night with a stranger into your busy schedule?"

My pulse quickens when Carey locks his dark eyes with mine. They don't look as pained as they did earlier. "Two strangers creating a memory they will share for eternity?"

Masking my excitement he remembered a quote I said months ago, I nod. "Although I'm not sure we can still use the term strangers. You've seen me—"

"Naked," Carey fills in, surging my excitement out of the stratosphere.

I hold my breath, eagerly anticipating his answer. I swear my heart is pounding against my chest so fast, the bearded man standing on his glass patio eyeballing the exchange between Carey and me will be able to hear it.

I nearly throw a fist punch into the air and squeal in delight when Carey nods. "But I refuse to drink tasteless beer," he declares, his voice no longer having the smear of uncertainty it held earlier.

"Fine," I holler with a roll of my eyes, the excitement in my tone incapable of being missed. "You bring the beer; I'll supply the food."

Desire scorches my veins when slipping off Carey's lap makes him expel a throaty gargle. I would have said a moan, but since he tried to stifle his response to my loss of contact, it came out more sounding like a gargle.

After curling out of his car, I dip my torso back into the passenger window. My heart beats triple time when my eyes drink in his ruffled appearance. I don't think I've ever seen anything as beautiful as a rough brute of a man with lust-filled eyes and kiss-swollen lips.

"Thanks for the lift." The huskiness of my voice exposes my excitement.

"It was my pleasure," Carey replies with a smirk. "I'll see you soon, Gemma-the-tasteless-beer-drinker."

My heart nearly bursts. This is the first time I've experienced a playful and carefree Carey. *God, I hope it isn't the last.*

"Not if I see you first, Carey-you've-never-experienced-life-until-you've-drunk-beer-that-tastes-like-your-grandma's-undies," I reply before cringing. *Seriously, "grandma's undies" was the best line you could come up with?*

My insides dance like a hooker on crack when Carey throws his head back and laughs. "I've always had a thing for Betty White, but that's just taking it one step too far."

"Thanks for the heads up. I'll be sure to delete any *Hot in Cleveland* episodes on my DVR before you arrive. I wouldn't want you getting all hot and bothered," I jest, my tone tainted with girlish giggling.

My smile inches higher when I spot the disappointment on Carey's face. Clearly, he likes me making him hot and bothered.

"Wesley can smell a man in *need* a mile away. He may not be able to control himself," I explain.

Carey's confusion blasts into the next galaxy even more quickly than our somber moods disappeared. "Is he as protective of you as Hugo is?" he asks, confusion heard in his tone.

My heart warms. Not just because of his admission Hugo is protective of me, but because he believes Wesley will need to hold him back from me. Does that mean he's planning on doing something scandalous? *I can only hope.*

"Wesley won't be holding *you* back from *me*. It will be *me* holding *him* back from *you*," I clarify.

It takes a few seconds of quiet reflection before the reality dawns on Carey's face. I can't tell if the smug grin etching onto his mouth is because he's flattered by my compliment, or because he just realized if Wesley was given the choice between me and him, my bed companion would be my pillow.

"Goodnight, Carey," I say, fighting not to invite him in like a loser who can't control her libido.

A grin tugs my lips high when I spot Carey's indecisiveness. I don't think he knows if he's coming or going. I'm glad to see I'm not the only one struggling. Although most of my time with him has been spent in a lust-filled trance, thankfully, my outward appearance gives no indication to the absurdity happening inside my body. I respectfully hold in my excitement, even with my body screaming at me to pretend I'm filming an episode of *Girls Gone Wild*.

"Night, Gemma," Carey eventually grinds out.

After waving at each other like we are in middle school, Carey glides his car down the gravel driveway.

CHAPTER 27

HAWKE

Gemma has a look in her eyes—a raw pain that causes the area in the middle of my chest to ache. I knew the instant her declaration about having everything snatched away left her mouth she wanted to take it back. I won't lie, her words stung. Normally, I'd happily accept the pain. I'd appreciate it, but this time was different. The hurt in her eyes wasn't being projected at me because of what I had lost; it was reflecting something she went through. *Something I'd give anything to help her heal from.*

I wait for the grief to arrive for my silent thoughts. It doesn't come. I shouldn't be shocked. My connection with Gemma is so odd. It is happening at a lightning pace that is both scary and dangerous, but it feels so good. Better than I'd care to admit.

My grief the past five years has seen me at my weakest. It took everything I thought I knew about life and morphed it into a hideously bland and lifeless canvas. Gemma is changing that. She's adding speckles of color back onto the black canvas I used to call my life. Every minute I spend with her has me craving another.

I'll never fully get over my grief. My love of Jorgie and Malcolm will never go away; they will forever be in my heart, where I will cherish and love them every single day, but Gemma gives me hope that one day I'll wake up without so much heaviness on my chest I can barely breathe, that I'll laugh without feeling pain, and that I'll act on my desires to kiss her without a single thought passing through my mind first.

Before Gemma came into my life, any contact I had with the opposite sex was an attempt to fill the void Jorgie left. I don't want that from Gemma. I want to be the man she comes to in a crisis. I want to be the man who fully wipes the mistrust from her eyes.

I want to be the man who can look at her without feeling guilt.

CHAPTER 28

GEMMA

"That was low. Really, really, low," I grumble while digging one of the fake apples out of the fruit bowl on the entranceway table and pegging it at Wesley's snickering face.

After dodging the wildly flung plastic fruit, the smug grin on Wesley's face grows. "I was protecting your virtue."

"My virtue doesn't need saving." *My heart. . . that's a completely different story.*

I place my handbag and keys on the entranceway table before pacing into my bedroom.

Pushing off the sofa, Wesley follows me. "Do the foggy windows mean you guys are a *thing* now?" he asks, his voice a unique cross of intrigue and concern.

I shrug my shoulders. "I don't know. What do you think? You had a prime view of the entire event from your stalker perch on the front patio."

Wesley balks, shocked I knew he was watching us just as eagerly as the bearded stranger living in the glass house next door.

When Wesley remains quiet—neither denying or admitting my claims—I walk into my closet to replace my summer dress with a nightie. The vast range of emotions pumping out of me today has made me so exhausted, I can hear my bed calling me.

While dressing, I consider Wesley's question. I really hope tonight was the beginning of something between Carey and me. I know our story hasn't been one that would grace the pages of a steamy romance novel. We haven't had innumerable sexual encounters or acted recklessly, but that doesn't make the quality of our story less impressive. Our story is as unique as both of our predicaments. I don't need to be swept off my feet in a whirlwind relationship that fizzles out before it even begins. I want a man who will see past my past. A man who understands there will be days I'll be bouncing around like I've taken too many of the pills Dr. McKay prescribed me, and there will be days where I may not be able to move from the couch. With everything Carey has been through, I truly think he's that man for me.

I said earlier tonight that Carey and I are the equivalent of lightning and thunder, and that if we got together we could be catastrophic, but how often do you have a thunderstorm without lightning? They may be destructive, but that doesn't mean they don't belong together.

After throwing a spaghetti strap satin negligee over my head, I pace to my bed, pull down the cover, and slip inside. The softness of the high thread count sheets comforts my weary muscles while also placing wicked thoughts in my devilish mind. *They're as soft as Carey's sinful-tasting lips.*

The blood drains from my cheeks when I lift my eyes from the comforter and spot Wesley's downcast face. Smiling, I pull back the covers and gesture for him to join me. When he shakes his head, my brows stitch. Wesley is an affectionate type of guy. He never turns down an opportunity to spoon.

"You're not the only one stuck in a sexual rut. I've barely had the time to jack one off in the shower. If I climb into bed with you, I can't guarantee I'll keep my hands to myself," he admits, his voice gruff but truthful.

"I don't know if I should take that as a compliment or an insult. From the disgusted look on your face, I'm leaning toward insult."

Wesley grins while waggling his brows. "If I didn't believe you've already fallen for Carey, I'd have no worries proving it was a compliment." He aims for his tone to be playful, but it still comes out with a touch of uncertainty.

My mouth moves as I attempt to deny Wesley's assumption that I'm falling for Carey, but my words stay entombed in my throat. I learned a hard lesson from lying that I don't plan on making twice. As much as I wish our night ended differently, the respect Carey showed me tonight tethered my heart to him even more. A sexual connection is great, but there's much more required for a lasting relationship. And although I've never been in love, I do know one thing: I want much more from Carey than just a few nights between the sheets.

I scoot up the bed to lean my back on the headboard. Once I've ensured all my body parts are respectfully covered, I pat the mattress, offering for Wesley to join me. The stranglehold around my heart eases when he does as requested.

"What's wrong?" I question when he rests his cheek on my shoulder.

His lips form into one of the sexiest pouts I've ever seen. "I don't know. This all just feels a little weird. For years, it's always been me and you. Now I've got to make room for another man to come in and take over the role I've been doing the last three years. It's like forced retirement. I'm not even twenty-nine for fuck's sake."

Unexpected tears prick my eyes. "No one will ever replace you, Wesley. They couldn't. It won't matter what happens; we'll always be in each other's lives. Besides, if anyone should be worried about being left behind, it should be me." I nudge him with my shoulder, silently demanding his attention. "From the praises I've heard about you the past few weeks, by next year, you'll be saying 'Gemma who?'"

The hurt in his eyes dissipates. "That will *never* happen. Everything I've been doing the past three years is so I could give you back what you've given me."

"Wesley..."

"No, Poppet. I had nothing before I met you. Not a single thing. Now look at me. I freeload in an apartment in New York; I'm living it up in a kickass cabin on the cliffs of Bronte's Peak, all while I'm recording a collaboration with the number one band in the country. The world's strongest drugs couldn't conjure up this shit."

"Everything you have, you earned yourself. I didn't give you anything but love, which you gave in return just as much. Love is not something you can put a value on, Wesley. So don't *ever* feel you haven't contributed to our relationship. You gave me way more than I could have ever hoped for. You gave me a reason to live."

The reasoning behind Wesley's uncertainty is revealed when he murmurs, "And now I have to pass the baton onto another man. There's this weird sense of achievement when you're someone's crutch. I don't know if I'm ready to hand over that power yet."

"It's not that serious between Carey and me. For all I know, when he finds out my secret, he may not want me anymore." My words come out brittle since I forced them through the bile sitting in the back of my throat.

"You've never been a liar, Gem; don't start now. I heard what he said about wanting to know you as well as me. He wants to know you—the real you. You've just got to decide if that is what you want."

"I want that," I reply without pause.

Wesley drapes his arm around my shoulders. "Then when you're ready, tell me, and I'll step back."

Panic clutches my throat. "You don't have to step back, Wesley."

"A three-sided relationship never works, Gem; trust me, I've tried. If a relationship with Carey is what you truly want, we both have to make sacrifices. You might be the baddest bitch in the US, but you can't keep all the handsome men in the country at your beck and call."

Smiling, I drop my head on top of his. "If I didn't have this horrible neurosis of being a bitterly jealous and demented woman, I'm sure we could work around your concerns, but since the thought of Carey being with anyone—let alone a man as wickedly handsome as you—makes me want to break out my Kung Fu moves, we're going to have to work out another solution."

Wesley tries to hold it in, but the quickest chuckle escapes his lips.

"Here I am for the first time in my life trying to be serious, and you bring out the corny Kung Fu jokes."

"Who said I was joking? My moves would be so suave, they wouldn't see me coming. A paper cut can kill if inflicted in the right area." Half of my statement is lost when Wesley wraps his arm around my neck and playfully holds me in a choke hold.

"You're lucky you've got a rock ass body, Poppet, or Carey might have taken your ninety-day rules and worked it out on one of the numerous women I've seen begging for his attention the past two weeks."

The playfulness is wiped from my face as blood roars to my ears. "Women? What women?"

Wesley's lips crimp as he shrugs his shoulders.

"What women, Wesley?"

Even on edge that my possessiveness of Carey is already so potent, it's taking all my strength not to straddle Wesley and torture him until he spills the beans.

I keep my eyes planted on Wesley when he slips out of my bed and heads for the door. "Wesley? I swear to god, if you leave me hanging, I won't be held accountable for my actions."

When he spins around to face me, reality smacks me in the face. He's taunting me. "Did I say women?"

I grit my teeth and nod.

"Oops. My bad. I meant to say me."

His brisk pace has him halfway down the hall before I've even scrambled off the mattress.

CHAPTER 29

GEMMA

"And that's a wrap!" I squeal, my voice laced with excitement. The noise of my camera clicking sounds over the excited cheer of the band members of Rise Up. I can't stomach the idea of missing candid snaps of their jubilation that their grueling four-hour shoot is finally over. They're not the only ones excited. My feet have never been so sore. A glass of red wine and a long soak in the tub are the only plans on my agenda this evening.

"I think that will be a great cover."

I finish placing my camera in my bag before raising my eyes. Although nervous someone managed to sneak up on me unaware, I respectfully hold in my frightened squeal—barely.

"Thanks, I think so too."

Cormack smiles before thrusting his hand into the pockets of his expensive tailored trousers. Cormack is a handsome man, standing a little under six feet tall. He has thick, luxurious blond hair, blue eyes and a face that could earn more dividends than his massive bank balance if he found the right person to photograph him. He has an approachable demeanor that successfully conceals the fact he's stinking rich.

My brow bows into my hair when Cormack rocks back and forth

on his heels. I can tell he wants to say something, but for some reason, he's being super quiet.

"Is there anything I can help you with?"

Cormack smiles a sheepish grin that sets my heart racing. "No. I'm just undertaking a bet."

My brows stitch. I'm more confused than ever.

"Jenni bet that within thirty seconds of me talking to you, Hawke would magically appear," he explains to my bemused expression. "She believes he has a *thing* for you."

I shake my head, praying it will hide my inanely smug grin. "I think you've both overestimated my appeal, but thanks for the. . ." My words trail off into unintelligible jargon when Carey magically appears by Cormack's side.

Cormack's smile enlarges. "You're welcome." After issuing me a cheeky wink, he spins on his heels.

"What did Cormack want?" Carey asks while removing my camera bag from my grasp and slinging it over his shoulder.

I blink three times in a row. "Umm. . . he was just praising my photography skills." *And playing matchmaker*, but I keep that snippet of information to myself.

Ignoring the snickering faces of Jenni and Emily as we saunter by, I follow Carey into the parking lot of the warehouse.

"Do you have any plans for the weekend?"

With the band's schedule about to turn hectic, they decided to take a weekend off from the limelight to spend it surrounded by family and friends like they did before their first album launched. Thus meaning, I not only get the weekend off, so does Carey.

"No. I don't really make plans," he replies, his tone low.

He unlocks his Camaro and places my camera bag in the backseat. I smile at his thoughtfulness. Ever since our heated kiss in his car four nights ago, he has given me a ride home every night. Although our make out sessions haven't gone beyond what they did the night we met, they're certainly hot enough to steam up the windows of his Camaro.

Dust from the gravel driveway kicks up under my feet when I

stray my eyes to the ground. "Did you want to hang out?" I question, my words uneasy.

Carey's brows stitch when he hears the unease in my voice. Clearly, I'm not the only one confronted with spending an entire two days together—*alone*. The band members of Rise Up aren't the only ones spending the weekend with family. Wesley flew to Tiburon early this morning. At first, I was pleased. Then reality dawned. Most of my time with Carey the past three weeks has been closely monitored by others. It's never been just me and him.

Carey's eyes drift between mine as he contemplates my offer. I love his indecisiveness. Others may see it as a sign of disinterest. I don't. Carey is a man struggling with loss. I'd be more concerned if he didn't take his time configuring a reply. The best things you have in life never arrive in haste.

After taking a few moments to ponder, he mutters, "I'd like that."

"Great," I reply, glee evident in my voice.

As I slide into the passenger seat of his car and fasten my seatbelt, my cellphone vibrates in my pocket. My heart beats triple time when Carey's cell rings at the same time. In unison, we pull out our phones and hit the call button.

Before either of us can issue a greeting, Hugo's deep timbre voice comes barreling down both lines. "Ava's in labor! She's early! My mom isn't even here yet. What the hell am I supposed to do?"

My eyes rocket to Carey. He's standing at the side of his car frozen solid.

"Hugo. . . Hugo!" I shout into my phone, attempting to interrupt his panicked rant. When he pauses long enough to gasp a jagged breath, I say, "Don't panic. We'll be right there."

I disconnect my call and throw my cell into the center console. After sliding into the driver's seat, I roll down the window. A dull ache hits my chest when I spot the raw panic flooding Carey's eyes.

"Hop in; I'll drive."

Seemingly on autopilot mode, Carey pulls his cell away from his ear and clambers into the passenger seat. He remains quiet the entire four-mile trip, not even flinching when I grind the gears of his beloved Camaro.

When I pull into the driveway of Hugo's new home ten minutes later, Hugo rushes out of the house with an ashen-faced Ava under his arm.

"Oww. Owww. Owwww," Ava winces, her small voice getting louder with every whimper she makes.

Clutching her stomach, she bends over and exhales a deep, long-winded grunt. Hearing the absolute terror roaring through her body sets me on edge. My frozen stance mimics Carey's to a T. He managed to climb out of his car, but he hasn't moved out of the doorframe.

"That looks really, really painful," I mumble to anyone listening.

Hugo waits for Ava's contraction to end before he scoops her into his arms. I snap out of my trance when he locks his panicked eyes with me. "Joel goes to bed at 8. Don't let him eat sugar after 7 or he'll be up past midnight. My mom and dad are on their way, but they're hours away. Our emergency contact numbers are on the fridge..."

I place my hand over his clenched fist. His pulse is racing through his body so furiously, it pounds my palm. "We've got this," I assure him.

After bouncing his eyes between me and Carey, he curtly nods.

"Good luck." It was a pathetic set of words, but I have no clue what you're supposed to say to someone who is going to experience pain equivalent to having every bone in your body cracked.

My head slings sideways when the cutest little voice I've heard tingles into my ears. "Aunty Gem! Unky Hawke!"

Joel, Hugo's four-year-old son, comes charging across the freshly trimmed grass. The unease festering on Hugo's face eases when Joel immediately leaps into Carey's arms. Heat blooms across my chest when Joel's affection for his uncle causes Carey to topple onto his backside, sending his gorgeous laughter into the late afternoon air.

"HE'S FINALLY ASLEEP," I whisper, tiptoeing out of Joel's room.

Joel is a great kid, but I didn't realize his personality was an exact replica of Hugo's until now. I'm even more exhausted now than I was earlier. Who knew Monopoly was such a tiresome game? After slipping into the vacant seat next to Carey on the couch, I instinctively place my head on his shoulder. The quickest flex of his thigh muscles is the only objection cited from my closeness.

Carey has been wonderful the past three hours. Seeing him with Joel exposed sides of him I had not yet been privileged to witness. He's a wonderful uncle, and I have no doubt he would have been a wonderful father.

"Are events like today hard for you?" I question before I can stop my words.

Carey inhales a large breath that expands his chest before briefly shaking his head. I swallow a lump in my throat as I lift my head off his shoulder. "If I were to give you something. . . *sentimental* would now be the wrong time?"

He drifts his dark eyes between mine for several seconds before he once again shakes his head. Smiling to ease the anxiety in his eyes, I slip off the couch and pad to my handbag. My hand rattles when I slip it into my bag to remove Malcolm's perfectly restored ultrasound picture. I run my index finger across the glass to make sure there are no smears before pacing back to Carey. When his eyes zoom in on the photo frame in my hand, a vast flare of emotions pass through his eyes. He knows what I'm holding without even needing to see it.

Sneaky tears well in my eyes when he gasps in a shocked breath as I hand the picture frame to him. Compared to the photo in his wallet, this image shows all Malcolm's perfect little features. His ten little toes and fingers, the grooves of his chunky thighs, and even the curve of his plump lips.

I press my fingertips under my eyes, desperately trying to push my tears back when a sheen of moisture forms in the corner of Carey's eyes. His hand shakes when he lifts the frame to his mouth and gently places it against his lips. That is all it takes for my first set of tears to fall. *I'd give anything in the world to take away his pain.*

Spotting the wetness on my cheeks, Carey seizes my wrist and pulls me onto his lap. I bury my head into the curve of his neck, hoping the scent of his skin will ease the heaviness on my chest so I can secure an entire breath. I can barely breath through the tightness clutched around my throat. It is so surreal how beautiful and cruel the world can be to one man.

I don't know how much time passes before Carey mutters, "Thank you, Gem. This means the world to me." It was long enough that my tears have dried, but not long enough to inhale a full breath.

"You're welcome." My heavy words bounce off his neck and fan my lips with my warm breath.

With Carey running his hand down my back and my emotions at an all-time high, exhaustion soon overtakes me.

My tongue delves out to replenish my dry lips before I slowly crack open my heavy eyelids. My pulse quickens when I take in the strange environment surrounding me. From the virile, manly scent I know whose room this is, but what I can't fathom is, how did I get into Carey's bedroom? Don't get me wrong, I couldn't think of a better place to wake, but I still find it peculiar that I'm so carefree around Carey, I don't even wake when he moves me—*over two miles*.

I clutch my chest when a deep voice greets, "Morning."

Swinging my eyes to the side, I spot Carey standing in the doorway. His large frame and tall height fills the narrow gap. He's dressed down in a pair of cargo pants and a plain blue tee. His face appears freshly shaven, but his eyes have the signs of a tired man.

"Did you sleep?" My voice is groggy from just waking up.

He cringes. "Breaking in a new couch is never fun."

"You slept on the couch?" I grimace when my high voice bounces off the wall and shrills into my ears. My voice is loud with both shock and disappointment.

Carey nods. "I didn't want to startle you," he murmurs, his eyes softening with understanding.

My heart swells from his attentiveness. "How did you get me here without waking me?"

A smirk graces his beautiful lips. "Years in the military," he replies, like his simple response answers all my questions. It doesn't.

I'm about to ask for further information when reality dawns on why I'm waking up in Carey's room. "Did Ava have the baby?"

The most breathtaking smile I've ever seen carves onto Carey's lips. "Yes."

"Was it a girl?" My voice is high with glee.

Carey nods.

"What did they name her?" I can barely contain my excitement. Ava is my one and only female friend, so I've never experienced anything like this before.

With a glint in his eyes I don't recognize, Carey takes his time replying. "Elouise Marjorie Marshall," he eventually responds. He lifts his eyes from his twisted hands. "Marjorie was Jorgie's christened name," he explains, his tone a unique mix of pride and sadness.

"It's a beautiful name. I'm sure Elouise will honor it well," I push out through a solid lump in my throat.

The pain in Carey's eyes dulls. "Jorgie would be honored as well."

A few minutes of silence passes between us. I wouldn't necessarily say it is awkward, but it is full of palpable tension. Carey isn't a man of many words, but with each day we spend together, the man hiding behind the protective shield is slowly emerging, so he doesn't need to speak for me to know what he's thinking. And although I'd do anything to ease the uncertainty and guilt his eyes get every time he looks at me, I'm so incredibly grateful his guilt isn't as strong as his desire to spend time with me—and I'm not just talking between the sheets.

My attention snaps back to the present when Carey's deep voice booms through my ears. "Hmm, did you want something?" A flash of heat creeps up my neck when my croaky voice makes my words sound more like a suggestion than a question.

Carey scrubs his hand over his recently trimmed chin. From the gleam in his eyes and the delay in his reply, I have no doubt he also took my question with the hint of suggestion I didn't mean to issue, but am now glad I did.

After delving his tongue out to lick a set of lips I've fantasized about more than I'd care to admit, Carey says, "Visiting hours started ten minutes ago if you want to visit Elouise."

I dive out of the bed and race into the attached bathroom before the word "ago" escapes his lips.

I CAN FEEL the weight of Carey's tension every mile we travel to the hospital. I know he said last night that he doesn't find events like this hard, but I can't see how that is true. I'm not saying he isn't happy for Ava and Hugo, but it would have to conjure up old memories, ones he'd rather keep buried.

Just like every moment we've spent together, I allow my heart to guide my actions. Carey turns his eyes from the road to me when I curl my hand over his clenched fist resting on his thigh. I don't say anything. I let my eyes talk on my behalf. The pain in my chest lifts when he unclenches his fist so he can run his thumb along the edge of my palm.

After finding a vacant spot in the expansive parking lot of Ravenshoe Private Hospital, we curl out of the car and make the trek to the main entrance. The dull ache in my chest fully clears away when Carey rejoins our hands. To others, it may seem like a friendly gesture, but for a man living with grief, it is a gigantic leap in displaying my importance in his life. *Who needs grand gestures like candlelit dinners and bunches of smelly flowers when you have a man with a guarded heart willing to hold your hand in public?*

The ghastly scent of disinfectant lingers in the air as we walk down the bustling hospital corridor in silence. Only the noise of chuckling nurses and doctors being paged sounds through our ears. My heart melts into a puddle on the floor when Carey pushes open door 34A in the maternity suite. Ava and Hugo are sitting side by side with a little bundle of pink nestled between them. They're so immersed in categorizing every little inch of their daughter, they fail to detect our presence.

Keeping my eyes planted on Hugo's beaming smile as he peers down at his daughter, I pace deeper into the space. My efforts are less than stellar when Carey's feet appear to be the weight of concrete. His stiffened stance is even more forceful than the one he used on the church stairs months ago.

Clearing the pain from my eyes, I raise them to Carey. He looks down at me with the same amount of panic flaring in his eyes he held the day we met. It is a beautifully tormented visual that displays there are so many sides to this man I can't wait to explore.

"Don't think. Just breathe," I encourage.

Heat blooms across my chest when he follows my instructions by inhaling a large breath. His chest rises and falls three more times before he crosses the threshold of Ava's room. The euphoria pumping out of me in invisible waves is so intense, Ava and Hugo jerk their heads up in sync. The smile on Hugo's face grows when his eyes dart between Carey and me. It turns blinding when his happy gaze drops to our interlocked hands. Any chance of calming my wildly beating heart is lost when Hugo's inquisitive stare doesn't loosen Carey's grip around my hand. If anything, it strengthens it.

"Congratulations," I say, walking further into the room. Thankfully, with Carey clutching my hand, he follows closely behind me.

Our hands only unlock when Ava offers for me to hold Elouise. When I accept the wriggling bundle of pink, a scent I'll never forget fills my senses. There's nothing sweeter than the smell of a newborn baby. I lift Elouise closer to my face and inhale a deep, undignified whiff.

"I've been doing that all morning," Hugo admits, his voice heavy with sentiment.

After absorbing every perfect feature of Elouise's little face—which takes a good twenty or so minutes—I hand her to Carey, completely ignoring his brisk shake of his head for me not to. Sensing Carey's unease, Elouise whimpers in his arms. A barrage of emotions slam into me when the hard lines of Carey's face soften as he tries to subdue her little cries. The unease in his eyes completely clears away when his gentle pats on her bottom soothes her whimpers. My heart that melted on the floor completely evaporates when Carey draws Elouise in close to his chest and she falls blissfully asleep.

"You're a natural," I whisper, ensuring only Carey will hear me.

When he lifts and locks his eyes with me, I'm bombarded with numerous silent thanks. Smiling, I ran my hand down his arm, more than grateful to help him through this. My smile grows when the hairs on his arms bristle from my briefest touch.

AFTER NUMEROUS SQUISHY CUDDLES, two slices of bland cafeteria pizza, and a few hours of laughter, Carey and I leave Ava and Hugo in the capable hands of their numerous guests and pace back to his Camaro.

"She's really cute," I gush, loving the miracle of life.

Carey smiles a grin that gains him the devoted attention of a group of giggling nurses. "She is," he agrees.

The warm fire glowing in my chest combusts when we merge onto the sidewalk of the hospital and Carey interlocks our hands. We walk through the parking lot with the same amount of silence we did hours ago. This time it is void of any awkward uncomfortableness.

After unlocking his Camaro, Carey opens the passenger side door to me. There's no chance I can hold in my smile, so I just set it free. "Thank you," I blubber.

Remaining quiet, he closes my door, runs around to the driver's side, and slides in his seat. While fastening our seatbelts, our eyes connect for the briefest moment. The shift between us is dense and quick. It goes from a friendly vibe to being fired by lust. Our unique connection surges into uncharted waters when he runs the back of his fingers down my cheeks before locking his eyes with mine. They don't look as pained today as they normally do.

"What now?" he questions. His two short words express way more than he intended.

I rub my hands together as I turn my eyes to the brilliant blue sky. My heart rate kicks into overtime when an awesome idea formulates in my tired brain. "Are you up for a challenge, Mister? An ultimate afternoon of gear head activities?" I lock my challenging eyes with his. "Or is your ego too fragile to sustain another massive hit?"

Carey tries to act unexcited. I'm not buying it. His eyes flared the instant I stuttered "gear head." I'm glad he didn't hear the deceit in my tone. I don't just want us to create another day of memories. I want to do anything in my power to ease his pain during this no doubt difficult time.

"Depends," Carey replies, his voice low and tempting. "How do you handle defeat?"

My eyes roll skywards. "*Please.* I kicked your butt on the NASCAR simulator at the arcade."

My mouth gapes when Carey says, "Only because I let you win."

I try to refute his claim. My mouth moves, but my words stay entombed in my throat. I can't deny his statement as his eyes are relaying that it was nothing but gospel. My excitement swells. That means he wanted to spend time with me months ago, that he purposely lost so our night didn't have to end. I knew I wasn't the only one feeling our undeniable connection that night.

Laughing at my shocked expression, Carey reverses out of the parking lot.

"We will see who is laughing when I whip your butt. I've been practicing." That's not a lie. During my month-long stint in my apartment, I became addicted to online NASCAR games.

The heat on my cheeks from Carey's beautiful laugh flames more when he says, "Spanking ass is Hugo's thing. I prefer to issue my punishments in slow and tortuous licks."

My entire body shudders.

CHAPTER 30

GEMMA

Carey and I stumble into his apartment, bumping into the entranceway table and knocking a picture off the wall. Our movements aren't because we spent our afternoon acting like teens playing arcade games and racing around a go-kart track. It is because neither of us are willing to detach our lips from one another to gather our bearings. Our entire afternoon was like prolonged foreplay. Gentle little touches, a few sneaky kisses, and creating memories that will last longer than a lifetime. It has been a wonderful day that has only tethered my heart to Carey more.

With his fingers weaved through my hair and his tongue dueling mine, Carey kicks his front door shut and steps backward. Not willing to relinquish his delicious mouth from mine, I tighten my grip around his shoulders and curl my legs around his hips. A grin crimps my lips when we fall like a heap onto his lumpy couch with a thud. The thickness of Carey's cock in his shorts is barely contained, brushing against my aching core and wiping the laughter off my face.

His mouth captures my breathy moan when I rock my hips forward, dragging my soaked sex along his wide rod. Excitement tingles my nerve-endings as a rush of lust scorches my veins. By the time Carey's fingers have made quick work of the buttons on my shirt, I'm panting, wet, and on the verge of combusting. My breathing turns greedy when he cups one of my breasts in his large hand and squeezes it gently. His index finger and thumb roll my nipple into a firm and hard peak.

No longer able to leash my excitement, I pull my lips away from Carey's sinful mouth with the intention of wrangling his thickened shaft from its tight restraints. My almost frantic movements stop when for the briefest moment my eyes connect with Carey. The shift between us is fast and resolute. Just as quick as our fire-sparking union commenced, it ends. The rapidly forming cloud of guilt building in Carey's eyes makes quick work of the wooziness hindering my astute mind.

I place my hands on the curve of his sweaty jaw and peer into his eyes. "Don't." My one word expresses everything I want to say. *Please don't feel guilty. Something as magical as this should never have guilt attached to it. Don't let your past guide your future.*

When Carey remains quiet, I say, "If you want me to go, I'll go. I understand."

Little nicks hit my heart when he faintly murmurs, "I don't see Jorgie when I'm with you." He locks his remorse-filled eyes with me, his gaze both shocked and aroused. "Why don't I see her when I'm with you?"

My right shoulder lifts into a shrug. "I don't know," I respond truthfully, my low voice displaying my heartache at the pain in his eyes.

I want to kiss away his pain before promising he will never experience that type of hurt again. I want to never leave his side so his haunted memories will be forever lost, but I can't do either of those things. All I can promise is that I'll help him work through his grief until he reaches a stage where he feels comfortable being around me. It won't take away his pain or make him forget his past, but it will give him the opportunity to live without guilt.

"Do you want me to go?" I ask, my voice barely a whisper.

Relief engulfs me when he briefly shakes his head. It's short-lived when he murmurs, "But maybe you should."

"Then I'll go," I whisper, attempting to climb off his lap.

A breathless moan escapes my lips when he strengthens his grip on my backside, successfully pulling me back into his lap. "I don't want you to go."

"Then I won't."

He flexes his fingers on the globes of my ass. "If you tell me you want to go, I'll let you go," he informs me, sheepishly peering at me through a set of thick lashes.

"I'm not going to say that," I reply with a soft shake of my head. "I will never say that."

He slowly rocks his hips forward, his movements so agile, they're almost imperceptible. "I'm broken."

I lean forward, flattening my breasts against his sweat-slicked chest so I can't see the remorse in his eyes when I reply, "So am I."

His lips brush the shell of my ear when he mutters, "I may never recover."

"I know. Me either."

I want to kiss him, but I won't. I'm not going to do anything that will risk ending this conversation. Our sentences may be brief, but they're jam-packed with emotions not even the world's best poet could replicate.

Carey slowly drags his hips forward again, allowing me to feel it isn't just his emotions swelling. "This won't be easy."

My lips tug into a small grin. "Nothing worth having is."

"Hugo said one more crack could completely break you. I don't want to break you." The promise in his words alone ensures that will never happen.

"Hugo doesn't know how strong I've become. I'm not the same Gemma I used to be."

Excitement heats my blood when his hand creeps under my skirt and he snaps my panties off my body. "Why me?"

"Why not?" I reply, my two words long and breathless.

He slides his hand between our bodies and releases his cock from its tight restraints as my teeth graze my bottom lip. "Why me?" he asks again before bracing the tip of his cock at the entrance of my pussy.

My hot pants of breath hit his neck as I mutter, "Because you make me feel whole. I want to do the same for you."

A wave of euphoria overwhelms me when he sinks the first inch of his cock into me. He takes his time, gently delivering every inch in a painstakingly slow thrust.

"Why now?" he asks once every inch of me has been filled to the brim. Not just my pussy, but my heart as well.

I draw away from his chest and glance into his eyes. They aren't as tormented as they were before. "Because we've suffered long enough. It's time for the pain to stop."

He withdraws his cock at the same tortuously slow speed before sliding it back in. "The pain will never stop."

"No, I guess it won't." My lungs saw in and out with every breath I take. "But it will never ease if we don't try."

My head lolls to the side when his thrusts quicken. He works me into a frenzy using a slow and controlled pace, like a man who knows my body in intimate detail. "Will you try as well? Will you do it with me?"

Lost in the race to climax, I nod. "Yes. I'll be right by your side every day if that is what you want. I'll never leave your side."

"Promise." He drags his cock all the way to the tip before guiding it back in in a mouthwatering thrust. "Promise you'll never leave. I can't go through that again." He said his last sentence so quietly, I can't even be certain he said it.

Oh, god— Carey.

The pain in his voice cuts me raw. I can't take this. I can't handle so many emotions at once. I flutter open my eyes, preparing to tell him that isn't something I can give him. I can't promise him that any more than I can promise his grief will end. Grief never ends. It may ease over time, or become less painful, but just like love, it lasts a lifetime.

Tightness spreads across my chest when I see the pain in his eyes. He needs this promise more than anything. Even more than his next breath. How can I pledge to ease his pain, then the next minute break his heart by denying the one thing he needs more than anything?

"I promise," I mutter, deciding that breaking a promise to a broken man is better than shattering his heart beyond repair. "You'll never go through that again."

CHAPTER 31

GEMMA

"You dawg," Wesley says with a chuckle. "Using your daddy to ensure your sexual rut doesn't return."

I snap my eyes to the small living room of our cabin to ensure my dad and Carey didn't hear Wesley's statement. Although what he's saying is one hundred percent accurate, I don't want either my dad or Carey knowing it.

Happy we've failed to gain their attention, I return my eyes to Wesley. He finishes scooping the avocado dip I made earlier into a white ceramic bowl before locking his eyes with mine. "What happened to the 'dating exclusively for six-months before you meet my daddy rule?'"

I pull the fried tortilla chips out of the oven while replying, "The math is simple. Even a layman like you won't have any trouble following it."

Squealing, I leap out of Wesley's reach when the crack of a tea towel sounds through the kitchen. "Who needs math when you look like this?" He runs his hand down the front of his body while waggling his brows.

I slant my head to the side and quirk my lips. "True."

There's no use denying the truth. Wesley is gorgeous, and I'm beyond obsessed with Carey. The past week has shown a side to Carey I knew was hiding beneath his grief. He's a caring and gentle man who was handed a horrible life sentence. I won't pretend I understand what Carey is going through, but I do understand nothing I could say or do will ease his pain. The best I can do is accept that there will be ups and downs, days filled with sadness, and times when his grief will take him away from me. If I can control my selfishness as well as my understanding, I can work through these troubles.

Snapping his fingers in front of my face to break me out of my trance, Wesley says, "But just for us *laymen* you better give me the details."

Smiling, I say, "Everything with Carey happens at a rate 90 times my set limit. So, we only needed to have two dates before he could meet my dad. Although our first night together wasn't technically a date, I'm counting it as one."

Wesley's brow arches into his hairline. "So a one-night stand and a nookie on a couch equals a parental meet and greet? I'm so fucking glad we sorted our shit out before my cock got anywhere near your pussy."

"*Please*. If we ended up twisted in the sheets, you'd not only be begging to meet my dad, you'd be pleading for round two."

This time Wesley's crack of the tea towel hits me right on the backside. Even nursing a stinging butt, I grin like an idiot when he doesn't attempt to refute my claim. Although my confidence is already at an all-time high from numerous fire-sparking exchanges with Carey the past seven days, no girl in their right mind would knock back a compliment from a man as handsome as Wesley and not get giddy about it.

Wesley leans his shoulder on the doorjamb of the kitchen. "For two strangers, they seem to know each other well."

"They've met before, although I don't think my dad remembers," I explain, grabbing a six pack of beer out of the fridge. "Carey did two of my dad's advance driver training courses."

Wesley's lips extend to the tip of his nose. He appears shocked by my admission.

"You should see Carey on the track, Wes. My god, I swear my panties nearly combusted."

Wesley twists his neck to the side and eyes me with an impish gleam. "Those sexy, if you survive these, you'll get to meet my daddy after two dates *contouring* panties you were telling me about?"

I cringe. "Don't remind me."

Wesley pushes off the doorframe and ambles deeper into the kitchen. "It must be love, as I can sure-as-hell tell you, if a chick I took home was wearing those hideous fuckers I begged you not to buy, I would have called Miramax Films and told them *Bridget Jones* had escaped the mental hospital she should be locked up in. I don't give a shit if it turns sausages into steak, no one should wear panties like that."

"It isn't the panties that make a woman. It's what they're covering," I retort, my voice doused in laughter to hide my embarrassment. Part of me wears contouring panties as I want to ensure all my body parts stay where they belong, but the major reason is the little niggle in the back of my head wondering if it was my clothing selection that caused the shake to my core six years ago.

Not noticing the quick switch in my demeanor, Wesley grins while asking, "It's the treasure behind the material that is the ultimate prize?" His voice is low and tempting.

I nod.

"Then why are you wearing a racy little red thong today?"

My eyes rocket to his. My mouth is gaped, my eyes bulging. I've always said Wesley knows me well, but I didn't realize he knew me *that* well.

Bending down so his six-foot frame can meet me eye to eye, he says, "Just a suggestion: unless you want your daddy to lock you up in a nunnery, don't bend over in front of him."

After yanking up the waist of my low-riding jeans, I follow a snickering Wesley into the cozy living room. Although my dad has spent the last three hours ensuring he is always positioned between Carey and me, I wouldn't change a single thing. Carey's face alone when he walked into the cabin and spotted my dad rearranging the living room is worth putting up with my dad's overbearing protectiveness. Carey didn't act as flabbergasted as Wesley did when we met the members of Rise Up, but his eyes were the brightest I've ever seen, and the smile he issued me when I greeted him on the patio with a daring kiss is still stretched across his face.

My dad's eyes lift from the TV when I place the dip and fried tortilla chips on the coffee table. I'm not lying when I say my dad is a handsome man. Even being in his fifties doesn't dampen his appeal the slightest. He has inky black hair that falls around his chiseled face. His eyes are a few shades darker than Carey's, and his skin more tanned, but that is where their comparisons end. Actually, come to think of it, they have a lot more similarities than I'd care to admit.

Any concerns that I've fallen into the trap of dating a younger version of my dad flies out the window when Carey's hand skims past my thigh as he reaches for the tortillas. His touch wasn't on purpose, and I'm standing next to my dad, but it doesn't stop an upwelling of desire to create havoc with my libido.

The fiery rage in my core nearly combusts when Wesley hooks his thumb into the loop of my jeans and yanks me backward. "Your ass is blocking the TV, Poppet."

His yank has me toppling into the small space left between my dad and Carey on the three-seater couch, leaving them no option but to scoot to the side so I can sit between them. Although my dad's jaw gains a tick it didn't have earlier, he admirably holds in his annoyance at me practically sitting on Carey's lap.

I'm not surprised. That is just like my dad. Carey has been nothing but respectful to him the past three hours, so my dad will do the same. My dad has always believed that respect is not hard to gain, only easy to lose.

When Carey adjusts his position so his splayed thigh presses against mine, I turn my eyes to Wesley. "I love you so much," I silently mouth.

I nearly giggle like a school girl when he mouths back, "I want every *explicit* detail."

My efforts to act my age become impossible when Wesley uses his tongue to push out the side of his cheek, mimicking a gesture only a teenage boy should make. Overcome with dizziness from sitting so close to Carey, and the three bottles of beer I've had, I decide to play along with Wesley's childish game.

After making a circle with one hand, I push my index finger on my opposite hand in and out of my clenched fist. Adding to my immaturity, I screw my face up to replicate expressions only the world's worst porn stars should make. Wesley sinks deeper into his chair, his chest thrusting up and down as he battles to hold in his laughter.

"Hmm," I say when my dad calls my name.

His big, worldly eyes take in my inclined cheeks and heavily dilated gaze. "Are you okay? You look a little flustered."

Tearing my hands apart like they're opposing magnets, I strangle out, "I'm fine."

My words are husky, choked by the mortified lump sitting in the back of my throat. Wesley and I have been known to have moments of silliness, but with my brain busy categorizing every movement Carey makes, I've gone into full-on moronic mode.

The faint chuckle seeping from Wesley's mouth vanishes into thin air when my dad swings his eyes to Wesley. "You're not corrupting my daughter again, are you?" my dad asks him. I can't tell from his low tone if he's being serious or witty.

"No, Sir, not at all," Wesley replies, his face whitening with every syllable.

My dad loves Wesley as if he's his own son, but that doesn't mean he isn't going to put him in his place if he believes he's being disrespectful. Several heartbeats of uncomfortable silence later, four sets of eyes turn back to the television.

The heat on my cheeks doubles when Carey inconspicuously leans to my side and whispers, "Is that your prediction for post-race entertainment?"

He may have only said one little sentence, but my god, it was strong enough that the remaining hours of the race were nothing but a blur to me. I was too busy fighting to control my unbridled desire to pay attention to a group of cars charging around a race track.

CHAPTER 32

GEMMA

"Are you sure I can't offer you a ride?" my dad offers Carey, gesturing to his black SUV parked next to Carey's Camaro. "My driver can arrange for someone to collect your Camaro tomorrow morning."

Carey spent the last half hour answering my dad's broad range of questions regarding the restoration of his pride and joy. I was shocked to discover Carey fully rebuilt his Camaro with his own two hands using nothing but spare parts from junkyards scattered around New York. That little snippet of information exposed a side to him I can't wait to fully unearth. Knowing he had the patience to take something others had seen as worthless and restore it to its former beauty fills me with hope that he will do the same thing with me.

After dropping his eyes to my teeth grazing over my bottom lip, Carey murmurs, "Thanks for the offer, but I wouldn't want to put you out."

Every muscle in my body tightens in anticipation.

"You wouldn't be putting me out," my dad fires back, his tone lowering to a depth he hasn't used thus far tonight. "It will be my utmost *pleasure*."

"Daddy," I whisper when I hear the silent statement in his reply. He pretty much just told Carey he isn't leaving until he does.

"I understand your concerns, Sir, but you don't need to be worried," Carey assures him.

Disappointment slashes me open.

Blood stops gushing from my invisible wounds when Carey adds on, "Gemma is a very respectable woman. You can be assured I won't do anything to taint that."

Time stands still when my dad assesses Carey's soul from the inside out with his worldly eyes. I release the breath I'm holding in when several uncomfortable minutes later, he thrusts his hand out in offering.

I fiercely suck it back in when my dad mutters, "You were an admirable young man twelve years ago; I can only hope time hasn't changed you." I shouldn't be shocked my dad remembers Carey. He never forgets in general, let alone a man who has as much driving talent as Carey.

Carey briefly nods before accepting my dad's handshake. My pulse quickens when my dad pulls Carey in so they're standing eye to eye. Since I've always looked at my dad in a different light than I do Carey, I never realized he was so tall until now. The size of a man isn't a concern to a child when all they can see is the heart of a lion.

"But in saying that, if you hurt my daughter, they'll never find your body," my dad warns.

Before I can reprimand my dad for his inappropriate threat, Carey says, "I understand. I don't want to add to the pain in Gemma's eyes." I stop breathing when he swings his eyes to me and testifies, "I want to clear it away."

I expect Carey's admission to cause a rush of panic in my veins. What I don't expect is for it to bolster my excitement. That's not something a man only interested in a night off from his grief would say. That's a man laying foundations. A man who doesn't just want to know my façade; he wants to know everything about me. That notion alone is equally terrifying and exhilarating.

My mind snaps back to the present when my dad says, "I appreciate your honesty, but I don't trust words. I trust actions." He flicks his eyes to me. "In saying that, I trust you and your judgment."

My heart swells as sentimental tears prick my eyes. "Thank you, Daddy. I love you." My dad may not have said the words, but he just gave Carey his seal of approval.

"I love you too, sweetheart." After pressing a kiss to the side of my cheek, my dad drifts his eyes to Carey. "Don't let me down."

He waits for Carey to nod his head before he slides into the back of his chauffeur-driven SUV. Once his taillights disappear into the horizon, Carey encloses his hand over mine and guides us back toward the cabin. The sexual tension firing between us is great enough to spark a fire. I'm not shocked. There's nothing sexier than discovering someone wants you just as much as you want them.

When we enter the living room, Wesley stops gathering the empty beer bottles and darts his eyes between Carey and me. "I'm going to call it a night. I have an early recording session tomorrow."

My excitement hits an all-time high. Not only did Carey just get my dad's nod of approval, he also got Wesley's.

Pushing to his feet, Wesley paces into the kitchen. The clattering of beer bottles being dumped into the bin sounds through my ears shortly before he walks back into the living area. He awards my kiss blown through the air with a cheeky wink before spinning on his heels and ambling down the hall. The throb between my legs grows with every step he travels.

The instant his door clicks closed, I pounce. My abrupt push on Carey's chest sends him stumbling onto the couch and spreads a broad smile across his mouth. This day has been seven long hours of torturous foreplay. I could smell Carey and feel the heat of his body, but I wasn't allowed to touch him. That was pure torture.

After straddling Carey's lap, I slide one of my hands beneath his shirt as the other yanks on the drawstring of his shorts. Not in my wildest dreams have I ever been so forward, but I can't wait any longer to feel his skin against mine.

"Seriously. You need to get naked, like *now*," I demand, my voice husky and crammed with need.

My frantic movements stop the instant Carey grasps the hem of his shirt and yanks it over his head. My god. . . I'm speechless. I'm certain even seeing his perfect body in the flesh for the hundredth time won't dampen its appeal the slightest. Broad shoulders, defined and smooth pecs, and hard slabs of muscles jutted in six tight bumps on his stomach, the man is a work of art, one I'd happily spend hours perusing every single brush stroke.

My eyes divert from absorbing Carey's magnificent torso when I feel him growing beneath me. His cock is hard and extended, stretching the material of his shorts as they struggle to hold in his impressive package. Spirals of pleasure twist in my core when I rock against him. He grows even more, getting thicker and longer with every grind.

I love this. I love how all the insecurities I've been harboring since my attack disappear when I'm with Carey. I'm not evaluating every look that passes his eyes or striving to be the dominant one in our partnership. Nothing is on my mind but enjoying every second of our unique connection. That's a real rarity for a victim of assault. I never thought I'd have these types of feelings again during sexual contact, but just like every moment I spend with him, I'm discovering sides of me I haven't seen in years. . . and sides that are completely brand new.

I increase the pressure of my grinding, ignoring the fact my rampant horniness has driven me back to my teen years where dry humping was perfectly acceptable. Carey doesn't seem to mind. He curls his fingers around my backside, strengthening his grip before he rocks his hips forward, meeting my grinds stroke for stroke. I'm so turned on, I'm certain I'll have a wet patch on the front of my jeans by the time this is over, but for the first time in my life, I don't care.

Carey's fingers flex against my backside when I mumble, "More. Oh, god, I need more."

Drawing me in closer, he sways his hips upwards in long, sensual strokes, adding to the cluster of lust surging through my core. I love that he can drive me wild with desire all while being gentle and passionate. Don't get me wrong, Carey knows how to fuck. The night we shared together weeks ago proves that without a doubt, but I appreciate his gentleness.

I sling my arms around Carey's shoulders to tether myself down as my breathing switches to low, shallow pants. The coils of my womb tighten as a wave of pleasure vibrates through every inch of my skin.

"Fuck, Gem. Are you about to come?" Carey grates out, his words raspy.

I should be ashamed. I should feel embarrassed, but I'm not. I've floated too far into orgasmic bliss to be ashamed.

The spark of lust in Carey's eyes ignites when I briefly nod. His thrusts become firmer and more precise, demonstrating he has no qualms about satisfying me while I'm still fully clothed.

With the rim of his mouthwatering cock pressed against my throbbing clit, and his eyes void of a single ounce of guilt, it doesn't take long for my climax to hit fruition. I come with a breathless moan that adds to the passion firing between us. My orgasm is long and welcomed, fully clearing away any haunted memories lingering in the back of my mind.

Carey slowly brings me down from orgasmic bliss by slowing his strokes. My body is acutely aware of every inch of his glorious cock rocking against me, but his leisured pace slowly drags me from a lust-filled haze to reality.

Any chance of stepping back into reality vanishes when I lock my eyes with Carey. For the first time in months, his eyes aren't carrying his usual level of guilt. Don't get me wrong, they still hold both remorse and guilt, but they're nowhere near as strong as normal.

A girly laugh topples from my lips when Carey stands from the couch, taking me with him.

"Time for round two," he mutters, pacing toward my bedroom with my limp, sexually drained body flopped over his shoulder.

CHAPTER 33

GEMMA

Basking in the glory of a wonderful summer morning and waking up without the aftereffects of a nightmare for the sixth night in a row, I pace towards the warehouse my studio is set up in. I'm teeming with excitement. Today I get to reveal the cover Cormack has chosen for Rise Up's commemorative CD. It is also an opportunity to show the band the photos I've captured of them. I'm in love with them. I can only hope they feel the same way. They're a set of images that showcase the band in a light the public has not yet seen. It displays that they are brothers and men of high integrity, not just handsome musicians with extensive musical talent.

My mood is also riding the crest of euphoria as the past two weeks with Carey have been staggering. Our time together has taught me that intimacy is not just purely physical. It's a deep and powerful connection between two people. His kisses alone reap a more intense connection than any man I've slept with, making me realize every encounter I've had before him was nothing but an emotionless transaction. With Carey's help, I intend to change that.

My brisk pace slows when the early morning sun unveils a man standing under the awning of the warehouse. He's wearing a dark blue suit and black polished dress shoes. Although a majority of his face is hidden, I don't feel as uneasy about him as I normally do when I'm confronted by a stranger alone. He has that humble Boy Scout look that places my usual concerns on the back burner. . . *or perhaps last night's libido-bolstering orgasms are playing havoc with my perception?*

"Can I help you?" My voice is a faint quiver.

The blonde gentleman stops peering into the window of the warehouse and spins around to face me. Even with his eyes shrouded by concern, miraculously, my panic stays at bay.

"Hello, Gemma, my name is Brandon James. I'm a local FBI agent in Ravenshoe," he greets me.

Masking my shock that he knows my name, I drop my eyes to his identification he's holding out for my perusal. I take my time checking its authenticity. Years of weariness have ensured I don't take people just on face value anymore. Carey is the only man who has broken that firm habit of mine the past six years.

Happy his identification looks legitimate, I return my eyes to his face. "What can I help you with, Brandon?"

His hazel eyes peer past my shoulder to a group of young teens mingling in the parking lot. "Is there somewhere private we can talk?" he enquires. His voice is calm and neutral, but it doesn't stop my panic from slowly climbing.

"Sure, umm... we could talk inside?" I suggest.

Brandon smiles as he timidly nods. I return his gesture while digging my hand into my bag. To Brandon it looks like I'm rummaging for my keys, where, in reality, I'm speed dialing Wesley's cell phone number and activating my speaker phone.

When the screen on my cell illuminates that the timer has begun, I pull out my keys and act surprised. "There they are."

Remaining quiet, Brandon shadows me to the entrance of the warehouse. His closeness doesn't conjure any thoughts—negative or positive. I don't know if that's a good or bad thing.

"If you don't mind me asking, how did you know to find me here? This warehouse isn't registered in my name, and I haven't publicly announced I'm in Ravenshoe." I keep my voice loud enough to ensure

Wesley can hear me, but not overly loud to raise suspicion from Brandon.

"I have a lot of resources at my disposal," he chuckles.

His charming laugh soothes some of the agitation twisting my stomach, but it isn't enough to stop me from protecting myself.

After sliding open the double glass doors, I gesture for Brandon to enter before me. You can protect yourself better if you face your attacker head on rather than having them sneak up on you unaware.

"Is this a personal visit or business-related?" I query.

Brandon's brows tack. "I guess you could say personal." The ricketiness of his words exposes his unsureness.

"Do I need my lawyer present?" The hammering of my heart can be heard in my voice.

Brandon shakes his head. "I'm not here representing the FBI," he informs me.

Dread washes over me. "Then why are you here?"

My hand delves into my handbag to seek my canister of pepper spray. This time, I don't attempt to conceal my intent to protect myself.

"I know Hugo. I'm a friend of his. I'm here on his behalf," Brandon adds on quickly, no doubt reading the panicked expression on my face.

I stop rummaging in my bag. "You know Hugo?" I ask, surprise lacing my voice. I shouldn't be surprised though. Everyone knows Hugo.

The dizziness plaguing me dulls when Brandon curtly nods. I don't know why, but his aura is telling me that I can trust him, but not his motives.

Hoping to ease the swirling of my stomach, I ask, "Does Hugo know you're here?"

I clutch my handbag close to my chest when Brandon reluctantly shakes his head. My chin quivers as he murmurs, "I'm not going to hurt you, Gemma."

"Y-you know what happened to me?" I don't know why I'm stuttering, but something about this doesn't feel right. My intuition is telling me something bad is about to happen.

Glancing into my eyes so I can see the truth beaming from his remorseful gaze, Brandon mutters, "Yes."

"How? You can't. No one knows. It's sealed. All my files are sealed." I stare him straight in the eyes. "Only those involved know what happened."

Sick gloom spreads through me as every nightmare I've had the last six years hits fruition. I haven't seen the faces of the men who attacked me since we had our day in court years ago, but even with Brandon having no recognizable features of my attackers, I'm still wary. The circumstances of my assault mean my recollection of the people involved are best described as hazy, so I can't one hundred percent testify Brandon isn't one of them.

I take a retreating step when Brandon paces closer to me. Spotting the panic flaring in my eyes, he stops and shoves his hands into his pocket. "You can trust me, Gemma. I'm only here trying to help Hugo."

I point to my office on my right. "I-I'm going to call Hugo. You s-stay right there. I'm going to call Hugo." My words are hoarse and sound like they were dragged through gravel.

My brisk pace to my office stops when Brandon says, "If you do that, you'll only make matters worse for him."

I grit my teeth before spinning around. "If you truly know what happened to me, you'd know things couldn't get any worse than they already are."

The remorse in Brandon's eyes triples. "Madden has photos of your attack."

I shake my head, refusing to acknowledge the truth glowing from his wholesome eyes. "That's not true. Madden wouldn't disclose that information to anyone. I don't believe you."

When Brandon takes a step closer to me, I wave my hands in front of my body, begging for him to stop.

He stops pacing mid-stride before disclosing, "My name is Brandon James McGee. I'm the youngest brother of Madden McGee."

My bag crashes onto the ground as tears I swore would never spill down my cheeks again roll out of my eyes unchecked. I can barely breathe through the tightness clutching my neck as my lungs wheeze to fill with air.

Closing my eyes, I count backwards from ten, utilizing one of the tricks Dr. McKay recommended when I'm trapped in the midst of a nightmare. This can't be real. This can't be happening. Not here. Not now. Not while I'm alone.

When I open my eyes and am confronted with the same pair of hazel eyes that frequent my nightmares, I scream, "Get out!" My loud voice bellows off the isolated warehouse walls and shrills into my ears.

"Get out!" I scream again at the top of my lungs when Brandon fails to comply.

"I'm not going to hurt you, Gemma. I'm trying to help you. I'm trying to help Hugo." His pleading eyes add strength to his admission, but I can't hear him. I can't hear anything through the blood roaring to my ears.

Overcome with a rage I've been harboring for six years, I charge for Brandon. My nails claw his arms before I raise my fists to pound his chest. "You ruined everything! You took everything away from me. I hate you. I HATE you!"

My face heats with anger as I put in the same effort I did when I fought my attackers six years ago. This time, I'm not outnumbered. This time, I won't let them win.

Tears fling off my cheeks as I continually pummel my fists onto Brandon's chest. He takes everything I'm giving, not once attempting to protect himself. "You might have thought you got the better of me, but you didn't! You'll never win!"

"That's right, Gemma. He didn't win. Make him pay."

Tears streaming down my face hamper my vision, but they don't stop my vicious onslaught. *My pain will never end, so why should his?*

With my mind stuck in the haze of the past and the present, the pounds of my fist become sluggish as my knees weaken. When the effort of my heaving lungs becomes too great for me to ignore, I fall onto my knees and gasp in ragged breaths. The pain of my knees hitting the concrete is nothing compared to the torrent of pain tearing through my chest. I can barely breathe as it hurts so much.

"I hate you," I mumble through a sheet of tears. "I hate you for hurting me. I hate you for making me feel worthless. I hate that scum like you get to breathe when good people like Carey's family don't."

I raise my tear-flooded eyes from the ground, wanting to ensure my attacker absorbs my gospel words. My mind spirals when the evil set of eyes I'm expecting to stare back at me have been replaced with a pair of remorseful eyes—eyes I'd never forget.

Carey.

CHAPTER 34

GEMMA

"Whose place is this?" I ask when Carey guides me into an expansive living area of a penthouse apartment in the middle of Ravenshoe. With the aftereffects of my meltdown still playing havoc with my emotions, my voice is hoarse and tainted with grief.

"This is the old apartment I shared with Hugo when I first moved to Ravenshoe," Carey informs me, his tone low and dejected. "I thought you'd prefer to talk somewhere private."

Smiling to ease the uncertainty on his face, I nod. Carey's suite is wonderful, but after seeing the concern in Jenni and Emily's eyes when they arrived at the warehouse minutes after Carey, my desire for privacy is at an absolute pinnacle. They're very sweet and kind-hearted girls, and I could tell just from the expressions on their faces they would give anything to ease my pain, but the remorse in their eyes nearly had me backpedaling on my decision to tell Carey the truth. My desire for him not to look at me like they were is so potent, I cashed in the last of my genie wishes on the way here.

After placing my camera bag on a large chair sitting at the side of a glass entranceway table, Carey throws his keys into a crystal bowl. He has barely spoken a word since he found me huddled on the floor of the warehouse nearly forty-minutes ago. He doesn't need to speak to express his sentiment. I can feel it radiating out of him. He's nearly as devastated as me. I've always said silence can speak volumes. Clearly, Carey has read my silence with acute accuracy.

Striving to keep my voice neutral, I ask, "Are Hugo and Wesley coming here?"

I release a relieved breath when Carey briefly shakes his head, grateful I can tell him my secret without additional witnesses. Although Hugo and Wesley already know the worst of my life story, I don't want them to sway Carey's response. I know my secret will be hard for him to hear, but I want to gage his true response, not one mimicked by those surrounding him.

Carey stops walking halfway down the hall. His heart is beating so furiously, the veins in his hand thrash against my lower back. "Did you want them to come? I can ask them to come if you don't feel comfortable being alone with me."

My heart aches from the pain radiating in his tone. "I'm perfectly fine being alone with you, Carey. I love our free time," I reply honestly.

The weight on my chest lessens when my confession clears some of the pain in Carey's eyes.

I lick my parched lips before saying, "I'd like to have a shower, though." I feel dirty. Not just from sitting on the filthy warehouse floor, but from the entirety of my day.

"Okay," Carey replies quietly, his eyes softening with understanding.

After switching on the faucet in a lavish bathroom and handing me a stack of towels, he paces to the door. "I'll meet you in the living room?"

Smiling to calm the heavy frown line between his eyes, I nod.

It isn't until I'm alone do my nerves really hit me. I'm not nervous about spending one-on-one time with Carey; every minute I spend with him has me craving more. I'm worried about what his reaction will be when I share my secret. He has been patient and kind the past two weeks, but I saw the disappointment in his eyes every time I shut down his efforts to discuss my past. I want him to know everything about me, but the idea of him looking at me differently stops me from sharing.

Dr. McKay has often quoted that sharing my secret frees me from the pain associated with it. I somewhat agree with his statement. Secrets in any form aren't a good foundation for a relationship, but being stripped bare is a terrifying thing even the world's strongest person would have difficulty doing. Just knowing it is the right thing to do doesn't make it any easier.

That's why even with my astuteness being buried in anguish, I know why Brandon approached me today. He believes unearthing incriminating evidence against my attackers will cause justice to prevail. What he isn't aware of is that the likelihood of that happening is nonexistent. After numerous botched attempts at having my attackers charged in Military Court, my dad went one step further—he went after the men he believed were responsible for the failed attempts of justice. He won, meaning not only was a settlement of 3.5 million dollars wired into my bank account three years after my attack, I signed a non-disclosure statement, which ensures I cannot discuss any of the events leading to the lawsuit with anyone—not my attackers youngest brother or the man who pled guilty to a crime he didn't commit just to save me. That was the biggest mistake I made since my attack. It is one I've regretted every day since.

After taking my time in the shower, I dress in one of Carey's long-sleeve shirts left slung over his bed. It feels comforting being surrounded by his unique virile scent. While standing at the side of the room, sucking in lung-filling gulps of air, I swing my eyes around the space. The sluggish beat of my heart kicks up when I spot Carey's wallet sitting on the dresser.

Allowing my inquisitiveness to get the better of me, I push off my feet and pace towards the mirrored dresser. Warmth fills the hole in my chest when I spot Malcolm's ultrasound picture I restored tucked safely into the corner of his wallet. My heart rate kicks into overdrive when I discover another picture slotted next to it. It is the photo I took of Carey and me the first night we spent together. It feels like years has passed since that memory-creating day, but it has only been a matter of months. *There's no right time or place for love. It can happen at any time.*

With every second I stare at the Polaroid picture, the agitation swirling my stomach eases. Carey not only kept the picture I snapped of us, he stored it with a photo that means the world to him.

That alone makes what I'm about to do a whole heap easier.

After placing Carey's wallet back on the dresser, I slowly saunter down the elegant hallway. For every step I take, I exhale nerves and inhale courage. Courage is one muscle in your body that never stops growing.

My eyes stray away from my bare feet when my body's perception of Carey activates. He's standing at the side of the living room wearing a pair of shorts and a plain cotton tee. He has a glass of amber-colored liquid in his hand, and his hair is wet as if he has also showered. Sensing my presence, he lifts his downcast gaze to me. Something deep inside me shifts when I see the glossy sheen coating his eyes.

Seeing him stripped and vulnerable forces me to blurt out, "I was raped six years ago."

He sucks in a jagged breath, his eyes widening, his jaw tightening.

"What?" His one word is so weak I barely hear it.

Fighting against my wobbly legs, I push off my feet and pad closer to him. He stares at me, his eyes icy and aloof, his fists balled.

"I was raped six—"

"I heard what you said. You don't need to repeat it," he interrupts, his voice as brittle as my composure. The repulsion attached to his words cuts through me like a hot knife through butter.

"Maybe you should sit down," I suggest when I notice the heavy shakes hindering his large frame.

He runs his hand across the scruff on his chin before he steps deeper into the living room. He doesn't go to the couch. He heads straight to the liquor cabinet on the far wall to refill his drink.

His shaking hands impede his efforts. Fragrant liquor spills over the rim of the glass before sloshing on the expensive-looking carpet.

Once his glass is full to the brim with an auburn-colored liquid, he downs the overgenerous serving in one gulp.

After following the same routine another two times, he spins to face me. My greatest nightmare confronts me.

The pity.

The shame.

I see it all reflected in his eyes.

"Please don't look at me like that," I plead through a sob sitting in the back of my throat.

He tightens his grip on his glass so much it nearly shatters. "Like what? How am I looking at you?"

"Like I'm a victim," I mumble as tears burn my eyes. "I'm not a victim, Carey. I'm a survivor. They may have taken away my right to say no, but they did not take away my dignity."

"*Jesus, Gemma.*" I've never heard so much pain expressed by two short words. "They?"

He grits his teeth when I briefly nod. I can see his anger—*or is it disgust?*—twisting all the way from his stomach to his face.

"I'm going to go." My jitter voice exposes I'm on the verge of tears.

He locks his eyes with me. His wintry gaze sends a chill down my spine. "Why?" The stabbing ache in my chest doubles from the desolate look in his eyes.

"It will be better for us both if I leave."

"No, Gemma. It won't," he replies, shaking his head. "I'm sorry if I am not responding how you want me to, but I'm not completely fucking heartless. I just found out the woman I am falling for was *raped*. Give me a few minutes to absorb this. Give me a few minutes to work out a response."

No longer trusting my legs to keep me upright at him declaring he's falling for me, I perch my backside on the couch and watch him in silence.

He runs his hand down the side of his face several times while guzzling the amber liquid in his glass at a rate slower than his first three.

I hate this.

I hate that I'm now a contributor to the remorse in his eyes.

This is the reason I didn't want to tell him. My desire not to cause him anymore pain was even more potent than my wish for him not to look at me in pity. Unfortunately, it appears that both of my wishes have gone un-granted.

"I didn't tell you my secret because I want your pity. I told you because I want you to know me. *All* of me. The good and the bad, but now I understand that was stupid of me to do."

"Why?" Carey's remorse-filled eyes bounce between mine.

It's hard to force the words past the tightness of my throat. "Because you'll never look at me the same now."

He shakes his head. "That's not true." He stares me straight in the eyes. "You know that's not true. I thought you'd never look at me the same again, but you did. Give me a chance to do the same."

I want to believe what he's saying. I want to believe nothing can come between us because we've already had more than our share of heartache, but I can't.

The pain in his eyes tells me I can't believe that.

"Gemma, I..." His words trail off into silence.

"It's okay. You don't have to say anything. This is my shame, my embarrassment. You don't have to take responsibility for it."

His fists clench into firm balls at his side. "Your *shame*? Your *embarrassment*? You were *attacked*. You have *nothing* to be ashamed of."

Tears trickle down my cheeks. "I'm not ashamed about my attack, that wasn't my choice. I'm ashamed about the person I became after my attack, and that I didn't tell you earlier. I'm ashamed I didn't give you the chance to back out at the beginning." My voice cracks with emotion. "That was selfish of me to do. I should have never taken that right away from you. I should have let you see the true me."

"I see *you*, Gemma! I see *you*," he replies, his voice getting louder.

I viciously shake my head, sending tears springing off my cheeks. "You haven't seen the ugly and scared Gemma. I kept her hidden from you as I couldn't stand the thought of you hating what you saw."

I shake like a leaf when I stand from the couch and unclick the heavy set of bracelets lining each of my wrists. They drop to the floor with a clatter before scattering around my feet.

Carey gasps in a sharp breath when I turn my wrists over to expose the thick red scars slashed up each wrist.

"Gemma..." My stomach lurches into my throat from the devastation in his voice.

My lips quiver as I begin to speak. "I wanted them to stop lying. And I wanted to save him."

His confused eyes bounce between mine. They're brimming with moisture. "Who?"

He takes a step back like he's been physically punched when I mumble, "Hugo."

The confusion in his eyes grows, right alongside his anger.

His face is red, his fists balled.

I run my fingers under my eyes, removing the tears flowing down my cheeks faster than my hands can clear them. "When they charged Hugo with my rape, I tried to stop them. I did everything in my power to stop them, but they twisted everything I said. They made it out that Hugo was threatening me, and that my fragile *emotional* state was playing tricks with my mind, but that wasn't true. Hugo's DNA was only under my nails because he saved me from the men hurting me. He *didn't* hurt me."

Gratitude replaces some of the anger lining Carey's face.

My lungs rattle when I struggle to fill them with air. "They were going to find him guilty. He was going to spend time behind bars for helping me." I drop my eyes to the ugly red scars on my wrists. "I thought they wouldn't be able to falsely prosecute him if I wasn't alive."

When Carey steps towards me, I violently shake my head. If I don't finish my story now, I may never build up the courage again.

"Hugo found me. He found me before I bled out. That's why he pled guilty. He knew I wasn't strong enough to go back into that courtroom. He knew I had let my attackers win."

Carey crosses the room so quickly, he's nothing but a blur. He wraps his arms around me and draws me into his chest.

The furious beat of his heart blasts my eardrums when I press my damp face into the curve of his neck, desperately hoping I haven't broken us before we've truly begun.

"They never won," he growls in a low and menacing tone. "If they did, you wouldn't be here."

Steam from my earlier shower billows around us as he throws open the bathroom door and steps inside. Still clothed, he twists the faucet on and stands us in the middle of the shower recess.

Lukewarm water trickles down my locks, drenching them from the roots to the very end.

I close my eyes, letting the warmth of Carey's body and the heat of the water wash away the negativity drowning me. I can barely breathe through the torrent of tears flooding my cheeks.

My eyes flutter open when he places me on my feet before fiddling with the buttons of my shirt. After undoing the top two buttons, he grasps the hem and pulls it over my head.

The modest cotton bra I'm wearing does nothing to hide my aroused state. The wet material clings to my breasts, exposing my rosy pink nipples that are pulled taut and aching with need.

Even drowning in despair, I can't stop my body responding to Carey's closeness.

Banding his arms around my back, he unlatches the three clips fastening my bra. Not even two seconds later, it joins my shirt on the shower floor.

The bristle of his recently trimmed hair grazes the skin on my stomach when he lowers my saturated panties down my quivering thighs.

Now my outside matches my inside.

I'm stripped, naked and bare.

After yanking his shirt over his head, Carey releases the drawstrings of his pants. They slump to the floor with a thud.

The urge to cry overwhelms me when I notice his penis is thick, heavily veined and jutted, extending well past the rigid bumps of his six pack.

Relief clears away some of the heaviness sitting on my chest.

Even after I've exposed my hideously ugly insides, he still finds me appealing enough to get hard. It gives me hope that maybe one day he will look at me without pity in his eyes.

We stand huddled together for several moments with nothing but steam between us. Carey doesn't speak. He doesn't need to. I take comfort in his silence. Sometimes silence is more powerful than a million meaningless words.

I don't know how much time passes before Carey tightens his grip around my shoulders. "This is the exact shower I stood in trying to convince myself that what I was feeling for you months ago couldn't have been real. That there was no way a stranger could fill me with so much hope that not every chapter of my story had been written."

I push my face into the space between his pecs, praying the smell of his skin will keep my tears at bay.

My efforts are useless when he continues speaking. "I never thought I'd be strong enough to move on after losing Jorgie and Malcolm. What I didn't realize was that the strength I needed wouldn't come from me. It would come from a person who had a heart strong enough to love me even when I pushed her away."

He places his hand under my chin and lifts my head. "That person is you, Gemma. You have the heart of a warrior. Nothing you said today has changed my opinion on that. Nothing you will ever say could change that."

Fresh tears prick my eyes when he stares at me in admiration, a look I swore I'd never see beam out of his eyes. "You were right. You are not a victim," he confirms, quoting what I said earlier. "You're a survivor, because the fire roaring inside you was greater than the one that tried to destroy you."

EPILOGUE

HAWKE

Two months later...

Life breathes into my soul when a frisson of awareness jolts through my body. I can't see Gemma, but I know she is close.

Is that wrong of me to say? Is it wrong of me to admit that every minute she spends with me resuscitates me from the man I used to be?

For the longest time, I truly believed I died with Jorgie and Malcolm. That my life was over the instant Jorgie took her last breath.

As much as it kills me to admit, I don't feel that way anymore.

Gemma is slowly guiding me out of the sheltered life I've lived for the past five years. She's carefully piecing back parts of me I thought I'd lost, pushing me out of the shadows and exposing the man I was before I lost everything.

I'm not saying I'll ever recover from losing Jorgie and Malcolm. Grief isn't something you simply get over. It's like an ocean. Sometimes the waves come in hard and fast, other times, you have nothing but a flat and calm current.

Gemma understands this. She doesn't expect an instant switch in my persona, or to take away my pain. She just wants to ease it.

Just like I want to do for her as well.

I may not be a man of many words, but I express myself in other ways. Although I now know why Gemma's eyes are filled with mistrust, I'll never stop trying to remove it. Every gentle touch of my hands on her skin is a silent promise that I too am working on piecing back the shards of her broken heart.

I'm going to be honest: when Gemma told me she was raped, it killed me. I knew from the mistrust in her eyes that she'd been badly hurt, but I never realized it would be something so horrific.

Just the thought of anyone hurting such a beautiful, kindhearted person like Gemma cut me deep. I never wanted to kill a man as much as I did that day. I'd give anything to go back and stop Gemma from being hurt, but I can't. All I can do is stand by her side and support her when she's having a rough day, and constantly remind her that the men who assaulted her never won.

They will never win.

Although I'm mad at the way Brandon confronted Gemma two months ago, I understand he was trying to help Hugo, but what Brandon needs to recognize is, Hugo's desire to protect Gemma outweighs his desire to clear his name.

That alone guarantees I will forever be in Hugo's debt.

Gemma is the most courageous woman I've ever met, but there are only so many knocks a fragile soul can take before it shatters beyond repair. I care about her so much, I will do everything in my power to ensure that never happens.

Gemma and I would never wish what we've been through on our worst enemy, but something good came from our tragedies. No one can truly believe another's pain until they have experienced it. That is why Gemma and I connect so well. One selfish heart can break another, but two broken hearts can only join to become one.

My body's perception of Gemma's closeness is proven on point when she enters the wings of the stage Rise Up is currently performing on.

To the pleasure of both Cormack and myself, Gemma agreed to digitally document Rise Up's first official tour. Although my request to have a minimum of three floor spaces between Nick and Jenni's hotel room was not fulfilled, Cormack was gracious enough to grant my request to be roomed with Gemma.

It's been both a bumpy and joyous two months.

Gemma is proof I didn't need someone to complete me. I just needed someone to completely understand me.

She does.

She knows me better than anyone.

A smug grin curls on the corners of my lips when Gemma stops talking to her studio-assigned assistant and lifts her head. Her eyes don't even wander around the room. They lock straight on me, proving I'm not the only one who can feel the earth shifting beneath my feet when we're together.

At times when the guilt attached to my grief becomes too great for me to ignore, I'd like to say my interest in Gemma is nothing but a sexual connection, but that isn't true. Months ago, I woke up every day calculating the hours I had left until I could go back to bed. I lived my life as if I had a timer over my head counting down the seconds remaining until I got to see my family again.

Now, I don't even look at the clock on my bedside table when I wake. My time is better invested. I take a quiet moment each morning remembering those I loved and lost before I spend the rest of my day with a woman who shows me that you can care for someone without needing to forget your past.

Gemma not only breathes air into my life, she frees me. I'm not half the man I was when I lost my family, but I'm a better man when I am with her.

Gemma's wild berry smell conjures up memories of our first night together when she leans in and places a kiss on the edge of my mouth. "You're early," she whispers like we're surrounded by hundreds of nosy onlookers.

Her reaction can't be helped. Normally, that's exactly what happens. If it isn't Emily and Jenni meddling in our affairs, it's Wesley.

I never understood the bond Wesley and Gemma had until after Gemma revealed what happened to her. Although I will always be a little jealous of their close bond, I will never voice my concerns.

This may hurt to admit, but Wesley is the reason Gemma is so strong today. If she didn't have Wesley, I'd hate to think of the struggles she would have endured alone the past four years.

I also have no reason to be jealous.

Their bond is odd for a different sex couple, but when you look closely, you realize it is no different than the connection I have with Hugo.

A thankful smile graces Gemma's lips when I remove her camera bag from her grasp. "What the hell have you got in here?" This bag is a lot heavier than it looks.

"Cameras, photo processing equipment. Standard work stuff," she informs, shadowing me out of the stadium.

I cock my brow and peer into her pretty green eyes. "You're supposed to be taking the weekend off."

"I know," she replies softly, her words tainted with guilt. "But you look so sweet when you're sleeping, I can't help but take a few sneaky snaps."

Laughing, I pull her to my side and quicken my pace. There's only one thing better than watching Gemma sleep: watching her sleep while she's naked.

Gemma stiffens when we merge into the back alley of the stadium.

"*Gem...*"

I don't need to say any more than I did. That one word expressed everything. My relationship with Gemma is still fresh, which means we are treading through the muddy waters every new relationship goes through. The getting to know each other stage. This process has been a challenge for us both. I don't like talking about my past—particularly the parts that include Jorgie and Malcolm. Gemma has no trouble sharing stories of her childhood, but the instant her timeline shifts to adulthood, she clams up, and the mistrust I've been fighting to clear from her eyes returns stronger than ever.

"I'm trying, Carey. Some habits are just hard to shake," she whispers into my shirt while firming her grip around my waist.

I lock my eyes with hers. "Like biting toenails?"

A weird thudding noise comes out of the area my heart used to belong when the faintest giggle sneaks past Gemma's lips. "Yes! That's disgusting. You should *really* stop that."

We make the short four block walk to our hotel in silence. Silence never used to bother me, but tonight I can't stand it. I thought silence was a way of solving problems. In reality, it only makes more.

"Pizza or Chinese?" I question when we hit the entrance of our hotel. I'll say anything to break the uncomfortable silence.

Gemma shifts her eyes to me. They aren't as haunted as they were in the alley. "Hmm. Depends. Are we eating in or out?"

I nudge my head to the hotel. "In."

"Wine or beer?" she questions, her lips quirking into a sexy pout.

I arch my brow, allowing my actions to speak on my behalf.

Wine is for pansies. Real men drink beer.

"No brainer. Pizza it is." She drags her eyes slowly down my body. "That also means there's more chance of me getting you a little tipsy." She tilts toward me, connecting her massively dilated eyes with mine. "Are you a loved-up drunk, Carey?" She waggles her brows before she glides into the lobby of our hotel, stealing my chance to reply.

I chuckle. That's one thing I love about Gemma. She recognizes when she's struggling, but instead of letting it drag her down, she takes a few moments to absorb it before she pushes it to the side, deciding it isn't worth wasting her precious time.

She's the strongest and bravest woman I've ever met.

As I enter the elevator a hotel staff member named Ralph is holding open for us, the entirety of my statement crashes into me. My heart rate climbs as the words I just spoke ring on repeat in my mind.

That is one thing I love about Gemma.

Love?

Gemma laughs when I stumble out of the elevator once it arrives on our floor. "Did someone start their weekend festivities early?" she jests, her brows waggling.

I try to formulate a response, to act like guilt isn't clawing at my chest, making it hard for me to breathe, but all I manage to strangle out is, "I'm going to grab a quick shower."

Gemma throws open our hotel room door. "All right. I'll order the pizza," she responds, thankfully not noticing the erratic switch in my composure.

"Use the credit card in my wallet," I mumble before charging for the bathroom.

"They don't take credit." I can hear the confusion in her voice. Usually, I'm more on the ball than I am right now.

"Then use cash," I suggest before closing the bathroom door and ensuring the lock is in place.

After switching on the shower, I fill the vanity sink with cold water, and then scrub my eyes, trying to rid the guilty look from them.

I didn't mean what I said.

It was just a metaphor.

Everyone does it.

"Look at those drapes. I *love* them."

"I *love* what you've done with the place."

"I'd *love* a few more hours of sleep."

People toss the L word around so freely, it doesn't mean anything anymore. Right?

After clutching the vanity in a white-knuckled hold, I lift my eyes to the mirror.

It takes me several moments staring at my reflection before reality dawns.

It isn't guilt in my eyes.

It's love.

What the?

I should be freaked out. Bile should be burning my throat, but all I am feeling is euphoria.

Gemma is fierce.

She is strong.

And out of all the women in the world, she deserves to be loved the most.

It won't be easy. Guilt will always play a part in our relationship, but I think we have what it will take for two broken souls to become whole again.

I will never not love Jorgie, but maybe Hugo is right. I don't have to forget her to love Gemma. I simply need to stop fighting fate.

The End

The next story in the Enigma series is on **Ryan**: Detective, best friend of Brax, and known associate of Isaac's. It is called: The Way We Are

Facebook: facebook.com/authorshandi

Instagram: instagram.com/authorshandi

Email: authorshandi@gmail.com

Reader's Group: bit.ly/ShandiBookBabes

Website: authorshandi.com

Newsletter: https://www.subscribepage.com/AuthorShandi

If you enjoyed this book, please leave a review!

AFTERWORD

Please note suicide is never an option. If you're hurting or feeling anything like what Carey and Gemma experienced, please reach out for help. You are not alone. There are services that can help you rebuild your life. Just like Carey and Gemma's story shows, no matter how dark it is, there is always a light at the end of the tunnel.

Your life matters. It matters to me, and it should matter to you too.

Suicide prevention support numbers:
USA: 1-800-273-8255
Australia: 13 11 14
UK: 0800 58 58 58

ALSO BY SHANDI BOYES

* Denotes Standalone Books

Perception Series

Saving Noah *
Fighting Jacob *
Taming Nick *
Redeeming Slater *
Saving Emily
Wrapped Up with Rise Up
Protecting Nicole *

Enigma

Enigma
Unraveling an Enigma
Enigma The Mystery Unmasked
Enigma: The Final Chapter
Beneath The Secrets
Beneath The Sheets
Spy Thy Neighbor *
The Opposite Effect *
I Married a Mob Boss *
Second Shot *
The Way We Are
The Way We Were
Sugar and Spice *
Lady In Waiting

Man in Queue

Couple on Hold

Enigma: The Wedding

Silent Vigilante

Hushed Guardian

Quiet Protector

Enigma: An Isaac Retelling

Twisted Lies *

Bound Series

Chains

Links

Bound

Restrain

The Misfits *

Nanny Dispute *

Russian Mob Chronicles

Nikolai: A Mafia Prince Romance

Nikolai: Taking Back What's Mine

Nikolai: What's Left of Me

Nikolai: Mine to Protect

Asher: My Russian Revenge *

Nikolai: Through the Devil's Eyes

Trey *

The Italian Cartel

Dimitri

Roxanne

Reign

Mafia Ties (Novella)

Maddox

Demi

Ox

Rocco *

Clover *

Smith *

RomCom Standalones

Just Playin' *

Ain't Happenin' *

The Drop Zone *

Very Unlikely *

False Start *

Short Stories - Newsletter Downloads

Christmas Trio *

Falling For A Stranger *

One Night Only Series

Hotshot Boss *

Hotshot Neighbor *

The Bobrov Bratva Series

Wicked Intentions *

Sinful Intentions *

Devious Intentions *

Deadly Intentions *

ACKNOWLEDGMENTS

Thank you to the following individuals who without their contributions and support this book would not have been written.

First to my husband Chris, when I said I wanted to write a book he simply replied with "Ok great." No hesitation, not even a small amount of consideration, he just offered his full support. This is very much in tune with exactly how my husband has been our whole marriage. I have an idea, and he supports me 100%. I'm so grateful to have him in my life and I wouldn't want to have it any other way. He is my most valued gift in life.

Second to my darling mum Carolyn Wallace. She sits and reads the entire first drafts while attempting to assist in editing. I've never been good with anything grammatical related, but she assists me where she can.. For this, I will be eternally grateful.

My first book was originally written to be shared amongst my friends, in a hope that others may enjoy the story that I've created, but with the support of the people mentioned earlier, I decided to self-publish my story to share with others. I hope you enjoyed them!

Please remember to leave a review of my book.
Cheers
Shandi xx